DAGGER AWARD FINALIST

COSTA FIRST NOVEL AWARD FINALIST

ELLE LETTRES READERS' PRIZE WINNER

PRAISE FOR

THE GIRL IN THE R

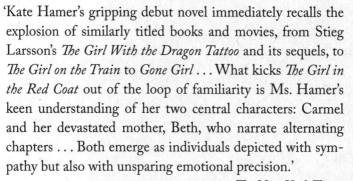

'Kate Hamer's gripping debut novel immediately recalls the explosion of similarly titled books and movies, from Stieg Larsson's *The Girl With the Dragon Tattoo* and its sequels, to *The Girl on the Train* to *Gone Girl* . . . What kicks *The Girl in the Red Coat* out of the loop of familiarity is Ms. Hamer's keen understanding of her two central characters: Carmel and her devastated mother, Beth, who narrate alternating chapters . . . Both emerge as individuals depicted with sympathy but also with unsparing emotional precision.'
   – MICHIKO KAKUTANI, *The New York Times*

'This stunning debut . . . has the propulsion of a thriller.'
   – KIM HUBBARD, *People*

'Every sentence in Kate Hamer's debut is so perceptive that you're torn between wanting to linger on the thought and itching to learn what happens next . . . The taut plot alternates between Carmel's emotional struggle to survive and Beth's refusal to believe that her daughter is gone forever. Meanwhile, their complex yet unbreakable bond is rendered with honesty and love.'   – DAWN RAFFEL, Oprah.com

'Keeps the reader turning pages at a frantic clip . . . What's most powerful here is not whodunnit, or even why, but how this mother and daughter bear their separation, and the stories they tell themselves to help endure it.'

    – CELESTE NG, author of *Everything I Never Told You*

'Hamer's book is a moving, voice-driven narrative. As much an examination of loss and anxiety as it is a gripping page-turner, it'll appeal to anyone captivated by child narrators or analyses of the pains and joys of motherhood.'

    – *The Huffington Post*

'Riveting. Worth the hype.'   – *Book Riot*

'Compulsively readable . . . Beautifully written and unpredictable . . . I had to stop myself racing to the end to find out what happened . . . Kate Hamer catches at the threads of what parents fear most – the abduction of a child – and weaves a disturbing and original story. There is menace in this book, lurking in the shadows on every page, but also innocence, love, and hope.'

    – ROSAMUND LUPTON, author of *Sister*

'Gripping and sensitive – beautifully written, *The Girl in the Red Coat* is a compulsive, aching story full of loss and redemption.'

    – LISA BALLANTYNE, author of *The Guilty One*

'Mum and Carmel share the telling of this tale, which takes a direction you won't be expecting. Best read in a single sitting.'

    – VIOLET HENDERSON, *Vogue*

'Unpredictable and moving.'   – *Marie Claire*

'Page-turning yet beautifully written.'   – *The Huffington Post*

'*The Girl in the Red Coat* keeps the reader hooked – and awake into the small hours.'
— ISABEL BERWICK, *Financial Times*

'[A] spectacular debut . . . Telling the story in two remarkable voices, with Beth's chapters unfurling in past tense and Carmel's in present tense, the author weaves a page-turning narrative. The trajectories of the novel's two leads – through despair, hope, and redemption – are believable and nuanced, resulting in a morally complex, haunting read.'
– *Publishers Weekly* (starred review)

'Hamer's lush use of language easily conjures fairy-tale imagery, especially of dark forests and Little Red Riding Hood. Although a kidnapped child is the central plot point, this is not a mystery but a novel of deep inquiry and intense emotions. Hamer's dark tale of the lost and found is nearly impossible to put down and will spark much discussion.'
– *Booklist* (starred review)

'Poignantly details the loss and loneliness of a mother and daughter separated . . . Fast-paced . . . Hamer beautifully renders pain, exactly capturing the evisceration of loss . . . Exquisite prose surrounding a mother and daughter torn apart.'
– *Kirkus Reviews*

'Reading this novel is a test of how fast you can turn pages.'
– *Library Journal* (starred review)

THE GIRL

IN THE

RED COAT

THE GIRL

IN THE

RED COAT

a novel

KATE HAMER

MELVILLE HOUSE
BROOKLYN • LONDON

THE GIRL IN THE RED COAT

Originally published by Faber & Faber Ltd. in the
United Kingdom, February 2015

First Melville House hardcover printing: February 2016
First Melville House paperback printing: February 2017

Melville House Publishing   8 Blackstock Mews
        46 John Street   and   Islington
        Brooklyn, NY 11201   London N4 2BT

mhpbooks.com   facebook.com/mhpbooks   @melvillehouse

Paperback ISBN: 978-1-61219-561-2

THE LIBRARY OF CONGRESS HAS CATALOGED
THE HARDCOVER AS FOLLOWS:
Hamer, Kate.
    The girl in the red coat / Kate Hamer.
        pages   cm
    ISBN 978-1-61219-500-1 (hardback)
    ISBN 978-1-61219-501-8 (ebook)
    1. Missing children—Fiction. 2. Single mothers—Fiction.
    I. Title.

PR6108.A52G57 2016
823'.92—dc23
                                        2015019006

Design by Christopher King

Printed in the United States of America
    1 3 5 7 9 10 8 6 4 2

To Mark

THE GIRL IN THE RED COAT

I

I DREAM ABOUT CARMEL OFTEN. In my dreams she's always walking backwards.

The day she was born there was snow on the ground. A silvery light arced through the window as I held her in my arms.

As she grew up I nicknamed her 'my little hedge child.' I couldn't imagine her living anywhere but the countryside. Her thick curly hair stood out like a spray of breaking glass, or a dandelion head.

'You look like you've been dragged through a hedge backwards,' I'd say to her.

And she would smile. Her eyes would close and flutter. The pale purple-veined lids like butterflies sealing each eye.

'I can imagine that,' she'd say finally, licking her lips.

I'm looking out of the window and I can almost see her – in those tights that made cherry licorice of her legs – walking up the lane to school. The missing her feels like my throat has been removed.

Tonight I'll dream of her again, I can feel it. I can feel her in the twilight, sitting up on the skeined branches of the beech tree and calling out. But at night in my sleep she'll be walking backwards toward the house – or is it away? – so she never gets closer.

Her clothes were often an untidy riot. The crotch of her winter tights bowed down between her knees so she'd walk like a penguin. Her school collar would stick up on one side and be buried in her jumper on the other. But her mind was a different matter – she knew what people were feeling. When Sally's husband left her, Sally sat in my kitchen drinking tequila as I tried to console her. Salt and lime and liquor for a husband. Carmel came past and made her fingers into little sticks that she stuck into Sally's thick brown hair and massaged her scalp. Sally moaned and dropped her head backwards.

'Oh my God, Carmel, where did you learn to do that?'

'Hush, nowhere,' she whispered, kneading away.

That was just before she disappeared into the fog.

Christmas 1999. The children's cheeks blotched pink with cold and excitement as they hurried through the school gates. To me, they all looked like little trolls compared to Carmel. I wondered then if every parent had such thoughts. We had to walk home through the country lanes and already it was nearly dark.

It was cold as we started off and snow edged the road. It glowed in the twilight and marked our way. I realised I was balling my hands in tight fists inside my pockets with worries about Christmas and no money. As I drew my hands out into the cold air and uncurled them Carmel fell back and I could hear her grumbling behind me.

'Do hurry up,' I said, anxious to get home out of the freezing night.

'You realise, Mum, that I won't always be with you,' she said, her voice small and breathy in the fading light.

Maybe my heart should have frozen then. Maybe I should have turned and gathered her up and taken her home. Kept her shut away in a fortress or a tower. Locked with a golden key that I would swallow, so my stomach would have to be cut open before she could be found. But of course I thought it meant nothing, nothing at all.

'Well, you're with me for now.'

I turned. She seemed far behind me. The shape of her head was the same as the tussocky tops of the hedges that closed in on either side.

'Carmel?'

A long plume of delicate ice breath brushed past my coat sleeve.

'I'm here.'

Sometimes I wonder if when I'm dead I'm destined to be looking still. Turned into an owl and flying over the fields at night, swooping over crouching hedges and dark lanes. The smoke from chimneys billowing and swaying from the movement of my wings as I pass through. Or will I sit with her, high up in the beech tree, playing games? Spying on the people who live in our house and watching their comings and goings. Maybe we'll call out to them and make them jump.

We were single mothers, almost to a man – as one of the group once joked. We clustered together in solidarity of our status. I think now maybe it was not good for Carmel, this band of women with bitter fire glinting from their eyes and rings. Many evenings we'd be around the kitchen table and it would be *then he, then he, then he*. We were all hurt in some way, bruised inside. Except for Alice who had real bruises. After Carmel had gone – oh, a few months or so – Alice came to the house.

'I had to speak to you,' she said. 'I need to tell you something.'

Still I imagined anything could be a clue to the puzzle.

'What is it? What is it?' I asked, frantically clutching at the neck of my dressing gown. What she told me disappointed me so much I turned my face away and looked at the empty shell of the egg I'd eaten yesterday on the kitchen drainer. But when she started to tell me my daughter had a channel to God and could be now at His right hand – how I hated her then. Her false clues and her finding of Jesus, those wrists in identical braided bracelets turning as she spoke. I could stay silent no longer.

'Stop it!' I yelled. 'Get out of here. I thought you had something real to tell me. Get out of this house and leave me alone, you stupid cow. You crazy stupid cow. Take your God with you and don't ever come back.'

Sometimes, just before I fall asleep, I imagine crawling inside the shell of Carmel's skull and finding her memories there. Peering through her eye sockets and watching the film of her life unfold through *her* eyes. Look, look: there's me and her father, when we were together. Carmel's still small so to her we seem like giants, growing up into the sky. I lean down to pick her up and empty nursery rhymes into her ear.

And there's that day out to the circus.

We have a picnic by the big top before we go in. I spread out the blanket on the grass, so I don't notice Carmel turn her head and see the clown peering from between the tent flaps. His face has thick white make-up with a big red mouth shape drawn on. She puzzles why his head is so high up because his stilts are hidden by the striped tent flap. He looks briefly up at the sky to check the weather, then his red-and-white face disappears back inside.

What else? Starting school, me breaking up with Paul and throwing his clothes out of the bedroom window. She must have seen them from where she was in the kitchen – his shirts and trousers sailing down. Other things, how many memories even in a short life: seeing the sea, a day paddling in the river, Christmas, a full moon, snow.

Always I stop at her eighth birthday and can go no farther. Her eighth birthday, when we went to the maze.

2

FOR MY EIGHTH BIRTHDAY I want to go and see a maze. 'Carmel. What do you know about mazes?' Mum says. If I think hard I can see a folded puzzle in my mind that looks like a brain.

'I've heard things,' I say. And Mum laughs and says OK. We don't have a car so we go on the bus, just the two of us. The windows are steamed up so I can't see where we're going. Mum's got on her favourite earrings which are like bits of glass except colours sparkle on them when she moves.

I'm thinking about my birthday, which was last Thursday, and now it's Saturday and I'm thinking about how my friend gets cards and presents from her nan but Mum doesn't talk to her mum and dad even though they're still alive. I don't mind so much about the cards and presents but I'd like to know what they look like.

'Mum, have you got a photo of your mum and dad?'

Her head shoots around and the earrings flash pink and yellow lights. 'I'm not sure. Maybe, why?'

'I just wonder what they look like sometimes and if they look like me.' It's more than sometimes.

'You look like your dad, sweetheart.'

'But I'd like to know.'

She smiles. 'I'll see what I can do.'

When we get off the bus the sky is white and I'm so excited to see a real maze I run ahead. We're in this big park and mist is rolling around in ghost shapes. There's a huge grey house with hundreds of windows that are all looking at us. I can tell Mum's scared of the house so I growl at it. Sometimes she's scared of everything, Mum – rivers, roads, cars, planes, what's going to happen and what's not going to happen.

But then she laughs and says, 'I'm such a silly old thing.'

Now we're at the top of this hill and I can see the maze below and it *does* look like a brain. I think it's really funny I've thought about a brain inside my brain and try to explain but I don't do it very well and I don't think Mum really gets it. But she's nodding and listening anyway and standing there with her long blue coat all wet from the grass at the bottom. She says, 'That's very interesting, Carmel.' Though I'm not sure she really understood, but Mum always tries to. She doesn't just ignore you like you're just a mouse or a bat.

So we go in.

And I know all of a sudden it's a place I love more than anywhere I've ever been. The green walls are so high the sky's in a slice above me and it's like being in a puzzle but in a forest at the same time. Mum says the trees are called yew, and spells it out because I laugh and ask, you? I run on ahead down the path in the middle where the grass is squashed into a brown strip and Mum's far behind me now. But it doesn't matter because I know how mazes work and that even if I lose her, we'll find each other sooner or later.

I carry on around corners and each place looks the same. Bright red berries pop out of the green walls and birds fly over my head. Except I don't see them fly from one side of the sky to the other – they're above the high green walls so I only see them for a second and then they're gone.

I hear someone on the other side of the wall.

'Carmel, is that you?'

And I say no even though I know it's my mum – it doesn't sound quite like her.

She says, 'Yes it is, I know it's you because I can see your red tights through the tree.'

But I don't want to go so I just slip away quietly. It starts getting dark, but I still feel at home in this place. Now, it's more like a forest than a maze. The tops of the trees stretch up, up and away, and get higher, like the dark's making them grow. There's some white flowers gleaming and once I see a piece of rope hanging from a branch, I think maybe a child like me used it as a swing. It's in the middle of a path and I go right up to it so my nose is nearly touching the frayed bit at the end and it twists and turns in the breeze like a worm. Dark green smells are all around and birds are singing from the middle of the walls.

I decide to lie under a tree to rest on the soft brown earth because I feel tired and dreamy now. The smell of the earth comes up where I'm squashing it and it smells dark and sweet. Something brushes across my face and I think it's an old leaf because it feels dead and scrapy.

The birds don't sound like they're singing now, more like chatting, and the breeze is making the trees rustle. And I hear my mother calling me but she sounds just like the rustling and the birds and I know I should answer her but I don't.

3

I RAN DOWN hallways of yew. Each one looked the same and at the end, every time, I turned a corner to see another endless green corridor in front of me. As I ran I shouted, 'Carmel, Carmel – where are you?'

Eventually, when there was only enough light to just about see I stumbled on the entrance. I could see the big grey house through the gap and the front door looked like a mouth that was laughing at me.

Across the field was the man who had taken our money, leaving. He was walking toward the brow of the hill and already a long way from the house.

'Please, come back.' My ragged shout didn't feel like it had come from me.

He hadn't heard. The sound was swept up by the wind and carried away in the other direction. Only crows answered me with their caws.

I began running toward him, shouting. He seemed to be walking very fast and his figure was disappearing into the last of the light.

Finally he must have caught my cries and I saw him stop and turn his head. I waved my arms about and even from such a distance I could see his body stiffen, sensing danger. I must have looked crazy, though I didn't think about that then. When I caught up with him he waited for me to get my breath back as I rested my hands on my knees. His face under his old-fashioned cloth cap was watchful.

'My little girl. I can't find her,' I managed to say after a minute.

He took his cap off and smoothed his hair. 'The one with red legs?'

'Yes, yes – the little girl with red tights.'

We set off toward the maze. He switched on his torch to show the way.

'People don't just go into mazes and never come out,' he said reasonably.

'Has anyone else been here today?' I asked. My throat closed up waiting for his answer.

'No. At least, there was a couple here this morning. But they'd gone by the time you arrived.'

'Are you sure? Are you sure?'

He stopped and turned. 'I'm sure. Don't worry, we'll find her. I know this maze like the back of my hand.' I felt so grateful then to be with this man who had the plan of the puzzle imprinted on him.

As we approached the maze he switched his torch off. We didn't need it any more. A big moon had risen and lit up the place like a floodlight at a football match. We went in through the arched entrance cut into the woven trees. In the moonlight the foliage and the red berries had turned to black.

'What's the little girl's name again? Karen?'

'No, no. Carmel.'

'Carmel.' His voice boomed out.

We walked fast, shouting all the way. He turned the torch back on and pointed it under the hedges. There were rustlings around us and once he pointed the light straight into the eyes of a rabbit that froze for a moment before bolting across our path. I could tell he was working through the maze methodically from the plan.

'I think we should call the police,' I said, after about twenty minutes. I was becoming frantic again.

'Maybe. We're nearly at the centre now, though.'

We turned another corner and there she was, in the crook of the hedge. The torchlight flashed over her red legs poking out from underneath the black wall. I put both hands into the gap and dragged her out. Her body felt pliant and warm and I could tell at once she was asleep. I lifted her into my lap and rocked her back and forth and kept saying to the man smiling down at us, 'Thank you. Thank you. Thank you. Thank you.' I smiled back at him and held her lovely solid warmth.

How many times I was back in that place that night. Even after we were home and safely tucked into bed, I kept dreaming I was there again. Walking around and around in circles and looking. Sometimes the rabbit bolted away – but sometimes it stopped right in the middle of the path and stared at me, its nose twitching.

4

I LIKE PLAYING in the garden on my own, making dinners. There's a tree at the bottom with twigs that if you skin off the bark looks just like chicken, white and flaky. So with twig knives and forks I can put out dinner. There's old leaves though – black and slimy left over from ages ago – so I kick them away to make a gap on the grass.

I'm super safe here. Around the garden there's a stone wall and I can only just about see over the top. Over the wall there's fields and hardly any houses. But I can see smoke from chimneys puffing far away. There's a long way I can see as Mum says Norfolk is flat like a pancake.

As I'm playing I see two big white birds flying side by side. One's a bit in front of the other like he's the leader. Their necks are stuck right out and they're flying low down, wings flapping away like it's hard for them to stay up. I climb onto the bottom of the wall to see better and, guess what? They fly right over my head and I have to laugh at their big tummies wobbling in the air and their orange legs dangling down flappy and useless.

But that's when I turn around and see Mum's face at the window. Oh, she tries to go back but it's too late. I've caught her checking I'm still there, like she does since the maze. Then she comes out of the back door with her coat on like it's nothing at all and I never caught her. She smiles the sort of smile people do when they want you to stop being grumpy.

'What was funny, Carmel?'

'What was funny, what was funny, Carmel?' I mutter under my breath but so she can't hear. But I feel bad because her smile looks a bit broken. Anyway I want to tell her about the birds.

'Geese,' she says.

'Like snow geese or like goose that Alison had for Christmas dinner?'

'Yes, both. They mate for life. That would be a male and a female you saw.'

I have to ask as I'm not sure. 'Mate for life . . . ?'

'Yes, they stay together forever like they're married.'

So not like you and Dad then. I don't say that *of course*, even though she's annoying me again, crouching down and pretending to play with my leaf plates because she doesn't want to go back inside and leave me alone. She fiddles around with the twigs I've put down for knives and forks, making them all untidy. One of her brown boots stands on a plate and crushes it though she probably can't realise and thinks it's just a leaf.

I sigh and kneel down and straighten it up again as best I can. But *now* she says, 'Carmel, you're getting your trousers wet.' And she starts stroking my hair and her hand feels very heavy on my head and I'm wishing she'd stop though I don't say. I just carry on putting bits of chicken back onto plates and waiting for her to go away.

She goes in the end but now I feel mean because perhaps she just thought she was being nice playing with me. Being mean goes right into my stomach, sick and uncomfortable, like I've swallowed a stone. After the maze I've been feeling mean a lot. Last week we went to McDonald's. I was so excited because we were taking Sara. Sara's mum smells nice and so does their house and her mum wears the most gorgeous shoes with gold bits on them. We were in McDonald's and me and Sara were laughing together about a silly secret but Mum's there watching and listening. Oh, she was pretending not to but she kept looking at me without turning her head, just out the corner of her eyes like a spy. And then I had such a mean thought it made the McFlurry I'd just had go all hard in my stomach. It was – I wish Sara's mum was my mum and I was Sara's sister and we could all live together in their little warm house in town and maybe I could have some peace.

After we'd taken Sara home and we were on the way back on the bus to our house I was still feeling horrible. I was thinking maybe she wasn't spying like I thought at all, maybe I'd just wanted it to be me on my own with Sara – more grown-up like, so I said, 'I wish I could buy you some gold shoes.'

Mum turned and smiled a lovely smile.

'What a nice thought, Carmel, but where would I wear them? To Tesco's?' And she laughed. 'Tell you what, we could both have gold shoes and we could just wear them for shopping.'

I started laughing too at the thought of us trying to walk around Tesco's in high-heeled gold shoes, tottering behind the trolley. Then I looked down at her feet on the bus floor. She was wearing her big brown boots she's worn for so long there's toe shapes in the leather. I remembered she has quite big feet with lumpy toes and I imagined seeing her there on the bus with her feet squeezed into tiny gold shoes like Sara's mum wears and it made me feel a bit sad. So I looked out of the window so she couldn't see my face.

5

THE MAZE WAS FADING to a distant memory.

It was Saturday and we'd been shopping. We were walking down the lane with our Tesco bags when we saw Paul's red Peugeot parked outside the gate. He got out of the car when he saw us and stood with his arms folded, smiling at Carmel. Then he opened his arms up wide as she raced forward and flung herself at him.

'Daddy,' she screamed.

'My girl,' he almost shouted. 'My lovely girl.'

He never looked at me once the whole time, but maybe, after all, I was relieved. I'd tried to keep myself together in the time since he'd left, for my own sake and Carmel's – flowers on my blouses, deep berry colours, or summery yellows. A dash of lipstick, cheap and cheerful. The same with the house – I'd put bright orange curtains at the windows and hung little mottoes up on the walls, to try and fill the gap he'd left. But typically Paul had caught me on the one day we'd rushed out to catch the bus, me still looping my hair into a haphazard ponytail. And Carmel was ecstatic to see him and I didn't want to spoil that so I unlocked the front door to let us in and waited till she went to hang her coat up.

'What's going on?'

He sat at the kitchen table looking bigger than I remembered. Tall and handsome with his legs lolling about like our little kitchen chairs were from a schoolroom. He smelled strange though, the chemical scent of fabric conditioner hung about him.

'I've come to see our daughter, that's OK, isn't it?'

Then I heard her coming down the hall so I didn't mention access agreements or how he was supposed to see her every weekend and hadn't been near us for nearly five months. I was just glad for her that he was there. Carmel was bringing armfuls of things to show him – a cushion she'd made at school with her name painted on it; her last report; her new umbrella which had ears sticking up in little flaps when you opened it.

'Never mind all that.' Paul stood up and he looked so strong and handsome that I had to harden my heart. 'Let's you and me go and watch a film in town and you can choose a place to eat afterward.'

He leaned down and unpeeled a strand of hair stuck to her cheek and tucked it behind her ear. Such a tender gesture. I wondered how he could have borne to stay away for so long. Then, like he'd been reading my mind: 'I've been wanting to see you so much, Carmel. I've just been waiting till everything was settled . . .' I realised he meant till *I* was settled. 'We'll have a lovely evening now. We'll stuff our faces with popcorn.'

'And Mum?' Carmel was looking over at me. God, how alike they looked: clear hazel eyes; curly hair; strong bones.

'No, let's leave Mum in peace for once. Just you and me.'

I chimed in with a smile as bright as a piece of tin, 'Yes, you two go. Enjoy yourselves. I've things to do.'

Carmel looked suspiciously at my tin smile so I softened my face and said, 'I've got lots to do here, Carmel. I'll be able to read in front of the fire without the television on.' So she slowly put her things down and went to get her coat.

'You could come, but probably for the best, eh? It would only spoil it for her, wouldn't it? I mean, if us two fall out again.'

I said, 'Yes, Paul,' and turned away, conscious that my hair was in a scruffy ponytail with scrappy bits falling around my face and hating myself for caring. 'You go,' I said, and willed myself not to ask about Lucy, and whether they still lived together, but I didn't need to ask really. It wasn't just the smell of fabric conditioner that was new, anyone could see he'd been dressed by a woman. Pink-and-green polo shirt, sweetie colours. A chunky Patek Philippe watch gleaming on his wrist.

'I needed to talk to you anyway, Paul.'

'OK.' He braced himself.

'About Carmel.'

'Oh, yes.' He relaxed.

'We've had a parent–teacher meeting. They think, well, they think she's quite special.'

His face dropped and he frowned, then looked around at the space where she'd just been. 'What, like special needs?'

I let my breath out in a slow one, two, three.

'No,' I said. 'No, the opposite. Clever, you know. Very bright . . . but . . .'

'What?'

'Dreamy. Too dreamy sometimes. Have you not noticed?' Was it just me who saw those absences? When she stood rooted to the spot and her eyes became strange and stony – then as soon as they came, they went. Fugues, I began to name them. I wanted to talk to someone about it. Perhaps Paul was closer than he realised in his meaning of 'special.' But after all, I couldn't be sure – how can you tell when you only have one child, when there's nothing to measure these things against?

Paul didn't want to talk about this, I could see. I remembered how he used to be on accepting people as they are. 'Maybe. But . . .'

'What?'

'I've always thought it was more like she has an old soul. The Chinese say that, don't they, or the Hindus?'

'Oh, Paul. She's so pleased to see you,' I burst out.

He looked uncomfortable. 'I'm sorry I felt I had to wait until, you know.'

I did. Divorce is never pretty. Ours wasn't.

'But now. Now it's all settled.' For him I suppose it was. 'Now things have settled we can do this more often, all the time.'

'Look, Paul. I need to go over it with you, the meeting, there's more.'

That's when we heard Carmel coming down the stairs, so the conversation ended.

'C'mon, curly mop,' he said. 'You and me hit the road.'

I watched their tail lights disappearing down the twilight road. Then once the last blink of red had gone I went and fished out some tobacco from the dresser drawer. The tobacco was old and had hardened inside the plastic pouch so it looked like chocolate-flavoured sugar strands. When I rolled the cigarette I had to twist both ends so the tobacco didn't spill. I lit it and sat next to the window, smoking and looking out.

It wasn't just a marriage with Paul – we'd run a business together buying and selling ginseng and specialist teas. When he'd left I'd been proud and angry and told him I'd rely on the reception job I'd found – not quite full time. We agreed that he would have the business and I would have the house. He had no need of a house now he was moving in with Lucy and it was better for Carmel to stay in the same place. Lucy had a small new build on the outskirts of town. I knew, because I found it one night, mad with jealousy. To her credit, she asked me in. So much younger than me; I burned at the cliché. As I was following her I looked at her behind, tiny in tight-fitting white jeans. My eyes followed the contours of her backside down to between her thighs and I thought, 'Paul has put his cock inside there.' And the thought made me feel sweaty and ugly.

Her feet were bare, with tiny pink painted shells of toenails, and I realised – remembering the shoe rack by the front door – that this was the sort of house where you'd take your shoes off in normal circumstances. Would Paul really do that? I looked down at my feet and wondered if after I'd gone, she'd be there with dustpan and brush and squirty carpet cleaner, rubbing at the cream carpet where my boots had been.

She told me they were in love and she was sorry. She seemed nice enough – I'd wanted her to be heartless and hard-faced and she wasn't either of those things. But as I left I couldn't help saying spitefully to her, 'He's unreliable and untrustworthy. He'll do the same to you.'

She tried to still her face but I saw the movement flick deep behind her eyes, knowing what I'd said was possibly true. And I relished that flicker – took it home with me and turned it over later, Gollum-like, as though it was something to be treasured. It shames me now, to say that.

After Paul had gone the house slowly emptied of his presence. Every time the door opened the wind blew in and took with it a bit more of him. The smell of tea faded. We'd kept the dresser full of stock and it exuded smoky smells of Lapsang and deep stately tannin with a flowery trill of jasmine riding its wake. The smell of tea still makes me think of Paul. Even passing the tea section in the supermarket or taking the lid off the pot in a café to check the contents brings back our time together and the feel of him. After the dresser was emptied these tea smells faded away until it was strangely only the thin scent of jasmine that remained. I'd catch its sharp delicate breath in odd parts of the kitchen. Occasionally I'd find a piece of ginseng in a kitchen drawer, the rude rooty stub a reminder of something base and earthy. Once I came across a knotted ball of Japanese tea that had rolled behind the log basket. The dense packed ball looked like a form of root too but would reveal itself when boiling water was poured, growing in the cup into the form of a chrysanthemum.

The house became very quiet. The noise I made as I blew out smoke was a rushing wind in my ears. Sometimes the floorboards would creak upstairs or the old heating would clink rapidly for a few seconds. I stayed there until I saw the headlights of Paul's car returning. I must take her out more, I thought.

6

WHEN I WAKE UP in the morning, everything's wonderful. For a moment I can't understand why. Then I remember: Mum's said if the weather's good we can go to the storytelling festival and that's today.

My bed's under the window. I look through the glass, in the shape of diamonds, at the sky.

It's blue, blue, blue.

I lie here, warm under my quilt. I can hear Mum downstairs – the big old kettle clanks getting put on the stove and then *pop* when the gas is lit. When Dad was still at home I could hear his voice rumbling the floorboards. Or sometimes I could hear him arguing with Mum and they sounded like two bears snarling. When I went downstairs they'd stop and smile at me but they were making their faces smile, I could tell. People think when you're a child that you're just a mouse on the floor with a tiny brain.

My headmaster thinks that – that you won't understand things. On parents' day Mum was a bit late. My teacher – Mrs Buckfast – told me I could wait outside the classroom until Mum got there. While I was waiting in the corridor I heard Mr Fellows the headmaster inside the classroom say to Mrs Buckfast that *my* mum was 'yet another single mum.' This made my face go a bit red with crossness because I didn't think it was his business to say things like that. When Mum got there she was out of breath and saying, 'Sorry, sorry, sorry. I couldn't get away from work.' But I didn't mind, I knew she was only late because she had to walk when everyone else had cars. So I held her hand and said, 'It doesn't matter. It's only ten minutes.' When in fact it was more like fifteen.

When we went in together Mrs Buckfast said I was 'highly intelligent but sometimes on another planet.'

Mr Fellows kept looking at my mum and I knew why – because she's much prettier than the other mums. She's got thick brown hair and blue eyes and a nose that goes a little bit up and very pretty big lips that look nice when she puts some lipstick on them.

The headmaster started talking. 'Carmel's vocabulary is extremely advanced. Her imagination is amazing, I don't think she quite sees the world like the rest of us.' Then he looked at me and said, 'But you'd forget your head if it wasn't screwed on.' Which I thought was rude. Especially with what I'd heard him say about my mum. When I didn't answer he said, 'Like last week on the school trip when we couldn't find you and when we did, you were sitting on a bench on your own looking like you were a million miles away. We were very worried, Carmel.' And Mum said, 'What's this?' I sighed then and stopped liking them talking about me. I started feeling upset and I was really glad when Mrs Buckfast smiled and said I'd grow out of it she was sure, so it didn't matter too much. And Mum told me not to worry too and afterward she took me for a pizza in town – not planned or anything – and we had a lovely time. She told me knock-knock jokes until I was laughing so much some Coke came down my nose.

These days I don't miss Dad's shouting but I do miss his rumbling voice. But Mum says it's just the two of us so we can do anything we want. She says, 'We can be two nutters together.' Sometimes we dance in the kitchen around the old wooden table. We turn the radio right up and use big spoons for microphones.

Right now, I don't try and stop listening, like I did when Mum and Dad were arguing. It's like I'm all ears and they stretch toward any tiny sound. I think of Mum right under my bed in the kitchen, sitting down and drinking her morning cuppa. It makes me laugh – that I'm seeing exactly what she's doing in my mind and I'm lying right over her and she doesn't even know. Then I hear a noise like someone's humming in my room.

I look up and that's when I see a bee at the top of my window. It's buzzing more than humming now and I kneel up. It's the biggest bee I've ever seen in my life and it's got white bits on its fur like it's an old man – or, as Mum would say, 'in the winter of its life.' Every time it bounces against the window it makes an extra loud buzz like it's getting angry. It doesn't know about the glass in its way – it can't understand why it can't just fly out free into the garden. So, very carefully, because I know bees have a sting like a poison dart, I open up the window. It bumps against the glass once more and then flies out. At first I think it's going to fall and crash onto the ground but it soars up into the air and away into the garden over the top of the apple tree.

I get dressed in my leggings and my favourite purple-and-red stripy T-shirt that feels so soft and lovely against my skin and it's got long arms and I can feel the day in front of me. Before I go downstairs I decide to draw a picture of the storytelling festival. I find a piece of paper and draw with a thick pencil a man sitting down. He's wearing glasses and I imagine the story he's telling so I put scribbly words coming out of his mouth. Then I do a rabbit at his feet with its mouth open because it's listening so hard.

Downstairs there's a toast smell in the kitchen and Mum's wearing jeans and a flowery top – she told me flowery tops are her 'haute couture' and I got her to write those words down because I want to put them in my word collection – and I ask, 'Are we still going?' Because you never can be sure.

She turns around and smiles at me. 'Yes, Carmel, yes.'

7

DAY 1

WE TOOK THE TRAIN that day. I wanted it to be special for
Carmel and taking a train rather than the usual bus was a treat.

She had crazes for things then, like any kid. Passions that
flared up and then fizzled and died as quickly as they came but
her love for the colour red seemed to be enduring. I'd bought her
a red duffel coat and that's what she was wearing. She'd asked if
she could have red shoes the next time she needed shoes and we'd
seen a pair in the window of Clarks. We looked at them every
time we went into town to check they were still there. My wages
didn't go far, but I figured I might be able to buy them before she
returned to school after Easter and prayed they wouldn't be sold
before then. So far, miraculously, every time we went into town
there they were – on a little green felt-covered stand, like two big
fat ladybirds waiting on the grass – even though the rest of the
stock changed around them. As she put on her coat that morning
I made a decision.

'Tomorrow, we'll go into town and if those shoes are still there,
we'll buy them.'

'Really?'

'Yes. Really.'

To hell with everything, I'd put them on my credit card and

worry about it later. That morning with the spring wind blowing through the back door anything seemed possible. Perhaps I could even ask Paul to pay for them, now he'd made a reappearance. I'd felt he wanted the connection back with his daughter, even if he didn't want anything to do with me. Perhaps it was time to accept the contribution he'd offered that I'd recklessly turned down, insisting that we'd manage without him.

That day on the train, for a while at least, the past got swept away by the spring, the sucking hot air from the trains as they speeded through the station and the excitement of a day out, just the two of us. I thought: I've been in such a state, such a terrible stupid anxious state this past year since Paul left. It's time to stop it now. Time to start afresh.

Carmel sat opposite me bundled up in her duffel coat. The train was crowded. A tall young man with a dirty denim jacket and the tattoo of a spider's web creeping up his neck from his open shirt got on and took the seat next to Carmel. He fiddled with his mobile phone for a while and then the guard looked at our tickets. I could see from the start the man in the denim jacket was desperate to begin a conversation. Words began to form in his mouth that he kept swallowing at the last minute, but after the ticket collecting he couldn't hold back.

'Good little girl you have.' He was speaking to me.

'Yes. Thank you.' I smiled at him. It was peaceful and comfortable on the rocking train with Carmel right opposite me.

'Day out, just the two of you?'

I nodded, then was it my imagination or did his sharp darting eyes glance at my ring finger? Though ridiculous that anyone should note such things these days – especially at his age.

'Left the old fella at home?'

'That's right.'

Maybe it was just me conscious of my finger, as naked as a root, where less than a year ago a thick gold ring with a circle of silver flowers had gleamed. Either way I was relieved when he got off.

'I'm glad he's gone,' I said.

'Who?' asked Carmel, her mind clearly on other things.

'Mr Spiderman, of course.'

She didn't laugh at my silly name-calling, just patted my hand – once, lightly.

'You nutter,' she smiled, dreamily. Then it was just the two of us again, sitting opposite each other. The train went through an avenue of trees. Carmel's hair splayed out with static across the nylon headrest of the seat as she looked out of the window. As we passed through the trees they made a pattern so her face was one moment in bright sunlight and the next in darkness. This is the image I remember most from the day. Carmel's face being stripped with light and dark, flickering on and off, like at the end of a spool of film when it's about to run out.

8

GREAT FLAPPING LINES of flags are blowing upward at the festival to the blue sky. While we're queuing a woman dressed as a dragon walks up and down on stilts.

'How do they walk?' I ask my mum. 'Can I have some stilts?'

I can imagine myself walking around the garden in them and being able to see right over the wall. Though I don't tell Mum that bit.

'They strap their legs up and have to practise a lot,' Mum says.

The dragon goes past again, she looks down at me, and against the sun her golden face turns dark. She drapes her frilly dragon wings over me and I tip my head back so they can fall over my face and everything goes green and gold, then black. She walks on and I can see her bottom moving under her shiny tight green leggings. When a man dressed as a fly comes near I swap sides with Mum, in case he does the same, because I don't really like the fly.

When we pay and get through Mum leans over me. 'What d'you think?'

And I'm just nodding and nodding because I can't say what I think except I love it. I love how everything seems weird, or too tall or upside down. That there's people with sequins on their eyelids or dressed as bears and a giant book open on a page with the corner curling up – though when I touch it with my finger, it's not paper but hard plastic. It's like the place in *Alice* on the other side of the mirror, a place where I might be able to grow as high as one of the tents or talk to a cat. Mum's explaining how in each tent there's stories being told and when she says that I can feel words come shooting out of the tent doors and I just want to stand there at the openings and let them fizz on my brain.

Mum's reading the book now that tells you everything that's going to be happening. The programme she says it is, though I thought that was something on the telly.

'What kind of story would you like to hear?'

I say fairies because I can't put into proper words the things in my head: swords glinting in the dark; pirates with hard yellow eyes; things that happen under the sea; creatures with furry mouths that whisper secrets.

We find a tent called 'Once Upon a Time.' Inside, there's a pretty woman with silver glitter on her face and little pink wings drooping down her sides. The tent's lit up with coloured lights that twinkle on and off. When everyone's sitting cross-legged on the mat on the ground she reads this story about a fairy that has to earn her wings by doing good deeds. But all the time she's reading out loud it's like she's trying too hard and it's making her worry. Her forehead keeps crinkling up and when she puts on the voice of the fairy it's high and squeaky and her wings start looking sadder and sadder. And as well the fairy's just too good to be true, especially when she swears never to let a bad thought cross her mind ever again. Bad thoughts happen in everyone's mind – I know I've got them. So when the story finishes I start pulling on the sleeve of Mum's green jacket.

'Did you like that?' she asks.

'Yes, it was lovely.' I don't want to say about the sad wings or the too-good-to-be-true fairy. 'Can we go somewhere else now?'

We find another tent where a story's going to start in half an hour.

'Let's bag a place,' says Mum and because hardly anyone's there yet we can be right at the front. I sit on the floor mat under the wooden stage and the empty chair that's ready for the storyteller.

Mum's looking at the programme again. 'You'll like this one, Carmel. It's a real writer and she's going to be reading a story she wrote herself.'

The tent's soon full to bursting, even people standing at the back.

I look over my shoulder and it's then I see the man.

He's standing against the wall – if you can call it a wall as we're in a tent – he's got white hair and glasses and he looks *just like* my storyteller in the drawing. And I smile at him because he looks like that and he smiles back. He's staring right at me.

The writer comes in from a gap in the tent behind the stage. She's old with short spiky grey hair and she's got on this long glittery pink skirt with little blue boots poking out from underneath and her dangly earrings are the shape of question marks. She's got a basket too. It's a long time before she settles in the chair. She takes a big blob of pink bubblegum right out of her mouth and glues it onto a piece of paper in her basket. In the basket there's books and her knitting showing out of the top with the needles stuck into a ball of red wool. I'm getting the feeling she's been knitting right up until it was time to start the story and then afterward she'll go straight back to it.

The first words of the story are: 'The day her dad left Cassandra was so upset she went out into the garden and buried her favourite doll . . .'

I listen and listen because it seems to me that the girl in the story is just like me. I can feel Mum looking at me sometimes but I don't let that take my listening away. The story finishes and the writer looks right over her red glasses and says, 'Would you like to ask me any questions?'

There's quiet for a bit then a woman at the back puts her hand up and asks, 'Where do you get your ideas from?' Though I can tell she only asks this because the quiet is embarrassing and she's filling it up so it won't be so bad for the writer. But the writer answers anyway. Her ideas, she says, come drifting toward her, and she's got no way of knowing where they came from. They just come floating right toward her like out of a fog. It's not much of an explanation but I can tell she's telling the truth as best she can.

Other children start asking questions. 'Why did you call the girl Cassandra?' and 'What happened to the dog that was in the beginning of the story and not the end?' This question makes the writer smile and she says the dog was there through the whole story but she's only written about him at the start and maybe that was a mistake. That's very interesting to me, because I never thought you could make mistakes in stories. She starts saying things about who you can talk to if you are upset like Cassandra – teachers, friends and of course there's always your nan and grandad.

That's when I put my hand up.

She points to me straight away – like I knew she was going to, because all the way through I can tell she's been interested in me. She kept looking over at me when she was reading and finally I think I have something quite interesting and unusual to tell her.

'I don't know any of my grandparents at all.'

She's smiling and leaning forward, she *is* interested. 'Why, dear?'

'Because my dad's parents are dead and my mum hasn't spoken to hers since I was a baby.'

Mum pulls her arms in the green jacket around and hugs her knees.

But the writer understands, she leans forward even more and says, 'How fascinating! I just knew you'd have something out of the ordinary to tell me.'

My question seems to finish everything and people start leaving.

'Did you like that?' Mum asks. But I just nod; I can't really say anything after speaking like that in front of everyone.

'Let's go and have a bite to eat then, Carmel. You must be getting hungry. I know I am.'

And I'm grateful to her because I know she probably wants

to ask if I felt like the girl in the story when Dad left, and I did, but I don't feel like talking about it.

We buy hot dogs and eat them sitting on the grass on top of a little hill so we can see everything below: the tents; the big book; the crowds with the people on stilts standing up taller than anyone else. We chew for a bit then I look down again.

'What's that?' I ask. There's smoke on the ground and the people are sticking up out of it with their legs invisible.

'Seems like there's a sea mist coming.'

'Oh, I thought there was a fire.'

'No, just a bit of old fog and look, it hasn't reached us here.' She laughs and her blue eyes light up all bright.

I put the last bit of hot dog in my mouth and squish it with my teeth. I decide I like the mist. It makes everything seem even stranger than before and I like that.

'I love it here,' I say, because I do and the feeling of it has suddenly rushed through my body.

'Do you, honey?' Mum's finished her hot dog and she's sitting with her face turned up to the sun. 'I do too.' And she looks happier and prettier than I've seen her for ages.

But then she turns into a spy again.

9

DAY 1

HOW MANY TIMES have I gone over what happened next? How many times more? Fated for it to run and run, a tape that as soon as it ends rewinds back to the beginning to start again.

After lunch it got busier – the prospect of a children's story-telling festival a magnetic draw for parents of bored holiday kids. The lovely weather of the morning that had lured so many people on a day out was changing. The sun kept trying to break through but the cold mist poked its fingers into us, so we kept our coats on. I felt the first pricklings of a panic attack – something I imagined I'd left behind – but Carmel was still excited, buoyed up with being somewhere new and the ancient magic generated by the stories. We walked among mothers pushing buggies and families studying their programmes and the people in costumes handing out leaflets or free bottles of water. At first I just kept glancing down to check for the flash of red beside me.

It became noisier. There were bangs and smoke from fire-crackers being let off, the smoke mingling with the creeping mist. Cheers as a mass of yellow balloons was let off and careened across the sky like a crazy wayward double of the sun dislodged from its mooring. Smoke from burning burgers infiltrated its meaty smell into pockets of the crowd. Thoughts of the school trip started coming back to me, where the teachers had lost her. The maze where she'd disappeared.

So I held on to her hand but it felt slippy, always at the point of breaking loose, so sometimes all I had was a finger or two. Don't fuss, I told myself, just make sure she's next to you. She wants to be a big girl now. But I looked for that flash of red and it was gone, replaced by a fat woman who didn't seem to feel the cold, the jellied weight of her arms hanging down beneath the short sleeves of her pink T-shirt, silver stars bursting across her breasts. She leaned down and stabbed a shiny blue helium balloon on a stick inside a pushchair. 'Here,' she grimaced. 'Now shut up.' Then the red of Carmel's coat appeared and I could breathe again. I reached for her hand, feeling just thin air and this time a man in a Fair Isle jumper, carrying a little girl in pink boots on his shoulders, had come between us. 'Can you see the bear?' he called upward. 'Can you see the bear?' Then some leaflets were thrust at me and there was Carmel again and I dropped the leaflets onto the churned-up ground and found her hand and held it tight, so I couldn't lose it. Then the air began to get more and more lacy with fog.

'Just keep hold of my hand,' I shouted down.

My resolve on the train, how quickly it had been dismantled. And everything, I know, would have been forgotten if that day hadn't been preserved forever, my panic a brick in the building that was made, hour by hour, of events – standing there for all time instead of crumbling away into memory. I didn't mean to but maybe I sounded cross too – I expect so. So sometimes the very worst thought becomes a train that doesn't stop.

The thought: Was it my fault? Was it my fault? Was it my fault? Was it my fault? Was it my fault? Was it my fault? Was it my fault? Was it my fault?

10

MUM'S VOICE TURNS SHARP and cold like the fog. We cross the field to the biggest tent where they sell books. The fog comes in the tent with us like it really is smoke. There's some thin rain too, the kind that gets you very wet, so everyone is coming inside. And I seem to be able to hear her better inside, exactly what her voice is saying: 'Carmel, stay here. Stay so I can see you. I nearly lost sight of you then.' When all I've been doing is stopping to look at books.

There's tables piled high with them and she buys me a couple. While she's paying I turn around and I'm facing the stomach of a man. I look up at his head and it's the man from the tent and from the drawing again. He's tall and old-fashioned in a way I can't really explain. There's nothing like a top hat or long hair or anything but he's not quite the same as the other men around him, like he could have stepped out of olden times. He's got on a white shirt very ironed and with no collar and a black rough suit. I smile up at him again but he's gone.

I turn around back to Mum and she's taking a plastic bag of books from the lady behind the stall.

But even inside she wants to hold my hand tight, tight every second. That's OK at first but if I want to stop at a stall and hold a book it's annoying.

'Look.' I point over. 'Look over there.' There's puppets of knights and horses hanging up and jiggling about by themselves. I want to go right up to them and see how they work.

She doesn't even hear and her hand's feeling sweaty and slippery so I make mine stiff like a claw so it'll be difficult to hold.

'If you don't hold my hand, we'll have to go straight home.' She's sounding tired and cross and I'm really angry with her now for spoiling our lovely day. I try to nip the anger back in and explain.

'It's just that I want to look at books and I can't because you won't let me go.'

'Well, we can stop holding hands when we get to a stall. How about that?' She smiles a stiff little smile that's not real.

I say, 'Oh, all right, then.' I still feel cross with her because it's not fun any more now I know she's not enjoying it.

We come to a stall piled up high.

'Let's look at this one.' I only say that because I want a rest from her.

I look at the books and they're so babyish – *Where's Spot?* and things like that. I don't want to go back to being yanked about so I look very slowly and carefully. Spot with his bone, Spot's day out. And the baby books make me feel even crosser but I carry on looking anyway, picking each one up.

'Why d'you want to look at those, Carmel? They're for little kids.'

'I want to look at those fairy stories over there.' I go moving up the table.

I turn over the pages of a fairy story book. The drawings aren't that good but I look at each one anyway: the princess with her pea; Cinderella in rags; the wolf looking silly in a frilly red cloak. I move up to look at something else. People press around me and I'm being whacked on the back of my head with someone's handbag.

I'm in such a bad mood now. It's not often I feel like this and I don't like it. It's like everything's wrong – especially me. Now I just want to be on my own. To go back to this morning in my room when the sky was blue and everything was lovely. Everyone has come into this tent now the storytelling has stopped for lunch and people want to buy something and get out of the rain. I'm getting so squashed I think the table is going to cut me in half.

Then I have an idea – to scrunch myself right down and walk like I saw a toad walk once, till I'm under the table. So I do – the tablecloth only comes halfway down but it feels free and safe and secret under there. I decide to look out for Mum's boots that she's got her jeans tucked into and then I'll come out.

There's a box of books and I take a peek into it and there's piles of the book I used to read when I was little about a skeleton. I take one out and it's not like when I was seeing Spot the dog. I don't feel babyish, it's like being back little again but I like the feeling it gives me this time. So I read *Funnybones* and look at the pictures. Sometimes I touch them too, I don't know why.

When I get to the end I realise I might have been ages. But I'm not sure. Sometimes things happen so it feels like I'm not really there at all. It's like the time the headmaster was talking about when I was sitting on the bench – looking at a tree blowing about – somehow my brain got slipped and in the world there was only me and the tree.

Then it slipped more and I was in a creepy dark tunnel where I'd been before but that day was the longest time it had happened for. Though I didn't want to try and tell them about that.

And just now the same thing happened with *Funnybones* and there was the book and me but I didn't go as far as the tunnel. I went back to being five for all that time and it had felt nice.

There's less legs now so I crawl out. I'm a bit worried that I might have been a long time, I'm not sure. I look about and can't see Mum.

I carry on picking up books. I don't know what else to do. I should look for her, I decide. Maybe I'll find her waiting for me at the end of the table but I get to the end and she's not there. I stand there for a bit. Then I think, she must have got pushed back by the people and I try to look but I can't find the back of where everyone's standing. They just seem to melt into other people and it's the opposite from earlier, I'm longing to see her now. My breath starts coming in and out quickly because I want to find her so much. I walk around the tent for a while. I go back to the same table where I lost her – twice, three times – and she's still not there so I walk out of the tent and across the field.

Outside, I can hardly see the tops of the tents any more or the flags – just people coming out of the fog. And only if they're close. All the sounds have gone thick and quiet like when I put my duvet over my head at home. I shove my hands deep into my pockets to try and stop me worrying and I think – our lovely day's gone and we may as well go home now, back on the train. I stop, wondering what to do, and the people I can't see, I can hear – muttering around me.

Then, stepping out of the fog right in front of me is the man from earlier with the round glasses. Because of the fog he comes out of nowhere, like a genie does.

'Oh, dear.' He looks upset, his face crumpling up. 'What's the matter?' I ask. There's a horrible feeling at the bottom of my throat. Sick and tight.

'Oh, dear. Oh, dear . . .' he keeps saying. 'Something's very wrong.'

People's voices muttering in the fog sound like the humming of the bee from this morning and I squeeze my hands tight and dig my nails into my skin because it feels like I might fall over.

'Where's my mum?' I nearly shout, except it comes out quite small because my throat feels so tight.

His face goes a bit less upset and straightens out. 'I need to check, what's your exact name?'

'Carmel Summer Wakeford,' I say, trying not to cry. But everything happening's so wrong I can feel a big sob blocking up my throat and the snot in my nose starting to run.

He's nodding, like he's got the right person, and says in a slow voice, 'Carmel, it's your mother. She's had a terrible accident.'

There's a rushing in my ears and the fog cuts us off so it's just me and him.

'Who are you?' I ask.

And he says to me, 'I'm your grandfather.'

II

DAY 1

IT WILL BE LIKE the day in the maze, I told myself. I'll run around this field looking, scared witless, but we'll find each other eventually.

The fog had grown cold and dense and I kept stumbling on empty plastic bottles and bumpy ground. 'Carmel,' I yelled at the top of my voice, 'where are you?'

I kept yelling into the fog but it never answered. It just sucked up my voice into its blankness. I wanted more than anything to catch a glimpse of that red, like a poppy standing proud in a cornfield. But there was just a jumble of colour, made milky, as if looking through a wedding veil. I thought I'd go to the entrance and ask for help: an announcement on the tannoy. Or to the St John Ambulance in case she'd fallen over and was there right now having a plaster put on her knee while someone in uniform was saying, 'All done. Now then, let's find your mum.'

People were getting fed up and wanting to leave. The field was emptying, they were all at the entrance – a temporary arch made out of plywood with shapes cut into it to look like battlements – so I had to push past them. I knocked against the bodies without caring, muttering, 'I've lost my little girl,' over my shoulder to the 'watch its.' Several people asked if I was all right but I couldn't stop to answer, I was too intent.

'Carmel, where are you, where are you?'

The ticket offices next to the arch were empty, the organisers probably guessing that no one would arrive so late in the day, so I had to find my way back again, all the time shouting, 'Carmel, Carmel,' till my voice was hoarse.

I found my way back into the tent where I'd last seen her. It's too soon, I told myself, it's too soon to panic. Stop it. Stop it now.

The trestle table where she'd stood was half empty – many of the books sold. I'd had the idea of asking the man with the till if he'd seen her but there was nobody there now. The thought came to me that the remaining books left out like this could so easily be stolen.

'Carmel,' I called. 'Where are you?'

A man put his hand on my arm. 'What's the matter, love?'

'My little girl. I can't find her.'

I realised my eyes were wet and stopped for a moment this time.

'Oh dear. Dear. You need to get to the main tent. They'll help you. She's probably waiting there for you.'

'Yes – thank you. Thank you. Where is it?'

'Ask one of the staff – they'll tell you.'

I rubbed at my eyes.

'Don't worry, love,' he said. 'You'll find her. Mine were always getting lost when they were young.'

I took his advice and went outside to look for staff. He's right, I thought. There must be an official tent or a place for lost children. But the fog was lacing the air so now it was hard to see the tents any more. Panic gripped my insides again. Even among so many other people I started to feel alone in some kind of new and terrible reality.

What if, what if . . . I never see her again? No. No, not that. I stumbled, then righted myself. Stop thinking it.

I tried to yell again but my voice had disappeared into a squeak and a sudden tide of terror washed over me. I reached out and wordlessly gripped a woman's bright red sleeve. 'Hey, get off,' she said. 'Get off me.'

She shook me off and got swallowed up into the fog.

Then one of the men on stilts walked right past me, his stilts close enough to touch. I could feel my voice re-gathering inside my throat in a shout – 'Please, help me. Help.' I didn't care any more what I said or if I sounded mad and frantic.

The stilts paused and started to move on so I shouted again and they stopped and the next minute a young man with corn-rows all over his scalp had jumped down and was standing right next to me.

'Did you ask for help?' His clothes were made of patchwork and underneath the multicoloured jacket his shoulders were strong, like he was active all day. I remembered the man with the cloth cap in the maze and I felt relief. The stilts man was part of the day, of the organisation. He could tell me where I needed to go.

'My little girl, I've lost her,' I said.

'Where did you see her last?'

'In the place where they're selling the books.'

'I bet a lot of people are getting lost in this. It's bad luck it should happen today when we've been planning it for so long. A sea mist is always the worst. It must have been the hot weather this morning that brought it on.'

It made me feel a bit better when he said he expected lots of people were getting lost and separated, like this was just a mishap that would be sorted out.

'I'll take you to the admin tent and they can put a tannoy call-out. You two'll be glad to get home when you find her.' Then he was guiding me across the field with his stilts tucked under his arm.

Inside the tent the fog had crept in and lay low on the ground so it got kicked up into little clouds as we walked. There was a woman with bright dyed red hair – the kind of red not even meant to look real – walking up and down and speaking into a walkie-talkie and I noticed a flap of brown paper had got stuck to the heel of her boot. Across the squashed grass of the floor people were packing things away in boxes.

The man in patchwork steered me up toward the red-haired walkie-talkie woman.

'This lady has lost her daughter,' he said. He went away and came back with a fold-up chair for me to sit on. But I didn't want to sit down.

She looked up with sharp blue eyes and reluctantly re-sheathed the walkie-talkie in a leather holder on her belt that looked like it was meant for carrying guns.

'I expect she's just got lost in the crowds. How long is it since you've seen her?' Silver flickered from her tongue as she spoke from the piercing there. She sounded like this losing of a daughter was nothing more than a pernickety nuisance and could be sorted out with a snap of her fingers – meaning she could get on with something more important.

I looked at my watch and with a burning spurt of real sickness in my throat I realised it must have been just over an hour.

'Ages, an hour and a half. At least.' I wanted to exaggerate because I sensed she wasn't taking it seriously enough, that she didn't have a daughter and thought that kids just ran off all the time.

She was shifting a foot around and suddenly became conscious of the paper stuck to her heel. With a movement like a ballerina she forked a leg behind her, holding her foot with one hand and peeling off the paper with the other.

When she was done she said, 'I can put out an announcement.'

'Please. Could you? Her name's Carmel and she's wearing a red duffel coat.'

'How old is she?'

'She's eight. Eight years old.'

So she walked off to where a tannoy system was set up on a trestle table and the man with cornrows looked at me with kind big eyes and said, 'Don't worry too much. It's got a bit chaotic because of the weather.' I nodded at him dumbly.

I heard an electric gasp as the machine was switched on and then the woman's voice booming from the outside.

'Public announcement. Lost child. There's a lost child. Name of Carmel. Red coat. Eight years old. If you find a lost child please bring them to the large tent at the back of the field. Lost child . . .'

I ran outside and tried to scan the field, though it was hard to see much. I went back in and the woman was busy moving boxes now, stacking unused programmes away.

'Do it again,' I shouted.

'You don't have to . . .' A sharp spike of a frown had popped up between her eyes. The man in patchwork could see it was going to get nasty so he stepped in.

'You keep on the tannoy. We'll go and look around the field,' he told her. Then to me, 'My name's Dave.' He took my hand and his brown fingers felt hard and strong. 'What's yours?'

'Beth,' I mumbled.

Outside the ground was churned up into mud – a thick cakey mix of lolly sticks, leaflets and broken plastic cups. The smell of the mud rose up, dark, sweet and cold, with the odour of something uncovered that should have been left alone. I heard the announcement again from outside the tent but no one seemed to pay much attention. Dave helped me to retrace our steps, holding on to my arm. Back to the sales tent – he called Carmel's name in a deep booming voice and looked under tables and I did the same.

'OK,' he said. 'Now we'll work our way around the field.'

After every lap around the tents we went back to the walkie-talkie woman to check if Carmel was with her. Each time I was willing myself to see the bright little spot of red waiting for me by the boxes, or peeping out anxiously through the gap in the doorway, and felt a sickening panic when it wasn't there. The panic rose in stages, so it was like someone singing the same note but at a higher and higher pitch.

Time was getting jumbled up and I found it hard to think if a long time or a short time had gone. I tried to look at my watch as we raced around the field again, but I was walking too fast, running really, and my brain was in such a state of shock I had trouble deciphering what the golden fingers meant.

Back again. Nothing. Headlines again, wasn't there . . . No, no, no. Yes, there was – nearby, about five years ago. I don't remember if she was found. I think she was, how terrible I don't remember. Paul, I need to speak to Paul. To tell him, get him to help. He'll be so worried, angry that I've lost her. I can't think about that, though, I just want her . . . '. . . back.' I didn't realise but the word came out of my mouth in a wail.

'What?' asked the walkie-talkie woman, confused.

'D'you have a phone?' It was just before the time when everyone possessed a mobile phone and I'd held off because of the expense.

'Yes.'

'Call the police, it's been too long,' I said over my shoulder as I pitched out once again to look. Then in again and she hadn't – some problem with the signal. A hole in coverage she called it – though I was sure I'd heard somewhere that emergency-service calls went through anyway and I imagined she hadn't bothered, thinking I was just a hysterical woman. But then she realised it was her battery that had run out so she made the call on one of the box-packers' phones.

The field was almost empty and I looked at my watch and focused. The time crystallised sharp and clear: nearly two hours. Really two hours, not the made-up time I'd given her before.

'Tell them it's been nearly two hours, tell them that,' I said.

'Yes, the mother's here with me, right here,' she said into the phone. 'Yes, that's right . . .'

I snatched it from her. 'Please, please, get here as quick as you can. It's been ages since she's gone – ages. And she's not like that, she's really not,' I said, not entirely truthfully. It was anything, anything I could say to make them take it seriously. My voice was rising higher and higher into a painful squeak so the woman took the phone back and gave the details of where the festival was and how to find us when they got here.

The atmosphere in the tent had changed. A few people carried on packing stuff up around me, but quietly, averting their eyes, like there'd been an accident they were now trying to ignore. I felt my legs trembling underneath me and I collapsed on the chair Dave had put out. The woman squatted next to me. She didn't look bad-tempered any more.

'They're on their way,' she said.

By evening the field had emptied of people, but the only way I knew that was because it was silent now. The fog held its stranglehold over everything: its white noise sliced up by powerful police torches. There didn't seem to be enough police cars; I wanted a whole fleet, an army there.

Sometimes the cars had their lights playing and that cut through the fog too and lit up the air with a crackle of blue lightning. The white-out made it a dream state: the strange sense of being underwater or wading through glue; the feeling that once the fog lifted she would be revealed, standing in the middle of the field, motionless with fright and with drops of moisture clinging to her coat. The feeling that this was a drama, using us as characters, unfolding on a roll-down screen made of fog and air in the middle of a dark field – the red of Carmel's coat flickering across the screen.

'I should go home.'

Soothing voices around me. There were three or four of them, ready to contain my terrible anxiety. To direct operations in the way they needed to go.

I found it hard to stand still so I perched on one leg. 'I need to go home, in case she's there. She doesn't have a key. She won't be able to get in.'

One soothing voice now. It was the tall bony man with ginger hair who had arrived a bare half hour ago and now seemed to be in charge. What was his name? My mind fumbled – Detective something . . . Andy.

'What we'll do, Beth, what we'll do is we'll send someone over there. You let us have the keys and we'll send someone over and if you tell us where we might be able to find a photograph of

Carmel then that's all the better, isn't it?' He smiled encouragingly, like he'd had a bright idea and wanted me to be part of the plan. His face looked waxy in the dim light; maybe it would melt away and I would wake, with a jolt and then flooding relief. Instead, a terrible surge of anxiety shot through me.

'Oh, please. Please find her. Please, please find her.' My voice was babbling in my ears. I looked at my watch – four and a half hours. But he was going on again about photos. 'Recent ones. As recent as possible. We'll take you home but we'll stop at the station and take a proper statement.'

'Oh no, no.' Now I felt a rising panic at the thought of leaving this place. It would be an admission: arriving as two and leaving as one.

'Beth, I want you to remember.' His pale brown eyes – soft, vestigial lashes – looked right into mine. 'You need to know that you are not alone. There is this.' He gestured behind him, the torches, the muffled voices through the fog, the blue police lights raking the sky. 'There is us on your side.'

I relinquished my keys and let myself be led to a waiting police car. Andy held on to my arm and carried a torch to light our way. It lit up the scene in fragments – the gouged-up mud filthy with litter, the flapping empty tents; the festive day now a Somme wasteland. The crew had had to hold off de-rigging and as I drew closer I could see the outlines of their shapes, smoking and kicking their heels around the entrance. I saw the orange points of light from their cigarettes through the fog and heard laughter, then, 'Sshh, sshh – she's coming through. It's the mother.'

In real life bad things can be fascinating, or very hard to look at. Some turned their eyes to the ground and others stared as I walked past. One, with a trilby-type hat and a Polish accent, called out, 'Bless you, mother; bless you and your little girl. I pray to the Virgin . . .' Then I was in the back of the police car. Andy slid in beside me, splashes of blue and red light from the cars on his face.

'Try not to panic,' he said very quietly and calmly. 'Children sometimes wander off.'

'She wouldn't do that. She wouldn't leave me. Not for this long.'

He turned and smiled, tight at the corners. 'Then that means she'll be all right, doesn't it?'

But nothing was all right. At the police station it was clear nothing was all right at all. Andy's platitudes were just a ruse to calm hysterics down. Already I could see some kind of action plan had swung into place. They knew . . . they knew a bright little girl of eight years doesn't just wander off and not come back. They didn't know how it had happened before. I wasn't going to tell them that. And at the station there were more eyes, sheathing their looks of fear and pity or reproach with their lids: the woman behind the counter; the man unlocking the interview-room door; the woman passing me in the fluorescent-lit corridor, going off duty after carefully applying her eye make-up in the locker-room mirror. Two quick flashes of turquoise as she rounded down her lids and looked at the floor.

'We need to take a proper statement,' Andy said. There was a woman already sitting behind the desk in the interview room: round-faced, pretty.

'This is Sophie, she's what we call a family liaison officer. She's there just for you, Beth, for whatever you want . . .'

She looked at me. It lasted only a moment but the look was deep, deep. I could tell she was reaching in and making some sort of assessment. Moment over, she smiled. 'Beth, any questions, ask. Anything you need, you must tell me.'

What I need is my little girl back. 'Hello, Sophie,' I said. 'Thank you.'

I sat facing them at the scarred wooden table and they began questioning me and writing my answers in their notebooks and recording my words on a machine. I tried to answer as best I could, I tried to keep my brain focused on the task, but it kept veering off at steep tangents of rising panic, so I would have to refocus and ask them to repeat the question.

'Tell us about Carmel's father, we'll need to get in contact with him quickly. We've tried the number you gave us and we passed by the house earlier but there was nobody home.'

I felt such pity for them then – for Paul and Lucy. The rosy flush of their lust was about to be transformed into something hard and brittle – one of those horrible wreaths of ceramic roses in a graveyard, a filthy sepulchre.

'Oh God – shall I call him?' I started scrabbling in my bag for my diary, where his mobile number was scratched on the front page. I realised it was the only one I had – no landline – and it seemed such a tenuous thread. Sophie gently put her hand on my arm.

'We'll keep on with that. You say you are separated. Any issues with that?'

'No, not really. I mean he's stayed away a lot. He's supposed to see her every weekend but we didn't see him for months, then all of a sudden he came around and took her out.'

'So there have been disagreements with access?'

'I suppose so. No, not really, it's nothing to do . . . it's just that he's got a new girlfriend and he's more wrapped up in that. We've only just started communicating again, I mean properly. It's been difficult.'

They exchanged glances.

'Is there any way, do you think, that he might have taken her?' Andy asked. 'I know it's hard to fathom, but dads can act in funny ways after divorces. Take kids off out of the blue and not tell a soul about it.'

'It couldn't have been Paul. He's too . . . too lax to do anything like this. Besides, I'm not sure he even knew we were there. No, no, no, you've got the wrong end of the stick, it's not him. You must look elsewhere.' All the same I grasped at the possibility that perhaps I *had* told him, and he'd taken it into his head to spirit her away.

I looked through the window at the dark. 'He'll probably be home now. I don't think they go out much in the evening.'

Sophie left the room briefly, I assumed to give instructions about hunting Paul down. Soon there would be a police car at their door. Blue lights through the window, sliding down their sitting-room walls.

My watch: eight hours now. I found it hard to sit still. Impossible. Every so often I would feel as if I'd been wired to the grid, a surge of electricity would jolt me forward, or even up to standing, so I was looking down at them. The rising panic – I forced it into my body so my mind could keep functioning and giving them what they needed to know. Kindly, they didn't comment. They let me pace or bang my head with my hand or slump in the chair with my arms hanging loosely by my sides, as long as I kept talking, kept telling them: when; who; school; friends; dads; any boyfriends of mine; eyes: blue or brown; hair: what colour – thin, thick, curly, straight, short, long.

When the photo albums arrived, it seemed peculiar to see them there, uprooted from the shelves at home to lie beside the blinking voice recorder.

They came just as I was describing, screwing up my forehead and trying to be as accurate as possible, the colour of her hair. Not blond, not brown; it was, I finally decided, 'the exact colour of a brown paper envelope.'

12

'QUICK, QUICK.'

We're running toward the car park and he's telling me to go faster. He's tall with long legs so he can run much better than me. He keeps looking back over his shoulder and saying in a panicking voice, 'No time to waste. Quick as you can.'

I do run as fast as I can but I can't help it if I keep stumbling. It's hard when I'm crying and my nose is running and I don't even have time to find the tissue I know's in my pocket. Then we get to his car that's white. I don't see it till we're right next to it as it's the same colour as the fog.

'We'll go straight to the hospital,' he says. Then he unlocks the door.

I slide into the seat next to him. The car's very clean and the seats are shiny and white too. It starts up and I rub my hands up and down my face and try and get rid of all the snot and tears. But it just mixes together and goes hard so it's like I've got a mask on.

We drive slow because there are other cars in front of us trying to leave.

'What h-happened?' I ask. I feel like the whole world is folding up around me and I don't think I've ever been so scared in my whole life. I feel like I'm living in a programme inside the telly or in a different country where they have bombs and volcanoes.

I can't see his eyes because of the white mist outside shining on his glasses. 'My dear' – his voice goes quiet and kind – 'she was looking for you in the car park and she got run over by a truck.'

'Oh no, no.' My hands go over my head like something's going to fall on top of me. 'Is she . . . is she alive?'

His mouth goes into a thin straight line. 'Alive, yes. But very badly injured, Carmel. She probably thought you'd run off.'

'I didn't,' I shout, and turn around in the car seat so I'm shouting right at him. 'I didn't run off. We just lost each other.'

Then I crumple up a bit because I have that sick guilty feeling. Only it's not a small stone in my stomach now, but a great big one taking up loads of room and pushing up into my throat. I have the horrible feeling that it's my fault, because I didn't want to hold her hand and be good. And I wasn't being good, if I'm being truthful. I imagine the truck with her brown boots sticking out from underneath, like when the house landed on the witch in *The Wizard of Oz*. Only not like that at all of course because this is real and terrible and my mum isn't a witch, she's lovely, even if we were having a small argument that didn't matter.

I cry for a good long time but my grandfather doesn't say anything. I cry most of the hard snot off my face until my eyes feel too big for my head. I scrabble around for the tissue in my pocket and blow my nose but there's too much and it goes over my fingers.

'Here, have another one.' My grandfather reaches into the back seat and grabs me a packet of new tissues. I realise then what's strange about his voice, it sounds Irish or something and I didn't know Mum's dad was Irish.

We're out on the road now and I stop crying for a minute and for the first time I look at him properly. The thing I notice most about his head is that it's pale all over. He's got white hair clipped neat and there's the fog reflections on his glasses so his face is like a white sheet of paper with just the thin silver edges of his glasses gleaming out.

Suddenly I think he looks like a ghost and I ask, 'Why didn't you say hello to us when we saw you earlier?'

'Oh, Carmel. You know how your mother and me have fallen out.' And he turns to look at me even though he's driving. 'The ingratitude of children is a terrible thing to bear.'

Even though I don't really understand I don't like it much because it sounds like it's a bad thing about my mum and it doesn't seem right to be saying bad things when a truck has just run right over her.

'How did you know we were even there?' I ask. I hadn't thought about that before. Now I've stopped crying my brain is trying to understand the day that's turning into a terrible broken puzzle with jagged edges and bits missing.

'I didn't. I just saw you and thought – there's my little Carmel.'

'But how did you know it was me?'

Mum doesn't talk much about her mum and dad, just – 'We don't get on. It's a shame.' I miss having a nan and grandad when my friends tell me about the things they do with theirs. Days out and making biscuits, stuff like that.

'Your mum sends me photographs every year. At Christmas.'

'Does she?'

'Yes, and we talk on the phone sometimes. I like to hear the news, even though we don't get to see each other.'

I guess that must be after I'm in bed because I've never heard her.

He turns and gives me a little smile and I can see his eyes then. They're pale blue and misty-looking but there's kindness in the circle of blue and his voice sounds like he cares about when they talk on the phone.

'I know you must have a lot of questions. But there's not much time right now. It's very lucky I happened to be there. I'm awful glad I was.'

I just stay quiet because nothing feels lucky today. Nothing's felt lucky since those dragon wings went over my face and turned everything black.

The car bumps on along through the fog so I can't even see where we're going and I start getting this odd feeling that we're the only two people in the world and driving not on the road, but through the clouds. It seems like anything is possible today, me and Mum saw birds disappearing into a man's hat even. I can feel something knotty under my fingers so I look down and see there are black stitches in the white seats. I keep running my fingers over and over them. I breathe slow and deep like Mum showed me how to do when I fell over when I was little and there was blood everywhere.

'Are we nearly at the hospital?'

'Yeah, nearly there.'

But we keep on driving for ages and I start feeling panicky again. 'Tell me in minutes how far we are,' I say.

He does a little laugh and it's a rattle noise in his throat. 'I tell you what, dear. Shall I call the hospital and see how she is? Is that a good idea?' He turns his head and smiles.

'Yes please.' My voice sounds small in the car.

He drives onto the side of the road and we park on the grass. He gets a phone out of his pocket and opens the door. 'Better signal out here,' he says. He starts to get out, then stops. 'Have you got a phone, dear?'

'No.'

He nods and climbs out of the car.

I can see him through the window – just the bottom half holding the phone in his hands and pressing buttons – then the fog disappears him. That's what I wanted for my birthday but Mum and Dad said NO, and I could only have a phone when I'm older because it fries children's brains. I told Sara about this and she made a noise like frying bacon and grabbed her head, because she's having one for her next birthday.

He's parked us about an inch from a stone wall so there's not much to see out of my window except crusty stuff growing over it and the bits between the stones crumbling out. I think about getting out of the car but the wall means I wouldn't be able to open the door on my side. And I don't want to get the white seats dirty by climbing over them and getting out on the other side. I feel frozen into a lump and now Grandad is outside the car and not with me I'm frightened because I don't know him. I wonder what my mum would think about me being with him, and the idea that she doesn't know where I am gives me shivers all over. Then the door opens and makes me jump and Grandad can see I'm afraid. He sees it on my face and the way I'm holding my hands together, one inside the other.

'Now, then, Carmel, I don't want you worrying away.' He slides in next to me and puts his hand on my shoulder. His voice has gone soft and kind.

I nod. I feel a bit better now he's back and he knows what to do and where to go and everything.

'I don't want you worrying but I have to tell . . . I'm afraid I have to tell you we can't go to the hospital right now.'

This makes me sit bolt upright. 'Oh, why? Why?'

He shuts the door on his side with a click.

'Your mother's been taken to theatre. We can't see her now.'

This is another big hole opening up in the puzzle. 'Theatre? Why would she go to the theatre?'

He smiles a little crooked smile then, more on one side than the other.

'No, dear. Not that kind of theatre. It's what they call the place where doctors do operations. They're going to try and fix her. Isn't that good news?'

I lean back, tired out. 'Oh.'

He doesn't think I'm being happy enough about it. 'It's very good news, Carmel.'

'I suppose,' I mumble. But I don't like to think of my mum having an operation with a big light shining on her while she's asleep.

'There's no point us going there now. They said to call tomorrow. Are you thirsty, dear?'

I nod. My throat feels scraped out. He opens the glove box and gets out a bottle of water. It's only half full like someone else has been drinking from it and I don't like the idea of that so I try to drink without my mouth touching it too much.

'We'll go back to my place for the time being. Just until we've heard something. I'll fix you something to eat.'

'All right,' I say, even though what he's just said wasn't really a question.

He starts the car again and it's so big it sort of flops back onto the road.

I think of something. 'What about Dad?'

'Well, I've just spoken to him too. He's on his way to the hospital and he's very pleased there's someone to take care of you. He said he can't think straight right now.'

'Oh.' That sounds like Dad. I lean back feeling sleepy and trying not to be. All I can think is that I wish I was at home with Mum and everything was back to normal. That this wasn't worth a stupid story about a fairy who has to earn her wings. Or even meeting the real writer. Where are fairies and writers now when you need them? If I was with Mum, and everything was OK, I wouldn't try to get away from her again. I'd stay close to her all the time. I wouldn't even try looking over the wall at home, not ever.

13

WE DRIVE for a long time. Then it turns into night and there's blackness around the car. I get so tired I fall asleep.

When I wake up I see the car windscreen and for a minute I think I'm looking at a big broken TV and the swirling outside the glass is the picture trying to come through.

'You've been asleep, little Carmel.'

I turn my head to look and Grandad's hands are still stuck tight to the steering wheel as if he hasn't moved all the time while I've been asleep. It's not a surprise to me he's there because I didn't forget about him even though I was asleep, if that's possible. But something's made me go prickly, I think it's the way he said 'little.'

'It's fine, dear, to sleep. It'll help you with the shock you've had.' And he sounds kind again and I decide he's probably the sort of person who's not used to talking to little girls – like Dad's girlfriend – and it makes everything coming out of their mouths sound wrong and squeezed.

He doesn't seem tired at all. There's a sort of sparkly energy coming from him now. Mum told me once that can happen if you don't get much sleep. You stop feeling tired and get . . . 'wired up.'

I sit up in the slippy seat that's warmed up I've been in it so long.

'It's very dark here.' I'm trying to see where we are.

'I've taken the B roads. They're always more fun,' he says.

Though I can't think what's fun about it when it's so dark you can't even see, except some long grasses lit up by the headlights reaching out and whipping at the car either side. Then he starts singing, 'I'll take the B roads and you take the low.' He laughs at his song like he's done something clever.

'Come on, join in, Carmel. I'll teach you the words. *I'll take the B roads and you take the low . . .*'

'No thanks.'

He clutches at the steering wheel and laughs again. 'It'll be fun. Singing always makes a journey go quicker.'

'No thank you.' I'm trying to be extra polite but I really don't want to sing his song. I just don't feel like it.

He keeps on trying to get me to join in. But he gives up in the end and says, 'Not far now.'

I stare into the dark, being like a cat, and I start seeing some black hills. It looks like countryside with not even a single house. 'I thought you lived in London,' I say.

'Well . . . Carmel. The fact is, the fact is – we did. But when your grandmother died I couldn't settle. Then I met Dorothy, a true gem of a woman, and for the moment, well – we're staying in Wales. Waiting to see where the wind will blow us.'

'My grandma died?' I sit up. '*When* did she die?'

'Several years ago now – did your mother never tell you, dear?' And he tut-tuts like it's really sad and the saddest thing of all is Mum not telling me.

'No, I don't *think* she ever told me.' I'm trying to make it better for Mum, by making out I can't remember whether she told me or not.

'I think you would have remembered that, Carmel.' He's right.

I decide I can't really be upset about someone I don't know – even if she had been my grandma. But it's funny that Mum didn't tell me. I'm really wanting to ask why they argued but it seems too rude. Then a thought comes to me that Mum wouldn't have fallen out with someone for no reason and I make a decision to keep my eye on him, and find out what that reason might be.

I'm so tired now my eyes are burning but it doesn't stop me worrying about Mum.

'Can we phone the hospital and see what's happening to Mum again?' I ask.

'It's too late now. All the staff will be in bed because it's the middle of the night.'

'Is it?'

'Uh-huh. We'll phone in the morning and God willing they'll have some good news waiting for us. Besides, we're nearly there now.'

Then we're driving up a hill and around and around a winding road and I can hear wind blowing on the car.

'Here we are at last,' he says, and in the car lights there's the tallest pair of iron gates I've ever seen.

'Is this where you live?' It's a scary place, but I don't want to say.

'Yes, for the time being. It looks very big, Carmel, but we're only renting a tiny part of it. The rest is empty.'

'OK.' I swallow.

He rubs his hands together like people do when they're thinking of the next thing that has to be done. He gets out of the car and unlocks the big padlock that's hanging off the gates. With the car lights shining on him it makes his white hair glow around his head. He opens up the gates and comes back into the car.

We drive into a sort of yard and the headlights flash over a great big stone building that looks like a castle. He stops just inside the gates and goes back to lock them up.

When he gets back in I ask, 'Is this a castle?'

He's smiling as he switches the engine off and when he does that the lights go out too and everything goes black. Now he's sitting next to me in the dark and I don't know if he's still smiling or not. I don't know *what* the look is on his face.

His voice comes out of the dark. 'No, dear, it's not a castle. It used to be something called a workhouse in the old days. But developers started doing up part of it, before they ran out of money, and that's the bit we're staying in.' His voice sounds like he might be smiling.

I've heard of workhouses. We did them in school for history.

They were for people that . . . that 'fall over hard times.' But I don't ask anything else.

'Time to get out of the car, dear.'

I do but I'm so tired and it's so dark I'm stumbling around. There's a cool wind on my face, fresh, that smells of grasses and flowers.

'Here, let me help you. I thought there was a flashlight in the car but I seem to have mislaid it.' He laughs. 'Silly Grandpa.'

I feel his arm around my shoulders, guiding me somewhere, but I keep nearly falling over because I can't see my own feet and what they might be stepping on. But somehow, even though there's not one tiny star in the sky to show the way, I know we're getting near the building because I can feel a kind of heaviness or a great big weight in front of me, like the way bats can.

Then a door opens and light spills out and down over a row of big stone steps leading up to the door and onto the old-fashioned stones the ground's made of. This one patch of light is so bright it makes the woman standing there look like one of those cut-out paper puppets where you can only see their black shape.

'Ah, there's Dorothy. Waiting for us.'

She's wearing a skirt that nearly comes down to her ankles and she's got long hair whipping about in the wind. She looks so much like a puppet of a black witch standing there in her castle that under my breath I say what Mum told me to say whenever I'm frightened.

Courage, Carmel. Courage.

And it always works, well, nearly always. Dorothy doesn't seem so frightening once we're inside and I can see her properly in the light coming from a bulb hanging in the hallway. She's got light brown skin and sort of sleepy but clever eyes. She leans down toward me and says, 'So this is little Carmel.'

I nod. And even though I don't know her it's nice to be with a lady again. She smells of cooking and spices and looks a bit like something from the olden days too with her long black skirt and red blouse tucked into it.

She takes my hand. 'Come, child, you must be starving.' I realise she sounds foreign.

We go down the hall and she opens a door and there's a place with coats and boots and she opens *another* door and there's a kitchen with a long wooden table running right down the middle of it. It's much, much newer than the big hall; it's got shiny new white cupboards.

'This is our part of the house, Carmel. Isn't it nice?'

I nod, even though nothing seems very nice at the moment.

'The rest isn't finished so we rented it good and cheap, they did us a real good deal.' Her face looks very pleased about this. 'Now, would you like to use the bathroom?'

I nod and she takes me through a big living room and up a staircase that goes around and around to where there's a bathroom. The room next to it is a bedroom and the door is open so I can see there's suitcases stacked on the floor at the bottom of the bed. She waits for me outside and then we go back down to the kitchen.

'Sit here, child.' Dorothy pulls a chair out from the end of the table. 'What would you like? Would you like cookies and milk?'

'Yes, please.' Dorothy puts a glass of milk and three chocolate-chip biscuits in front of me. I realise how hungry I am and I gobble them down quickly. It's only when I'm picking up the crumbs on my wet finger I see I'm alone in the room. I feel very strange, sitting at this great big table in such a great big house, like I'm the princess in one of the Grimms' fairy-tale books at home. I start crying then, I feel so strange and lonely. The fat tears get mixed together with the crumbs on the plate.

Dorothy's back. Because my eyes are full of water the red of her blouse grows down and sideways. I blink and she goes back to normal.

'Now then. Child, child, what's the matter?'

'I didn't know where anyone was.' She sticks her hands up in the air. 'Lord. What a girl. I was just getting a bed ready for you. Now there's no need for this, is there? Everything will come out A-OK in the end.'

'Will it?'

She nods. 'Sure it will. Let's get you into your bed. In the morning, you'll feel much better. Everyone always does. Now,' she puts her hands on her hips, 'there's only one bedroom in this apartment, and that's where me and your grandpa sleep. So, I've found a bed for you in the other part of the house. It's not done nice and new like this part, but it'll have to do for now. Thank the Lord they gave us the keys for us to keep an eye on it.' She winks at me.

We go back to the hallway with the bare bulb again. I follow her up the big wooden stairs that our feet clatter on and the echoes go up into the ceiling. At the top of the stairs she unlocks a door to a long corridor with lots of doors. She's holding a candle which is just as well because it starts getting dark the farther down it we go. First she shows me a toilet I can use that has a wood seat and an old-fashioned chain. Then she opens the door next to it.

'This is your room, in here.' Inside is nearly empty – just a bed with sheets and blankets and an old chair by the window.

'There is no electricity in this part of the house,' she says. 'Here, I have found one of my petticoats for you to sleep in.'

I look at the bed. 'Dorothy, am I allowed in here?' It doesn't look like anyone's slept in this room for about a hundred years. And the way it was locked up, it feels like we shouldn't be here at all.

'I won't tell if you don't,' she winks again.

I don't want to change while she's standing there. So I sit on the bed and hold the petticoat in my hand. Then I hear behind my back her going out and the door shutting – *clunk*. So quick, quick I change into the petticoat, which is white and has frills around the bottom. The door opens again.

'Are you ready, Carmel?'

'Yes.'

The petticoat's so long I nearly fall over it as I take my clothes over to the chair. But Dorothy just laughs. 'Here – we must make it fit you.' And she ties the shoulder strings up into bows so it only comes down to my feet and doesn't trip me up like before. She tucks me in and I'm about to ask her to stay but then I hear the door closing. It's so dark I can't see my hand in front of my face, even.

'Goodnight Mummy. I'm sorry for everything,' I say, although I never call her Mummy now. And I can hear Dorothy's footsteps getting farther and farther away and I shout out quickly in a panicking sort of voice.

'Dorothy, don't go. Please come back.'

The door opens so the light comes through in a slice.

'What is it, child? Are you afraid?'

'Yes.' I'm glad she's said it and I don't have to explain.

'Would you like me to sit on your bed awhile?'

'Oh, yes. Yes please.'

The bed's creaky and old so it makes a noise when she sits on it. She puts her candle down and holds my hand and strokes it with one of her thumbs.

'When I was a child I was often afraid.'

The voice she uses is like she's going to tell me a story. I hope she does, it would take my mind off everything. When she doesn't say anything for a while I ask, 'What of?'

She's quiet for a bit. 'Things that moved too quickly. My mother said I had bad nerves.'

'Oh.'

'So I understand what it is to be afraid. You must have courage, Carmel.'

And her saying this and sounding like Mum makes me feel a tiny bit better and I can't hold off any longer and start feeling myself going into sleep.

When I wake up in the night she's gone. The thick blankets on top of me aren't light and soft like my duvet at home, they're heavy so they push my legs into the bed. It's cold. But not inside the bed – that's steamy and warm like the sheets weren't dry enough when Dorothy put them on.

I feel achy and tired all over – even my brain. There's a little bit of morning in the window and I roll over and watch it growing because it helps. I try to understand everything that's happened. But then I give up. Sometimes, it's easier to think of things as stories – not real, even. I've practised it before – when Dad went away, and another time when two bullies at school were saying words to me – words like 'wanker' and 'weirdo' that shot out of their mouths like dirty spit. If I made these things into stories I could float away from them, and look at them sideways, or like they were happening inside a snow globe.

All the same, I can't stop pictures flashing up in my mind. The main one – my grandfather's face as he unlocked the metal gates, turning to look at me as if he was checking I was still there. I remember how he looks exactly like the man in my picture, his white hair bright in the car lights and his pale owl eyes with their little specs. It seems a million years ago I did that drawing – even though it was only yesterday. I wonder about the rabbit in the picture, listening at his feet, and I wonder who the rabbit is and why he's there. And then just before I go to sleep again I have a very odd thought. It's that I know who the rabbit is, and the rabbit is me.

14

DAY 2

I FELL ASLEEP for about an hour, sitting on the sofa with my head tilted sideways on a cushion. God knows how I managed it, but then it wasn't really like sleep. Sleeping should be forgetting and I didn't forget at all. Not when I was asleep or when I woke up. I felt gratitude I'd been spared at least the terrible painful jolt of remembering.

When I opened my eyes the police liaison officer – Sophie – was sitting in exactly the same place, on an opposite chair, reading texts on her phone. She looked neat and tidy despite being up through the night; her blond bun hadn't come loose, even a little bit.

'Hello,' she said.

I threw off the blanket and swung my feet to the floor. 'Any . . . any news?' I asked, my breath coming quick and fast.

'Not yet.' She leaned over and briefly touched my arm and went to fill the kettle.

Then I was suffused with a kind of pain I'd never experienced before. It ran through me, as if I was made of fibre-optic wires, flowing into my hands, my throat, everywhere. I sat for a few moments, wondering how it was possible to function with such pain and dread.

Stand up, I told myself and amazingly my body obeyed.

Behind me I could hear Sophie filling the kettle, pouring milk. I went to the back door to breathe in some fresh air. The fog from yesterday had lifted completely. It was early, but already it was the most glorious sunlit morning. The tree shone with drops of dew and a scented steam rose from the grass as the sun dried it out. It seemed incredible to me that the world had turned once again on its axis and carried on *as if not one thing had happened*: the sun had risen and the birds were singing and bees and insects were busy buzzing away in the trees and grass.

On the washing line were the clothes I'd hung out the morning before, just before we'd left to catch the train. Carmel's striped pyjamas, her T-shirts, and a row of her knickers – candy pink, white, and yellow – danced about in the breeze. My head hurt, the sunlight sliced bright curved beams into my eyes and the clothes seemed to perform a jig in the wind – *where's Carmel?* they mocked. *Have you lost her? Is she gone? Have you lost her? Wha-hee.*

A wave of nausea engulfed me and I doubled over, there by the back door. There was a startled shout and the sound of the kettle banging down and Sophie was beside me and one arm was going around my back and the other one cradled my head and she gently, gently helped me to stand up again.

She looked out into the garden. 'Shall I get those things in?' she asked.

I nodded. 'Yes. Yes, I'll help you.'

15

WHEN I WAKE UP for the second time it's properly light but I've got trouble remembering where I am. I blink a lot on purpose which is the trick I do when I want to wake myself up properly.

The room is huge with a high ceiling and bare floorboards, like I'm ill and in an old-fashioned hospital except my bed's the only one in here. There's no curtains and the sun shines right onto me and feels warm on my face. On the windowsill there's a lot of dust and black bits mixed in with chunks from the ceiling fallen onto it.

Bits of yesterday start to come back to me in flashes. But they're jumbled up: the black-and-green shiny face looking down at me; the man with owl eyes jumping up out of nowhere; the long dark time in the car; the giant book; Mum on the train saying 'nearly there, nearly there'; biting into a hot dog and snapping off the head of a long red worm of ketchup.

Mum's brown boots sticking out from under a truck.

I don't need to blink any more when I remember that. I sit up straight and a scream comes out of me I didn't even try to make. It jumps out of me like a sneeze does.

The scream goes, 'Oh no, no.' And the sound flies up into the air and bounces around the ceiling. My legs kick up and down and the horrible thick blankets fall onto the floor in a lump and I jump right out of bed in one go. Footsteps come running down the corridor and Dorothy rushes in. She looks even darker in the daylight, like an Indian and with the same dusty black skirt as yesterday that comes down nearly to her ankles. Today, there's a blue blouse tucked into it and a wide leather belt around her waist. Her hair is in a straight ponytail that goes right down her back and she reminds me of a woman in a cowboy film I once saw.

'Now, now. There's no need for that noise,' she says. Though really I stopped screaming when she came in, I'm so glad to see her.

She starts picking up the blankets off the floor and folding them tidily. She's very quick and neat doing this. Then I hear more footsteps and they don't sound quite right. They go clump, clump and on the second clump there's a dragging sound.

'Thank the Lord, there's Dennis,' Dorothy says, and my grandad appears in the doorway. His sleeves are rolled up and he's sweating on his face like he's been working in the garden or something.

'I want to talk to my mummy,' I say. I'm clenching my fists without even meaning to.

Grandad walks toward me and I see now what's been making the dragging noise. There's something wrong with one of his legs and he has trouble lifting it properly off the ground, so it scrapes across the wooden floor when he walks. He wasn't doing that yesterday, not when we were running to the car or when he was unlocking the gates. And I know it was that sparkly energy that had somehow stopped him limping for a while. I don't know how I know, but I just do.

His big pale eyes are on me and I feel hot and strange standing there in Dorothy's see-through petticoat.

'I want to talk to Mum,' I say in a quieter voice, which feels fluttery like there's butterflies in my mouth.

He scrunches down on the floor in front of me which I can see is hard for him because his leg hurts. Then his face is right in front of mine.

'Of course you do, Carmel, but you must remember it's important to stay as calm as we can. We need to be very grown up and calm for your mummy.'

I think about this for a minute and see it's true, and I feel a tiny bit better.

'You get dressed, and I'll go and phone the hospital to find out the news,' he says. He gets up and I can see it hurts again. Him and Dorothy are standing around me, like I'm going to run off any minute, looking at me to see what I'll say.

'All right,' I say.

I stand by my clothes on the chair and wait for them to go so I can get dressed. I'm looking out of the window at trees when I hear the door close behind me.

I can see now that the black bits on the windowsill are the crispy bodies of dead wasps. They're dried up and their thin spidery legs are bunched and pointing up to the ceiling. When they were alive they must have been more heavy: like the bee who escaped from my window and dipped down so low when he was flying out I thought he was going to crash. Now these wasps are dead all the heaviness has gone out of them and I think – how strange that being alive seems to make you heavy.

My clothes from the day before feel thick and dirty in my hands. But I put them on anyway, even my knickers. Even though my mum says, 'Always start the day with clean knickers.' I realise I don't even have a toothbrush to brush my teeth with and decide to ask Dorothy if she has a spare one and hope she won't suggest using one of theirs because using other people's toothbrushes is gross.

Outside my room there's the long corridor that's painted green to halfway up the wall and then dirty white above. I follow the way I've heard their voices go till I'm at the top of the wooden stairs again. Down below the front door is wide open and outside there's a stripe of blue sky above the metal gates. The sky looks the same as it always does – like it's another normal day – and that's a relief.

Grandad and Dorothy's voices are coming from their apartment downstairs and they sound like insects chatting away – up and down, up and down. Dorothy's a little grasshopper – rrrupp, rrrupp, rrrupp. Grandad's bigger and deeper. I think 'cockroach' at first but that doesn't seem a very nice insect to be. So I change that to one of those big black beetles with pincers. I listen again to check if I've got it right: beeep, beeep, beeep. I hear one of them moving toward the door and I don't want them to find me listening so I start to come down the stairs. Then my grandad is standing at the bottom.

'Ah, there she is – little Carmel. I've spoken to the hospital. Come down and have some breakfast and be welcomed properly to our humble abode.' Humble rhymes with bumble and I think it means small but I can't see what's small about living here.

I rush the rest of the way downstairs then because I want to find out about Mum. Dorothy's at the cooker.

'Come, sit down.' Grandpa walks over to the table with his funny limp and Dorothy puts a pancake in front of me and sprinkles some sugar on it.

'Blueberry,' she says, and winks and for some reason the way her eyelid rolls ever so slowly over her eyeball reminds me of an animal. She sits next to me and folds her hands in the lap of her black skirt.

The blueberries pop as I chew but it starts making me feel sick that I'm gobbling lovely pancakes when Mum's in hospital, so I put my spoon down. Grandad sits at the top of the table.

'Carmel, there's good news and bad I'm afraid. Which would you like first, dear?'

They've both gone quite still and they're looking at me carefully.

'Bad. No, good.' I hang on to the sides of my chair so hard it hurts my hands.

'Well, your mother had a very long operation. It went right through the night because she was so terribly injured. Oh dear, my poor daughter.'

He gets a white hanky out of his pocket and wipes his face with it and I have the funny feeling he's trying to hide his eyes and I wonder if he's starting to cry behind the hanky. I know I am, I can feel my eyes filling up again even though I cried so much yesterday I didn't think there'd be any water left in my head.

After a while he puts his hanky back in his pocket.

'What about the good news?' I ask. My voice comes out tiny. I'm an insect too now – but a quiet little baby one that's crept under my plate to hide.

'The good news is that she's finally out. The wonderful skills of the surgeons have put her back together as best they can.'

Put her back together as best they can. I don't like the sound of that. It makes me think of a doll or a puppet that's been taken to pieces and put back all wrong so they've got legs coming out of their head and an eye looking out of their bottom. But I tell myself that's silly and that's not what he means. I tell myself I need to pull myself together.

'When can I see her?' I say, still in the baby insect's voice. 'Can we go now?'

Grandad looks worried and lifts up his hands from the table and holds them in the air in front of him so I can see their insides.

'Oh no, no, Carmel. She's very sick, she's . . .'

'I won't bother her. I'll let her sleep . . .' I'm sounding more like myself now, more like Carmel.

'No, no. That's just not possible, not possible at all.' I can see he's getting upset and fidgety now.

But so am I. 'Why? Why isn't it possible?' I stand up with my fists squeezed like I'm going to hit something.

'Well, you see, she's in a place called intensive care. It's a very quiet place for people who are really sick. And it needs to be quiet so the people can get better.'

'But I won't be noisy. I won't, I won't.'

'Maybe not, Carmel. But you see the doctors say there are no visitors allowed, especially not children.'

'So I'll creep up and peep around the door.' I'm shouting at him. 'Or if there's a window in the door I'll only peep through that. And if it's too high you could hold me up to look . . .'

'*No*, Carmel.' The shout from him is so big and frightening the tears that have stayed in my eyes come popping out and I put my hands up to my face. I fall back to sitting on the chair and Dorothy reaches out her arms and pulls me toward her. She smells of pancakes and her clothes feel very soft as if they've been washed a lot and I push my face into her and sob.

Her voice goes sharp. 'Now, Dennis, that's enough. Leave us alone and the child will be fine.'

After a while I hear my grandfather leave the room and the door shut behind him. I don't want to move from Dorothy's lap so I put my arms around her and cling on like a monkey. She starts stroking my hair.

'There, there, Carmel. Everything will be A-OK. It's all A-OK. We're here to look after you, that's all. As soon as your mommy starts to get a little bit well again you can see her.'

It seems much more normal and makes more sense when Dorothy explains. I start to feel better and even take my arms from around her so I can blow my nose on the pink tissues she's given me out of her skirt pocket.

She smiles at me. When I see her eyes the word 'amber' comes into my head. The colour of them makes me think of a necklace Mum's got with big yellow-brown stones and when I was little I used to like to put one big bead in my mouth when no one was looking because they looked like sweets. No sweet taste ever came off it, but I liked the feel of it in my mouth and Dorothy's eyes look exactly the same as those beads – even the little brown bits in them.

She makes me another pancake. Then she tells me to go outside and get some fresh air while she does the dishes, and she gives me my coat which she hung up with theirs last night.

I stand at the top of the big stone steps for a moment and sniff at the air like a fox. I want to see where we are but the gates are still chained with a shiny padlock. I look through the gap and my face goes cold from the metal and all I can see is blurry green. Around the house in a circle is a high wall made of stones bigger than my head and in one place there's a tree growing straight out of it, its roots clawing into the stones. I sit underneath the tree and the shadows make nodding shapes on my coat.

I start feeling like I'm a picture or in a film, flat and made of the same stuff as the people on TV. My hands start feeling sticky and I open them up and look at them. Dirt's got into the cracks and I sniff my palms. They smell salty-sweet like peanut clusters only there's just dirt and sweat.

I walk some more. I don't think anyone's lived here for a long time before Dorothy and Grandad. There's broken tiles and stuff at the back that crunch under my feet. There's even some rusted farm machines.

I stop feeling real again. There's nothing I know here except the clothes I'm standing up in. This time, I feel like I'm about to be switched off – like I really am on the TV. I sway from the feeling and I almost go back inside to try and make it stop.

After a while I decide the best thing to do is to put my brain to work to try and get to know Grandad and Dorothy better before I see them again, so they'll be more familiar. Grandad's energy was still around the gates when I went past. It was hanging about there like the fog from last night. Dorothy's different. Hers is folded up tight and neat inside of her. I think about Grandad's limp and how it was gone and now back again. That makes my leg hurt and I nearly fall over. So I stop thinking about it. I don't think about Mum in hospital either. I'm keeping it in a snow globe.

I sleep in the same bed for another night. I really want to go home now. I say that and they say, 'Not quite yet.'

I don't like the nights but in the day the house feels better. Dorothy and Grandad's apartment is nice and new and they sleep upstairs in it, where I went to the toilet the first night. Their sitting room next to the kitchen has got a big leather sofa and it smells of new carpet and has a huge window that looks out of the front of the house. It's so big I can sit in the window and I do. But where I sleep is not done because people Grandad calls developers ran out of money. The good thing about it is they got their apartment cheaper – Dorothy's told me that twice. This morning I heard them talk about what it would be like if they owned the whole building, not only renting their bit of it. How they'd turn it into lots and lots of apartments and make piles of money out of it. They'd be like the developers. But the way they talked about it you can tell they're dreaming about the idea, it's not real.

There's no television anywhere. I ask Dorothy about it but she just laughs and says her family didn't have a TV when she was little and when they got one the people moving about inside of it frightened her and that reminds me of the feeling I had before.

I ask about Mum again. They say I can see her soon. I say I want to speak to Dad, and they say they've tried his phone but it was switched off because he's inside the hospital. They've left a message and he'll call back when he can, they're sure. But in a funny way I'm excited about him being there because it means he cares about what happens to Mum. If he's with her maybe, you never know, it'll make them be together again. I don't know what will happen to Lucy if they do. I can't worry about that.

My clothes feel mucky I've been wearing them so long. I sit on the big steps by the door and cry into my hands. But after a while of crying I tell myself that I'm turning into a cry baby, like the girl at school called Tara who I feel sorry for because she's special needs and drips tears onto her desk all day so her desk's wet by home time. I go quiet and listen to the birds singing. And then – even though I know it's not possible, not possible at all – there's something speaking in the air, and it's my mum's voice. And I know it's only in my head but I hear it muttering around in the tops of the trees. At first, I can't make out what the tree-voice is saying but then it sighs and I hear clear as a bell: *'Courage, Carmel. Courage.'*

And it calms me down and I know all of a sudden whatever's going to happen I have to have hard bits of courage inside me to help. If I carry on crying every five minutes I'm going to get weaker and weaker until I turn into a lump of soggy tissues scrunched up with snot and tears.

I make a decision. I know workhouses are places no one ever wants to go so I decide I'm only going to think of it as a castle from now on.

I ask about Mum and they say: not long now.

16

DAY 3

WHEN THE POLICEWOMAN SAID, 'I'm so sorry, I have a problem with childcare,' I could see she instantly regretted her words by the way her incisor bit into her full bottom lip, staining it deep pink. Two policewomen – family liaison officers – shared looking after me in shifts. I felt more at ease with Sophie – she was clever and sweet-faced. I never felt under investigation with her, like I did with the other one.

'I'm so sorry. I should never have said that, of course I shouldn't.' Sophie bit her pretty lip again. 'It's the childminder – something about her husband being taken to hospital. I don't know what to do . . .'

She had the anxious, intent look of a parent needing to be in another place.

'It's fine. Please, don't worry about talking about your family, it feels normal – nice. Go, you go. I'll be fine for five minutes.'

I was exhausted and quiet for the moment. The next shift were a little late – the police car would be nosing through the country lanes as we spoke, pollen softly falling on its bonnet from the plants in the hedgerow. A television appeal was being organised for that day. It made me feel better when I had something practical to think about.

Then I was alone. I sat at the kitchen table with a cup of coffee. The house became very still and soft and I felt it was holding its breath, watching me, waiting to see what would happen next. I tried to drink my coffee. 'You must drink,' Sophie had said yesterday. 'You must eat. You have to keep yourself *alive*.'

While I drank I made wild plans of what I'd do on her return – I'd seal up every crack in the house. I'd bring in workmen to build a gate that locked with a golden chain as thick as my wrist. I'd mix mortar in a bucket and drag stones back from the fields to lay on top of the garden wall until it reached the rooftop. Never again, I'd declare, as I worked through the night, never again will that be allowed to happen.

I'd been looking for a patch of bright red since the day she'd gone so when in my side vision a sudden flash of it slid through these crazy imaginings and past the fence outside my teeth started chattering on the cup.

As I flew to the window I spilled my coffee on the table and it splashed across the newspapers onto Carmel's black-and-white face.

But when I looked out it was just Paul coming up the path. Through the front picket fence I could see his car parked on the road – the red through the window as he'd driven past. We hadn't spoken since Carmel had vanished. Once, my heart would have leapt at the sight of him, even after he'd left me. Now, it throbbed painfully with adrenaline and disappointment.

His walk, everything was different about him – strangely both stumbling and purposeful. From a distance I don't think I would have recognised him. I answered his hammering on the door and he stood there – arms hanging by his sides. He pushed past me and we stood for a second, looking wordlessly at each other.

He went and sat on the sofa. 'Tell me what happened,' he said, not looking at me. 'I need to know from beginning to end. Exactly. What. Happened.'

So I did, as best I could.

'You lost her.'

'Yes, yes I did, Paul. It was foggy and – yes, Paul, yes, I lost her. And now, now I don't know where she is.'

Again, like on The Day It Happened I got the sense of the ground opening up and releasing something that should have stayed compressed: the smell of mud; a deadly mustard gas seeping about the room. Our pain had a colour and a smell, it shimmered dark yellow in the morning light around our feet.

'I've been questioned. They thought it might be me.' He was angry now, like men are when there's no action to be taken.

'Paul, they have to do that. It's just procedure. You must understand. I've been questioned too. Oh God, I'm glad to see you.'

He cut across me. 'You lost her.' Then: 'It's your fault. It's all your fault.' That cold chaotic stare again.

'Paul, how can you say that? How can you be so cruel? When you haven't even been near us for an age.'

He stood up. 'How could I come here? It wasn't good for her.' He was shouting now. 'Not with you, you looking at me so tight-lipped and hating. Children pick up on things you know – she did. She always got these marks under her eyes when I came around, dark circles. It was the stress of it. Oh, what's the point?' He made for the door.

'Are you going already? Paul, please don't leave.' I was whimpering almost. 'Please don't leave me with this. She belongs to both of us.'

'I have to.' He pulled his palm across his eyes like he was trying to rub it all away. 'I just . . . just can't stand this. You don't realise.'

'But Paul, we have to stick together.'

'No, you don't understand.'

'Forget about before, everything. None of it matters. Let's concentrate on getting her back, Paul.'

'No,' he shouted. 'I just can't. I can't. I can't. I can't.' He spoke one word at a time again. 'I. Just. Can't. Stand. This.' Then, without warning, he pushed me against the wall. He pushed me so hard I was pinned, my feet lifted off the ground. I looked over his shoulder through the window and saw the police car had arrived.

They hadn't got out – maybe they were talking into their mobile phones or had seen Paul's car and decided to give us a moment alone.

'Paul, what are you doing?' I was having trouble breathing, his body was pressing on me so hard.

He didn't answer. I closed my eyes and hung there. In some funny way I felt that's how I wanted to stay – suspended forever, my feet pointing into nothingness. His head turned and for a moment I thought he was about to kiss me, but he pushed harder so his hips ground into me and his shoulder stuck into my collarbone. His breath felt hot on my neck and I could hear him making little strange noises, groaning.

When he released me I fell forward onto my knees on the floor. Without looking back he strode across the room, and in a second he was gone, the door slamming behind him in the wind.

Then I was alone, on my hands and knees, the sound of the slam echoing around the room. I heard the noise of Paul's car starting up and roaring away and I realised what he'd been doing. He'd been pushing as much of his grief into me as possible, to see if he could try and drive away without it – I could feel it, rooting inside and making itself at home.

But I could only feel sorry for him. Because I knew how it'd be chasing, speeding along behind until it caught him up, flying in through the window and surrounding him, like a swarm of bees. I sent my missive winging after him too, from there on the floor: 'Don't blame me, Paul. If nothing else, please don't blame me.'

17

DAY 3

I SAT HUNCHED in front of the TV watching me and Paul making the appeal on the evening news, bright lights shining in our faces.

'You both did well.' Maria – the other police liaison officer – was with me.

'Did we?' To me, we looked like a pair of broken birds, folded into ourselves, our voices faltering and tiny. Paul had said under his breath, 'Sorry about this morning,' to me before we began. 'Don't worry,' I'd whispered back, 'I'm just glad we're doing this together.'

Now it was over I was becoming pent up, desperate. Maria seemed harder, spikier than Sophie. Her presence was acute and watchful and I felt like she was studying me for clues. Even though she wore plain clothes, the smell of uniform hung about her neat black suit and white shirt. She was reading notes, quietly. Her hair, cut in a businesslike brown bob, fell in two curves across her cheeks and the ends pointed their sharp tips to each corner of her mouth.

It was unfair, really, she'd done nothing wrong, but that evening she was becoming the target of my fear and wild anger: something in the professionalism of her manner, the sense that this was a job for her. I imagined her steadily climbing the career ladder: being involved in such a case would be a bright feather in her cap to put on her CV.

I switched off the television and paced and then dropped on a kitchen chair, another attack of the shaking that I seemed incapable of stopping rocking the chair beneath me. 'I can't sit here,' I said to her at last. 'Let's go out in the police car and look.'

She put down her notes neatly on her lap. 'Honestly, Beth, hard work is being done right now. All we can do is wait.'

'Wait for what?' I started pacing up and down the kitchen again.

'They're having a meeting now, as we speak. Be assured, Beth, everything is being done that can be. You'd be better off having a bath, or something to eat. What have you eaten today?'

Her retreat into platitudes felt learned and I ignored her question. 'What kind of meeting?'

'A strategy meeting. To plan out the way ahead.' I could tell she was picking her words carefully.

'Then why the fuck am I not there to hear about it?' I shouted, the words exploding out of my body.

She drew the ends of her hair back with her fingers and tucked them behind each ear.

'It wouldn't be the right thing, really, Beth. It would complicate things to have the family involved. It makes things . . . harder. You have to trust me on this, Beth.' I knew instinctively she'd learnt to intone my first name like this on some course or other.

'I'm her mother. What does that mean? Does that mean nothing?' I was yelling now, the words flaming from my mouth – a dragon mother.

But she only sighed and my anger fizzled away so I went to the front door and wrenched it open. From my cardigan pocket I took out the pouch of tobacco that I'd asked Sophie to bring and started rolling a cigarette. Around the front door were littered the flat butts of rollies I'd smoked and then extinguished with my heel. I'd gone back to tobacco with one swift and easy motion and it had welcomed me, through its smoky lips: *where have you been, away so long? I've missed you.*

Was the weather mocking me that week? What I wanted was hailstones burning the ground, gales that tore down trees, lightning that cracked open the sky. A sign from who knows what that something unnatural had been done. Instead it was the most perfect evening. The fields rolled away from me, shining in the light. The air was the colour of a golden peach. The leaves had opened their tiny fists on the beech tree. The lowering sun arched through the branches of the trees and new life seemed to lie just beneath the skin of the earth, impatient and muttering.

Soft footfalls behind me and I could hear Maria's breath.

'I'm sorry,' she said, quietly. 'I don't have children of my own. I had to have my bits taken away years ago. So you see, I can't imagine how hard this is for you. I don't want to pretend to.' It occurred to me that she must be going against the grain telling me such personal things and they probably weren't supposed to divulge private details.

'No, I'm sorry . . . I'm so sorry,' I said. 'Sorry for swearing at you. I know you're only here to help and I swore at you. That's awful.'

'Oh, fuck that,' she said. And I smiled at that.

Everything was quiet and still. The smoke from my cigarette curled upward and filtered through the branches of the tree, rising up and dancing away into the air. I imagined it flying as spirit matter across the fields. Carrying cells from my lungs: tiny curled, coded messages intended to strike fear into whoever had taken her – *war. You've started a war.*

I could feel Maria's breath on my shoulder. 'I want you to know when you have certain thoughts, thoughts you must be having . . .' She trailed off.

I didn't turn around. The sun slipped down a fraction and I stayed unmoving.

'Thoughts you can't bear,' she continued. 'Then, this is what you have to do.' Her voice was soft and low behind me.

'This is important. You have to see it in your mind as a place that you can't go. A path you can't go up, or a door you can't enter – are you listening, Beth? Can you hear me?'

Without looking around I nodded and her quiet voice went on – an urgent tone behind me. 'You must see it in your mind with a big NO ENTRY sign. Or with a gate you won't climb over. You must think of every detail.'

I pictured it. I saw a gravel path edged with weeds. It curved a little. At the end was a tiny house with ivy covering the windows. The door was bolted and a plank of wood was crudely nailed across it. Halfway up the path a snake lay, the rope of its body blocking my way. The creature was lightly dozing but had one primitive eye cocked at me beneath its lid, ready to wake if I took another step.

'Can you see it now, Beth? You see that place in your head, and you must promise never, never to go there. It's not for you, it's not a place you're allowed. Do you have it now?'

And I said, 'Yes. Yes, I can see it.'

I stayed there for a long time, smoking one cigarette after another. I could hear Maria behind me, folding up the newspapers on the table, clearing space. Then quietly laying out plates and cutlery.

I turned and concentrated on putting one foot in front of the other. This is how life must be from now on, I thought. I decide on the next action I need to perform and do it. Step, step, step to the kitchen sink. Bend down, open the cupboard door, take out the dustpan and brush. Back to the front door. Crouch down. Sweep, sweep, sweep. The front step, be careful not to miss under the stone lip. Sweep, sweep, sweep until it's clear.

18

THE SOUND MAKES ME stop still by the gate and my hair does a strange thing which is lifting off my head and going straight up.

Ting, ting, ting.

What is it? Not Grandad and Dorothy because their car is gone. I've been looking for them for *ages* and thinking, getting scared, about what would happen if they get squashed on the road like Mum. Thinking I'll have to eat grass until I die. That I'll be a ghost and trapped here forever.

Being on your own is terrible, especially when there's noises and you don't know what they are – though maybe it's just a bird or an animal. Quiet as anything I creep around the back where it's coming from and crawl behind some bushes on the corner and peep through the green stalks.

Then my hair floats down to where it normally is because it's just Grandad there. He's got his shirt sleeves rolled right up and he's nailing a metal lock to a door and that's what's making the sound. He grunts as he works – the way old men do – and mutters something under his breath. I'm *so* pleased to see him I nearly jump up and say hello to surprise him. But then I remember what I've told myself – that I want to keep an eye on him and the best way to do that is when he doesn't know he's being watched, and then he can't pretend anything.

I crouch, spying on him, until my feet start feeling pins and needlely. And I'm glad I do this because he starts singing a very weird song that could tell me a lot about him. It goes:

Are you washed in the blood,
In the cleansing blood of the lamb?
Are your garments spotless? Are they white as snow?
Are you washed in the blood of the lamb?

Ting, ting, goes his hammer as he sings. He's got a lovely voice, he really has, but the words make me think of people washing in lamb's blood and getting it in their eyes and up their noses and how it would smell and stick to you all over.

I must have moved because Grandad stops working and his arm – the one with the hammer – gets stuck in midair above his head.

'Carmel?' His head turns and his eyes are staring right into the bushes through his round glasses. 'Is that you?' His arm's still up.

I stay put.

'Carmel, I know it's you. I can see the red of your coat.' And I remember what I was going to do earlier so I jump up and throw out my arms. 'Ta-da. Surprise,' I say, to make him think I'm just playing a silly trick.

He frowns. 'Child, it's very naughty to spy on people. It's a sign of a *very* untrustworthy character.'

I feel guilty then because I know he's right – and I don't like the sound of being an 'untrustworthy character.' So I go and sit on the step and say, 'Sorry. I really am.' Then to change the subject I ask him what he's doing.

He looks at the hammer in his hand as if he's forgotten about it.

'I'm securing this door. Thieves and intruders are everywhere in this world, child, and we have to keep them out.'

He carries on hammering with his face tight and turned away. I think he's showing me he's still cross.

'I thought you'd gone out and left me alone.' I feel like crying when I say that.

'Of course not, we wouldn't do that.' He does one last bash with his hammer. 'I phoned the hospital again this morning.'

This makes me jump and go 'Oh' because I didn't know he was going to phone and now I feel I should've asked him about Mum.

'Too busy spying to think about that, eh?' Which is quite a nasty thing to say but the guilty feeling gets worse anyway. It also makes me think that Grandad was a lot crosser about the spying than he'd let on.

'What did they say?' My breath comes quick.

'Well, do you remember that place I told you about? The place called intensive care?'

He's talking to me like I'm a baby but I just nod.

'Well, your mother is still there, so I'm afraid we can't see her yet. But she is much better. Stable, in fact, that's what the doctors said.'

'Stable.' I like the sound of that.

He puts down his hammer and comes and sits next to me. 'Yes. We'll be able to see her soon, dear. Very soon.'

This relaxes my body all over. It feels quite nice then, the two of us sitting there together even if we had a sort of argument over the spying and I think how I actually sometimes miss having a nan and grandad, even if Dorothy's not my real one. I notice his eyes are nearly the same blue as my mum's.

'Where do you come from? Are you Irish?' I ask, because I want to carry on having a talk.

'Me and Dorothy? We've lived in America, dear, that's why you might think I speak so strange. I'm not particularly from any-where. Did you think we were Irish? That's funny.' And he laughs. It's the sort of laugh you see in a cartoon with an 'oh, ho ho' sound coming out of his mouth. 'But *my* grandfather, he came here to this workhouse when he was a boy, he used to tell us stories about it. So I looked it up when I was down this way and imagine my good fortune when I saw that part of it was to rent. I thought – perfect. That's just perfect.' And he laughs again.

I don't think any of this is funny and he stops laughing after a while.

I pluck up the courage to say this for a long time: 'Where's Dorothy, *Grandad*?' Saying that word makes me feel shy but he seems to like it and maybe he's thinking it's nice to have a granddaughter because he looks at me and grins.

'Dorothy's gone to town to buy you some surprises.'

'Oh. What sort of surprises?'

'Well, that would be telling, wouldn't it? And then they wouldn't be surprises any more.'

We sit there for a bit in the sun.

'Carmel, it's going to be simply wonderful getting to know you again. It's a crying shame your mother argued with us,' he says out of the blue.

I think: I'm not sure what my mother will have to say about *that*, but of course I don't say it because I don't want to upset him. I suddenly feel very tired about all the arguments and falling out and shouting and clothes coming out of windows that adults do right over your head, as if you're just the mouse on the floor and don't understand. 'Just a little tiff me and your mum are having,' they say, even when their voices didn't sound like they were having a little tiff, they sounded like they were going to kill each other with knives. Or 'nothing to worry about' or 'everything's A-OK.' Even when it's not A-OK: very far from it. So I do a big sigh and Grandad smiles at me again.

'C'mon. Let's go inside and see if there's any cookies in the cookie jar.'

And I take his big hand and we go together back inside the house, with him whistling and swinging his hammer in his other hand that's not holding mine. On the way back I see something I haven't noticed before.

'Look, Grandad.' It's a row of tiny houses, small enough for hobbits or elves, built into the side of the castle wall. Every single door has round holes cut into it. He just grunts like he's thinking about something else and I want to stop and look but he's got my hand so I have to follow.

Grandad leaves me in the kitchen with some crayons so he

can get on with his jobs, and being on my own makes Mum come back to me. I see her lying on the hospital bed like a broken spider. I see her cut up by doctors so she looks like bacon. I'm scared if I draw anything it'll be her with metal stalks and tubes coming out.

I look up at the high ceiling and I have the idea I could float up to it like a balloon and that Grandad might reach up and try and grab my string but I'd be way, way too high. The only time I'd float down again is when they said Mum's better and I can go home. I do some crying again, with my head on the crayons, so the snow globe's not working. Its stuff is leaking out.

The first I know that Dorothy's come back is when I hear her calling, 'Carmel, Carmel. Where is she?'

'In here, in here.'

She comes into the apartment with masses of carrier bags. She's got red lipstick on and a yellow blouse with bright pink roses. 'Provisions,' she says, and soon the table's covered with tins and lemons and boxes of cereal.

'Tonight is feast night.' She laughs and flings her hair back like a horse does with its mane. Her eyes look shiny and excited as if going out made her quicker and more awake.

'Dorothy,' I say carefully, because you never know what's going to make grown-ups act in funny ways or make them say no – no way, José. 'Next time you go out, can I come with you?'

She laughs and says, 'Maybe.' I pick up a tin of beans and it's silly, it makes me feel a bit wobbly and teary because it's such a relief seeing something so familiar: the same blue colour and the *57 varieties.*

'Now then, Carmel, something just for you.' She picks up the bag that says *British Heart Foundation* on it in red writing and starts taking out piles of lace dresses – six of them, like dolls or bridesmaids wear. They make a frilly mountain of lace in between the shopping, all ice-cream colours: yellow, peach, pink and white – made of nylon, that Mum never buys. Then she shows me another bag that's got new tights, knickers, a nightie and shiny patent shoes.

'Oh,' I say. 'Um – thank you Dorothy.'

'Don't you like them, Carmel?' Her face looks disappointed. 'This is how girls dress where I come from. When they go to church on Sunday morning they look like dozens of little flowers dancing down the street.'

'Usually,' I say, 'I wear things like jeans and T-shirts with pictures on them. And trainers.'

'Oh. But those things you're wearing are so dirty.'

I look down: it's true. The leggings have gone baggy at the knees and my cuffs are crispy with dirt from outside. Even my socks have started itching.

'Maybe just for now,' she says.

'All right,' I say, trying to keep polite, even though the clothes look exactly like how Alice dressed at the Mad Hatter's tea party. 'I will till I can go home.'

Grandad comes in rubbing his hands together.

'She's back,' he says, and he puts his arms around Dorothy's waist and they do a funny little dance together around and around that's extra funny because of his limp. He settles back in the biggest chair at the head of the table, smiling his head off, like a king expecting presents. 'And what is there for me?'

'There, your favourite.'

He twists open the top of the bag and takes out a peanut in its shell.

'We give those to the birds sometimes,' I say.

He frowns, as if I'm spoiling his lovely snack. 'Now that would be a crying waste of good food.' He makes a sound like bones cracking as he splits open a peanut between his fingers and thumb.

Dorothy says, 'Come, child. It's about time you took a shower and washed that grub and dirt away.'

She leads me up the stairs toward their bathroom and behind me I can hear the crack, crack, crack that Grandad makes, splitting open peanut shells.

•

When I come back down Grandad folds up the newspaper he's been reading and tucks it under his bottom so he's sitting on it. 'There she is,' he says. 'As pretty as a picture. As cute as a bunny rabbit.'

My old dirty clothes are in a ball in my hands with trainers on top. Dorothy dumps them into the little room with the washing machine and I feel a pang when she shuts them in there.

'You chose the yellow.' Dorothy clasps her hands together. 'How perfect.' She likes the dresses way more than I do; if there was one big enough she'd probably want to wear it. If Mum saw me now she'd laugh and say I look like a right nutter. But when I put it on I decided – whatever happens – I'll have to stay being Carmel on the inside, with my name printed like a stick of rock, which is something I've heard Mum say.

Dorothy's feast is in steaming bowls on the table and my mouth starts watering as I sit down. There's beer for Grandad too.

'And now, let's take a moment to say grace,' says Grandad. I copy what they do and bend my head and put my hands together.

'God, you have given us this wonderful food . . .' and he goes on and on about how lucky we are to be eating 'the grains from the land' and 'the flesh given up to us.'

I take a peep from under one of my eyelids. Grandad is frowning with his eyes screwed shut and I realise – with this praying and the song from the morning – he must be what Dad calls 'a God botherer' – the most dangerous sort, he says. Though Grandad doesn't look dangerous, just sweaty and upset. And he does end up praying for Mum too: '. . . and for our daughter, Beth. We pray that she continues on her path of recovery and that we will be reunited in love in the happy future.'

He finishes at last. 'Be careful,' Dorothy says, and winks at me, 'we like our food to have fire in it in Mexico.'

She helps me put things on my plate and I say, 'I thought you were from India.'

'No. Mexico is the country where I come from, Carmel, where

the beautiful earth is red and the sunshine on flowers makes them glow like they have lights inside . . .' she gives herself a shake, 'but I met your grandfather so everything is for the best. I needed a strong man, a hard-working man, a protector. I saw your grandfather preaching in America and thought how fine he was. So I never went back to Mexico but I can still have food with fire in it.'

I touch my tongue carefully on the chicken stew and it feels like it's going to go up in flames so I stick it out to cool. Both of them laugh at that.

'See, I warned you,' says Dorothy and wags her finger at me, her red lipstick smiling across her face.

I don't really mind them laughing. It's like we're our own family, the three of us, and if I'm a balloon I'm tied to the chair now which is better, I suppose, than flying off free to get lost. I eat three huge pieces of corn with butter dripping over my chin I'm so hungry.

But as it's getting later there's something worrying me and with us all talking and laughing I pluck up the courage to ask about it.

'Dorothy, do I have to sleep in that room tonight? I mean, is there a little bed that can go at the bottom of *your* bed perhaps?'

I can't remember exactly how many nights I've had in that room. But I can't stand the thought of another one because there's noises shuffling around my bed. In the day I mostly forget but now it's nighttime just the thought of it is making my hair stand on end.

Dorothy wipes her smile away with the tea towel she's been using as a serviette and the smile comes off onto the white cloth in a red mess.

'No, child. You see there really is no room.'

'Couldn't she have a nightlight? A little candle maybe? It would be a light in her darkness,' Grandad says.

'Would that help? Do you think that would help you, child?' Dorothy asks.

And I say I suppose so even though I don't think really it will help at all. Not with the flickering shadows that a candle makes leaping about. I even think it might make things worse. But Dorothy's already up and going through one of the kitchen drawers and looking.

'Here, I knew we had one.' She holds up a candle in its little metal tin. It's the same as the ones me and Mum sometimes put along both sides of the garden path at home when we have visitors. We light them all at once so the visitors can see their way to the house. But we use hundreds of them to do this and Dorothy is only holding up one.

'Perfect,' says Grandad. 'Just the thing.' And he helps himself to more beer.

'Time to say goodnight, Carmel.' Dorothy says this quickly. Perhaps she realises I was going to ask about changing where I sleep again. I sigh and try to pretend to myself that a little candle is going to make a big difference and how cosy it's going to feel now in that great big room.

She lights the candle then puts it in a china pot. 'Come, child. I'll tuck you in and say goodnight and see to it that you are as snug as a bug. Say goodnight to your grandfather.'

I say goodnight and he turns his cheek toward me. 'A goodnight kiss?'

I'm not sure if I want to kiss him goodnight. But I do anyway. I sort of touch my lips onto his cheek and it feels very hard and solid there and it makes me think of the skin of pigs that hang up – stiff and dead – in the butcher's shop.

'Night night, sweetheart,' he says, then gives a little burp.

I follow Dorothy up the stairs, dragging on my new shoes, because I want to put off going to bed as long as possible. In the corridor the flame in Dorothy's hand shines through her skin and blood so there's a big red hand floating up. Her shadow in a long skirt is on the wall. I look back and see my shadow, following behind, with my puffy shadow skirt sticking out. We *both* look like the paper puppets now and I wonder what story we'd be telling if we were.

I change into my new nightie by crouching on the other side of the bed and Dorothy tucks me in and puts the candle on the table next to me.

'There, my dear, dear child. Doesn't that make everything better?'

I'm about to say, 'No, not really,' but I realise there wouldn't be much point. I say, 'Yes, Dorothy,' and she smoothes my hair back onto my pillow and goes away.

When I can't hear her any more it begins. The shadows that the candle makes dance around the room and the dark places look like black holes waiting to eat me up. Every time I spend five minutes in this room it seems to come alive. It wakes up because I'm there and it's worse than ever tonight. There's shuffling and rustling all around. Then I hear quick footsteps running across the floor and I can't stand it any more. I'm so frightened it feels like my insides are freezing. So I pick up the candle with one hand and get hold of my blankets by the corners in the other and run down the corridor dragging them until I'm at the staircase with the light shining up it. I leave the blankets and take the candle and go back to my bedroom quickly to get my pillow. Then I carefully put the tea light on a post which is flat on top. I sort out my pillow and blankets to make a bed at the top of the stairs. I have some blankets above and some underneath and I crawl into the bed I've made. It feels a lot better there even if it is hard underneath.

Courage, Carmel. Courage.

I turn my back on my bedroom. All that muttering and shuffling can get along by itself, I'm not going to have anything to do with it. I put my face so some light can shine onto it.

Downstairs I can hear Dorothy and Grandad's voices rising and falling, rising and falling. Except after a while it's only Grandad's voice and Dorothy has gone quiet. Or when she does say something it's very small and flat. I close my eyes and think of home to make me feel better. I make pictures of it flash up in my head: the mugs hanging up on hooks over the sink; our two toothbrushes in a glass in the bathroom; the moon shining huge over the rooftop; the red bucket by the back door; the fire making crinkly noises in winter as a log burns.

Mum in one of her flowery tops. Daisies. She's hanging up a wooden sign we just bought, it says: THERE'S NO PLACE LIKE HOME, and when she's finished she dusts her hands off and says, 'What d'you think, Carmel?' and her eyes are shining out their lovely blue lights and I jump up and down and shout, 'There's no place like home, there's no place like home,' and she laughs.

I'm thinking of these things so hard I hardly notice at first Grandad's voice has got louder and louder. When I do realise I open my eyes wide and hold my breath listening, stretching out my ears. Grandad sounds strange, like he's in pain, or upset and angry. I can't help hearing now he's so loud, though I can't understand what he's shouting.

'I had to do it, Dorothy. I had to. I was compelled, how can I make you understand that? She's the one. The one, the one. You need to stop talking to me now. Stop your fearfulness. Be told. I had no choice in the matter. If I explained for a hundred years you still wouldn't understand.'

Then everything goes quiet.

19

DAY 7

'THEY'RE HERE.' Maria was looking out of the window. 'Beth, it's your parents, they've arrived.'

I peered out of the window and I could see my dad trying to open the door of the pearl-grey Jaguar. Two or three press people still turned up sporadically and now a photographer was flashing his camera through the car window.

'Remember,' said Maria. 'If we tell them about the sighting, they mustn't in any circumstances talk to the press. The last thing we want is a journo putting a spanner in the works. The information's very vague.'

A woman had walked into a police station somewhere in the Midlands. She'd been out with her dog and seen the figure of a girl in red looking out of a window. She couldn't remember which street. They were going to retrace her steps.

This was one sighting of the many. Each time they told me not to get my hopes up – I don't think they even told me about them all. Leads to me were silver wires that could reach out to where she was. I imagined us both tugging, one on either end, so we could feel each other's vibrations. They sent convulsions of excitement and anxiety through my body. It was like this now – I was in a state of high alert.

'I'll tell them – but they won't talk to anyone. They're not that type.'

Maria breathed out. 'Good.'

I looked out of the window again and a slim woman dressed in beige with hair carefully curled close to her head was coming up the path. It had been years since I'd seen her and she'd aged.

I ran to the door and as I wrenched it open I heard a sound coming from me. 'Mum, mum, mum' – the sound that starts with a pressing together of the lips and rounds the mouth in one convulsive seizure. I felt as if ancient cords were working my mouth independently into that shape.

My father finally came through the gate – the angle of his small, pointing beard on display, cross and harassed. 'No,' I heard him say, his voice carrying, tight and clipped. 'No. Get away from me.'

My mother's awkward embrace smelled of her familiar cool metallic perfume. Over her shoulder I looked into my father's face, set grim and folded.

I took them inside and tried to invoke my mantra to calm myself down – open the cupboard door, teapot out, lift the kettle with your hand, drop the bags into the pot . . . Maria was introducing herself in quiet tones behind my back.

Why did we argue? It seemed so ridiculous, irrelevant now in the face of this, this rending of the earth. They'd disapproved of Paul, called him a useless tinker to his face. I'd given up the idea of university to go off with him, set up our business, start a life. I was an only child too, maybe that played its part? They were more than disappointed, they were furious, acting as if Paul was some powerful Svengali who'd mesmerised me. I invited them to the wedding. My mother phoned and asked, why wasn't it Catholic? But even if it was, they wouldn't be coming anyway. Not to see me marrying him. Finally, after Carmel was born, even our phone exchanges fizzled out so they hadn't seen her since she was a baby. Paul gently aided me in this, I could see later. It must have been a relief to him, this cutting of the ties. They'd been so awful to him, putting down the phone if he answered, even – who could blame him? Later, I wondered if it had had a bearing on our marriage ending. If maybe the fissure hadn't gone away at all but ran through our lives, deep buried, black. Paul had told me a few days before he left it was a blessed relief to him, to be with Lucy and no one disapproving or disappointed.

I made the tea and Maria left us alone to sit around the table like three strangers, which we were. They'd had to fly back from Spain and their faces looked wide-eyed with shock behind their cheerful suntans.

'This is a terrible business. Terrible.' My father frowned. 'What can be done about it? What?' Nobody answered and he fell silent.

Mum put out her hand and placed it on my arm; I saw the liver spots on her skin. 'I've seen her picture in the papers. I've got a photograph of my mother as a child, all ringlets and great big eyes, and I couldn't believe how alike they look. She's beautiful, Beth. So lovely and innocent. Who would want to do a thing like this?'

'I don't know,' I said quietly. 'I don't know.'

My father still looked angry. 'And what's that husband of yours about now?'

'What do you mean?'

'What's he up to? Where is he?'

'Dad, Paul left me, about a year ago. He left me for another woman.' I let them absorb the information. Was it me, or did I detect a smirk on my father's face, a certain 'I told you so' in the jut of his small grey beard?

'Oh, Beth.' My mother's cool hand reached out again.

'I don't care any more. I really don't – all I care about is getting Carmel back. Everything else is . . . nonsense. The fact that Paul left me is nothing, absolutely nothing.' I trailed off.

'Anyway, maybe it was for the best . . . ?' my mother murmured.

I leapt to my feet; amazed they could be dwelling on this past history, even now.

'I've lost my daughter,' I bellowed across the tea things at them, 'do you not know that?'

My father buried his face in his hands and started sobbing.

'I'm sorry, Mum, Dad, but I can't have you alienating Paul. He may not be my husband any more but he's still Carmel's dad and she needs both her parents.' I moved over to my father, who was still weeping, and I put my hand on his arm. 'It's OK, Dad. Listen, they're out, they're out looking now. You mustn't say anything to anyone – there's been a sighting. A girl – in red – looking out of a window. The woman said, she said she looked like Carmel and she looked lost. They're taking her back there – right now. As we speak.'

Excitement was gathering inside of me. I knew it was tenuous but this one somehow felt real. I could picture her – dreamy and lost, staring through a sash window. Shadows on her face.

Maria appeared behind us. She'd been listening all along, I could tell. 'It's going to take a while, Beth. This lady is quite elderly. She's frail and . . . well, I'm afraid slightly wandering in the mind. I'm sorry, they're going to wait till six o'clock when her daughter can go with her. They're going to have to retrace her walk and knock on every door.'

Later, I could bear it no longer. They didn't want me to go but I told them I needed to get some fresh air, to phone me as soon as they heard anything.

Except I knew it wasn't fresh air I wanted but to be looking, looking, looking. Under stones, in rain barrels, in sheds or barns, down behind shop counters. I slipped out of the side gate mad with the desire to look. I imagined in my fever she might have shrunk to the size of a tiny red charm, small enough to hang on a Christmas tree, or on a bracelet. That's why I couldn't find her. She'd fallen without me noticing and now I'd have to search in holes in trees and in the cracks in the ground. I'd have to put my ear right onto the earth and listen for her calls no bigger than a mouse's squeak.

Out in the countryside I jumped over a low stone wall into a field of corn and walked, the green tips brushing against my fingers as I parted them to look on the ground beneath, like a hunting dog, moving my head from side to side looking: for a foot; a stray bead or hair; for that flash of red. It didn't feel useless in that moment, it felt like I was on a mission, that there was a purpose to this search. But when I reached the corner of the field and scrambled up so I was standing on top of the wall, the scale of my task dawned on me. I gazed over field after field, each one the same as this, extending out into the horizon as far as my eye could see.

I looked at my phone: nothing. It was as if she'd vanished into thin air.

'Where are you?' I screamed across the empty fields. 'Where are you?'

By day 30 we were a family again – me, Mum, Dad. They stayed with me, bringing carrier bags of supermarket food. Dad repainted the front fence; I told him not to, but he said he felt better with something to do. How ridiculous our feud felt now.

'Stop looking,' they told me as I left the house with my coat on. 'I can't,' I said.

The girl at the window never was Carmel. They found her, but it was the granddaughter of the people who lived there. And it was a red dressing gown she'd been wearing, not a coat.

That day I searched the woods. By now I was as exhausted as the princess who was made to dance, over hill and dale, by her slippers. The ones she couldn't take off. It was starting to get dark by the time I lay down next to a stream, pushing my face into the ground, not sitting up even to spit the gritty grains of earth from my mouth.

I lay there for a long time. So long, it seemed, that things turned from dark to light. Slowly, beams descended and soft silver light filtered through the trees. The silvery light reminded me of something and while my mind was groping toward the memory I was distracted by a humming. I lifted my head – there was a child across the other side of the stream. She was sitting, throw-ing pebbles into the water – each one tinkled as it fell – and I wondered what she was doing here in this isolated spot, what her parents were thinking letting her stray so far and all alone. And as I watched there was a slow dawning realisation. This little girl wasn't a stranger, I knew her. It was Carmel. It was my daughter.

I sat up.

'Oh, it's you,' she sniffed, and threw another stone.

I wanted to laugh then, at her being so sniffy, because relief was flooding into my bones like the most health-giving balm possible, an elixir.

'Carmel, where have you been all this time, my love?'

She stood up. She wasn't wearing her duffel coat but a little red jacket over a white dress, and the jacket was stitched with discs that shone out ruby red in the silver light. 'I'm not too sure. You lost me,' she said, and threw another stone into the water. 'You lost me as if I was nothing but a bead. Or a ten-pence piece. You kept taking me to places where it could happen. You were doing it on purpose.' More stones plinked into the stream.

'No! That's not true. You wanted to go to those places; the maze was your idea. Remember?'

She wrinkled up her eyes, then looked troubled. 'Maybe. So did we both want to lose each other?'

'Of course not – don't say that or we won't stay found. Now come to me and we'll go home.'

She shook her head. 'I won't be able to get over this water, especially with my new shoes.'

Then she turned and started walking into the trees and I could see the wind blowing her hair so the strands lifted around her head.

'Carmel, Carmel . . .' I shouted at the receding figure. Then of course I woke, the shout with the soil in my throat, and stood looking at the bank opposite that seemed to vibrate with her presence still.

'I will see the real you again,' I vowed across the water, as if she was still there. 'In this life or the next I *will* see you again.'

That was the last dream I had of her when she wasn't walking backwards.

97

20

I KNOW NOW I DIED the night of the feast. The knowing comes to me, quick, like a light being turned on. I stagger into the kitchen and fall into a chair and bang the table with the flats of my hands.

'No, no, no. I don't want to be a ghost. Save me. Save me.'

Dorothy stands in front of me with both hands up to her face. 'What in the world is the matter, child?'

'You mean you can really see me right now?' I howl. 'I'm not dead?'

'Of course not – oh, sweet Jesus, and Dennis out too. What's happened?' She sits next to me and puts her arms around me tight.

After a long time I stop crying and sit up.

'I found some old photos with children and I realised they must all be dead by now and I just started thinking it.' It sounds silly to say that now.

She sighs. 'You've been alone too much, that's the trouble.'

'Dorothy, how long do I have to be here? I probably should be back in school now.' Days are like beads and I've lost count of how many there's been but I think by now there's been necklaces and necklaces of them. Lots of nights too, each one sneaking out onto the landing.

My question makes her give a little jump and the thought comes to me that maybe something terrible has happened to Mum and they haven't told me yet.

'Why, do you not like us, child?' Her eyes peep at me from the corners. 'Perhaps we should think of something nice to do. Take your mind off things.'

'I want to talk to my dad. Grandad has the number.' I didn't see him for so long I don't know if I can remember it myself.

'Mmm. I guess.'

'Why can't I?' I feel like banging my hands again.

'Now then, this will upset your grandfather,' she mutters. She's looking at me like she's scared of what I'll do next.

'I want. To talk. To Dad.' Crying has made me hiccup when I talk.

She pinches her forehead between her fingers. 'Ah, I remember now. I do have the number – in case of emergencies.'

'You do? Can you ring it, please? Ring it now.'

She takes a phone out of her bag and presses the numbers and hands me the phone and I'm trembling at the thought of speaking to Dad. Dorothy carries on putting saucepans away but she keeps looking over at me. It rings about two hundred times.

'Carmel. You've been doing that for twenty minutes. This is what's been happening. We didn't want to tell you – but he hasn't answered for days.' I shoot out my arm to throw the phone down but at the last minute I pretend to just drop it instead. It spins on the table and stops ringing.

Dorothy says, 'Carmel, that's naughty.' But I'm collapsing on the chair and burying my head in my arms because Dad being like I'm not even alive is making me feel like a ghost again.

'What if we go outside?' says Dorothy quickly.

I lift up my head. 'Outside the wall?'

When we get to the gate Dorothy puts her hand down the front of her blue blouse and feels about. Then she pulls out a long piece of blue cord and on the end of it is a silver key. So that's where they keep it, I think, right next to them.

'No telling about our little adventure to your grandfather

now. It'll be our secret. He's overprotective, he thinks it's not safe around here. Do you know what "overprotective" means?'

I nod, and this being a secret makes me think something I've thought before – that Dorothy's a little bit afraid of Grandad, that she does what he tells her to do on the outside, but on the inside her thoughts are different. I can see them sometimes, in her amber eyes, flittering away with tiny brown butterflies. Then she rolls down her eyelids and blinks to make them go away.

She gives a push with her fingers and the metal gates swing forward.

'Oh,' I breathe. Then 'Oh' again because it's a kind of funny shock for me to see the outside and I feel dizzy as if I might fly off into the air. But the strangest thing of all is, for a flash, what I really want to do is to creep back inside the gate again and for it to be closed and locked behind us.

Dorothy is already stomping out, carrying the orange plastic Sainsbury's bag with a picnic in it.

She turns. 'What's troubling you now, Carmel?'

'Everything looks so big.' It's not flat as a pancake like where I live but as though waves have rolled along under the earth and pushed up, making hills as far as you can see.

'Do you want to go back in?'

I say, 'No,' quickly and step outside the gates onto the grass.

'We'll walk right around the wall,' Dorothy says. Her black skirt flicks up into the air as she walks. We start following the path. Soon we're so high the forest and the silver river below look as small as a farm set. I put my hands on the wall for balance and the stone feels hot from the sun and the wind whips into my face and I want to shout out:

'I'm alive, I'm alive, I'm alive.'

After Grandad gets back, I wonder if he can guess we've been outside. If something gives us away – the fresh air clinging to our clothes, perhaps, or the look in our eyes. He's more serious even than he usually is. He's still got his limp, but now it's just a nuisance to him – something he has to drag around like a bike or a heavy bag. His thoughts are big and heavy too, I can tell. His forehead gets tight like a garlic bulb with a little blue vein raised up on it.

He tells Dorothy to 'prepare.' I want to ask, 'For what?' But there's something about Grandad that stops you asking things these days. The way his big owl eyes look at you as though you've done something wrong. Something bad, snooping and spying again. Being untrustworthy.

Me and Dorothy tidy up the kitchen and he keeps making calls on his mobile phone, always going out of the apartment or into another room. Dorothy's quiet and peeps over her shoulder at the door. Sometimes she gives me the tea towel or the broom and says, 'You stay here and carry on.' When they're both gone I try my trick of stretching out my ears. It doesn't work this time and all I can hear are mashed-together words that sound like a washing machine going around.

I start drying the dishes slowly, keeping as quiet as I can, so the sounds coming from me won't cover their conversation. But I still can't hear. I feel prickly all over, even in between my toes and inside my bottom. I think I'm scared of Grandad now with his pale eyes and his garlic-bulb head and the way he has of watching me. And he gets worked up really easily, and when that happens you'll do anything you can to make things better and get him calm again, to make him sit nice and quiet and crack away at his favourite peanuts. But I realise all of a sudden listening won't make that happen, because of being untrustworthy again.

Now there's feet shuffling toward the door and they both stand looking at me.

'Carmel, child. Put the dishes down and come sit down.' Dorothy says it kindly but for some reason this makes the prickles worse, so they're running down my back in rivers.

I do as I'm told and Dorothy tidies the colouring things they've given me into a pile. Grandad sits at the head of the table in one of his black suits. Dorothy's in her soft red blouse, the one she was wearing the night I came here. Both of their mouths are turning down at the corners. Grandad keeps fidgeting on his hard wooden chair and I can see his sparkly energy is back and it's flying around the room and that's what's making him fidget so much.

'Carmel. Dear, dear Carmel.' Grandad wipes his hanky over his face and I'm getting scareder and scareder.

'What? What is it?' My voice rushes out of me like a little wind.

'I'm afraid I only have bad news today, Carmel. Bad, terrible news,' says Grandad, and my throat squeezes tight like he has his hands around it and he's choking me half to death.

'Mum?' I whisper.

Grandad nods. I turn to Dorothy but she's looking away. 'I'm afraid so, Carmel. I'm afraid I've heard – and there's no easy way to say this – that your mother died in the night.'

And even though I knew this was what they were going to say I jump up and scream, 'No.'

'Carmel, dear. You have to be calm. Listen . . .'

I won't listen. My hands push at the table and I don't know how – it's so huge and heavy – but the legs screech across the floor and it smashes right into Dorothy's ribs.

'No, no, no.'

What can I do? I don't know where to put myself, even. I run out of their apartment. Grandad shouts out, 'No, child, listen,' but I can't stop – up and down the stairs. Bashing myself into the walls on purpose. Hitting my head with my own hands.

'It can't be true. It can't be,' I'm yelling down the big stairs. 'I want to see her right now.'

Dorothy's face is a floating blob below. 'Please, child. It's a terrible cross to bear but you must face it. We must face it together.' She starts walking up the stairs with one hand out in front of her like I'm a squirrel she wants to feed.

And Dorothy saying it makes it really true. With Grandad you never know what's going to come out of his mouth next – blood of lambs, taking the B road – but Dorothy's realer, like a mother or a teacher. When she says it, that's it. I rush past her and she falls back against the wall, her eyes and mouth three round Os. Behind me I can hear their shouts and Grandad saying, 'After her, Dorothy. After her.' There's Grandad's slide, drag of his bad leg and then the thud of his good one. Dorothy's quicker. I hear her patter and I imagine her bunching her long skirt up in her hands so she can run better.

But they're no match for me. My terrible hurting pain's like petrol so I'm a burning car tearing through the building, wailing as I go. Back up the stairs and past my bedroom, past rows of windows and a broken one where I've seen fast birds fly in and out of the hole – to a part I haven't been before, a staircase with carved handles. At the top is a big brown door and it gives way with a whoosh like the sound of a fridge opening.

And I fall inside a room I just know has had no human being inside it for about a hundred years. There's velvet-covered chairs bunched around the fireplace and when I fall in shrieking I feel them turn toward me, like real sitting people would do if someone came in wailing their head off. The thick red carpet swallows up the noise of my footsteps.

This room is the pain room, I think. This is the room of death. There's black wallpaper covering the walls and in it I can see evil buds of pink flowers patterned over and over again – a thousand flesh eyes all looking.

'My mother's dead,' I gasp at the room.

It freezes at first and doesn't know what to say back.

'She's dead, she's dead.'

I run in circles, pushing over wooden tables with pots of plants that died years ago and they crash to the floor and empty ashy stuff across the carpet. And after not knowing what to say, the room wakes up with a roar from being dead and frozen. It goes after me, chasing behind as I kick chairs and rip at old dirty velvet on the cushions with my teeth. I scrabble at the wallpaper with my nails but it's so thick and glued on my fingernails slide across it.

'You're just furniture,' I yell, and start shredding and kicking again because I want to turn it into lumps. I'm knocking myself against heavy things and crying out for Mum: 'Mum, Mum, Mum – don't leave me here, don't leave me here.'

The room's half destroyed when I hear Dorothy and Grandad's shouts. I've shredded it in five minutes flat after it staying the same – like a tail or an eye in a jar – for a hundred years, but I wanted to do more. I wanted to put every single wall eye out. There's a mirror above the fireplace and I catch myself in it – panting and spitty – and I look so white and strange, with glittering eyes, I hardly know it's me for a second.

As I fly out of the door Dorothy is lifting up her skirt and putting one foot, in her old-fashioned black lace-up shoe, on the bottom stair but I'm down and past her and she tries to grab me but misses. She looks up, with her mouth falling open, like I'm just a blurry ball of hair and teeth and skirts screaming by, then gone.

Outside I'm halfway through the garden when the electricity that's been making me run lifts out of my body and I fall, panting and tired out, until I manage to lift up my head and see I'm outside the hobbit houses. A big plop of rain falls – and I'm so close it looks huge – and I watch it land on a leaf, wobble and shine, then drip down. I crawl to the hobbit house at the end. There's a bench on the back wall but I curl up on the floor on the lumps of stone there and push the door closed with my feet. A spider twinkles over to me, stops for a second, then dances into my hair and I don't even shake it out.

Slowly, the light goes greyer. There's a patter of rain outside and puffs of fresh air that smell of green weeds come through the holes. 'Mum,' I gulp – and think I sound like a fish.

There's a feeling I've got, an idea that won't go away: that if I'd never found that flower death bud room, none of this would have happened. It doesn't make sense because they told me about Mum before I'd even set foot inside but the feeling of that place is clinging to me like a gas that's crept inside the holes in my skin. I tremble and cry for my old life: walks, Christmas, garden, you're a right nutter, Mum's friends drinking wine around the kitchen table, the kettle going on in the morning and Mrs Buckfast at the front of the class. Most of all though – the kind blue lights in Mum's eyes.

I hear a tramping and one real amber eye appears and hangs outside, looking through a hole in the door like the moon.

'Child, where have you been? We've been so anxious, so worried. What are you doing there, covered in dirt? You've been gone so long, we thought you'd vanished into thin air.'

I look at the talking eye but I'm just a frozen lump.

'Dear, dear.' I can hear Dorothy shuffling around, pushing against the door and panting, but I'm behind it so it won't open.

The eye pops up again. 'Child, you will have to move. I can't budge the door. Oh my, this is very bad, a bad business.'

More heaving till she's pushing so hard I'm being shoved like a stuffed snake that gets put on the backs of doors to stop the draught. Arms come around the door and a hand grabs my shoulder and I get shovelled out from my hidey-hole.

'There, there.' A sudden whoosh into the light and I'm lifted up into Dorothy's arms – my head rolling backward and my feet bumping up and down as she carries me.

'There, there, child. Oh, what good can come of this? Really, really. Fool,' Dorothy mutters as she heaves me up higher and struggles to balance herself on her two thin legs.

I get wrapped in a blanket that night, and put to bed. In a camp bed this time, at the bottom of theirs. So they can keep a watch on me.

Then I'm on their bed, wrapped in a sheet this time. It's morning. Bright daylight comes through the window falling on suitcases with coloured tickets tied to the handles. I move my head and it hurts. I blink and it hurts. I pinch my lips together and *they* hurt.

I don't hear them come in.

Grandad smiles down at me. 'How are we feeling? Are we feeling better?'

I shake my head. 'Dad,' I mumble.

He sits on the bed beside me. His face is very sorry and concerned.

'We've been in contact with your father. He's cast down to the depths about what's happened, Carmel. But you know, you know you told us he lives with another lady now, a lady that's not your mum? You know you told us you don't see him a whole lot . . .'

Clothes, floating out of the window, with no body to them and coming to rest on the ground, where I can't see.

Dad's sneery voice, out of sight: 'You think you're so middle class, but now you can shove it up your arse. Stone me, that sort of rhymes.' Then his laugh. Not like his, but someone I don't know – a demon.

'Well, he thinks it best . . . he thinks we should, I'm sorry . . .' But I know already. Getting excited about Dad going to the hospital was babyish – silly and horrible because he still loves Lucy. Mum tried to make me feel better when we didn't see him for weeks and weeks on end but all the time I knew, I knew what was happening. Clothes don't fall out of windows for nothing.

Dorothy is wearing the yellow blouse with pink roses, scared thoughts beating behind her eyes – *what will come of this?* Grandad doesn't know about these thoughts she has.

'Dorothy?' I ask. 'Dorothy, can I come and live with you?'

There's a hiss of escaping air, the sound of joy? From Dorothy? No, it's Grandad.

'Why yes, dear, yes . . . Oh, gladly, gladly . . .' From him.

But it's to Dorothy I turn. She leans over me and catches me in a hug against her bony chest. I hold on to her, tight, and get covered by bright pink roses.

Then later, in the kitchen. I'm dressed and Dorothy's trying to get me to eat something. I turn my head away from the egg – 'sunny side up' – feeling sick to my stomach. She shrugs and leaves me to it. I want her not to turn away and to cuddle me again but she's busy, scooping things out of cupboards and throwing them in a black plastic bin bag. 'The trash can,' she calls it.

This is before the tablets. Before: 'This'll help you to relax, Carmel. Just swallow them down, honey. Take them with a little water . . .' Before all that . . . the heavy drop down into the land of dreams. To the bottom of the sea where hardly a thing moves.

She's gone off somewhere and I'm left sitting at the kitchen table, the plate of egg sticky and gross in front of me, getting cold. I notice a bright spot on the grey tiles on the floor. A purple stripe against a red one. I get up to look. Closer, I see it's my T-shirt. It's been wet and now it's dried into a hard dirty ball. Dorothy's been cleaning the floor with it. It's like a thing from ages ago. Something you see in a museum in a case with a label up against the glass – 'Carmel used to wear this.'

Once, near a place called Stonehenge, we went for a walk. There was a hill Mum called a 'burial mound.' At the bottom of the hill was a tree, and the tree had tied to its branches a hundred waving scraps of cloth and ribbons and bits of paper with writing on, some in plastic things to keep them safe from the rain. I tried to read some but the rain had got in anyway and made the ink dribble down the page. 'Wishes,' my mum said, 'that people have left here, even the ones that are a scrap of ribbon. It represents a wish.'

I get some scissors from the drawer and snip, snip I have a piece of purple-and-red stripes.

I hurry, before anyone can stop me, to the wall tree and climb right in among the branches and tie the strip up high, wrapping it around twice, three times with a double knot for safety. And I make my wish, even though I know it's impossible – impossible for this not to have happened and for Mum to be alive again. I make it anyway because not even Grandad can stop you wishing. It hangs down limp for a moment then a little breeze makes it stand out sideways like a dirty flag.

I climb down from the tree. By the door there's a spade stuck into the ground. Grandad's black coat is hanging on it. I can tell from the heaviness there's something in the pocket. And I know it's untrustworthy, but I reach my hand in and it's a phone. Dad,

I think. Maybe he's changed his mind. Maybe if I speak to him he'll come and get me in his red car. I pick up the phone and stare at the numbers. Someone seems to have taken out my brain and put something else there, slow and stupid. I stare at the phone and try to concentrate. I knew the number before, ages ago. I did. I did. Remember, I tell myself, remember. Then – 0-7-8-1. I frown – what comes after 1? It's curled up – 6.

I look up. Grandad's standing at the door and he's got his arms folded and I get shivers all over because I know I'm doing something I shouldn't. My hand goes tight on the phone and I press the buttons without meaning to so lots of little beeps come out.

He doesn't get cross like I'm expecting. He goes down on the ground, bending so he's on one knee and that hurts him. 'Carmel. Honey, child. What are you doing?' His voice is soft and kind.

I hold tight onto the phone.

'Carmel?'

'Dad . . .' It's a squeak that's come out.

'I'm sorry. I'm so sorry about your dad, honey. Maybe he'll reconsider one day but he says – and I know how hard this is – he says he must start a new life now. As must we.'

Then he takes my hand and curls my fingers back and takes the phone away.

21

DAY 51

SOME DAYS WERE WORSE than others. Day 51 I hadn't managed to get dressed so when Alice came she found me still in my dressing gown.

'Beth, I've been meaning and meaning to come.'

She stood on the doorstep, hesitating, gifts in her arms – home-made blackcurrant jam and a bunch of sweet-smelling hyacinths, the purple petals stiff and bristling like a hairbrush. The daylight seemed to shift behind her and the breeze lifted her fine reddish-brown hair as if an invisible child was hovering above and tugging. The braided bracelets she always wore peeked from under the cuffs of her pink jacket as she handed over her gifts.

'How kind, how kind,' I said, juggling with flowers and jam, and asked her in and offered tea even though I felt in such a way that day that it was almost beyond endurance.

'I'm sorry I haven't been before,' she said.

I peered at her. What was she doing here? Alice had been more or less tangential to my life, not even really one of my friends. I'd felt sorry for her, I suppose, for her terrible life – put that down as the reason why she came across as a bit of an oddball and tried to include her when I could. Even if she did seem to fancy Paul a bit, I didn't take it seriously, and after all, he was attractive – lots of women fancied him; I found *that* out to my cost. I suppose I'd had the thought I should talk her around to doing something about the sporadic domestic violence. Though all she'd ever do was give a smile that slipped around like a fish in water, change the subject or insist she was all right.

But it's kindness, I chided myself. It's kindness that she's here today, and that made me exert myself.

She looked around the kitchen, clean and passable enough except for the empty shell of the egg on the kitchen drainer. 'I'm glad to see you're looking after yourself,' she said, and I didn't tell her that was from yesterday morning and I hadn't eaten anything since.

'Sorry to burst in on you,' she said as she sat at the kitchen table. She seemed highly anxious, though it didn't really register. Or if it did I blamed it on the stress of seeing someone whose daughter had vanished.

'No, that's OK, it's fine, please don't worry.' The teapot breathed fragrant steam as I lifted the lid and stirred. 'And I know it's difficult for people. They don't always know what to say.' But it was me having to force myself to speak this time.

She drank in little bobbing sips.

Then out of nowhere – 'Beth, I've been plucking up courage for ages to tell you this. I had to speak with you. I need to tell you something.'

'About Carmel?'

'Yes.'

'What is it? What is it?' I clutched at the neck of my dressing gown, suddenly excited and alert, imagining how this could be a clue to the puzzle – the one I'd been waiting for, the one I'd missed.

'Your girl . . . Carmel.' She stumbled and started again. 'Well, I was battered, you know, covered with marks. He'd gone mad two nights before, you know, like he got.'

'Yes, yes, I remember.'

'And the night we were here she saw me. Everyone else was

talking too much to take any notice but she put her hand on me, and the next day – honestly, Beth, I'm not making this up – the next day they were gone. Not a single mark and the day before I'd been black and blue. You remember, you must remember. Please, don't be angry, but I think she had a channel with God.'

She stopped with a gasp.

'A channel with God?' She didn't hear it, the sharp disappointment in my voice, burning in my mouth.

'Yes, it happens, you know, when children are close to Him that way. And I wanted to say . . . to reassure you that she would be with Him now, I mean . . .'

'What?'

'An angel, one of the angels, Beth.' Tears were shining in her eyes. 'Can't you see it? I think . . .'

My fury was a white heat building behind my eyes. 'Are you telling me my daughter is dead?' A horrible thought occurred to me: that I wanted to hit her too.

'Please don't be like this. It's just . . . if she is, then . . . I thought it would give you comfort, to know this . . .'

'Stop it.' I stood and put my hands over my ears. What I'd thought was to be a vital clue was turning into the outpourings of a crazy acquaintance. 'Please, stop it.'

'You've got to believe it, Beth. You have to.' As she spoke her wrists in those bracelets turned in front of her and hate rose up in me, thick in my throat.

'No. Get out of here. I thought you had something real to tell me. Get out of this house and leave me alone, you stupid cow. You crazy stupid cow. Take your God with you and don't ever come back.'

So, those leads, luminous and silver. How was I to know that Alice – of all people – held one in her hands, shining and spilling through her fingertips. And that even as we spoke, it was getting thinner, runnier – its silver lustre falling away into darkness.

22

WHEN I WAKE UP I think I must have died again – my eyes glued tight and my mouth stuck together. I'm lying down, but moving too – forward, the same way my head's pointing. Inside my body, there's a great big stone pinning me down.

I think I must be in that tunnel on my way to the pearly gates – I've heard people talking about what it's like to die. It's a long black tunnel then you see a bright light at the end and there are all your friends and family waiting for you who have died before and pearly gates come into it somewhere but I'm not sure how.

I really see some gates right in front of my face but they're not made of pearl. They're grey metal with cold coming off them. I've seen them somewhere before. Then they go away and red flowers start opening out on black behind my eyes instead. I go back down into a sleep that's like falling into a pile of pillows.

When I wake up I remember my name is Carmel.

I'm being rattled around now. I'm in a sort of factory maybe, rolling forward like an engine or a chocolate to the place where metal arms will pack me up into a box. Once I think I'm going to fall off the moving belt but I don't know what onto – I feel like I'll carry on falling. Farther and farther and forever.

Then another long sleep then awake again.

I try to make sense of what I see. After a long while I decide it's a ceiling, but with light and shadows rushing over it. I rest my eyes then – I'm tired to my bones – but I don't want to fall asleep again so I roll around till I'm on my side.

There's shadows and I start seeing four eyes in them, amber colour, looking at me sideways. Not one next to the other, like they should be in a head, but one on top of the other. I don't even know if I'm scared. I watch the four eyes lined up in a row. They watch me back, blinking sometimes.

Then a voice: 'We've been waiting for you to wake up, like – for ages.'

One of the pairs of eyes moves upward and around and then they're next to each other – like they should be – but floating in the air. The other pair down below stays the same, blinking and watching.

'I didn't know anyone could sleep like that. It's like you've been dead or something.' It's a television voice: a squeaky American cartoon.

I mumble something. Not real words, just a silly croak and there's the noise of both pairs of eyes laughing.

'You sound so funny.' The top pair of eyes seems to be doing all the talking. The ones down below just watch.

I properly pop back into myself for the first time. Lying on bunk beds there's two girls looking exactly the same. They could be two of the exact same person. The one below's got her head on a pillow but the one above is sitting up and leaning down to look. She swings her feet over and dangles them over the edge. She's wearing black patent shoes and a flouncy dress with lace that puffs up around her like she's landed there in a parachute.

The one down below speaks for the first time.

'Silver – you shouldn't have your shoes on when you're in bed. You'll get into trouble again.'

'Oh, who cares about that? She won't know anyhow.'

Top-bunk girl stands up. She has to crouch so she doesn't bang into the ceiling and she looks like she'll fall over we're jolting about so much now.

'I don't care. I'll dance on the bed, I'll do the moonwalk.' And she starts to lift her knees up and down, pounding her feet into the bright cover. It doesn't look anything like the moonwalk to me.

'Hey you, you girl – watch me dance in my shoes, watch me.' She carries on dancing so I'm afraid she might shoot off the bed and land right on top of me.

The one below starts laughing and smacking her hand on the bedpost in time.

'Dance, Silver, dance. Kick your legs right up so you show your panties.'

The dancing girl brings her knees up higher and higher. Her lacy dress bounces and her long black hair flicks up and down. She stops all of a sudden and flops down on the bed.

I want to talk to them but my words don't seem to make sense.

'What's that?' says top-bunk girl. 'What does she say?'

I look around me. My bed's on one side with the bunk beds against the other wall. Behind us there's a curtain hanging up. It's got red, pink and green in the pattern and the word 'paisley' comes into my head from out of nowhere. There's a window, very high up. That's where the light's coming from, streaming over the ceiling.

'I'm Carmel,' I manage to say. But I'm not really telling them – I'm reminding myself of something I nearly forgot.

Bottom-bunk girl says, 'I'm Melody,' but the top-bunk one says, 'We know that, of course. Carmel – it's kind of funny.'

I want to say – not as funny as you, with your horse names and your squeaky voices. But the box we're in jolts hard, enough to nearly tip the three of us off our beds. It comes to a slow grinding stop.

23

DAY 90

I WAS ALONE for the first time.

Mum and Dad had finally decided they needed to return home to London and I'd urged them to go. Reconnecting with Paul was always going to be harder while they were around – I needed to convince him I was no longer the vengeful ex-wife, I needed somehow to enlist his support.

I'll stay in the garden, I thought, for as long as I can. Somehow it felt better to be without ceilings, without paintings and furnishings and familiar patterns on mugs and throws and cushions.

The garden in contrast felt new. Unseen, it had transformed itself into summer – the flowers had sprung up without any tending and reds and oranges splashed against the wall. Bees bounced from petal to stamen, disappearing inside as if gulped at by the blooms.

I liberated the tools where they waited patiently for me in the shed and plunged my trowel into the collars of weeds around the flowers. I worked, moving down the long bed, until I looked up to see a section of the wall that had tumbled down, leaving rocks like unexploded devices half buried in the soil. I stopped to wipe the sweat from my face then lifted up the smallest rock and weighed it in my hands, looking for its cleft in the wall. There it was – the exact shape of the stone in my hands. I slotted it into place and looked for another match. I worked methodically, slowly, until the tumbled gash was repaired. The final stone was bigger, flatter than the others, designed to hold the rest in place. I dusted off my hands and stood to look at the perfect puzzle I'd put back together.

Something itched at my consciousness. What? Then it dawned on me that at some point any thoughts of Carmel had left me. That for a while my being was so connected with my task that's all there was in the world: me and the stones, their undersides cool and damp from the earth and their tops warmed by the sun. How long had this lasted? Two minutes, five – ten? A wave of guilt at forgetting hit me and I knelt on the grass and sank back onto my heels. It seemed impossible, but possible – that there might be a time ahead where I could drink a coffee, get immersed in a book, laugh with a friend, exclaim over a pair of new shoes, choose a paint colour, brush my hand over a velvet curtain and take pleasure in the sensation.

By now the sun was slipping downward and dusk was dusting the air and I had no choice but to turn to face the darkening house.

Inside, it seemed impossibly quiet and still like time had been pinched out, its golden hands buckled. Now I was alone I felt adrift in it, like it was an abandoned, half-sunk ship full of discarded possessions.

I padded upstairs and sat on her bed. Next to it was one of her most prized things – a china bedside lamp in the shape of a spotted toadstool, the front hollow to reveal the scene inside: a family of china badgers in their cosy kitchen. We'd found it in a charity shop and borne it home, then – clever Mum, I'd thought at the time, clever independent resourceful single mum, who needs him? – rewired it.

I flicked the switch. There was Father Badger, in checked slippers, reading a newspaper at the kitchen table, where a loaf cut in half and a tiny yellow triangle of cheese waited. Mum, in flouncy blue apron, holding a frilled pie just taken from the oven. Baby, also at the table, with a spoon in its mouth. A perfect vision of family; no wonder she loved it. I flicked the switch on and off, each time half expecting another china figurine to have joined them – Carmel, tiny and immobile, standing by the stove on the miniature striped rug. *It's all right, officer, she's taken off to live with the badgers. She drinks out of tiny cups and warms herself against tongues of painted fire. No alarm. At least she's where we can keep an eye. She'll be back; you can't live on brown painted bread forever.*

Underneath the lamp was a piece of paper – one of Carmel's drawings. I pulled it out to look: a man sitting with a babbling pencil loop of words coming out of his mouth and a long-eared creature at his feet. I lifted the lamp to tuck the picture back and the bulb clinked against the china inside, threatening to shatter.

I left her room, all the breaths she took in there, her thoughts that still bumped around the ceiling. She seemed to flit around me. I wondered for a split second – was she ever real? Have I dreamt up a whole life? I went into the bathroom and pulled the cord so the harsh bulbs above the mirror showed me in a blaze. I pulled up my T-shirt; there, there she was, in the tracks spreading across my belly, marks made as if by small skeleton hands – fine, silvery.

Around the house there was a buzzing, a smell, a sickness. A memory? Carmel throwing up across the table after a day out. Never mind, never mind – mop it up. A broken toy – a duck that wouldn't stop nodding and making mechanical quacks; Paul tried to mend it, then gave up and took the batteries out, silencing it for ever. Memories grew out of the darkness; their quick grow-ing webs crossing my path so I walked into them unawares and felt their skeins across my face. Carmel looking up at me: 'Can we still go?' Expectation in the air. 'Yes, we can go. We're catching a train.'

I reached her room again, realising I was almost panting, and I opened the window to gulp fresh air. Moonlight flooded in. The moon's swollen face looked down, heavy with something – water, blood – its mouth a fissure across the surface that might at any minute open and emit a high thin scream. I grabbed on to the window frame to steady myself. Get a hold of yourself, I thought.

I found the art materials in the bottom of her cupboard, a plastic crate with a slurry of felt pens, brushes. 'I need a map,' I announced to the room. 'I'll make a diagram of everyone we know and who knows them – there must be a clue hidden in there somewhere.'

I unrolled a ream of paper and stuck great sheets of it to the wall next to her bed. With a red pen I started in the centre of the blank whiteness.

Carmel.

Purple lines for our friends. More and more, a growing mesh of people and connections: Paul, his brothers Sean and Darren. Lucy. My friends – Belinda, Nessa, Julie, and the rest in a bird's nest under her name, runnels of felt pen linking us all together. Alice. The man at the maze. Then her friends – I struggled to remember as many of the names from her class as possible and arranged them in choir rows by the side of her.

'Where are you?' I asked the map. 'Is this the line that will take me to you?' I traced my fingers over the leads. 'This one? This one? There must be something.' All the time staving off the knowledge that it might have nothing to do with these names: a random lone event with no leads. Finally, I leaned back on her bedside table, exhausted, but with the realisation that even in this task I had again been absorbed, briefly, in that zone of forgetting.

My first night alone and I slept soundly, not one single dream penetrating the dark night. In the morning I wandered into her room with my tea in hand and faced the spiralling chart on her wall. The map of my daughter, I thought – it looked like a giant tangled spider ready to grow its many legs and wrap them around the world, its feathery feet feeling for where she was.

As I stood back and examined the coloured lines, the connections that ran between people, I saw also that it was a map of myself, of everyone I'd ever known and who'd known me, and it was a kind of funny shock to be reminded of that. I was a chunk of something split apart. I was going to have to find a way to survive alone – that, or shrivel and die.

24

I HEAR VOICES. Doors are flung open and light comes flooding inside. The two people standing outside are black against the orange sky.

I realise I've been in a truck all this time.

One of them leans forward and the bulb of his head gleams in a splash of light and I recognise Grandad. My eyes sharpen up – they're both there. Dorothy and Grandad.

Oh, I'm so pleased and relieved to see them I nearly cry out. My memories of them come rushing back, but I can't say a word. I lie there and watch Grandad fold out metal steps from the floor of the van. Dorothy's standing way behind him.

Grandad opens out his arms wide, welcoming. He looks bigger and more powerful than I remember. His head's held high and before it was always bent down with his eyes looking upward from the corners. He's pleased with himself now – strong and happy – lit pinky-orange from the sky and his white hair is longer and it's moving about in the breeze and his pale eyes are full of light. His hands are as big as spades and he seems excited to be alive.

I look at Dorothy.

It's strange. If anyone asked me which one I like best, which one's more friendly, I'd say Dorothy, she gave me hugs and once took me on a secret picnic, but she's changed too. I don't know how you can tell all this just by looking one time, but I do. Straight away. I see her with her face turned backwards from the sun and her eyes like black holes in her head. I know in that second she's a person who puts herself in shadows.

Behind them, the sun is low down and lighting up a place that's not even fields – just countryside with huge rocks sticking out of the ground. My brain reaches down inside of me and I feel the great big stone egg there: I know it's called 'my mum is dead and everything has changed for ever.'

This looking and knowing happens in a few seconds.

The twins run down the metal steps in great leaps. They run around Dorothy and talk in a different language to her I don't understand.

I feel I'm not afraid. I don't even want to cry. I'm an insect that's been put in a jar and shaken so much it's lying at the bottom, too battered to fly up. Slowly I climb out of bed and come down the steps – not like the twins, dancing and leaping, but like a little old lady, creeping, creeping along like her legs will break.

Grandad puts one arm around me to help me down. 'Carmel, how lovely to see you back to yourself and up and about again,' he says.

I want to say I don't feel very much like myself and I hardly call this creeping around being up and about.

'Welcome, welcome to our little family. I see you have already met Dorothy's girls. Her lovely twins, her flower buds.'

I nod. Why didn't Dorothy tell me she had twins? Why didn't she say, 'I've got two girls about the same age as you'? Why didn't she say, 'I can speak a different language?'

Dorothy is bending down over a pile of stuff on the ground and the twins are running around her like dogs let out after being shut up for a long time.

I feel a stab through my heart then and the stone egg gets heavier. I'm longing for Dorothy to come up to me and put her arms around me and say everything's A-OK and be back to how we were before. But she's opening up boxes and taking out saucepans and tins and the light is glowing on her brown skin and it's like she's turning her face away from me on purpose.

I come down the last step and my hand is on Grandad's sleeve. He's got on his usual white shirt, but over it there's a short coat. One like Dad had and used to call a 'donkey jacket.' It feels thick and felty on my fingers.

It makes Grandad look strong and tough.

'Hello, dear,' he says to me in a quiet voice.

'Hello,' I say back, and it feels like the hellos are private between us, away from Dorothy and the noisy twins. 'How are you feeling?' His face is serious, and he's looking at me as if I'm the most important thing in the world. And the look makes me want to cry because I haven't seen anything like it for so long. It's a kind of Mum look. But I won't let myself cry. I think about how I need to break the hard stone egg inside me into tiny bits – *Courage, Carmel, courage* – because it's so heavy I don't think I can stand to carry it around for very long.

The bigness of outside is making me dizzy. 'Grandad,' I ask, 'do you *live* inside this truck?'

He smiles and the wind whips his hair into his eyes then out again.

'For the moment, for the moment. It was provided to us and in it we make our home. But it's better than a house because it moves around.'

I feel a pain, right down below. 'Is there . . . is there a toilet in it?' I ask, and then I wish I hadn't because I can see from his face the answer's no but he doesn't want to think his truck's no good.

'I'm afraid this is no Hymer motor home. This is no fully kitted luxury vehicle. We have no need of that. If we need to relieve ourselves we do it in nature.'

I look around. I think he means for me to wee out on the grass but there's not a house or even a hedge in sight to hide behind. I step down, and when my foot touches the grass Grandad says to me, 'Welcome to America.'

And I look up at him amazed. I even forget about needing a wee.

'We're in America? Is that really true?'

He smiles, all dreamy. 'Yes, it's really true. You've been sick, Carmel, for a very long time, but I can see now that you are going to get better. The prayers we've said have finally been answered and Carmel is back in the land of the living.'

I shiver when he says that, because if there's a land of the living there must be a land of the dead – and what it looks like flashes up inside my head. It's thousands on thousands of eyes all squashed together in a pink meaty lump with every eye blinking and watching separately. Grandad doesn't notice the shivering.

'Go behind the truck, dear, and then join us. We'll light a fire tonight and eat our supper out in the open under God's great sky.' He smiles all kind down at me. 'Go, dear, go.'

I walk to the other end of the truck, the driving bit. My legs hurt and feel weak and strange. I crouch on the stony ground and lift up my nightie and wee. I don't recognise the nightie. It's white with pink roses and it comes right down to the ground. Someone else must have put this on me, I think. The wee rolls away from me, steaming and gathering up little bits of dust as it goes. It feels not right, with my bottom bare in this huge wide place, like I could be a little naked rabbit on the ground, ready to be jumped on.

Then I go around to where the others are. Dorothy's touching the flame of a match to a heap of sticks. I stay around the corner of the truck, peeping for a moment, because I suddenly feel shy. I see Dorothy settle back onto her stool and take out a carton of juice from a bag on the ground. She pours it into four plastic cups and passes them around. The air's turning bluey-black and the flames from the fire leap up and light their faces. My bare feet feel cold on the stones and scratchy grass and I shiver inside my nightie. Grandad turns around.

'Whose is that face? Looking out like a new moon? Come and join us, dear.' His face looks so pleased, and I can feel *his* feelings, calm and sugary thick, rolling around the campfire. Grandad opens up another camping chair for me to sit on. Then he goes and gets one of the blankets made of crochet from the beds and wraps me up in it.

Dorothy sticks a big fork with three spikes into the cool box next to her. She lifts it up and out and there's a snake hanging off it, stuck through the neck with the fork.

I scream and jump off my chair. 'What's that?' I'm trembling all over.

They all laugh at me.

'It's a sausage, child. Whoever was scared of a sausage?'

She waves the snake about and it turns into a sausage – but a great long one. 'What did you think it was?' she asks.

'A snake.' And they laugh again. I climb back onto the chair.

'Don't worry, dear.' Grandad gets up and tucks the blanket around me again. 'You don't have to fret about anything. Would you like some juice?' His hands are patting me, making the blanket right. I'm so grateful to him I get a lump in my throat.

'Yes, please.'

'Let's cook the snake,' says Dorothy.

She dangles the sausage above a frying pan on the fire and twists it around and around so it coils up in the pan. Quickly, it starts to sizzle and spit and send out puffs of meaty steam. She smiles at me but the smile's not right.

When the sausage is cooked she puts bits of it into long bread rolls, the soft kind. She shakes on sauce from a tiny bottle and it spits out, thin and red. I'm hungry. But when she plonks the big meaty chunk on a plastic plate on my lap I'm not any more. I nibble at a corner but something rushes through my mouth, a dragon, and I drop the roll back on my plate.

'Carmel, we like our food with fire in it. Have you not remembered?' Dorothy's face through the heat of the fire has gone wavy.

'Yes.' I do, but before it was fun. I'd touched my tongue on things and we'd laughed at the face I'd made. Now the spice seems a bad spell Dorothy's put on the food. I look at Dorothy and think:

please – won't you offer to make me some mashed potato, or one of the *57 varieties*: tomato soup, with crackers on the side. Dorothy, why don't you like me now? It could just be mashed banana in a cup. I think of vanilla ice cream and my throat burns.

But even through the fire I can see the thoughts in her eyes. The thoughts say – you're trouble. You spell trouble with a capital T for me and Melody and Silver. Though what this trouble is, I don't know.

The others eat their rolls. Then Grandad gets out his bag of peanuts and cracks away and soon there's a pile of empty shells at his feet, the nobbly ends the shape of ladies' nipples. The twins have been eating and talking with their mouths wide open so I can see their mashed-up food inside. Now their big eyes, the same colour as Dorothy's, are getting sleepy. They both lean on Dorothy, one on either side. I'm tired too. I feel very tired and weak and tiny in this great huge place.

It's getting darker and stars burst out of the sky, and they're so big and hard and glittering, I can hardly believe they're the same stars that shined down on me at home. They shimmer away and the whole sky feels like it's moving and whirling above. And there's just us in the world, sitting around this little fire.

I've spotted the difference between the twins. It's something even they don't know about. But I don't let on.

Before we got out of bed this morning they were fooling me about who was who. They kept swapping their names. So finding out about the difference is really useful. The secret clue is at the corner of Melody's mouth. When she talks or smiles or sometimes when she's not doing anything, the corner of her top lip on one side flicks out, it does a tiny twitch and lifts, so the tooth in the corner goes bare.

Then her lip catches on the tooth as she closes the gap. It's over in a flash and that's probably why nobody else knows about it. They're dressed now but I'm in my pink-and-white nightie.

Melody can't stop staring at me. 'Mom's been gone such a long, long time. Was she with you?'

'Yes.' It feels like she might be upset I took Dorothy away from her.

'We had to stay with Pastor Raymond forever.'

'Who's he?' I ask.

'He baptised us. He's got a gold phone and a big car.'

Silver says she doesn't care about that, she says the truck's the best thing on four wheels and she's glad to be back in it. She shows me around. 'This is my bed, and this is Melody's.' Silver stands square on the strip of red carpet in between the beds and points. 'And that's yours.'

'I know that. I woke up in it yesterday. And I went to sleep in it last night.' Melody does her tooth twitch from where she's sitting on the bottom bunk.

'After the snake?' says Silver.

'It was a mistake.' I can't think of anything else to say.

She points up. 'There's the window.'

I sigh now, then Silver's frowning because I'm spoiling her tour. She's telling me things I know already because there's nothing to show.

'OK, then, Miss. Little Miss. You don't know about this, do you?'

With a big yank, she pulls open the paisley curtain. Behind is a wooden bed with a patchwork cover. There's a shelf of books above it with a golden clock next to them. On the floor is a pretty rug in the shape of an oval with blue fringes around the edge and a bunch of red roses in the middle. It's in the right place so it'll be warm to stand on when you get out of bed in the morning.

Silver stands by the bed with her back to me and puts her hand up to the shelf and touches a green leather book.

'Pa's notebook.' They call Grandad Pa. Even though he isn't their dad, they've told me that.

'What's that for?'

'Sometimes he writes and writes for hours in it,' says Melody.

Silver whips her hand away and puts it behind her back. 'We're not supposed to be touching it.'

I like the bedroom. 'It looks like the granny's bedroom in *Little Red Riding Hood*,' I say.

Silver's nose lifts up and the two holes there sneer at me. 'I've heard about that. Fairy tales . . .' she says. Like she's way too old for all that.

'Silver. I think you're being mean,' says Melody. Me and Silver both turn to look at her and her tooth flashes quickly.

'Fairy tales are for babies,' Silver says, 'and the ungodly.'

I giggle then, because I can't imagine God, if there really is one, bothering about 'Three Billy Goats Gruff' or bears eating porridge. But both girls can't see what's funny, they stare at me with blank faces and their four shiny shoes pointing toward me.

I think of something. 'What do you speak with Dorothy?'

'What d'you mean?' asks Silver.

'I've heard you talk in a different language.'

'Spanish,' says Silver. 'Of course.'

I turn away. The back doors of the truck are open. Outside I can see the great sky and Dorothy blowing on the ashes of our fire from last night.

I shiver and put my hands up to my neck and feel bare skin.

'My hair,' I cry out. 'It's gone short.' I can't believe I didn't even notice the night before.

'It looks good on you,' says Melody from her bunk. She's touching her own hair, that comes right down to her waist, with love.

I feel all over my head, and my hair's got scrunched up into curls from being so short.

'When did this happen?'

Silver shrugs and her frilly skirt goes up and down at the bottom.

'You'll need to get dressed,' she says. 'This is your closet.' She opens a wooden cupboard at the top of my bed and the ice-cream dresses are there. I see a picture in my head then, of myself running through a great house, running and screaming. It hurts me to think about so I turn my face down to the floor so the twins won't see.

'You get dressed,' says Silver, 'and then we'll play together.'

I put on the yellow dress.

I think of something important to ask Melody. 'How did I get here?'

She's playing with a doll on the bunk bed, brushing its long gold hair over and over.

'I don't know,' she says, not interested. 'The same way everyone does I s'pose.' She goes back to the brushing. Now I have a terrible thirst in my mouth so I go to ask for a drink. But there's something I've heard about called 'being disturbed in the head.' And I really think it might be happening to me. I'm putting one foot in front of the other and a horrible thing is happening. Someone's pressing fast forward and I'm going into a speeded-up film. My feet are so quick they're wheels like there's an invisible bike I'm riding. In a tick I'm next to Dorothy, wondering how I got there so fast.

'Please could I have some juice?' I ask.

She pours some orange juice into a blue plastic cup and hands it to me. I don't recognise the writing on the side of the carton. It's not *Tropicana* like we have at home. I loved that word and sometimes I'd be looking at it for nearly an hour. Till Mum said – 'Maybe I should put it back in the fridge now, it'll be going off.'

This is different. It's called *365 Everyday Value*.

I take the cup. Thinking about Mum has made my throat hurt really badly.

'Could you drink any more slowly?' Dorothy's watching me, waiting for the cup back. I thought I was drinking at normal speed but she's there, tapping her foot, like I'm taking ages.

'You're like Old Father Time himself and there's dishes to do and all manner of things. I can't be standing here watching a girl drink for an hour.'

I hand the cup back, half full, not knowing what she means.

I'm shivering, freezing cold. 'Where's my coat?' I ask.

'It had to be thrown out, child. You'll have to make do with one of the twins' old things till we get you something else.'

My throat feels like it's about to burst. 'I wanted that,' I say, but she's moved away and doesn't hear.

I make a silent promise to myself and Mum that when I get a new one it'll be red. Somehow it's the most important thing.

The speeding up and slowing down keeps happening. One minute I'm in the truck and in a flash I'll be miles away, standing by the tree with no leaves that sticks out of the ground and has black burn marks. Far away there's the four of them, waving and calling me back. Or I'll be in bed and watching a drop of rain slide down the window – but it takes a whole day. Outside, a mush-room grows up out of the ground in front of my eyes. I play tea sets with the twins on a fold-up table and their voices go very fast and gabbling like chipmunks and they lift the cups to their lips and pretend to drink, over and over, and their hands move across the table, swapping things about so fast I feel dizzy. Silver speaks to me and the only thing I understand is my name at the end. I hang on to the pillowcase they're using as a tablecloth and I close my eyes and their angry chipmunky squawks ring in my ears as the tea set things crash down.

Tonight, in bed, there's light still in the air. I watch the twin in the top bunk and see her hair grow. Her long black plait flops over the edge and the tassel end of it goes downward like black oil dribbling.

What's happening? I ask myself. I'm seeing the hair grow right out of people's heads.

25

I MAKE FRIENDS with the twins. They go off sometimes and Silver won't talk to me. But even then Melody comes into the truck and holds my hand. We're playing with dolls when Grandad takes me outside.

'I want to know, dear. What you are thinking.'

We're sitting on the spiky grass and I can feel the pointed ends of it poking through my thin dress. It'll make holes in my tights, but I don't care that much.

'Right this minute? You want to know what I'm thinking right this minute?'

'Yes, dear.'

I've been staring at the white painted side of the van. There's black words showing through the paint, it says: *Drakerton's Fine Quality* . . . I don't know fine quality what because the paint's thicker after that, so you can't see the words.

'I'm wondering what the fine quality things were.'

'Oh.' Grandad's voice sounds disappointed, like it's not a good thing to think about at all. But I have the feeling everything's about to go speeded up or slowed down again and talking feels like it might be a way of stopping it happening.

'What do you think, Grandad? There's biscuits with tartan on that say "fine quality," d'you think . . .'

He interrupts. 'I don't think you should call me Grandad now.'

I turn to him. 'But why? You are my grandad, aren't you?'

'Yes, of course, dear. Except here, people don't really . . .' The twins think it's odd. And other people might, you never know.'

'But what should I call you then?' I think of the word *Dennis*. I don't like the way that word is shaped.

'How about Pa? It's what the twins call me. You could call me that.'

'Pa?'

'Mmmm?' He answers, like I've already agreed to say it. But if you say a certain name, a name like *Father* or *Pa* for instance, it feels very strong. It could change how they are to you. And how you are to them. My father's a bit rubbish, he's a dad who wants to be with his new girlfriend rather than coming to get me in his red Peugeot. It doesn't stop him being my dad.

I purposely prick my fingers on the spiky grass. 'No, I don't think I can do that. I don't think I can manage that.'

'Oh.' His face goes cloudy. 'Well, what about Grandaddy, then?'

This sounds awful.

'Mmm. Sounds a bit like . . .'

'Yes?'

'. . . like a daddy-long-legs.'

He sighs, he's getting annoyed now. 'Grandpa?'

'Mmm. Not sure about that . . .' I try pulling up a stalk of grass. But it's too strong and doesn't want to come out of the ground.

'What about . . . ?' I ask.

'Yes?'

'What about Gramps? I could call you Gramps. That's what Sara calls her grandad.' This makes me think about Sara. 'D'you think I can send my friend something? I could write a letter to tell her where I am and maybe you could post it?'

He goes quiet and his head turns slowly one way then the other like he's looking all around for things coming in the distance.

At last he says, 'Yes, yes. But concentrate on the issue at hand, child. This is much more important.'

'I said, Gramps.'

'I guess that'll have to do then.' He seems disappointed. I smile at him, so he'll feel better about it.

'I like it. It sounds friendly.'

'Well, I guess that's important . . .'

'Do I have to call Dorothy anything else?'

'No.' He's sighing again and heaving himself off the ground. I can tell his leg is hurting him bad today. 'No, I guess Dorothy can be Dorothy. Seems to have been enough trouble calling me by something decent.'

I didn't mean to be trouble. But I didn't want to call him Pa.

He's standing above me, in front of the sun. It makes him black, so I can't see his mouth moving when he talks.

'Come, dear. I think we should have a little walk. Just the two of us together.'

I shake my head. I don't want to be on my own with him. 'Why, child? Why ever not?'

How can I tell him he gives me the creeps sometimes? It'd be rude, upsetting. Specially after how he's looked after me.

'I want to stay here and play.'

He leans down and pulls me up out of the ground – pop! – like a weed. And he keeps hold of my hand and he's strong.

We set off across the great wide earth and I can feel three lots of eyes in our backs as we go, wondering where we're off to.

The sky is so big and the ground with huge rocks sticking out of it seems to go on for ever and ever. Miles away in the distance is a misty blue that could be mountains, or clouds. We pass a tree sometimes, sticking up out of the ground, but each time the tree looks like it really doesn't want to be there. And some of them are burned, like the one I've found myself at when the speeding up happens. Even Grandad – *Gramps* – seems tiny in this great big place and because the ground is either rocky or covered with bumpy grass he has trouble walking over it with his bad leg. He's sweating and every now and again he has to stop and wipe his glasses with a hanky. The jolting makes his face screw up with pain. I look back. The truck is a white spot far away and I can't even see Dorothy and the two girls.

We stop by a tree. It's bare jagged wood, black and burned. Gramps leans against the tree and closes his eyes. I think he must be resting, so I sit on the grass away from him and flick the seeds off a stem. I keep an eye on him though. Keep looking back over my shoulder.

'Come here.' I hear his voice behind me at last.

I sit still.

'Come here,' he says again. I don't want him to get angry so I do, but I can feel my heart going fast inside me. Children are like the zombies I once saw in a film at Dad's. We have to do as we're told and obey like our brains have got eaten.

There's not much room for both of us to lean on the tree. I stand there, a bit away from him, and look down at the dust on my shiny shoes.

He says, 'C'mon, c'mon,' and makes me move so we get squashed close together, our sides touching. He's taken off his glasses and he must have put them in his pocket because I can't see them anywhere. His pale eyes are shiny-bright.

'We need to have a very special and unusual talk, Carmel. We need to have a conversation.'

'What about?'

He looks at me hard. 'Pain.'

'Pain?'

'Yes, dear. Pain. My pain.' He touches his side. 'You've seen how I walk? Well, sometimes it's bad. Real bad.'

'How did you hurt your leg, Gramps?' I ask.

'A motor vehicle went into me.'

I have to stop myself from crying out because the picture of a pair of brown boots sticking out from under a truck flashes in my brain.

'Oh, oh,' I gasp. 'How?'

'That's not important. What's important is the here and now.'

He's looking at me so hard I feel I'm going to fall over. Then he sighs a little, but it's a happy sigh. Excited.

'Please, Grandad – Gramps. Can we go back now?'

'No.' His voice is sharp. 'It's high time, you know.'

'Please, Gramps.' I put my arms behind me and cling onto the tree. 'I don't know . . . I don't know what you're talking about.' That comes out wrong.

'Oh yes? I think you do.'

Behind his eyes reminds me of trees waving about on a stormy night. The muscles on his face are so tight, if I touched it my hand would bounce right off his skin. My short curly head prickles all over.

I suddenly have the idea he could murder me out here.

I don't know where the idea has come from but it makes my muscles move, to run off, but he catches me by the arm and pulls me back.

He holds my arm tight and I see him moving his face about. Making it nicer.

'Don't run away, Carmel. Why did you do that? Promise me you won't do that again.'

I don't say anything.

'Promise?'

I nod. I can't tell him it's because I had the idea he was going to murder me.

'I don't know if you know it, but you are a very rare person. Exceptional might be the way to name it. Not everyone can see it, but I can. I know how rare and special you are.' He lets go.

I don't want to be rare. I rub at my arm where he's hurt it.

Perhaps Gramps knows about how time keeps changing for me, and that's what he means. But I haven't said about it happening and I don't think he can read my mind. I rack my brains because Gramps is staring like he's waiting for an answer. The only other secret thing is how I see the energy in people and how it goes up and down, how they can be empty or full like a glass of milk. I haven't told him about that thing either. Both are private and I wouldn't know how to start talking about them.

'I, I don't understand, Gramps.'

'Yes, yes, sure you do.' He's nodding away to himself.

I can feel myself wanting to cry. 'I don't, please. Please can we go and see Dorothy? I'm thirsty.'

'The first time I saw you, I knew about this rarity and I've waited. I've waited and waited to talk about these things. I've been as patient as Job and it hasn't been easy, Carmel, knowing how wonderful things can be and having to wait. But sometimes that's what you have to do until the time has come. This morning, when I woke up and the day was so fresh and clear, it felt like the world had been washed new. And I thought: now's the time, today's the day – give me your hand.'

I don't want to.

'Carmel, your hand. Give me your hand, stop shallying.'

I want to put my hand behind my back and not let him touch it even. I want to run off to Dorothy, even though I know she doesn't want me now she's got her twins back. But if I try to run he'll grab me again so I'm trapped. I start to cry little sniffling sobs.

Slowly, he crouches down. It hurts him a lot to do.

'Carmel, dear. This is not a time for sadness. It's a joyful, joyful thing, this gift you have.'

His face is close to mine. 'What gift?' I sob.

He sighs. 'Calm down, will you? I can't tell you. I can only show you.'

He stands up again and his face has to scrunch up because it hurts him so much. He takes my hand, very slow and gentle. His hand feels cracked and rough at the fingertips, then very smooth on his palm.

'In this hand . . .' He stops and seems to get stuck with his eyes raised to the sky.

After a while I must be fidgeting because he snaps out of it and bends over me.

'Carmel, stay still. You're jumping around like a cricket. How can I concentrate?'

'What are you doing, Gramps?'

He looks right at me then with his eyes gone big. My head starts prickling again. My hair feels now like it's waving about on its own like tentacles.

'Put your hands on me, child. Oh Lord, see this girl who is a vessel of your grace . . .' He stops and mumbles to himself.

I reach out and put my hand on his arm, scared everything will slow down and I'll be stuck in this awful time forever. It'll be like when Dad's video gets put on pause and the picture stops, but jumps from side to side.

'Now, not there. On my leg, on the site of my pain. Oh God . . .'

And I do as he says because I know the sooner I do, the sooner I'll be allowed back with Dorothy. I put my hand very light and soft where he's showed me. On the rough black stuff his trousers are made of, by the side of his hip. He goes quiet and screws his eyes up tight.

Then everything does speed up, like I was scared of, in a terrible way. Clouds rush overhead and the sun chases them across the sky. It gets hot as the sun flies up to the top of the sky then cool again as it falls down. The grass flaps and waves, following the sun and everything grows – even the tree waggles its branches and goes upward.

When time goes back to normal the air is orange. The glowing sun is halfway past the edge of the world, so there's only its huge top half shining at us. Gramps's face has sweat on it. Slowly, he opens his eyes.

'Take your hand away now, Carmel.'

My hand's gone stiff and clamped to his side like it's been there for hours. I try to wiggle my fingers around but my hand's turned into a claw. It waves uselessly in the air with the fingers curled up.

Now Gramps has got a different face – he's so calm and smiling. Like there'd never been any pain in his whole life.

'*Now* we'll see how I've been right all along. How I've ignored the railings of my wife because I've known in my heart what's true. What we're about to witness, here together, is beyond mortal powers. It comes from heaven, child. It comes from heaven.'

I'm hoping what he says means this is nearly over. I don't think I can stand being here with him, all alone, for much longer.

'Don't look upset, dear.' He puts his hand down and strokes my cheek. 'We should be jubilating. It's a fine and a tender thing. Now then.'

He makes some grunting noises. He's got stiff too, leaning against the tree for so long.

'That's the way.' He stands up proper and straight and puts his shoulders right back. 'Now then.'

He pats himself up and down and then smoothes his hair back with both hands. He puts one brown lace-up shoe in front of the other like he's testing something out.

'With the grace.' Then his voice goes very low and quiet so I can't hear what he's saying.

He starts taking steps away from the tree, slow and stiff. He walks five steps, stops and smoothes back his hair, and starts off again back toward the way we came.

But his limp is worse now. The ground's so bumpy it's jolting through his whole body. He gets slower and slower and I think, if I was on the other side of him, I'd see his head pressing out tight into the garlic bulb.

He stops and slowly turns around until he's looking at me.

'What are you, child?' My legs start shaking so much I think they're going to crumple up underneath me.

He limps toward me with his feet slipping everywhere and his face ugly with temper. I can hear little whimper noises coming out of me even though I didn't know I was making them. I'm pressed into the tree so hard it's hurting.

'Are you really a child?' he yells over to me, his voice scattering over the rocks. 'Are you really?'

'Of course I am. You know I am. I'm your granddaughter.'

He charges right up to me and puts his hands on my shoulders and his face right in front of mine. I can't see anything except his eyes and the two of them keep joining up and making one great big purple-blue one. I can't help it, I scream. I scream right into his face.

For a second I think he's going to slap me. But he doesn't. He straightens up.

'You will reveal yourself.'

'Please, Gramps, you're squashing my shoulders . . .'

'Tell me who you are.'

'I'm Carmel. You know who I am. Gramps, let's go back . . .'

'You will show yourself as we all have to in the end. I wasn't mistaken in you, I know I was not. What I've gone through – I mustn't be wrongfooted. I've gone through hell. I've been tested to the limit. I've committed sins . . .'

He lets me go and I nearly fall.

'When I first saw you . . .' He's looking at me hard, up and down and side to side. He'd cut me open and look inside if he could. 'What can that mean? What does it all mean?'

'I don't know, Gramps. I really don't.'

'You stay there and think about it. Contemplate, Carmel, contemplate.'

'Don't leave me.'

'Yes. You need to think hard, to contemplate and pray. That's the only thing that can be done for you now. When I think of . . .'

He limps off but it's an angry limp, skidding over the stones, and worse than ever. He shouts something angry back but he's too far away for me to hear. Then something really awful happens: he falls and crashes to the ground and lies there on his back like an insect that's got stuck.

My legs and hands are shaking and I know I should go and help him. But it would be like going up to a scorpion that might sting you if you get too close. He rolls around trying to get straight and I think he must be swearing and cursing even though I don't hear the exact words.

Then: 'Carmel. Carmel – come here.' I can hear that, he's roaring it.

I stay where I am and cling onto the tree, watching him rolling around until he manages to heave himself up by his arms and get to standing.

And he stares at me, the garlic bulb bit of his head stuck forward, until he turns and limps off, scattering stones he's going so fast.

After a while everything goes silent. He's a dot far away and I can't hear his footsteps any more. All I can hear is the wind. I turn to the tree. It's got three main branches and where they meet in the middle they make a sort of dish, or a cup.

'The crying cup,' I say. Because sometimes it makes me feel better to give names to things. I lean over and let the tears fall down there. They splash onto the hot dry wood and it makes the burn smell stronger. The little puddle there is like Tara's puddle on her desk. And I try not to let them, but thoughts of Mum come rushing into my head and I can't make them stop. Only now she's not saying *Courage, Carmel, courage* or anything like that.

She can't say anything because she's dead.

When there's only a slice of sun showing above the ground I walk back to the truck. The white dot of it gets bigger and bigger until I'm there. Melody comes rushing up and puts her arms around me and hugs me tight.

'Oh, Carmel, I've been so worried about you.'

I put my head deep into her neck and hug her back.

'It's OK,' she says. 'He isn't mad any more. He came back and couldn't talk for a while. But he's fine now.'

I look over my shoulder and Gramps is there. He shuffles around, looking at his shoes.

'C'mon,' says Melody. 'Come inside and we'll play.'

Gramps is extra nice to me after. He says he's sorry he got

'carried away.' But every now and again he tries to get me to put my hands on his side.

I say, 'That's not how people get better. They have to go to the doctor.'

'Yes, Carmel, they can. It's something that can happen and it's a gift – a gift you should not keep to yourself. That would be a selfish act. Would you like to try again?'

'No, thank you.'

I cry and tell him I don't want to do it any more. I put my hands behind my back. I say, 'Gramps, I don't think I can make you better.'

He smiles at me and says, 'But I know you can.' Maybe he's right. I start feeling guilty that I can't help him, like he says I can. I hold out my hands in front of me to see if they look different to other people's. They don't, but looking at them so hard seems to make them float like they don't belong to me.

Gramps sometimes makes me feel I don't do it on purpose. And he looks after me – I don't know what would happen if he didn't, or where I'd go. He starts seeming more like a dad than a grandad and I wonder whether to start calling him Pa like the twins. But then I change my mind again and I don't.

One day we wake up and everything is getting packed.

26

DAY 100

I WROTE IT in my diary with the thick red felt pen I'd been using all along. I stared at the number. The act of writing those twin os had sent vibrations up my arm that now flew – wrapping themselves around my heart and pulsing into my brain.

I flicked backward and forward in the diary as I sat on the edge of the bed, the red numbers descending and increasing, animating – like one of those games where a figure is scratched on the edge of every page and can be made to walk by flipping the pages with your thumb. When I turned the page back to today the number 100 appeared to me as binoculars that she could be spotted through. I needed to take action; I needed Paul back.

He answered on the first ring.

'Paul, don't make some excuse not to talk to me.' The phone fell silent but I knew he was still there. I could tell by the faint electrical hum like a bee breathing down the line.

'I'm sorry, Beth,' he said at last.

'You've been avoiding me.'

'I know, but I – I don't even want to talk about it, it's too awful. Talking about it makes it real.' His voice sounded weak, like he'd been catastrophically sick or involved in a car accident.

'That's because it is.' The energy that had somehow breathed itself into my body overnight I now sent spiralling down the curly cord of the phone toward Paul, as if it might jump-start him too. 'Listen. I'm about to call Julie. I'm going to ask her to bring everyone around tonight that can make it.'

'Everyone?'

'Yes, all my friends. You know – from before. Nessa, Belinda.' I paused. 'Not Alice,' I muttered, though I don't think he heard that. 'They've all been trying to get in touch but I've put off seeing them.'

Paul snorted. 'Why tonight?'

'It's one hundred days, Paul.'

'Oh, I'm sorry.'

'Don't apologise for everything, you don't have to. I'd like you to come, and Lucy too. We need a leaflet, Paul.'

'A leaflet?' His voice was fading in and out. I imagined him lying on the sofa with his hand over his eyes.

'Yes, to hand out. Or put through people's doors. Stick up on lamp posts. You remember Nessa's a graphic designer? Well, I'm going to ask her to help me design one on the computer.' I tapped my fingernails on the hall table in a drumbeat. 'Well, try and come.'

Julie, Kirsten, Rosie, Lynne, Nessa, Belinda – the old gang. Most had tried to contact me. Not all, though, not Sally. There were a few that stayed away but it was Sally's silence that hurt. It was that memory of her, Carmel's fingers kneading her scalp and Sally's head falling back, her arms slumping by her sides – *Oh my God, Carmel, that feels amazing. Don't stop, don't ever stop.*

After I put the phone down I looked around the house and saw it as if for the first time. The illusion of tidiness was only because nothing was being moved about much. I walked around flicking switches in every room until light flooded the house. Everything was coated in a layer of dust. Cobwebs had sprung up around the doorways and it amazed me then that these spiders had been knitting away all the time in my grief-stricken presence. I made bucket after bucket of hot soapy water and scrubbed everything down, the floor, the table. The house was a stage – the thought came to me – a ritual would be played tonight. It needed to be ready. It needed props. I delved into the cupboard under the stairs and all I could find were Christmas decorations. I chose a few and draped artificial fir arrangements, clanking with pine-cones, across the mantelpiece and looped coloured bulbs around the mug hooks.

Julie arrived first and I ran down the front path and embraced her plump pink-coated figure.

'I'm so glad to see you,' she said. 'You're so thin . . . Look, I've brought food.'

She'd come with cake and wine. Nessa arrived with soda bread. Goat's cheese. Plump purple grapes. All of them brought something, until there was enough food to fill the table. A strange banquet. They reminded me of birds gathering around and lifting up the broken one of their flock onto their shoulders, bearing it along. They saw the decorations and didn't comment – even though it must have seemed I'd gone crazy. Anyone passing, and seeing so many cars, would have imagined a party inside, and it was – of sorts.

Nessa brought her printer that could spew out thousands of coloured leaflets at a time. Candles, too, they brought candles, their baskets and carrier bags stuffed full of them.

'They're for after dinner,' said Nessa, 'if you're OK with that. We didn't know what else to do.'

'Oh, oh . . .' I thought: how weak these vigils look when you see them on television – the reedy singing, the dim light – anything sad and pathetic will finish me off.

'We don't have to – it's fine. It's just an idea we came up with.' Her dark eyes, almost black, looked worried.

Something melted or collapsed within me. 'Yes, yes,' I said, tearing chunks of bread and cramming them in my mouth be-cause at last tonight I was starving. 'Yes, that's good – we'll light them all. Like we used to do.'

Outside, the night was cool and clear. My friends set to work laying candles up the path, around the front door, like they were planting hundreds of stubby life forms – mushrooms – in the ground. Then with a taper each we lit them. I thought, oh God, they're going to start singing or something. Please don't let them do that. I won't be able to stand it or to hold it together. They won't be able to cope with what they see when I don't.

But they just stood behind me as we watched the creeping glow of the candles burning brighter, reaching into the shadowy recesses of the front garden. Television can't convey the spirit of candlelight – it was a means to ward off bad spirits, a challenge to the night. The smell of hot wax perfumed the air and the light flared, reaching farther still until the picket fence was illuminated, and the dark figure standing there, watching.

'Paul.' I broke into a loping run toward him.

He stood on the other side of the fence. The candlelight was faint here but I was shocked by what I saw. He'd aged – I didn't know that could really happen – he looked like a Paul ten years in the future standing there.

'You came, I'm so glad. And Lucy? Is Lucy here too?'

'No. She wanted to but I'm trying to protect her from this as much as possible.' Who was I to point out how futile that would be? 'I didn't bring the car, I walked here,' he added, as if this would somehow explain something.

'Shame. I wanted to apologise about how I've been with her. Come in,' I said. 'Come and have something to eat.'

He shook his head and I saw he felt a compulsion to stay outside and that if he entered the world inside there might be no possibility of escape. We stood, either side of the fence, watching the light and my friends wandering among the candles and re-lighting any that had been blown out by the breeze.

'Why are you doing this, Beth?'

'I've been frozen in ice, Paul. I had to make some kind of – movement. Or I was going to be frozen to death. One day someone was going to find me and I would be dead and stiff in bed. Something, surely, is better than nothing? Don't you think that?'

He didn't answer. I wondered what it looked like from the air – this bright flaring glow. I looked up and imagined my daughter as a moth, invisible against the dark sky. I started laughing and Paul stared at me as if I really had gone mad.

'I've just realised.'

'What?'

'What it is we're doing here tonight. We're luring her back with light.'

'With light?'

'Yes, yes.' I reached over and grasped his arm. 'Can't you see? We're trying to show her the way home.'

Two weeks later I stood with Paul in her room. We held hands, as if locked in a séance where we could channel our daughter's whereabouts. The evening of light might have brought Paul back instead of my daughter, but we were no longer husband and wife – or even ex-husband and ex-wife. We were brother and sister united in this strange bond.

Nothing. Only the creak as the wind tugged on the open window. I went to close it.

He turned and studied my map and then rested his forehead against it.

'I'm so sorry, to have left you in all this. Saying it was your fault, that was unforgivable.'

'That's OK.' I laid my hand on his back. 'I want you to know, it's not about us any more, it doesn't exist. I don't want you to worry about that but I need you back – as a father.'

'I'll drive you to the counsellor,' he said, finally.

'Thanks, Paul. That's really kind.'

In the car we stayed silent for a while. I wound down the window and let the warm summer breeze blow over us.

'There's been nothing for weeks,' said Paul eventually. 'No new leads, nothing.'

'I know.'

Leads – those invisible wires that could take us to her. Or Hansel and Gretel's trail of bread crumbs. The wind seemed to have scattered them and time snipped them off. He was right, there'd been nothing.

The country lane was now turning into suburbia. Nineteen-thirties houses lined the street. Paul pulled up.

'Is this the one?'

I peered out of the window. Number 222. 'Looks like it.'

'Where did you find him?'

'Out of the Yellow Pages.'

'So the other psychologist not doing it for you?'

I shook my head. 'Yes. No – I mean sort of.' The police had put me in touch with a man who specialised in this sort of thing. It was helpful to some extent. All the same, I felt like it was part of a 'process.'

'I feel like I need to talk to someone fresh. Who doesn't know me. You should talk to someone too, Paul.'

'Maybe.'

I crunched up the gravel path and rang the bell, then studied the sunburst pattern on the stained glass. The man who opened the door was younger than I expected. At first I wondered if it was him, or if he was the door-opener for the real counsellor.

'You must be Beth, come in.' He wore jeans and a red T-shirt with *Slinky* written on it, no shoes, just socks. We shook hands awkwardly in his hallway. 'I'm Craig. Come through.'

The room was neutral – cream walls, oatmeal carpet. Two chairs facing each other and a coffee table in between. There, tissues fluffed out into a pink rose: the only spot of colour.

'Now, Beth.' He settled back in his chair. 'What would you like to talk about today?'

I looked through the French windows to the garden. A statue of Pan peeped with sly eyes from underneath a leaf. Craig appeared in his twenties. Could I really talk to him?

What could he know about having children, or anything else for that matter? I looked at him; his dark brown eyes were patient, kind – why couldn't the young know as much as the old? I learned that from Carmel.

I felt a welling inside of me. I had to unburden myself to someone.

'My daughter . . .'

'Yes?'

'She's missing.'

He started in his chair. 'What d'you mean?'

'She vanished. Four months ago. Nobody knows where she is.'

'Oh God . . .' He wiped his hands over his eyes. He looked suddenly even younger, his dark eyes and brows under hair bleached by the sun.

'I'm sorry. I should have warned you.' It hadn't occurred to me to do that. The bubble I'd been living in was so complete, so intense, I'd almost forgotten anyone outside of that bubble could be affected – was real, even. 'You haven't read anything in the papers?'

'I've been in South America for a year. I mean, I'm sorry.' He let out a shaky breath. 'There are probably people who specialise in this sort of thing.'

A flare of anger puffed in my chest. 'Are you trying to palm me off?'

'No. It's just . . .'

'I'm sorry. I shouldn't have said that.'

'No, it's fine. Let's start again. What happened?'

I told him, briefly. 'What sort of things do you normally see people about?'

'Oh, unhappiness, you know, the human condition. People who need to reframe their lives.'

I shifted my eyes and looked at the single picture on the wall behind his shoulder. I hadn't noticed it before. It was a forest, light filtering through the trees.

'People don't know what they have. But it's easy for me to say that now.'

We sat in silence for a minute.

'I'm sorry about that,' he said. 'I didn't mean to be shocked. But it is . . . shocking. I'd really like to help you, if I can.'

I glanced at his face again, he looked . . . like a good person. I nodded. 'Yes, yes. Please.'

'You tell me. You tell me where you'd like to start,' he said.

I sat silent for a minute. 'OK, then. I want someone to tell me it was my fault.'

'I can't do that, Beth.'

'Nobody will say it. My husband did, at first. Then he took it back. I think it constantly and I want someone to say it.'

'Why do you think it was your fault?'

I stayed quiet for a long time with my eyes closed. 'Since the day she was born, I've thought I was going to lose her. Then I split up with my husband and the feeling overwhelmed me – and she did keep going off, so it wasn't completely in my imagination, was it? Oh, it's so difficult to fathom, but I *do* know the thought was in the back of my mind and then it happened and now I feel like I made it happen.'

I hadn't told anyone this.

'Then let's talk about that.'

'No. I can't.' My voice had turned tiny in the room. 'Please, can we just sit for a while?'

We sat until the clock told us the hour was nearly up. I stood abruptly.

'Thank you,' I said.

He showed me out. 'I'd like to help if I can and see you again,' he said, standing on the doorstep. 'Can I ask if anything gives you relief, anything at all?'

'Yes.' I put my finger on the centre of the sunburst. 'I thought it was going to be looking, but that's turned into a kind of addiction. There's also holes, forgetting holes I call them, but I don't know if they really help either. There is one thing I keep coming back to though. Yes, one thing – tiny actions.'

27

THE NEW PLACE is a forest.

We help Dorothy unpack the van. She's got a cooler that plugs into a hole at the front and keeps the food nice and cold. She's got a special cupboard above Melody and Silver's bunk where the food is in plastic containers with clip-on tops. There's a wooden box where she keeps her tin openers and knives and spoons lined up very neat. The extra-big saucepan she uses to heat up water for us to wash has all the dishcloths and tea towels folded up inside it. I like the way Dorothy keeps everything. 'A place for everything and everything in its place,' is one thing she says.

'You children go into the woods and get some more sticks to light the fire,' she says.

The three of us run into the woods with a basket she's given us that's made of pink plastic. Inside the woods there's so many trees it goes suddenly dark and quiet.

Gramps has told us there's a special event to happen here.

'What are you thinking the "event" is?' asks Silver. She finds a stick and pops it into the basket.

'I dunno. Maybe there'll be candy.' Melody sounds hopeful.

'You never know with Gramps. Might be nothing,' I warn them. All the same I feel *something's* going to happen here. I felt it as soon as we came.

The other two nod and we carry on picking up sticks.

'Look, Carmel. There's a great big one.' Melody picks up a stick as big as her arm. 'Why don't you carry it back? Then Mom will be pleased with you.'

'Thank you.' I take the stick, thinking how kind Melody is. I see her tooth gleaming in the dark.

'I'm glad Carmel's with us now. Aren't you, Silver?' Melody sneaks her hand into mine and holds it.

Silver's picking up a stick, holding it with the ends of her fingers and trying not to get her hands dirty.

'I guess . . .' She throws the stick in the basket and brushes her hands together to get rid of the dirt.

'And I'm glad you're here,' I whisper. It feels like we can say anything here, just the three of us under the dark trees. 'I'm glad I'm with some other children.'

Silver puts her hands on her hips. 'Why do we always have to be moving around? It's not fair. I want to be with lots of children and have schoolbooks and a lunch bag, like we used to.'

'You don't go to school? Everyone has to go to school.'

'No. That's not true. We don't. Anyway, it's better we don't have to.' That's not what she was saying before.

'What about having a lunch bag and learning things? How do you learn anything?'

'Mom teaches us. And Pa gives us Bible study, he says that's all we need.' Her voice has gone scratchy.

'What sort of things does Dorothy teach you?'

'Sometimes math. We have to add up numbers of the dollars she's saved. Or how many miles it is to Mexico.'

'I wish there was a library we could go to here,' I sigh. I've had a sneaky look at the books on the shelf above Dorothy and Gramps's bed, but they all seem like the Bible sort.

Silver snorts 'Huh,' like books are useless.

'Carmel's our friend now, though, aren't you? It's like we've got a school friend with us,' says Melody all shy.

I have an idea.

'Maybe we could start our own school,' I say.

They like that idea, I can tell. They both stop what they're doing and look at me.

'How d'you mean?' asks Silver.

'In the truck – we could have school time. We could get some books and do lessons from them. And have sandwiches in a lunch box at lunchtime. And do, I dunno, sums and things. And art projects.'

We did an art project in my school making a dinosaur out of papier-mâché – everyone in the class working on a different bit. It'd been finished for ages and was going dusty on top of the bookshelf but Mrs Buckfast said she was determined to get it hung by wires from the ceiling next term. I suppose I'm never going to see it dangling over us now. I made some of the scales on its tail.

'Yeah, let's,' says Melody. 'What d'you think, Silver?'

'Who'd be the teacher?' Silver asks.

I think. 'We could take turns. And if Dorothy has time, maybe she could teach us something too. Something she knows about.'

Melody says, 'Mom has pictures of skulls. She keeps them hidden.' The words shiver through my body.

'What? Human skulls?'

Melody nods. Her eyes have gone huge. 'Yeah, they look like this.' She bunches her hands around her mouth with her fingers pointing downward to look like teeth.

'Why does she have them?'

'I don't know,' she says through her fingers.

'That's got nothing to do with school,' says Silver.

We're quiet for a minute.

'You really want to do it?' I ask.

'Let's start tomorrow,' says Silver.

'C'mon. We've got loads now.'

We run back to the truck together.

'Good girls. Good girls,' says Dorothy when she sees our basket. She gets on her hands and knees and starts piling the sticks on the ground.

The tall trees saw up and down in the breeze and not far away is a wide river moving past us and next to it a beach made of pebbles. I slide over the pebbles in my stiff shoes and look out over the water. In the middle there's such great swirls of black it looks like there's no bottom to it. I feel it again, that feeling that something is going to happen, and a brown leaf blows in front of me and lands on my shoe.

Dorothy is busy organising things: 'Get the pan . . . no, not that one, the one with the long handle . . . bring the wood for the fire . . . see to it, girls . . . Now open those tins of beans, Silver. Put them in the big pan. We'll have a cowboy dinner. No fire in the dinner tonight, Carmel,' she calls over.

I think she might be liking me again. She gives me a proper smile and I try to forget about what Melody told me, about the skulls.

We all have something to do. My job is getting out the spoons and knives and putting them ready on a clean cloth on the ground.

That's when Gramps comes from behind the truck and says a word: 'baptism.'

Sometimes words have colours. 'Tropicana' is orange, *of course*. 'Baptism' is white, white, white. Except when it comes out of Gramps's mouth and then it's black. Black like his Bible. He seems to have grown. His shoulders are enormous and his great arms hang down either side.

Gramps takes off his shoes and socks and his feet are blue and bony on the pebbles. He gets me to do the same and holds my hand. 'Spirit's in the river, Carmel,' he cries out. Dorothy and the girls come over and line up on the shore, waiting.

The cold's such a shock it knocks words right out of me. I stumble, with Gramps's arm tight around me, until we get so deep my skirt pops up. Gramps reads from the Bible in the hand that's not holding me and there's a big drop of water hanging from his nose that jiggles about as he reads.

On the pebble beach Dorothy and the twins have started singing:

Are you washed in the blood?
Are you washed in the blood?
In the cleansing blood, the cleansing blood of the lamb . . .

The sound spreads over the water and mixes in with the rushing of the river.

Lamb's blood, river water – I smell them both. I can taste them.

Then the Bible goes in his pocket and his big hand goes over my face and I can smell lamb's blood on that too and the river pours this into my ears – 'And her old name shall be set aside. She will be named in the Lord, and the name she will bear will be Mercy . . .'

His hand shuts up my eyes. He pushes me hard, backward.

The spirit river must be strong. It snatches me off him and starts carrying me away.

I pop up, and they're bright puppets – Gramps walking toward me with his arms reaching out, shouting, 'She's banged her head.' Melody on the shore and crying something out through brambles and her getting scratched up by thorns and tearing her dress.

Then down again, just long enough to see a white face in the water, an arm, a swirling down below. And it's my mum, my mum, my mum. Her beautiful face, the sound of my name coming through the water, 'Carmel, Carmel.' Then nothing.

Everything black like I've been shut inside his Bible for good.

Gramps is on top of me pressing up and down on my chest and the pebbles press into my back.

'Mum.' Water bubbles out of my mouth.

'I got you, child,' Gramps is saying as he pumps. 'I rescued you. I rescued you.'

'No. Mum.' I try to fight him off and he has to hold down my arms.

Melody's got a long scratch in the middle of her face and it's bleeding hard. Dorothy carries me inside the truck. She has to peel off my clothes and wraps me in a blanket and puts me on my bed.

'Carmel nearly got killed,' wails Melody. She's standing there with slits cut in her dress and patches of blood from the thorns, I hold out my hand and touch one on her arm and my finger comes away red.

Dorothy takes off Melody's dress and there's scrapes all over her body.

'Oh my Lord, child, child.' Melody starts crying even louder. She's standing there just in her yellow pants.

'Hush, hush,' says Dorothy. She goes to the fire and pours hot water into a bowl. Then she comes back in and drips something from a blue bottle into the water and starts dabbing at Melody's cuts with cotton wool.

'It's all right. It's surface cuts is all.' But still the water in the bowl goes pink and then red.

'Now stand very still, my girl. I can see a thorn.' She gets some tweezers and frowns hard as she picks it out. 'And another. And another. Child, you're a pincushion.' She picks them out one by one and I huddle into the blanket to keep warm.

When she's done she tells Melody to stand there in her pants with her skin in the air to make the bleeding dry up. It does really fast.

'You're a real quick healer, Melody,' she tells her. She puts on Melody's nightie for her and tells her to go sit by the fire. She picks up my dress from the floor. 'Ruined,' she says. She holds it up and I can see it's got stones and little shells and bright green weeds tangled through the lace. Dorothy's long hair is loose around her face. She's lost the smile she had earlier. I think of my mother's face, full of soft white light, and the word she sent through the water telling me my real name. I want to die then. I want to go back into the river and stay there with her.

'I wish Gramps never rescued me,' I sob.

'That's a foolish thing to say. Who doesn't want to be rescued?'

'Me.'

'Foolish and wicked and . . .' She rubs my hair hard in a towel, getting her fingers right into my skull to do it properly. I don't want her to stop. It feels like what's she's doing is the real rescuing, rubbing me back to life.

When she does stop I feel awful again. 'I want to be in the river, I don't want to be here.'

Dorothy looks into my face. 'You'll get used to it.'

I stay quiet.

'You'll even get accustomed to being called Mercy. I took a different name. I chose Dorothy from a movie. They wanted me to have a sacred name, but I said it's Dorothy or nothing.'

'What's your real name then?'

She doesn't answer, she just carries on: 'We can all get accustomed to most anything, names . . . anything.' I can see as her eyes turn inward and look at the things inside her brain. 'I have. When I came from Mexico we had only the clothes we stood up in and . . . oh, I miss the colours there.'

She stops rubbing me then and looks as upset as me. 'Why can't you go home?'

'Because I'm getting away from a crazy man. And I came here to make a better life, one with business opportunities.'

'What's business opportunities?'

'Well, for a start, you're one. All you need to do is be a good girl and do as you're told and everything will be very prosperous and A-OK and there'll be a lovely house and maybe even a car – Mercedes. Being called Mercy is not so bad if you're riding in the back of a Mercedes, is it?'

I don't know what she's on about.

'My name,' I say slowly, but trying not to be upsetting, especially as I liked the way she rubbed my hair so much, 'is Carmel. Mum said it's a name of a place that's supposed to be like paradise and it's Catholic like her mum and dad. Dad liked it because it sounds like *caramel*.'

Dorothy looks like she doesn't care what my name is or what

it means, as long as I stop causing so much trouble for her. She scrubs me so hard on my body with the towel it hurts but at least I feel dry and start to warm up. I don't even mind about being naked in front of her, except for the towel.

Then I'm wrapped in a blanket, sitting in front of the campfire, my teeth chattering away like they're trying to talk on their own. I can taste the river in my mouth and behind my nose. A big bump is growing out of my forehead that when I touch it feels a long way away from my head like it's been stuck on. They're all eating beans with spoons out of plastic bowls. Except for Melody, who says it hurts her to move. I've got on my nightie now, the one with the pink roses. And warm socks and a big thick jumper from the twins and one of Dorothy's cardigans over that and then a blanket around me and *still* I can't get warm, not right inside me.

Gramps has lost the lit-up energy. He's gone back to looking out of the corners of his eyes. Dorothy takes a ladle of beans from the pan hanging over the fire and puts it in a plastic bowl.

'Here. Have some beans, Mercy, build your strength up.'

But I thought I'd said to her . . . 'Carmel. I'm Carmel,' I say.

'I think Mercy is a beautiful name, don't you think so, girls?' asks Gramps.

'Can we have new names, like Mum and Mercy?' asks Silver.

'No,' Dorothy almost shouts. 'Your names will not change.'

Gramps says, 'Mercy is very special, Silver. Not all little girls need a new name.'

She's going to hate me now. Sure enough, her eyes turn into slits looking at me through the fire.

'Does this mean we can soon be putting down the deposit on a condo?' Dorothy's asking. And even though I've got no idea what a condo is I can see by the way she turns her head and looks at me when she says it that her having one has something to do with me.

Gramps raises both hands to quiet everyone. 'Stop. Isn't it enough to know that Mercy has come to us through fire, that she is part of us now and we have a new name to celebrate . . . ?'

That's enough. I jump up. 'I've got a name already and it's

Carmel. You're trying to make me forget it but I won't.' I don't tell them how Mum was there in the river to remind me and losing my name would be like pretending she'd never been alive. They wouldn't believe me.

'Sssh, dear,' says Gramps. 'No need to be upsetting yourself. Come, come and eat some of these beans. It'll do you good to eat something.'

'I don't want any beans,' I shout. 'I just want my mum. I want my mum. And you shouldn't give beans to the twins either. It makes them fart all night.'

Melody puts her hands up to her mouth and laughs when I say that.

I'll run away, I think. I'll run off and hide and they'll never find me. So I hug the blanket around me and take off toward the trees. I can feel the bottom of my socks turning soggy. There's shouts behind me, but it's too late. The blanket falls off but I leave it on the ground.

Inside the woods I crouch down, panting, behind a lump of ferns. I can see, through the leaves, everyone standing in the twilight around the fire and pointing toward the trees. There's Gramps – the size of a toy from where I am – going to fetch his donkey jacket from the truck.

I squeeze my eyes shut and try to keep quiet and stick my fingers into the soft earth. Then there's a tramp, tramp, tramp as Gramps gets closer. He makes the ferns brush against my face as he walks past them.

I can hear him for a long time walking around the woods. When he comes near to me he sounds like a wolf, hunting and sniffing. But, after a while, even the wolf gives up. It goes back to the fire and I can see him, looking into the flames. Sometimes Dorothy stands with her hands on her hips, looking into the trees too, her long skirt nearly touching the ground.

Then dark: I stand up, as quiet as I can, and turn to the woods. It's black in there and noises come out of the darkness, animals moving around. What do I do now? Do I wander about the night woods until I get eaten by a real wolf? Or lost, and starve to death? And the woods are so scary in the dark. There'll be ghosts in them, getting ready for fun and games – pulling my hair and pinching me with their skeleton fingers. I can almost hear them now, licking their bare teeth with invisible tongues.

I look back at the camp and the four people sitting around the fire lit up by the flames. I watch them for a long time as they talk and then boil a kettle and look at the trees again and stir the fire.

In the end I just go back out. I don't know what else to do. Dorothy makes me go to bed with nothing to eat and Gramps says I need to think about what sins I've committed by running away. But I don't. In the night Melody climbs in my bed with me and we hug each other.

'You'll keep calling me Carmel, won't you? You can do it in secret if you don't want to get in trouble.'

'Is it real important?'

'Yes.'

'Then I will.'

'Thank you for trying to rescue me,' I say.

'That's OK,' she whispers back.

28

DAY 150

I THOUGHT PAUL might phone on day 150. Then I remembered how he wasn't keeping track as I was – marking the red number in my diary every day. But I was vaguely relieved he hadn't. I'd had Nessa's leaflet updated with 'Missing – One Hundred and Fifty Days' across the top and I planned to leaflet Harwich ferry terminal – it was one theory that's where she'd been taken. Paul might try and stop me. He didn't think it was good for my health, this incessant looking. He was paying a private detective, who seemed well-meaning but lacked the urgency I felt coursing through my blood.

Day 150 I watched large stately ferries come and go; people in stretchy travelling clothes arrive with their kids and suitcases, bottles of drink in their hands and bum bags around their waists for their travel documents. I stood by a pillar and handed out my leaflets. Some stopped to talk to me.

'Oh my God, love, I hadn't heard about this,' or, 'I remember this, has she not been found yet? I'll light a candle for you both. What's the little one's name? I'll pray for her.'

Then walking away, looking at my leaflet and wheeling their cases, shaking their heads as they went. Holding their children's hands a little more tightly.

But mostly I didn't want to talk. Once I realised they knew nothing I wanted them to move on and let me find someone who did.

After an hour I saw one of the staff, a uniformed woman with a jaunty necktie, talking to a security guard. They were both looking at me. Tears welled in my eyes. Was this what my looking had become? Something people were tired of, a public nuisance. But they came over and read my leaflets and wished they could help. The guard bought me a cup of coffee and let me stay at my post beside the pillar.

Then my phone rang. It was Paul. 'Beth. Beth, where are you?'

'I'm at the ferry.'

'What? Why? Never mind. Look, Ralph has found something.' Ralph – the private detective.

'Oh, oh, what?' I crushed the empty coffee cup flat in my hand.

'It's from a holiday video that someone took. Where exactly are you? I'm coming to get you now.'

'And so what happened?' Craig asked.

'Ralph had the footage sent over by courier. It had been taken by a couple on holiday on a campsite. They thought they saw Carmel in the background.'

'When did you realise it wasn't her?'

'Oh, straight away. As soon as I saw it.'

'That must have been terrible. Disappointing.'

I nodded. I'd been so wild with hope and excitement.

There'd been a problem with the footage. It had been filmed on some ancient format and we'd had to travel to Ralph's office in Ipswich to look at it. It made the excruciating tension worse – the trip in Ralph's car. The smell of leather seats catching at the back of my throat. The stop to get petrol that seemed to last an age.

'It's the red, see. They see a girl in red and everyone jumps at it, which is ridiculous. This couple had come back from holiday and seen one of Paul and Ralph's adverts they've put in the press.

They'd videoed their kids playing cricket on the grass and there was a little girl walking through the frame in the background. She was wearing red and we couldn't see anyone with her. But it was a red anorak she was wearing anyway, not a duffel coat.'

'You say you didn't see her face?'

'No. She had it turned away from the camera, looking the other way. But I didn't need to. I know Carmel's shape like the back of my hand, the way she walks. They've taken it to the police – people want to help so much they jump at anything – but I know. I'd know my daughter. Paul wanted to be convinced, I think.'

Another lead, snipped off at the root.

'Beth, have you been thinking about what we've discussed several times before, your guilt at what's happened?'

'Yes.' I felt exhausted with it all.

'I think it might be useful to examine it.'

I looked through the French windows at the statue of Pan. The leaf behind him had grown since I was last there, so now it flopped over one of his eyes. His visible eye squinted at me.

'I try to stop myself thinking about it but I can't. Because – because I always felt I was going to lose her, maybe it made me overprotective.'

'Most people feel protective about their children, it's natural.'

'Yes. But, oh I don't know.' Then I was suddenly heated, sitting bolt upright. 'What if I influenced events? What if I did? I feel somehow I made this happen and I don't quite know how but the feeling won't go away. It's me, nobody has said I have but . . .' I trailed off and sat silent, thinking.

I remembered Carmel's words from the dream: *perhaps we wanted to lose each other.* I did sound cross the day she vanished, no maybe. I could admit that to myself now – *no, Carmel, stay with me, hold my hand or we'll go straight home, Carmel.* Cross and pissed off and harassed. With responsibility, with worry. No one tells you how it will be when you have a child. No one tells you it's going to be worry, worry, worry, worry, worry. World without end. How they hold your fate, your survival in their hands, whereas before you were free, free and didn't know it. How if anything happens to them you will also be destroyed and you carry that knowledge with you, constantly.

'No one will say it,' I repeated.

'Well, I won't either,' said Craig. 'We could sit here for a hundred years and I won't say that. I'm not saying we shouldn't talk about it. But I'm not going to back the idea up.'

We sat in silence for a while. 'All right,' I sighed, nearly sick of thinking about it. 'Shall we go back to firsts?'

'Do you think you're ready?'

I nodded. We'd been talking about the idea of firsts. First day back at work. First solo shopping expedition.

'That's it – I'll go into town on my own,' I said. 'Soon. Next week even.' I squeezed the arms of the chair. 'Or the week after.'

29

THE MORNING AFTER the baptising, I don't get out of bed.

I can still taste the river in my mouth. The bump on my head is bigger: it makes my eye half close up and I can't stop longing for what I saw down there.

I don't hear Melody tiptoeing up to the truck. The first thing that makes me know she's there is her voice floating in.

'Carmel, aren't you going to get up today?'

I open my eyes. She's standing outside, looking in and twisting her hands together. I can't see the scrapes on her body now she's dressed. There's only one I can see that goes all the way from her hair to her chin. It looks like someone's felt-penned her face.

'Don't you have to call me Mercy now unless it's secret?'

'No. Pa said we'll keep it for special occasions. For the time being.'

I sit up in bed. 'Oh.'

'He's scared you'll run off again.'

I lie back on the pillows. It feels like I've been in a fight with Gramps and that I might have won, though it's not certain.

She starts twisting her skirt around in her hands, holding on to the hem and sticking her fingers through the holes in the lace.

'We were wondering about the school?'

'Silver too?'

'Yeah. Silver wants to do it. More than me even. She just won't say, that's all.'

My eyelids feel heavy, they're going to drop down over my eyes any second now. I touch the bump on my head gently. There's crusty stuff in the middle.

'Maybe not today.'

'Oh.' She sounds disappointed. 'What about tomorrow?'

'Sure. Tomorrow . . .'

Then my eyelids clang down.

But it's tomorrow and now Melody's sick too but much, much worse than me. Gramps lays her on my bed.

'It's lockjaw,' Dorothy wails. 'It must have entered her body through the thorns. She needs a hospital, Dennis.'

He says, 'No insurance.' Then, 'God will look over her. God will look after her. Don't doubt it.'

Dorothy wails some more but he goes to the shore and reads his Bible. 'If only I could drive this heap of junk,' she mutters, and wipes the sweat off Melody's face. 'I'd kill us if I tried.' She looks with knives in her eyes toward Gramps's big back, then flies out to him and their voices spill out over the water that's flat today and smooth.

I wrap myself up in the crochet – pink, purple, blue squares – and kneel next to Melody in bed. When her eyelids flitter bright amber shows like two wet beads. Her jaw goes into a clamp, pushing out the scab lined down her face that's ugly pink.

There's a little wind blowing inside me. It goes into my mouth and blows around in there. My palms start to itch so I scratch them, trying to make it stop.

I lean over her and call Melody all the words my mum called me: 'Sweetheart. Angel. Darling. Love. Pumpkin Pie.' The wind in my mouth blows on her face and I add another one, 'Nutter,' because with us that was always a good word too.

'I love you, Melody.' I breathe it over her face.

Her hair is in black ribbons over the pillow and her face and arms are stiff like she's trying to turn herself into a doll. I climb under the quilts with her, it's fiery hot and I hold her in my arms and she feels like a doll too, until my eyelids clang shut.

Melody wakes me up sitting bolt upright. 'School, Carmel. When are we doing school?'

'Ugh.' I'm half asleep.

Her face has stopped trying to turn into a doll's. She's pushing off the bedclothes and I try to sit up, but I'm so tired I have to do it with my elbows. It's still the day outside.

Melody jumps over me and down the steps.

'Child, child.' Dorothy laughs and wipes her eyes and hugs Melody tight. 'Look at you. Let me get you something to drink.'

'You better, Melody?' Silver smiles at her.

I notice Gramps is standing quiet and serious. 'You know what this means, don't you, Dorothy?'

'What, Dennis?'

He looks to me and then to them. 'Only two hours ago Melody was a very sick little girl. In fact she could not move from her sickbed . . .'

'But kids get better all the time, Dennis.'

'See, I knew you doubted the truth of it. I know, woman, your thoughts.'

Dorothy has a plastic cup and rests it against the side of her face and taps it with her nail. She's thinking. Tap, tap, tap, tap. I wonder if Gramps knows *these* thoughts. They're going in and out, in and out.

'I believed you believed and that was good enough for me. You are the expert in these matters.'

'Can you not see it now with your own two eyes? Melody was too sick to move and look at her now. Will you look at her?'

Tap, tap, tap, tap. She smiles like she's just had something sweet and lovely to eat. 'Yes, yes. It could be . . .'

He stays serious. 'Carmel laid her hands on her and now she is well.'

Out of the corner of my eye I can see my hands pink and resting on the crochet cover, with the soft insides showing upward.

The fingers are shaking like there's shocks going through them. Is it possible? Gramps thinks it is, he's sunk onto his knees and started praying.

Dorothy cries out and her orange juice flies out of the cup in the shape of McDonald's golden arches as she opens up her arms. 'Oh, Dennis. True or no, I can see it now. How it can be – you clever, clever man – we're going to make our *fortune*.'

But he doesn't hear her. He's too busy praying.

'So who's gonna be teacher, then?' Silver's sitting on my bed.

'What about taking turns? You can go first,' I say.

'Mmmm. I think it should be . . .' She points right at my chest. '. . . you.'

'Oh, OK.' I frown. Now I'll have to think of something to teach.

We've made the inside of the truck look as much like a class-room as we can. I had the idea of putting books around but the only books are Gramps's Bibles and books with prayers. And we're not allowed to touch those so that's not going to work. Instead, we got out the drawing pad and sellotaped our drawings to the walls. It looks quite good. Dorothy's gone to walk to the shop. She left without telling anyone but Gramps. He told us it's five miles away and she's crazy, he would've driven her, but that she's used to tramping all over God's earth. She likes to.

The twins are excited: like something's really going to happen. I hope they won't be disappointed. I think hard for something to teach them. I remember. Just before, before – Mrs Buckfast was teaching us about the Tudors.

'OK. We'll do a history lesson. It's about the king.' I look over to Gramps. He's sitting miles away in one of the foldout chairs.

'What's his name?' asks Silver.

'Henry. Henry the Eighth.'

'Was he a good king?' Melody's brushing her hands up and

down the crochet bed cover, fast. The line down her face is pink biro now.

'No. He was not. He was a very, very bad king.'

Both of them breathe out together, an 'ooooh.'

'He had a red beard. And he used to feast. He used to eat a lot and that made him very, very fat.'

'Is that what made him bad?' asks Silver.

'No. Not that. It was because of his wives. He had six of them . . .'

'That's not possible,' Silver cries out. 'How can you have six wives?'

'No, not all together.'

'It's still not possible.'

'Look, what about your dad? I mean before Gramps.'

'Yeah, but he's gone. Not died. Just gone,' says Silver.

'See. So –'

'Mom says he was a work-shy Mexican pig. He got drunk so hard we used to hear him smashing the bowls downstairs. So Mom ran us away in the night, she said she was going to get a divorce. She said America is the land of milk and honey and if you're clever dollars will rain on you. Then she met Gramps.'

I black over the clothes flying through the air in my mind so I don't have to think about them. 'Yes, so you can get, um – a divorce. But Henry the Eighth didn't always get a divorce.'

'No?' Melody's hands are brushing up and down at super speed now.

'No. Some of them – some of them he had killed.'

'Are you making this all up?' Silver says it like she's hoping I'm not.

'I'm not.' I go quiet. Next term we were going on a school trip to one of King Henry's palaces called Hampton Court. Me and Sara were really looking forward to it because there's a maze and I told her what they're like. They've probably been by now. For a moment it's almost like I'm back home and I really did go to the maze with Sara and I'm remembering what it was like. Then I blink and it goes away and Melody and Silver are waiting, staring at me.

'Anyway, Mrs Buckfast told it to us, so it must be true. One had her head chopped off with an axe. And one had her head chopped off with a sword.'

Dorothy pops her head around the door and makes us jump. She's got an orange rucksack on her back.

'What are you kids doing?'

'We're having school.'

'Oh, well, anything that keeps you quiet, I guess.'

She goes over to Gramps and I hear her saying, 'Eleven dollars and fifty-one cents for your information.' Even though he hasn't asked.

We ask Dorothy if we can have our lunches wrapped up, like you would at school, and she agrees. Going out always seems to make her in a better mood. We help her make ham sandwiches and put them in three paper bags with an apple each. We have to have our cups in our hands, though, there's no mini cartons of apple juice with a straw you stick through like I used to have at school. So we decide to have our lunches there and then. Melody rings the bell around the neck of her teddy because I told them there was always a bell before lunch. After our lunch we get back to our lesson.

'We'll do art now, related to the topic.' It's something Mrs Buckfast used to say a lot but I can see they don't understand, so I say, 'We'll draw a picture about what we've been learning.'

'You're a good teacher, Carmel.' Melody smiles. 'Are you gonna be a teacher when you grow up?'

'I don't know. I might be.' I thought I might like to once. But Mrs Buckfast is very neat and organised, and I know how my thoughts fly away from me, so sometimes I hardly know where I am. And I don't think that would make me a good teacher. It might happen when I'm teaching with everybody looking at me.

We get out the drawing pad and have a sheet each. I'm drawing

Henry, gobbling on a chicken leg. I put bits of food into his beard. When I look over at Melody's drawing I see it's the queen having her head chopped off with an axe. There's blood everywhere.

We're packing up this morning and leaving again so I'm looking out over the river and calling for Mum quietly, so no one can hear. It feels so sad leaving – like I'm leaving her here in this river. 'Goodbye,' I whisper. 'I love you.'

The twins are calling out from the back of the truck. 'Hey Carmel, come and do school again.'

Inside, they're ready and waiting. They love this school game.

'Aren't we leaving? Where's Dorothy and Gramps?'

'They've gone for a walk in the woods,' says Silver.

'To have an argument,' adds Melody.

'Oh. OK. Who wants to be teacher?'

'Your turn again,' says Silver. That doesn't sound like a turn, but I don't mind. Not really. What else is there to do?

'Can we have the queens having their heads cut off again?' Melody's hands have started already, up and down over the cover.

'Mmmm. We did that. Perhaps we should do writing today. Do you do joined-up?'

'Not sure . . .' says Silver.

We get the paper out and make the sheets into two halves so it's smaller for writing. We have a pencil each and sharpen them so hard there's a pointy tip.

'Let's each write our own story. We need a topic,' I say. I guess it's not quite fair – it's what I want to do and I'm not sure teachers are supposed to do that – but the twins don't seem to mind. Their pencils are sticking up into the air, waiting.

'How about "all about me"?' I'm copying Mrs Buckfast again – that's one she gave us. 'You have to put your name at the top and your class number.'

'What's our class number?' says Silver.

'Um, it can be 5b.'

We settle down to writing. Sometimes I suck the top of my pencil to help me think. Soon, though, my hand's flying across the page. 'My name is Carmel. I'm eight years old. My favourite thing is reading. I've read *Alice in Wonderland* five times and I wish I could read it again. My favourite animal is Sara's Collie dog called Sheila. I also like small animals like bats and foxes.'

When we're done, I say, 'Let's look at them all and then read them out aloud.'

The twins lay down their papers next to mine on the floor and I can hardly believe it. I don't know what to say. Their writing is terrible – it looks like four-year-olds have done it – but good teachers shouldn't hurt feelings. Only horrible ones do that.

'That's very, very hard work you've done.' I pick mine off the floor. I'm embarrassed to see my joined-up writing next to their baby words. I worry it'll make them feel bad, or pick on me. I hold up Melody's to look. She's put her name at the top but after that it's just some odd words that don't really mean anything. *Cat. Dog. Mom. Truck* – except she's spelt it *truk*.

'Maybe we should do lots more writing lessons.'

Both girls are nodding, holding their pencils like they want to start already.

Then Silver says something.

'You're much nicer than the other Mercy, Carmel.'

I'm blowing the pencil dust off their sheets they've been pressing so hard.

'What other Mercy?'

Silver goes to the end of the truck and looks out, checking we're all alone. She puts her finger to her lips then climbs up on Gramps's bed and gets something down from the shelf. It's a tiny blue book with gold writing on the front.

'This one.'

She opens up the book and there's lots of typewriting in there and a tiny photo and some old bit of newspaper folded up inside. My hand flies up to my short curls.

'She looks like me! Her hair does anyway . . . and her face a bit. A lot.'

'She's Mercy too,' says Melody. 'We didn't like her, did we, Silver?'

Silver shakes her head.

'Who is she?' The prickles are back.

'She was with Pa, when Mom first went with him.'

I touch her little face in the photograph. 'What happened to her? Where is she now?'

They both shrug. Melody says, 'She went off with Pa. Then he called Mom up on the phone and said she's got to get on a plane and join him. Then you came back with them. We asked him where did Mercy go, and he tells us, "We've got Carmel now. We mustn't talk about Mercy no more. Never ever."'

Silver's nodding away, agreeing with her. 'So you mustn't say we told.'

'But.' I'm not sure 'but what.' I just know I've got my prickles back.

'You mustn't, Carmel. Honest, you promise? Or we can't show you nothing again,' says Silver.

'Was she my sister?' I don't know why I asked that. Except she looks like me and all.

Silver shrugs. 'We dunno.'

'But, but . . . why didn't you like her?'

'So quiet and praying. Always on her knees with Pa. She was boring,' says Silver.

Silver puts the little book with Mercy's picture back in its place on the shelf.

'Hey, I want to look some more, I want to read the paper in there.'

'No, they'll be back soon. We can't get caught. Promise you won't tell – or we won't play with you any more.'

'I need to look at her . . .' My hand flies up to snatch at it but Silver grabs my arm.

'No, I knew we shouldn't have told.' I start shoving her onto the bed but Melody is howling, 'Don't, don't, don't,' and pulling my skirt so hard I shoot back and nearly land on her.

Both their faces have gone the colour of milk. 'I knew you'd get us into trouble,' says Silver. 'If we even go near Pa's stuff he gets mad. We should never have showed you.'

'Promise you won't look again,' Melody says. 'Please. You might get caught.'

We're all panting hard. 'OK, I won't,' I lie. 'I promise.'

I walk down the steps and look over the bubbling river where I nearly drowned, thinking about the girl hidden on the shelf and who she is. She looks so much like me and now – now we have the same name.

Even from here, when I look back at the truck, it's like I can see the book winking at me from the shelf. 'One day,' I say under my breath, 'I'll look at you properly. *Detective Wakeford* will come and find you.' I'll need to carry out a search of everything, I think, and my stomach tingles.

'Mercy, who are you?' I say, as if she could hear me. 'I wish you were here now, so you could tell me. I'm Carmel.' Then a kind of shaking inside happens because when I told her my real name everything was so quiet – just the river bubbling and the river doesn't care. The sound disappeared in the air and I don't feel sure at all any more that I've won about my name. I take out the biro from my pocket and bash it with a rock till I have a plastic dagger. I pick three rocks and scratch, scratch. When I'm done I put them in a row but they remind me of gravestones like that so I pile them one on top of the other in this order:

Wakeford
Summer
Carmel

30

DAY 163

FIRSTS. FIRST DAY into town on my own.

I'll walk, I thought, it'll give me some exercise, though I knew really that way I could be looking too.

It felt peculiar to be alone out in the countryside. The wide sky, full of watery blue and grey, was still there. The cries of the birds echoed unchangingly around me. I was moving through a world that knew nothing except for the progress of the seasons. And was there, could I feel it, a nip of autumn in the air? Was it that time of year already?

The tramp of my footsteps marked out a steady beat. Every so often I would stop and lift my nose, and turn in a circle, scanning. I'd become a pair of eyes, a functionary being made for searching: my legs a forked vehicle, nothing but a looking post. Stop it, I scolded myself. She's not here.

I carried on along the familiar country road until I was on the outskirts of town. The houses, scattered at first, began to bunch closer together and form into streets. I stopped and tilted up my ear. The muted sounds of children playing drifted over me in a chattering cloud. With a convulsion I realised I was near Carmel's school and if I carried on I'd pass the red-brick Victorian building with the cheerful butterfly collages in the window.

'Oh my, oh my,' I muttered to myself, changing direction so I would skirt the little school entirely.

Then I was in the street surrounded by shops and people pushing past, some loaded with shopping bags, or smoking, or eating rolls from paper bags – little snow flurries of grated cheese cascading onto their lapels – or talking into their phones, or staring into space. Being among this mass of people felt as strange as being alone had done an hour earlier; so strange I moved close to the shops on the side of the pavement and crept along with my hand running along the buildings for support. Farther along I encountered an old man in a tweed coat who was employing the same method – creeping snail's pace – and we had to negotiate for a moment which one of us would part company with the wall.

But I knew what was ahead and it was getting closer and closer and I wanted to see but I didn't. Because I'd been playing a silly mind trick – if the red shoes are there, is that an omen that she's alive? But how could they be, after all this time? So I changed it to – if there's any red shoes in the window, I'll take that. That can be my sign.

All the while I was telling myself I couldn't live on omens and tricks of the light and signs from the heavens because if I did it would make me go mad. But still I had to see. I glimpsed the familiar Clarks green of the awning ahead and I crept and crept like a cripple toward it, until finally I was right in front of the window and looking at the green felt miniature landscape inside and the little ledge where the shoes had perched for so long. And the red shoes were gone: in their place a brown pair with ornate white zigzag stitching and a fat pink flower stitched to each toe. They were placed at a perky angle to each other, as though ready at a moment's notice to go running right out of the window and down the street. I scanned the window – blue, brown, pink, black, not a single pair of red, not one. I held on to the windowsill because for a moment I thought I'd fall and crash through the glass.

'Oh, oh . . .' My breath came out shallow and fast. I grabbed on to the brass column of the door handle and pushed, falling into the cool dark shop. Inside it was quiet, small shoes the colour of sweets displayed on white painted mountings. Bright plastic foot-shaped measuring devices with outsized tape measures and a plastic machine in the corner where Carmel had once laughed when the device tickled as it clamped her foot.

A young woman behind the counter, examining her nails.

'Is there something I can help you with?' she asked. 'Or do you want to browse?'

'Browse.' My voice sounded hoarse.

I went around the shop, stopping sometimes and picking something up, pretending to examine it. Though God knows why. My eyes took in children's shoes: little brown boots with fat laces; patent leather with round toes and a dusting of cut-out patent flowers; squashy blue sandals. It seemed the only thing I was looking for these days was red, red coats or red shoes, and sometimes I caught a flash of it – like sudden blood – across the room. But now, in my state, I felt it had to be *the* shoes, nothing else would do, and I'd pounce on anything red to see if they were the same ones, knowing I was torturing myself stupidly because so much time had gone. Each time I picked up a shoe, of course, it wasn't the pair I would recognise anywhere, with the twin diamond shapes cut out of the front and the tiny holes punched in the toes like a whiskerless muzzle.

When finally I had done a lap of the shop I found myself back at the counter again with the girl. Frosty white make-up gleamed beneath her eyebrows as she appraised me, and gratefully I saw I hadn't been recognised.

I cleared my throat. 'There was a pair of shoes in the window . . .'

'Oh yes?'

'Red ones.' I think I might have been whispering because she leaned forward to catch what I was saying. 'They were there for ages.'

'Boy's or girl's?'

'Girl's. With diamond shapes cut out. And a buckle. Sandals.'

'Sandals? Oh no, it's all back to school now.'

'Back to school?'

'Yes. No sandals any more. They were put on sale.'

'D'you think, d'you think it might be possible that some are still here?'

She sighed. 'Oh, I don't know. Hilary . . .' she shouted through an open door that led into gloom. Then Hilary came through – an older lady with glasses on a chain around her neck – and I had to explain all over again: the window, the diamond shapes, the buckle and the red leather.

'Yes, dear. Our sale is over now. But . . . why don't you go and look, Chloe? Look under the window there. I've been having a tidy up.' Chloe really didn't want to bother, I could see that. But she started lifting lids off the stack of green boxes piled beneath the window and each time she did, she said, 'No,' 'No,' 'No.' Like we'd sent her on a stupid mission that was doomed to failure.

'Doesn't your little girl need to be here to try them on?' she asked, after she'd opened the last box and delivered her 'No.' And the older woman said quite sharply, 'Chloe, go and look out the back. They could be there,' and I realised that Hilary had recognised me and was cleverly, discreetly not calling attention to it.

'We'll find them, dear. If they're here.' My throat closed up at the kindness of her manner and I stood there waiting for resentful Chloe to finish what I imagined to be a cursory search of the stock at the back.

'I'll go and help her, dear.' Hilary joined her colleague in the dark recesses of the stockroom and I imagined Chloe being told and her shocked face with its white make-up popping out of the gloom like two moonbeams.

After some rustling they walked back in a procession with Hilary bearing a green box in her hands and the other girl peeping at me in fascination over her shoulder.

'Now I can't be a hundred per cent sure. But are these the

ones?' She lifted the lid and there were the fat ladybird shoes nestling there as if they'd got fed up of being in the window and flown away to hibernate in the box amongst white tissue paper.

I put my hand up to my mouth and grasped at the counter with the other for support.

'Yes. Yes, they're the ones.'

'Well, isn't that lucky? Doesn't it just go to show what can happen? All the unsold summer shoes in the stockroom were about due to be sent back.'

'Can I buy them, please?' I grabbed at my shoulder bag and dipped my hand in it, fishing around for my purse. Hilary rang them up on the till.

'You're not going to . . .' Chloe hissed at her. But the older lady waved her away.

'That'll be twelve ninety-nine. Cash or card?'

'Card.' I remembered my PIN even, and Hilary folded the tissue paper gently and carefully, covering up the red, and bagged up the box.

'There we are, dear. We found them in the end, didn't we?'

We had. I clung onto the box in my arms. Was this my omen? If so, what did it mean? I'd told myself they had to be in the window, or something red at least. But they were here, the real ones, hidden in the back, in the dark.

I held the box tighter to my chest so I was nearly crushing it. 'Thank you. Thank you so much.'

I wrapped my arms around the bag with the shoes and hugged them as I set out for home. *I have the shoes, I have the shoes*, just the fact of them being in my possession made me walk taller, made my stride more purposeful. This time I took the route that went past the red-brick school – *first time past her school* – so two firsts today.

The playground was empty now and a dozing silence hovered over the building as I stood motionless looking over the wall at it. I could imagine the children inside, drowsy with lessons, ready for the end of the day. Soon the parents would be gathering in the playground to collect them and that thought made me stir myself to leave.

'There,' I told myself as I hurried away, hugging my carrier bag with the box of shoes inside, 'that wasn't so bad, was it? See what you can do?' It was the shoes, I knew, the incredible chance of finding them.

31

I'M HARDLY EVER LEFT on my own.

While everyone's off doing different things I stand in the truck and look out over the green lake we're parked next to and hum a little tune.

I go looking for the stone egg but all I can feel now is a soreness where it used to be. I'm guilty for a second but then I think: it doesn't mean I've forgotten about Mum, it means I don't have to die myself because that stone egg was killing me slowly.

Being on my own is making me think of being untrustworthy again. This truck is a whole box of secrets and they're all calling to me and want to tell me things. Skulls, Mercy – they get mixed up so sometimes I think of opening Mercy's book and seeing a skull where her face should be. It gives me chills.

'*Detective Wakeford* is here again,' I say, and just saying that the chills have gone and I'm shaking I'm so excited.

'Mercy, where are you?' I search with my eyes but because her book is so thin it must be squashed between the others. One by one I start slipping out the books to see if she's trapped between them. My hand brushes the leather of Gramps's notebook and then that calls out to me too, louder than anything else. Dare I? Dare I? I don't know how long I've got. I bite my lip.

Gramps's writing is large with lots of loops, pages and pages of it. I'm a good reader though. I was the best in my class. Mostly it seems to be prayers he's writing. My name – my eye catches on it and I stop breathing. Then I read and I can't stop because I've found a place where Gramps is writing about me and what he says gets the prickles going.

It was You, God, who told me to visit that island.

For a long time I did not know why. But when I first saw Carmel I knew. Oh Lord, I knew, I knew, I knew. Thank you. I'd been so troubled and confused. Forgive me for doubting. But I thought: I have a divine road but how am I ever supposed to take the first step along it, Lord, if you do not provide me with a map? I am lost. I was a doubting Thomas. I admit that now. But when I saw her I knew I had found my map, my compass, my way ahead. And maybe in time, she will release me from my own pain? Is that selfish? Is that wrong? I think not. No.

It took a long time. It took careful planning. Seeing her in that place called Boston was a sign, I'm sure of it. For I did not know there was even a Boston in that blighted isle and the other one is my birthplace so praise God. But I couldn't have her then, not that time. Softly, softly I told myself on that first encounter – you can wait a month, a year. You can wait a lifetime. She's truly my child and she belongs to me. I concentrated on the foolish woman she was with, her wrists covered in bracelets that looked like plaits and covering some Godless attempt at taking her own life no doubt. 'Paul and Beth,' she kept saying, 'Paul and Beth wouldn't take all this seriously,' and after some time I realised she was talking about the child's birth parents. She told me everything I needed to know, the riven family and their ways, so she must have been Your instrument without knowing that day. I clothed myself in dark disguise, planning even then, the notion forming as quick as a baby being conceived . . . so my voice flattened out to sound like hers, my hand over my face as I spoke. Little Carmel at the front of the church amongst the flowers and later when I saw her approach I could barely breathe and I shrank back into the shadows and made those my disguise – into a dark corner like a spider where I could observe the wonder of her.

It was an agony of waiting till I finally found myself outside their house. I can spend days, I thought, I have eternal patience. I am on fire. And seeing them leave and speeding along with them on the train, me and the holy ghost not two seats down. And into that Godless place – stories! There is only one story and that is the suffering on the cross.

No one was interested in my pamphlets – the ones spreading Your word. I saw people dropping them in the mud and then they'd be walked on. It made me so angry seeing the muddy boots pounding Your word into the ground. I could feel the wounds of Jesus opening up wider every time I saw it happen.

Mercy is lost to me now. She wasn't the real article, she was sent as . . . as a precursor. It's fitting she'll be ever hereafter left on that cold island. She was John the Baptist to Jesus and ordained she had to go the way of John the Baptist. She's lost to me. Lost.

I had to go back for the car and all the time of driving the terror that I might have missed my chance, it might be too late. I was so on fire with God's work I found it hard to contain myself – wandering the field in a ferment of pain and fear that she could be lost. Then I saw the blood-red garment and this time I kept it in my sight. It was my sign from You – however else would I have kept picking her out? Praise God.

It was as if she was on wires. Fine silver wires grew from her and around her like a divine cage. They shone out through the fog too. She couldn't see them, nor anyone else. Only me. This girl surrounded by the ignorant, ignorant of the Lord. By those wanting their heads filled with unbelief and base tales, when the only tale to tell, Lord, is the one of You, suffering on the cross – I say it again as it's the only truth.

I followed her, mortally terrified she would be lost to the crowd, by the great foul mass gawping and eating and counting out their money. But the red of her coat, that was my talisman, it enabled me to keep her in my sight.

She turned to smile at me and my heart felt pierced through with longing. For her gift, for her divine gift. Forgive me, Lord, but I was jealous then. I wanted it for myself – I thought again: a mere child? Except I can have her, I thought. I can have her. She'll work through me.

I never lost her once. Not even when she went under the table. I nearly made my move then . . . but 'wait, wait,' I told myself, and it was as if You were guiding my every step that day. No, I never lost her, not like her careless mother. That was my real sign, that and when she smiled.

Because when she smiled at me the silver wires throbbed around her, they grew and spun out, shining all around, arcing through the air.

And the red, it was Your divine heart, right in the middle of those bestial unbelievers.

It was there, just for me.

Thank you Lord.

As I'm coming to the end of the page I hear something outside and I shove the book back onto the shelf – quick, quick. Dorothy's face is at the open door and she's looking at me hard.

'What have you been up to, child?'

'Nothing.'

She stands staring at me and I'm trying to stop my face going red. I'm not doing very well though. There's burning on my cheeks and ears like I'm on fire.

'Well, if I find out you have – children in my country get whipped. They get whipped good and proper till their legs burn.'

Maybe she thinks I'm getting upset. Maybe I look it, though what I really am is scared and guilty, because she says, 'Have an apple.' She holds out a big yellow one with her hand flat, like you do with a horse. 'They're sweet and juicy . . .'

I shake my head. What she's saying is nice, but not the way she's saying it, trying to frighten me. At home there's a picture of Snow White's wicked stepmother holding out an apple with poison in it. If she bites into that apple, which she does, she falls asleep for a hundred years.

Dorothy snatches the apple back and walks off. I watch her long plait bouncing against her thin back. For a minute I hate her. I think, you don't even care about me at all – and I'm running after her. She hears me coming and whips around, quick, quick.

'I know about you. I know how you keep pictures of human skulls.' It's out of my mouth before I know it. I do a big gasp and clap my hand over my mouth as if I could shove the words back in.

She leans back on her feet and crosses her arms and looks at me.

'What you know, child, is nothing. Nothing about nothing. Go inside.' Light from the lake moves over her face.

Tears come into my eyes. Maybe Dorothy will be like a proper enemy now. 'What d'you want?' she says, when I don't move.

A big sob comes out. 'I want you to love me again. You're supposed to be like my mum. My mum never had any pictures of skulls.'

She's quiet. I can see she's thinking.

'OK, then.' She takes my hand and we go inside. Then she slides her hand under the mattress and pulls out squares of paper. Some of the skulls look like they're laughing, others are in screams. I hate them, they're the worst things I've ever seen. Now they'll be inside my mind forever.

'There, satisfied?'

'But Dorothy,' I put my hands up to my face, 'what, what are they, why d'you keep them?'

'The Day of the Dead. My ancestors.' She looks at them. 'Come outside, child.'

I follow her. She takes a blue plastic lighter out of her pocket that she uses for the fire and touches the flame to the corner of the pictures. Some birds out on the water start flapping and fighting and I nearly jump out of my skin because for a moment I think the skulls have come to life and started shrieking.

'Now, see, what is it you're talking about?'

The open mouths scream through the fire that licks their bony faces and then crisp up to burned flakes on the ground. Dorothy stamps on them so they turn into dust twirling away in the wind.

'There. Nothing can be made from nothing, can it, child?' That's what she said before. 'And if it is I'll tell him. I'll tell him you've been stealing from the Bible. He won't like that, will he?' As she walks off I watch as the ash blows in a puff out over the water.

I sit on the steps and I don't stop shaking for ages. Whenever Dorothy's horrible it makes me feel so bad I want to die. Tears trickle down the side of my face. But then I start feeling better, strong even. Dorothy had to burn her horrible skulls because of me.

I'm taking everything out one by one and looking at it like a policeman. I even think about looking for the book with Mercy in it again but then I change my mind. I've been in enough trouble for one day.

And I've read Gramps's secrets, even if I don't understand them. The way he talks in his book is weird like there's something wrong with him. Even if it is just Bibleish stuff, I remember telling myself about keeping an eye on him and when I stop shaking I go to find him. He's chopping wood with an axe and I watch him for a bit when he doesn't know I'm there.

He spots me at last. 'Carmel, what are you doing? Standing there and staring.' He straightens up. There's a pile of chopped wood next to him and the cut insides are leaking. There's some lazy flies swooping around his head.

'Nothing.'

He sees something in my face has changed. He's good at that, Gramps, but he does it different to me – he does it by watching and listening.

'Come on, dear. Tell me all about it.'

'Gramps, why did you and Mum fall out?' I ask it quickly before I have a chance to change my mind. He called Mum 'careless' in his book but I can't mention that because he'll know I've been reading it. Even though I could tell him he's wrong.

He pats a log for me to sit on. 'Now Carmel, we don't need to be dwelling on past history, we . . .'

'But why can't you tell me? Is it a secret?'

His eyes have gone very pale and I start to feel afraid then, but he puts his arm around me and says in a soft kind voice, 'I didn't agree with how she chose to live her life, her marriage. I regret it now, of course I do, I'm full of remorse in my prayers . . .'

His shoulders start heaving up and down and his hands go up to his face and his throat is making dry sobs. He's got his energy tight wrapped up inside him and tears ooze from under his hands. He starts looking like a big animal that's been hurt by a hunter.

'Gramps, don't cry,' I say at last.

'Child, what an exhibition I make of myself.' He rubs at his face with his arm.

I put my hand on his arm. 'You just miss her, that's all. Same as me.' And even though he's been upset I'm glad to know he does.

32

DAY 180

I BOUGHT THE TEXTBOOKS in a second-hand shop.

Biology books. I wiped the dust from the green covers and took them to the old man behind the wooden counter.

'All of them?' he asked. There were only three – he couldn't get a lot of custom.

'Yes, please.'

I opened the cover of the one on top of the pile. It had been published in 1969.

'Except . . . ?' Then I smiled. 'Sorry, I thought the information might be out of date. But of course – the human body – it doesn't go out of date, does it?'

It was a task I'd set myself. The 'tiny actions' I'd talked about with Craig had expanded. Now I told him: 'Tiny actions, for other people.'

I'd had an idea: maybe one day I could train to be a nurse. Maybe actions for other people would be a key. It was too soon, everyone said, and of course it was, but I made a deal with him. I would try and cut down on my looking and study some biology, if I could concentrate. The police investigation had gone quiet, for now, though I didn't know if that would make it harder or easier.

It helped, somehow, learning the human body: *the spinal cord consists of areas of white and grey matter . . . the back of the eye is filled with clear jelly . . . muscle contraction can be voluntary (controlled by will) or involuntary (automatic, i.e. reflex).*

On a good day I felt I was nearing some mystery of human existence: eyes, hands, feet, womb, fingernails. As if Carmel had not been taken but had shattered apart into fragments. An explosion of particles, fine like glass, and I could somehow learn to knit her back together again. I could feel her textures under my fingers. The slide of my thumb across a clean curl. The crispy skin of a healing cut. Bone, at the ankle – raw and knobbly. Meanwhile, her map grew. When a name came to me I hadn't thought of before – even some hardly known acquaintance I'd almost forgotten – I'd slip into her room and add it there. I'd had to stick two extra huge sheets of paper next to the others to cope with the burgeoning network. I kept at it but it never seemed to tell me anything that made sense.

Good days had tracts of calm. But on a bad day I wanted to visit violence on myself, at the same time knowing how I had to stay well and healthy. That, despite everything, I had to stay whole. So, I let myself wander there in my head. I'd have visions of severing my spine with bolt cutters. Cracking my head against the wall so a long spill of blood ran down and pooled on the floor around my toes. Smashing my hand through the window and scraping it back and forth on the broken glass. It gave me a relief, these visions. But I knew I couldn't linger in their technicolour for too long.

I had to stay sane.

Tiny actions. I planted up the container by the front door with bulbs for next spring.

'Well done,' my mother said when she arrived, a Waitrose grocery bag in each hand. My parents stayed often now, in my house. Mum cooked and Dad pottered around the garden. It was like time had gone backward and here we were, just the three of us again. Mum, Dad and Beth. They paid my bills too, for the time being, since returning to work still defeated me.

'That's good. I'll make you something to eat. Something light, we have to keep you alive, darling. We have to keep on going.'

We did.

The heart is a hollow, inverted pear-shaped muscle. Inside it is divided into four chambers . . .

Next spring, I think, then it will have been a whole year.

33

AT THE WHITE WOOD CHURCH Gramps's sparkly energy comes back, but it doesn't fly around this time. It's tighter, like a beam of light.

'Inside, room for everybody. Inside, and you folk make yourselves comfortable.' He reminds me of the man outside the circus tent calling everybody in.

In my school we went to an old church for harvest festival. We found a stone grave with the name *Elsie* and she'd died when she was only five years old and six months. But this church is painted bright new white and it's on top of a hill so you can see for miles around over yellow fields because it's the only hill that's there.

Gramps has got us all lined up by the door.

A woman in a dark pink hat says, 'Hello,' and, 'What a fine, fine day,' to Gramps. When she speaks the flowers on her hat – held on by wires – go up and down in Gramps's direction, like they want to talk to him too. She says, 'Such news has been coming our way. How blessed we are you made it so far up country.'

Gramps takes her hand and holds it against his chest.

He's been worried that no one would come. We got here early and a friend he knows called Bill was already there smoking, with the smoke going up in a line into the air. For a long time nothing happened and Gramps asked Bill if he put all the flyers out and Bill said yes, and not to panic. Then, across the fields, I started seeing people, tiny in the distance, crawling along like the bell going dong, dong, dong – rocking on the church roof – was calling feeding time for snails and they were crawling toward it. And when they got closer I could hear singing and some were in wheelchairs and some were walking with sticks.

'My dear, dear lady,' Gramps says to the lady in the hat, like he's about to cry. I do hope he doesn't. The way these people are – coming up to us so quiet, like we're really something special – I don't know what they'd do.

The woman in the hat's husband pops up in front of us and I have to jam my hand on my mouth to stop me screaming because one of his eyes is like a huge egg made of clear jelly spilling out of his eyehole.

'Pastor Patron,' he doesn't want to let go of Gramps's hand, 'we're awful glad to see you here, we really are.'

When he speaks you can see how it hurts his face. His eye pushes down on that side of his mouth and his words have to come out of a gap the other side so they whistle. The way I've been feeling about his eye, that it's disgusting and it looks like it's a home for a slug, that feeling melts away and I just feel sorry for him. Then the flowers hover over the woman's head as they go inside the dark church.

'Gramps, what are all these people doing here?'

But he's not listening to me. He's concentrating too hard, leaning down and tickling the faces of babies in their push-chairs and patting the hair of children in wheelchairs.

Dorothy doesn't say much. She's wearing a posh purple suit with a skirt that only goes to her knees, silky tights, shoes with heels and pearly earrings in her ears. Her hair is different too – in a bun – and it's hard to think it's Dorothy even.

When the people are inside Gramps says, 'Well, I guess our time has come.' He puts his hand on our backs one by one to make us go in. I can tell he wants to go in last.

Inside, the stage has got a microphone and chairs and a blue carpet that comes from the stage right down the middle to the front door. The record player playing the crackled-up music is up there too and every time it turns around the sun flashes off the record.

People turn to look at us and I see the man with the egg eye and the lady with the flower hat. I smile at them and they smile back and the lady's flowers nod hello to me.

Gramps walks up to the stage but we don't go with him. I sit next to Melody, at the end of one of the rows of benches; I want to stick real close to her. 'What's going to happen?' I ask her.

'You'll see. We'll sing and pray. Pa will do some powerful talking and spirit might come.'

Everyone stands up and I can hardly see, just the big back of the man in front with sweat coming through his blue shirt. Then I hear Gramps's voice – he must be talking through a microphone because it's booming out and it makes him super powerful.

'What a day. What a day for the healing spirit of the Lord to alight on this very place . . .'

Someone shouts in a loud voice from the back: 'Amen' – that nearly makes me jump out of my skin and it seems to set them all off, yelling out.

The church is hot and I start to feel dizzy and afraid. I creep my hand over to Melody and put it inside hers and she squeezes it tight. Then, Bill changes the record to one that's only music on it and no singing. He switches on a machine and it makes lit-up words go onto the wall at the back above Gramps's head and everyone sings about being a blade of grass cut down.

When the singing finishes, everything goes silent. I peep around the man's big back and up to the stage, but not letting go of Melody's hand. For a minute I think Gramps is crying. He's got his face in his hands and his shoulders are moving up and down and the crowd groan and shuffle around on their shoes. It feels like ages till he lifts up his head and holds his arms out wide and I can let my breath go at last. He looks up at the ceiling.

'Come, come and be moved by the spirit.'

The record gets to the end but keeps going around and around making scratchy noises. Nobody moves and it feels like a bomb is about to drop on us.

When I think I can't stand it any more a man jumps out of his seat and runs up to Gramps on the stage. He's black and young and he's wearing a shiny blue suit that looks too small for him.

Bill changes the record to deep slow singing.

Gramps holds out the microphone. 'Tell me, son. What is your name?' His blue eyes look over us as he asks, like we're all in it together.

A name gets said into the microphone but it sounds like 'Flim' so I don't think I've heard it right. He grins at the crowd.

Gramps asks, 'What's wrong with you, young man? What's ailing you today?'

There didn't look much wrong with Flim, not when he was jumping up onto the stage anyway. He doesn't answer, he just seems to like being up there and he keeps waving and smiling at us. I don't think he knows that Gramps is getting annoyed because he doesn't know him. But I do, I can see the signs. His neck seems to get bigger and grows out over his collar and he stands with his arm crossed over his chest holding his elbow.

But all Gramps says is, 'Take a seat.' Flim sits on one of the wooden chairs at the back of the stage.

Gramps says into the microphone. 'Now, son, stretch out your legs for me.'

Flim does what Gramps says. He stretches out his legs like a plank so everyone can see his shiny yellow socks and brown shoes.

Gramps gives the microphone to Bill and gets hold of both of Flim's brown shoes from underneath. He starts pushing and pulling, frowning a lot. Bill shoves the microphone between them so we can hear what Gramps is saying.

'Son, did you know both your legs were of differing lengths?'

Flim stops smiling then. He sits with his eyes popping out, looking at his feet as if he's seen the most amazing sight.

Bill holds the microphone so we can hear the answer. 'No, sir. I did not. I did not know that at all.'

Gramps looks up at the ceiling, with one of Flim's feet in each hand, and I can see his lips moving. At last he jumps up and throws his arms wide in a big ta-da and grabs the microphone back off Bill.

'Stand, Flim, stand.'

Flim does, slowly, and there's a great big smile covering his face. But when Gramps holds out the microphone to him he sounds like he's crying.

'Thank you, thank the Lord,' he's crying into the microphone. And then it seems to get too much for him and he covers his head over with his hands and runs off the stage.

Then something happens that makes me properly jump so my hand flies out of Melody's. The man in front of me with the blue shirt he's sweated into falls onto the carpet in the middle. His chins wobble and he opens his mouth and this comes out of it: 'Zoolawellatenchingfunkallahshoma.'

Nobody else takes any notice. Nobody says, 'Perhaps we'd better call an ambulance for this poor man.' They carry on shouting out and clapping as if he wasn't there and getting up out of their seats and moving to the front so I can't really see much of Gramps any more. The air has started to smell of sweat.

That's when Dorothy grabs onto my arm.

'Stop it,' I say, because I don't know what she's doing, but she holds my arm tight and starts pulling me up to the front. Through the crowd I see Gramps's face and he's smiling like I've never seen him smile before. All his teeth are showing and his face has gone pale red as he reaches out and puts his hand on a woman's head. She's thin with a long blue dress and masses of tiny curls that spring straight out of her head and Gramps has to cram his hand on because the curls try to bounce his hand right off. And I gasp because it's like a jolt of electricity goes right through her body and it's coming from Gramps's hand. She falls down flat on the floor. People stand around, looking at her. They mumble and someone even pokes her but she doesn't wake up. So two men with sweat on their faces pick her up and carry her off.

I don't want to be taken up to Gramps so he can make me fall to the floor. My heart's ticking very fast under my dress, it feels like it's gone twice its normal size and it's pushing right up into my throat. But Dorothy's got hold of my arm tight with her thin pinchy fingers. She's much, much stronger than she looks.

Instead she takes me to the side of the stage and a big fat woman in a dress with different-coloured triangles – yellow, pink and blue – fills up my eyes. Then she moves out of the way and there's a little boy, white and pale, in a wheelchair. He's tiny, this boy, with little twig legs – his brown trousers look nearly empty he's so skinny. His white hands rest on green plastic on the arms of the wheelchair. His hair is thin and golden like a baby's and I don't think I've seen anyone look like they're going to break so much in my whole life. Even the glass Christmas angels me and Mum used to hang on the tree with gold string looked stronger than he does. Dorothy shoves me right in front of him and he grips onto his arm things and looks up at me with his sweet face.

Dorothy takes hold of both my hands and clamps them around the boy's head, squashing her own hands over mine, so I'm trapped there.

His skull feels like I'm holding on to an egg. Don't let me crack it, I think. Don't let my fingers go through into the runny yolk inside. Dorothy's boobs are pressing into my back and I can feel her hot breathing through my body. His hair is soft and silky on my fingers and I can feel the shell underneath and for a minute I think I'm going to faint.

Just as I feel I'm going to crash on top of the boy and crush him like a bird's egg, the noise around me seems to get farther away. I open my eyes.

And it's only me and him. I forget even Dorothy and the people yelling and crying and the scratchy record. His lips look like they've been painted on – dummy in shop window lips – and his face is patient, as if he's used to having things done to him and not saying anything about it, just having to wait till it's over. His mouth is moving and I think he's trying to say something to me so I lean in but in my ear all there is is a shush, shush sound coming out of his mouth.

'What is it?' I say. 'Tell me.'

'Shush, shush, shush.'

What I'd really like to do is take him away from in here, wheel him outside into the sun so we can sit together and look out from the hill. I think he'd like that a lot more than being in here.

Gramps has appeared behind the wheelchair now.

Dorothy yanks my hands away off his head. She holds out my arms, her fingers tight around my wrists, so I'm opened up like she's showing me around.

Gramps leans over the boy from behind and booms at him. 'Look. See here. Now stand, boy, stand.'

Nothing happens for a minute, then the boy tries to move his twig legs and they tremble and shake.

'Stand, boy. Stand,' Gramps yells at him.

The little boy's really trying. He grips onto the green plastic arms of his wheelchair with both hands and goes even whiter than before.

'Yes. That's it – see. See how the boy is nearly standing.' Gramps does his funny little dance on the spot behind the wheelchair.

The boy manages to push himself a tiny bit more up out of the chair. His whole body is shaking and there's sweat on his eyelids. A crowd's gathering around to watch.

'Stop it,' I shout. 'Stop trying to make him.'

But they don't, they probably can't even hear my voice over the noise. What they want is for the boy to stand up and walk across the room and for everyone to be amazed. They keep telling him to stand up, telling him he's better. In the end I don't watch any more. I can't use my hands to cover up my eyes because of Dorothy holding me so I turn my head away. When I look back again the boy has gone.

As soon as Dorothy lets go I wriggle away to the door and take big deep gulps of fresh air.

Outside the white church it's still loud, like there's a storm happening inside. I put my hands over my ears.

'Where you going, child?' I hear Dorothy calling. I look back, she's leaning against the door.

'For a walk.'

Over the fields, it's yellow, yellow, yellow for miles and a plane in the sky.

'Don't go too far now.'

The shadow of wings moves over the yellow, getting bigger until it falls over me, cold and dark.

'D'you hear me?'

I'm remembering something.

A little window and engines roaring. A woman, with a tiny doll's hat sitting on her head. I'm wondering how it stays there it's so small. She's got a waistcoat with a silver badge on it. Her name's on the badge: Shelley. She's leaning down, her face is soft and pretty with shiny pale pink lipstick, and she's saying, 'Hey, is she OK?' And Gramps, he's sitting next to me and he gives her a great big smile. 'She's fine – not feeling quite herself is all.' But the lady doesn't seem sure about this and she leans in closer. 'Can I get you anything? Some water, what about a Coke? Would you like some Coca-Cola, sweetheart?'

Then for no reason, and I'm not even knowing why I'm doing it, I start laughing at her. I start laughing and a shocked look comes onto her face and she stands straight, holding a tray up with the ends of her fingers, and she moves away from us, saying as she goes: 'Well, if you need anything . . .'

The shadow of the plane is leaving, there's a black wing shape printed on the white front of the church.

I call over to Dorothy. 'Did I come here on a plane?'

She shrugs her shoulders. 'Sure. How else did you think you got here?'

'But, but . . . I didn't remember it, before.'

'Only travel is all,' says Dorothy, and when she says that I feel like a bug getting squashed because it's a big hole in the puzzle that just got filled up and nobody thinks it's important.

The plane's gone; just a noise that sounds like a Hoover getting quieter and quieter.

It's made me think of running away again – but then I look out over the fields. I remember the dark woods and not having anywhere to go and I know there's no point. I want to see Dad, but he feels about a million miles away, useless. Dorothy and Gramps and the twins are my family now. And Gramps is the one that cares about me more than anyone else alive. If I ran away I'd only be scared and on my own again.

I walk around the side of the church dragging my shoes in the grass. Two insects come and play around my eyes and I bat them away. 'Not today,' I say to them crossly.

Down the bottom of the hill a giant brown nut has landed there. I blink and it turns into a head.

I forget about the insects and lean over. 'Hello?'

A foot slides out. Brown eyes look up.

'Hi.' There's a hand too, picking at the grass, pulling stalks up.

I slide down in my stiff shoes. It's a boy in a black suit and tie but he doesn't seem to care about his clothes. He's sprawling around on the grass and there's bits of it all over his back.

'Were you in the church?'

He nods.

I flop down next to him. He seems like he wants to be away from it too. 'What's your name?'

'Nico.'

'Oh.' I can't think of anything to say so I peep at him. The sun shines on his dark skin and his black hair. It makes shadows on his face from his eyelashes. I'm thinking he looks – and this is a funny word to say about a boy – pretty. I look away again, quickly, so he doesn't catch me staring.

'I got hot,' he says.

'Me too.' I can feel the dinging in my head from the noise. My hands are still shaking.

I dig my black patent shoe down into the soft grass. 'My name's Carmel, I'm eight.' I feel silly then, he hadn't even asked but I told him anyway.

But he just says, 'I'm eleven. Two weeks ago.' He looks a bit sad and lonely then – but somehow that makes him even prettier – so I ask, 'What are you doing here? Are your mum and dad here?'

He jerks his head. 'They're inside. My sister, she's got cerebral palsy. They want to try and make her better. She's real bad.'

I look down at the floor. I don't know what cerebral palsy is and I don't want to ask, but I've been noticing how he talks.

'Are you from somewhere else?'

He nods. 'Romania.'

'I've never heard of that.' He smiles and I feel the sunshine warm on my skin. 'I'm from Norfolk in England.' I've done it again, telling him something he hasn't asked. I start pulling up grass too.

He doesn't seem to have even heard. 'They aren't ever going to make her better.' He's frowning hard. 'I wish they'd stop trying.'

'They might?' I say in a quiet voice. I want him to hope, but then I remember the twig boy in the wheelchair. 'It doesn't work for everyone. But Gramps says sometimes cripples get up out of their beds and walk. He says the blind can see with their own two eyes. He's seen it all happen. He thinks I can do it even . . .' I stop and bite my lip.

'Can you?' He doesn't sound sure, like I'm saying baby stuff.

I shrug. 'I don't know. That's what Gramps says.'

We hear people coming out of the church so we both scoot closer to the bank.

'I hope she does get better,' I whisper, fierce.

A voice from above makes us both jump. 'What are you two doing?' It's Dorothy. 'Get on up here.'

Nico stands up. 'Come on,' he says, and grabs my hand and starts pulling me up the hill. It makes me laugh being dragged like that – the feeling of his strong hand. I can see Dorothy's thin back walking away and I'm wishing and wishing she hadn't found us and we could stay there, on our own, for longer. But Dorothy stops and waits for us to catch up, and Nico lets go of my hand.

The twins are running toward us, their hair flying about.

'Come on Carmel,' says Melody. 'Mom says you did a healing. She says true grace was visited today.' I think of the twig boy in the wheelchair.

'Is that true?'

'Yes, yes. Come on.'

I look back. Nico puts his hands in his pockets and starts walking away. I want to fly to him then. To tell him maybe it is true. That his sister might really get better. But his mum's gone over to him now and she's got her arm around him. She's dark like him with gold circles hanging off her ears and a scarf with bright colours stitched onto black but Nico doesn't want to talk to her. He looks down at the ground like he wants to kill it.

Dorothy makes us line up by the door again as people come out, blinking and swaying. A lot of them have crispy dollars ready in their hands and – I can hardly believe it – they start giving them to her. She stuffs the money into a special bag with a zip at the top and she hadn't been wearing that when we came and I don't know where she got it from. They're saying, 'Thank you, thank you.'

After what Dorothy did with the twig boy I don't want to be near her. Whenever I look at her putting dollars in her bag I feel anger fizzling away inside. I stand next to Silver instead.

The lady with the flower hat comes out with her egg-eye husband. Her flowers have got squashed. I smile at her and she gives me a sad smile back and I watch them walking off down the path. The man is leaning on her and if she wasn't so big and heavy I think they'd both fall over.

Silver keeps looking at me. 'What's the matter, Carmel?'

'Sometimes I could *murder* your mom,' I say. I mean it.

I hold my breath. Now she'll probably go and tell. Instead, her eyes go sparkly and she giggles. 'I know. So could I.'

Melody's on the other side of her. 'What are you two clucking about?'

It's like they get jealous now if I speak to one too much.

'Nothing,' says Silver. 'Carmel, can we ask you something?

And you have to tell us, real honest and true.' They both lean in close. 'Are you an angel?'

Dorothy's behind us and she's heard. 'Girls, you leave Carmel alone now. She'll need a rest.'

'But is she, Ma?' Silver really wants to know. 'Pa says she is.'

Dorothy's eyes dig into me. 'Well, what are you, child?'

I look down at my palms. They're smudged dirty green from the grass. 'I'm Carmel,' I say. 'I'm just that.'

I have a burning wish to see Nico again before we leave, but he's already gone.

34

DAY 260

ON THE CUSP of the old year turning into the new I walked into the sea. I'd spent the early morning . . . looking, of course. What else?

I parked up. Even though I knew they thought it fruitless, my parents had bought me a car, the better to help with the looking. The biology textbooks gathered dust under my bed. I never went too far: all too soon I'd have that irresistible tug – *go home, go back, she could be there, waiting.* By now, was there a blade of grass I hadn't lifted in this county? Or the three counties around for that matter. It didn't matter; it might not be the right blade of grass. Not *the* one.

Cromer beach: a flat grey sky pressing onto grey sea; me: a mashed pink worm between the two. All the making of leaflets and maps; fund-raising to put adverts in the press; planting bulbs; the endless cups of tea and the phone calls seemed on that day to be useless flotsam to be smashed apart in an overpowering sea of circumstance. New Year's Eve took me back to new beginnings – I could almost feel the sharp, pleasantly acidic breeze that promised to blow the winds of change into our lives nearly a year ago. And it had, oh, it had. The thought of the new year yawning ahead seemed impossible.

I didn't even mean to kill myself but never had anything looked so inviting as that freezing grey sea. I shed my clothes as I ran toward it, scattering them across the pebbles. Then the plunge and the 'Oh, oh, oh, oh.' It felt exquisite – this pain that flooded through my body and punched everything else away. I swam, farther out toward the horizon, the waves pounding at my body till I went weak and slack. A thought drifted into my frozen brain. I could give up, here, now. The thought was enticing and refused to go away. It bloomed out like a growing flower speeded up by the camera until it was touching the sides of my skull and there was no room for anything else.

Maybe, if there was another world beyond that flat horizon, that's where she would be waiting. Not outside my house.

I let myself sink and my mouth fill up with seawater and the thick saltiness of it scoured out my mouth and nasal passages. I tried, I really did, I tried my very best to drown. But every time some involuntary convulsion of my body sent me gasping and choking to the surface, sucking for the life-giving air I didn't want. It was like trying to kill a machine.

Then after the sea had got fed up tossing me about it sicked me up onto the pebbles and in the distance I saw Paul scanning the beach and the horizon. When he saw me he started running. He was wearing a long black coat that flapped behind him as he ran and as he got nearer I could hear his words: 'Beth, for God's sake, Beth. Dear God, let her be alive.' Then closer, he could see I had breath in my body.

He lifted me up with surprising ease and carried me away from the sea's clutches. I had on my knickers but the sea had swallowed up my bra. Not that I cared. He was shouting as he carried me, not at me but at the world. 'What now? What more, for Christ's sake?'

I was dumped on the pebbles and then felt his big coat fold around me before he went to retrieve my scattered clothes. Numbed, I watched him whip them up quickly, angrily, and hang them over his other arm, for all the world like he was clearing up after a messy kid.

Then he came and dumped the pile at my feet and threw himself next to me.

'I could only find one of your shoes.' He looked at me and I could see the horror in his eyes. 'God, Beth, your lips are bright blue.' I let him tuck the coat more tightly around me and scrub at my face and feet with his big hands.

'How did you find me?' I asked eventually, my words sounding like a ventriloquist's dummy's through clenched teeth and cold-stiffened lips.

'I drove over to see you this morning.' He took my hand and held it there, putting his other on top to melt the iciness. 'And you weren't there, so I came looking for you. I wanted to see that you were OK. New Year is always a funny time. I drove around for a bit and saw your car parked back there.' He jerked his head backward. 'Christ, Beth. What the hell were you doing? What good did you think that was going to do?' He was almost shouting, and once again I marvelled at how often his go-to reaction had been anger where mine was grief. I almost envied him for it; at least anger had a burn.

'I'm sorry, Paul,' I muttered, the clenched teeth locking together. 'I wasn't even trying to kill myself . . . really. I wanted to be, I don't know. Blank, I suppose. For the relief.'

We had nothing to say for a moment and the shushing of the sea moved into the gap. Slowly, I watched the anger hiss out of his body, leaving him limp.

'Paul, do you ever wish we hadn't had her?'

He looked startled for a moment: he hadn't been expecting that.

'No. Never, not once.'

'I have.' It was true. I was sometimes plagued with the thought that if I'd never had her all this couldn't have happened. But now, now – I was destined forever to have a small red ghost following and chattering at my heels until the day I died and even be-yond . . . if there really was something there. A comfort? Maybe. Not really. Because even there she might elude me and I'd have to go on looking and looking and there would be no end to it, ever.

'I feel bad for thinking it. But I do, sometimes.'

'I don't think we should feel guilty for anything, Beth. Not for anything we feel or anything we think. No one else knows. No one. And if they say they do they're liars.'

'I think sometimes it was because I got distracted.'

'Distracted?'

'Yes. By my jealousy. By you. That it's my fault. My attention wasn't where it should've been and it wouldn't have happened if I'd been focusing on what I should have – other things too. The feeling I was going to lose her, they were all bricks, you see, bricks in what happened. Built one after the other.' My voice sounded rambling and hysterical, even to my own ears.

'Beth, it's not your fault.'

'You said before it was.'

'I've told you, I was distraught, I wasn't in my right mind.' Then a sudden urge seized me, like the one that made me walk into the sea, and I picked up a rock and smashed at the middle finger of my other hand, which was splayed out on a flat stone. Paul didn't move to stop me. When I felt I was done, and my finger was a bruised plum, I heaved the rock and threw it down the beach.

'Oh fuck, Beth. Fuck.' He moved in and put his arms around me. 'It's OK. I understood, I understand why you did that. Does it hurt? It must do.'

Instinctively I drew my hand up to my mouth, for comfort.

'Let me look.' He took my hand and gently examined it. 'Noth-ing broken.' I tucked it into the coat. He put his arms around me again and we both looked out to sea.

'I think about her all the time, all the time. I try and find answers. I . . .' He paused. 'Did you ever think, did you think Car-mel,' there, he'd said it, 'was a bit eccentric?'

'Sort of. I told you once, I think. Did you?'

'Truthfully, yes. It bothered me sometimes. I wanted her to fit in. I used to think maybe she was a bit, you know, like those Asperger's kids. She was so clever but in other ways really not.'

'I think she was on some spectrum or other. But I don't think it was Asperger's.'

'Then what?'

'I don't know.'

'Sometimes I wonder.'

'What?'

'If it could have anything to do – to do with what happened. But how can it have?'

I shook my head again. 'I don't know, Paul. I'm at the end of knowing, of thinking anything.'

'Lucy tries to help. She's been very understanding, but I think there's things only we can understand.'

'It must be hard for her.'

'Yes. She wanted kids, you know, but now . . .'

'It must be very hard for her,' I said again.

We sat together for a while and it struck me that we'd never had such an honest conversation in all our years of marriage. Then he helped me up and guided me to his car, tucking my clothes and one shoe into the footwell.

'Come home with me. We'll get your car later.'

Lucy greeted us at the door as Paul helped me up their neat little suburban path. If she was horrified at seeing me barefoot, covered in Paul's coat and with damp and matted hair, she managed to keep it to herself.

'She'll need a hot bath,' explained Paul.

'No. That's the worst thing you can do. I'll run a tepid one and we'll top it up slowly. The hot water's too much of a shock for the system otherwise.'

'Lucy's a care assistant,' explained Paul.

'Oh,' I said. I hadn't known that about her. In fact I didn't really know anything about her, save that I'd hated her in some dim past that didn't matter any more. I realised I was standing on the same patch of cream carpet where I'd put my boots before. This time, my feet were caked in sand and dirt.

'Sorry, Lucy,' I said. But she wasn't there and in the background I could hear bathwater running.

What is this thing that happens? When disaster strikes and women come, with their cakes and their bandages, with their cups of tea and their soothing fingers. It's the complicity of the birthing chamber, the laying out of the dead. They pick the bits of tragedy up off the floor and try to knit them together in some shape, the way I'd felt I could knit Carmel back to life. Not the way they were before, something lumpy and misshapen – but so there's a whole again. The tiny actions I'd been trying to make my mantra – sweep, bathe, pick up off the floor, drink, eat, straighten up that rumpled bed, dress the wound. Lucy took the coat from my shoulders and helped me into the bath. Even though I knew it was cool, and no steam rose from its surface, it burned against my skin.

'We'll wash your hair,' she said, and got the showerhead running and started sluicing water over my scalp. Sand flowed out of my hair into the bath and once a tiny snail creature plopped out. She lathered up my hair with shampoo and rescued the snail from the soapy water and popped it onto the tiles, where it stuck fast like a piece of bubblegum.

'Lucy, this is so very kind of you.' I started to cry.

'There, there,' she soothed, her deft fingers removing a tiny pebble from my scalp.

Paul hovered outside, not looking in. 'I'll make us something warm to drink.'

Lucy's tiny clothes were too small for me so she dressed me in Paul's – chinos and a fleece. I buried my face into the soft sleeve and breathed in the chemical flower scent again.

Then I was on her leather sofa, with one on either side. 'Paul.' I needed to ask this. 'Do you feel she's still alive?'

'Yes.'

His answer surprised me; it was so vehement it made him spill his tea on his legs.

'How?'

'I just feel it deep inside me, Beth. Don't you?'

No, I wanted to answer. All I feel is a big fat gaping mystery. A yawning vortex churning with coloured clues: crayons; red shoes; men on trains; the glittering skirt of a storyteller. They whirl around me day and night. It's a hole I stand on the edge of, always nearly falling in.

35

WINTER. WE SHIVER UNDER our crochet blankets and storms bash the side of the truck. Dorothy says our money's nearly gone. That it hasn't worked out like Gramps said it would. We haven't done any more healings in churches. Bill has got ill and Dorothy says Gramps couldn't organise a dead body at a wake. A hole comes in the roof out of nowhere and rain leaks over Dorothy's pots and pans and makes them rusty. She throws them out of the back door in a temper. She yells, 'Cheap trash,' and, 'When will I have a good set? A set made of stainless steel?' My grandfather doesn't answer her. He sits on the bed in a great big mood. The mood is so strong it comes out of him to about halfway down the truck and you think you're going to bang into it. The rain falls straight down in a sheet outside the open back doors. 'You and your notions,' Dorothy yells at him but it doesn't make him do anything except his head goes lower and he doesn't even look up out of the corner of his eyes.

The pans stay outside all night and in the morning they're full of rainwater and creatures, thin like the lines in my writing books at school, are using them as swimming pools.

Us three girls, we've grown. Our dresses are too short and the waists are squeezing our middles. Our tights, too, but they go downward. The elastic cuts into our bottoms and makes us look funny, like a balloon man's been making shapes with us. The other side of winter I'll be nine, though, and nine is when you're a Big Girl. So it makes sense I'm busting out of my clothes.

'The cold here is terrible,' moans Dorothy. She's sitting on their bed and she's wrapped herself up in blankets. 'There's no cold like this at home.'

When it stops raining for a minute, Gramps climbs onto the roof to find the leak, and mends it with squares of black stuff. We can hear him, moving around there like a bear. 'He's going to crash right through,' says Silver. But he doesn't, he gets down before that happens and the rain stops coming in.

Me and the twins shiver in our dresses and rain macs. Mine's an old blue anorak of Silver's with a zip.

'You'll have to get them new coats,' says Gramps.

Dorothy gives a shriek. 'Coats with what? Coats don't grow up from the ground.'

Gramps pulls a Bible down from his shelf and for a moment I think he's going to read from it – something about how coats actually do grow up from the ground and we should let God take care of it. If he does that, I think, Dorothy will hit him with one of her rusty pans. But when he opens it, it's scooped out on the inside like a melon, and there's paper money inside. I understand what Dorothy meant about stealing from the Bible now.

'Here, take this. Get them what they need. I can't have people seeing I don't take care of them.'

The town we go to is small, hardly one street of shops. But it's lovely to be here. People walk along with their bags of shopping, and smile. Dorothy doesn't like it though. One of the shopkeepers, he watches us through his grocery shop window as we walk by his store.

'They think we're itinerants,' says Dorothy and none of us know what she means but the way she says it doesn't make it sound like a good thing to be.

In the clothes shop I see straight away which coat I want. It's red, red, red. Even though I'm only looking at it hanging on the rail I can see it's warm and soft. I go up to it while Dorothy and the twins are looking on the other side of the shop. It's not exactly like my last one that got thrown away. This one is even better, it's got cushiony yellow lining.

I put it on and say, 'This one.' I'm doing the toggles up quickly I want it so much.

Dorothy's pushing Silver's arms into a purple puffa coat. She whips around real quick when I say that. When she looks at me her eyes go so dark and glisteny I think they're going to start dripping down her face.

'Oh no. No, not that one.'

'Why not?' I'm aching for it so much I'm talking back and I know Dorothy won't like it. But I remember how she's my enemy now so I don't care. I fold my arms tight and hug it.

'Oh no. No. No. It won't do at all.' She comes over and pulls the price tag from behind the back of my neck.

'There, it's too pricey.'

The lady behind the counter is listening to us now. She puts on her glasses that are on a gold chain around her neck and comes and looks at the ticket too.

'Now, let's see. It's been here rather a long time, that model. I don't know why because it really is a lovely coat. But there's no accounting for taste I guess and I'm prepared to make a substantial discount. I'll do it for the same price as those ones there.' She points to the twins standing in their puffa coats.

I smile at her, and she smiles back. She's old, with bright pink lipstick and lots of soft moles on her skin. Her hair is dyed a lovely gold that shines in the light coming through the window.

'Thank you,' I say. We like each other, I can tell.

But Dorothy's not pleased with me saying thank you, like it's really going to happen. 'Oh, I don't know. I don't know . . .' she says to herself. There's even a bit of red coming through her brown skin and I've never seen that before.

'Now then, I'm not meaning to be rude but can you tell me your objection? It's a real bargain,' says the lady, 'and will last much longer than those two. And I have to know,' she turns around to me, 'where's your lovely accent from, honey?'

'We'll take it,' Dorothy says all of a sudden and I feel amazed.

She starts hurrying then and counts out notes even before the lady's got back behind the counter. She's not slow and watching like she usually is with money. I wish I don't have to leave the shop ever. I could help the old lady tidy the pants that are in the trays underneath the glass counter. Or we could dress the children with the hard painted faces in the window and move their arms and legs about.

The shop lady follows us to the door. She stands there when we're outside on the street. 'Are you all right, dear?' She's looking at me.

Dorothy puts her arm around me. 'She's fine. She's our foster child is all. We've taken her in . . .' She starts pushing us down the street. 'Thank you for the coats. They'll be real warm and cosy now.'

When we're farther down I look back at the shop lady. She gives her gold head a shake and for some reason I think I see her shaking me right out of her head and me slipping out – away, down onto the ground. She bangs the door shut and the bell sound seems far away now.

Melody says, 'I'm hungry.'

Dorothy stops on the street. 'Oh, what the heck . . .' she says, and we go into a place with yellow and blue plastic tables and she orders burgers and milkshakes.

'You better make the most of this,' she says to me. But I don't answer. I'm getting used to her being sometimes nice, sometimes nasty. Mostly nasty. I stare at her, not saying anything, chewing on my burger with my new coat buttons all done up to my chin. I don't want to take it off ever.

When we've finished Silver starts crying and saying she never gets new stuff. It's because she's seen things in shop windows here. Dorothy would like to smack her, I can see, but she can't because there's people around. She hisses, 'This is the very last of it,' and gives us all some coins to spend. We go to a store that sells everything and spend ages choosing – Silver turning the carousels of toys around for hours. I start thinking Dorothy is going to smack her even if it is right in front of people. Silver ends up choosing a plastic pack of doll's things – bottles and paper nappies and a tiny potty – and Melody copies her. I choose some cards. When we're out of the shop I tuck them in my new coat pocket.

Dorothy asks, 'What are those for?'

'For sending to Dad and Sara,' I tell her.

Gramps comes from around the front of the truck where he's been fixing the engine. He's got oil on his hands and he's wiping a spanner with a cloth.

'Dorothy says you wish to send some greetings home, dear?'

Dorothy's told. I wish she hadn't because Gramps doesn't like it when I talk about home. He says things like, 'This is what we have to think about now, Carmel. Our new life.'

Instead he says, 'That's a great idea, Carmel. Need some help with that?' I nod slowly.

'Tell you what, you write what you like in your cards and I'll make sure they get posted.'

I spread the cards over the bed. The pictures aren't that good – squirrels and cats with hats on. The colour isn't always in the lines but they'll have to do. I write them nice and neat and in the one for Dad and Lucy I write – 'please come and get me if you can.' I seal it up because I don't want Dorothy and Gramps to see. I give them both to Gramps and think of something. 'How will they know where I am? I don't know the address here.'

'That's OK, dear. I'll write it real nice and clear on the back.'

Even with our new coats we can't keep warm enough. Gramps buys a stove you fill with petrol and heats the inside of the truck with it for an hour every night. Dorothy says he's going to kill us, but he says, 'What else d'you want me to do?' And the twins creep closer to it and say, 'Don't be taking this away, Pa.' They hold their fingers all nipped by the cold over it and make their eyes pleading and sad. Dorothy looks like she's given up. She starts doing her cooking on the stove.

South, we'll go south, Gramps says one day. He's been looking out at the rain all morning. Dorothy hugs him and starts looking better straight away.

'Yes, south.' She's nearly crying. 'I've heard there's true brethren there, righteous believers.'

'What about my letters?' I ask. 'They won't know where the new place is.'

'That's all right.' She starts laughing a bit through her crying like this is the last thing she needs to have to think about. 'I'll tell the lady at the post office here to send them on.'

I tell Gramps to do it too later because I don't think she'll bother.

One good thing – having my new red coat makes me feel like Carmel again. I wear it right up until bedtime. Dorothy says, 'Don't you want to take that off to eat dinner?' I shake my head. I want to be wrapped in red forever – it's the colour of Carmel. It doesn't look like the sort of colour Mercy would ever wear.

Though sometimes I do get mixed up with Carmel and Mercy, so I decide to steal Mercy's book because it's the one thing in the box of secrets I haven't opened yet. I don't even bother to play Detective Wakeford this time or wait until they're gone. They're only just outside when I kneel on the bed and poke my fingers in between the books and this time I find it easily. There's prickles going all over my head while I sneak off as far as I can to have a look at it on my own. I crouch behind a rock and look at her picture and touch her little face and the gold writing. Then I take the piece of newspaper and unfold it and I do a big gasp because there's a picture of her there, sitting down.

Behind her is Gramps. He's got his hand on the back of her chair.

It says: '*Church of the Truth Girl in Healing Ministry.*'

Mercy looks blurry and white in the picture. Gramps doesn't, he looks strong and clear. I read the words:

Truly blessed! One of our own children of the Church of Truth will soon be leaving us for foreign shores. Pastor Dennis who has been preaching at our little church these last three months has divined in Mercy Roberts extraordinary gifts of healing. He has agreed to develop these God-given gifts by taking her on and teaching her everything he knows of the power of the spirit in healing churches around the world. Our congregation has raised over seventeen hundred dollars toward the trip. We send our blessings with them both and hope whenever we see Mercy again, it will be as a fledged healer, come back to give help and succour to the afflicted of our community. Praise be!

I lie awake all night with the book in my hand and my heart booming in case they notice it's gone before I have a chance to put it back.

36

DAY 306

THE ONE THING THAT once I would have said could never
happen – happened. Me, Paul and Lucy became friends. More
than that, we became close. Paul's presence as a sexual being disappeared for me completely – the gap as vacant as the one left by
Carmel.

'You look thin,' Lucy said one night at the weekly meals that
had become our habit. The pink petal of her face floated in the
steam rising from her bowl of risotto.

'I'm all right.'

She stood and walked around the table and pushed the spoon
into the closed tunnel of my fist and patted my shoulder.

'There, eat,' she said. I did – for her. Each week was a blessed
touch of civilisation, she did everything properly: home cooking,
silver cutlery, napkins.

'Lovely food.' Paul smiled across the table at her.

She'd become a mother to us both. I wondered sometimes
how she could stand it, whether she'd stick around. I hated thinking of the nights I'd spent eviscerating her around the kitchen table with my friends, my mouth stitching bitter shapes as I talked.
The wall-to-wall cream carpets, I'd cackled. The sporty little car.
The hair straightened every morning, how mediocre. I'd cracked

her open and spilled her over the table, dabbing my fingers in the mess. I bet she'll have cosmetic surgery. I bet she wears those pads between periods that protect you from your own underwear. I bet she gets her home ideas from celebrity magazines. How would my Paul ever be satisfied with that – my volatile, romantic, outdoors-loving Paul? It wouldn't last.

Now, my fervent hope was that it would. Lucy was helping to save me, helping me to survive, and the generosity of her actions humbled me weekly.

The same time the following week my appetite was still dormant. Paul was late tonight and I was hoping he wouldn't bring anyone back with him like he'd done a few times before. I wanted Lucy and Paul to myself, my mummy and brother bear.

'Where's Paul?' I grumbled, cutting up asparagus into tiny slivers in the hope that would ease the transit to my stomach.

'He's started properly back at kayaking club – he must have stayed on for a drink. He'll be here soon. His food will keep.'

'Kayaking club? Oh no, that means he'll be bringing people back with him again. I hate it when he does that.'

The sound of Lucy's spoon rattling down on her plate startled me and I jumped. 'For God's sake, Beth. Honestly, you two may as well still be married.'

Her eyes were bright, sparky. I sensed mettle in her I hadn't seen before and how Paul would be attracted to it. I bowed my head. 'I've taken your generosity too far,' I said. 'I should stop coming here like this.'

'Stop it. No, of course not. It's not that. We want you here, but living with this is . . . he has to do things with his life. I know it sounds harsh –' She was swiping tears away with her napkin now.

'I'm sorry,' I said. 'Every day just seems like an act of survival and in the morning I have to get up and start all over again. It's made me selfish, hasn't it?'

She sighed. 'I wanted children, you know.'

I was sitting bolt upright now. 'You shouldn't let this stop you.'

'How can I? It would be like I was trying to replace her.'

There were raucous voices in the hall and I stood and started piling plates up. I went around the table and took her plate, repeating in an urgent whisper, before the others burst in, 'You mustn't let it stop you.'

Then there were three of them with Paul standing in their socks in the immaculate room, eyes slightly shiny from drink, and their antennae sensing atmosphere.

As I slipped away into the garden I heard, 'We're imposing, we won't stay. You're in the middle of dinner.' Then Paul's protests and them relenting, 'Go on, just a small one.'

Outside, I was licking the gummy flap down on my cigarette when I heard movement behind me. Childishly, I wanted to kick the leg of the bench I was sitting on. If it couldn't be just Paul and Lucy I wanted to be alone.

A tall figure came into view. I could see from the orange town lights it was Graham; I'd met him here before.

'Can I join you?' There weren't many who sought out my company these days but still I wished he'd go away.

'I guess.'

'I'm after one of your cigarettes actually.' He folded himself next to me. His beard jutting in profile resembled a carving in the half light.

'A sneaky smoker?' I handed him the tobacco.

'I'm afraid so.'

He began rolling so inexpertly I removed the makings of the ciggie from his hands and rolled him one myself. When it was lit we both sat smoking. I remembered the first time I'd met him he'd chatted to me, told me that he worked as an engineering lecturer in the local tech college, that he'd never married but had a daughter that he saw every other weekend. I didn't tell him anything about myself, even that I was Paul's ex-wife. How could I find the words for it all? But the next time we'd met he'd made me laugh and I'd become suddenly offhand. I didn't want men to make me laugh. I'd excused myself early, afterward realising there had been something in the humanity of his brown eyes that had overwhelmed me. I couldn't see them properly tonight in the weak orange light.

'I'm the mother of the missing girl,' I blurted out. That'll see him off, I thought.

'I know.'

When he turned up at my house two days later, I offered him tobacco again.

'I hate smoking actually; I haven't done it for twenty years. I wanted an excuse to talk to you. I was nearly sick afterward.'

He had a tall man's stoop even when sitting down. His beard, seen in proper light, was dark gold. I went to make tea and stood by the side window, looking out onto the gate, and I felt his presence behind me. The tremor that went through me was sudden, almost painful. I turned and started unbuttoning his shirt, quickly, before I had a chance to change my mind and the feeling that went through me was a warmth so intense I could almost feel the pain in my frozen bones as it splintered them.

Afterward, I wondered if I'd been trying to save my own skin again – if this was just another way of losing myself. Already my mind was reeling ahead, how I'd have to meet his family eventually, his daughter. The next thing would be eating at each other's homes, trips out. How one day he might talk about moving in and all the spaces that once held Carmel would get filled up.

'I'm sorry,' I said, sitting up, 'I think perhaps this can happen only once.'

'It's fine,' he told me. 'Don't explain.' And, relieved, I lay back down in the crook of his arm, smelling his skin, until we both slept a wonderful deep sleep.

37

DEAREST DAUGHTER,

The letter came this morning; Gramps has already opened it. Dad's written it on his computer.

I am not able to come and get you. Lucy and myself are due to wed. I'm so pleased that your grandfather and Dorothy have agreed to look after you. You could not be in better hands. Be a good girl for them . . .

There wasn't anything from Sara. I expect she'll have a new best friend now, probably Scarlet. I scrunch the letter up and go away from the camp without telling anyone. I climb a tree with no leaves and sit there on my own.

This place they call 'The South': it's the strangest place I've ever been. Clouds gather black and sudden when the sky's bright blue. Ropes of plants hang nearly to the ground from trees. Where we're camped is full of sand and dust. I can't understand why it's so hot here and it was cold before. That it was winter there and not here. I can't understand anything. At night it's so hot we don't sleep with any blankets. Sometimes on Sundays we go to churches where people sway and shout. Other times Gramps does his own church in the truck and gets us to kneel while he reads from the Bible. I think he likes it better that way.

Gramps says there's God all around us. Is that true? I thought I saw him once from the corner of my eye, but it was just Gramps's shadow on the ground. I look up into the sky and wish and wish God was there. I know I should think it's true. Am I naughty if I don't? I hold my hands up like I could stick my fingers straight into heaven and touch God's feet to check he's there.

I say to the sky, 'Who are you? Who are you? Show me that you're true. If something happens now, I'll believe, I promise.' There's a long time, but nothing happens. Insects squeak and I'm there under the hot blue sky waiting. In the sand down below *Carmel* is written in loops like a snake put it there.

Gramps says I'm an angel. Am I? Do angels sit in bare old trees like this? Mum used to call me that too, but she meant a different thing. When he says it, it scares me. I'm not, though. I'm not an angel. I'm a human being. My name is Carmel and I'm a human being. There's nothing else. God doesn't look down at you from the sky, checking you're all right. Dad doesn't either.

Dorothy comes to find me and walks right into the *C* and the *a*, messing it up. She doesn't even know she's standing on my name. She looks up to find me and I swing my patent shoe till it covers her face and pretend I'm stamping on it.

'There you are,' she says. 'We were worried about you. We thought you'd disappeared.'

Gramps is going to a healing. He's taking me.

'Do I have to go?' I ask. It'll be like before with the twig boy; I bet he's not even alive any more, that boy. He was so weak, I felt it when my hands were on his bony head. His life was a torch when the batteries are about to run out. But it's all arranged. Gramps is in his best white shirt and his black suit, and the Bible with glitteriest gold writing tucked under his arm. He blocks out the sun while he tells me I have to come.

Then we're holding hands and walking just the two of us. I can't choose. Choices, they all belong to Gramps and Dorothy.

They keep them in their pockets. The sky is blue, blue, blue and my feet make small marks on the dusty road next to Gramps's big ones. His prints look tangled because of his limp.

We come to a house. It's made of wood and trees are grown up around it and they flop their branches onto the roof like they've grown too much and they're tired now and need a rest. The grass on each side of the path is so high it's up to my head with insects that croak and buzz so loud my bones buzz with them. If I walked into the grass, even right at the edge, it would be solid with their bodies. They'd bite away at me so fast in five minutes I'd be a pile of white bones. Above us the trees make noises moving in the wind. Somewhere there's a stream. This place is full of noise. There's no cars, except a broken blue one rusting by the house, but it's louder here than standing in the middle of a road.

Gramps knocks at the door. His knocking makes a big peel of pink paint float down to the ground. There's no answer for a long time. Then a woman in an apron opens the door a little crack and stares with one eye pointing at us through the gap.

'What you want?'

Gramps coughs. 'It's Father Patron here. We've got an appointment.'

She opens the door wider and calls over her shoulder. 'Celia, preacher's here.'

Now there's more light on her I see she's black. Her apron has a top to it and there's a pattern of red and green apples all over.

I hear coughing inside the house. Then a big thick wind of illness blows through the open door and right over us. I get it in my nose, so strong it nearly makes me fall over. It's the smell of lamb's blood. Gramps can't smell anything, he's nodding and smiling at the woman. It scares me to look into the house where the smell is coming from, so I stay on the step. But Gramps is halfway in already. 'Come on, come in now,' he says.

I look back to where the biting insects are and force myself over the step into the house. I walk behind them and the dark in the hallway turns their heads into black shapes.

'. . . name of Mercy,' I hear Gramps say, his head bending down to talk to the woman in the apron. My throat goes tight and 'Carmel' sticks there this time.

We don't go upstairs but all the same we're in a bedroom now, at the back of the house. Against the back wall, in the bed, is a lump covered up by pink blankets. There's a chest of drawers with a wood cross hanging over it from a nail. The blinds are closed in here and the sun comes through them in stripes. One of the insects has got in and is sitting on the blind sunning itself. It feels like hardly anyone comes into this room. That the lump in the bed gets left on its own a lot. I think I'd rather be outside, even with the biting insects, and I go for the door. But Gramps is there first. He slams it shut and puts his hand on the back of my neck and pushes me into the room.

'Celie, they're here,' says the apple-apron lady.

The lump moves and groans.

'C'mon Celie. I don't be having all day.' The apple-apron lady sounds tired.

Then a big brown eye pops out from under the blankets.

Then a hand. The hand pulls down the covers and there's wild eyes.

'Oh Gramps, no,' I whisper.

'Shush, child,' he says back. 'She's afflicted.'

Gramps crosses the room, his black lace-up shoes clicking on the wooden boards. He uses my neck to take me with him. He sits on the wooden chair next to the bed, holding on to his Bible.

'Not today,' the lump mutters.

'Yes, today, dear. You have to take advantage, you know, when there's the holy spirit. You have to welcome it in and say, "Yes, today."'

He puts the Bible down on the bed and with his spare hand he reaches out and tries to move the blankets away but the lump grabs them tighter.

'If I let you go, Carmel, will you promise to stay where you are?'

'Yes,' I say. 'No.'

'Child don't want to be healing?' the apple-apron lady asks.

Gramps does his big flashy smile. 'Sure she does. Just gets overwhelmed by spirit is all.'

He decides it's safe to let go of me. I stay in the room but I step back from the lump's bed.

''Course *we* know it's a disease of spirit she has. But what does doctor say?' Gramps asks the lady.

She pinches her lips together. 'Multiple sclerosis.'

'She young for that.' Gramps has started talking like the apple-apron lady.

'Yeah, she young. Going to her mind now too.'

'That shows how deep the spiritual malaise has descended.'

The lady shakes her head and wipes her eyes on the apples. 'Poor Celie.'

'Do you think you could get her out of these blankets?'

The person in the bed shakes her head – I can see the top of it with hair jumping out thick and black. She pulls her blankets right to her face.

'Come on girl.' I wonder if the lady is her mum. It's hard to tell how old the lump is. Sometimes she looks like an old lady and sometimes like she could be my age. The lady puts her thin arms around Celie and tries to pull to make her sit up properly.

'Now then, Celie, maybe you could be helping me out a little.'

I feel: she's fed up of doing this. She's fed up of looking after this lump in the bed and she wants it all to be over. So she can go and sit on the broken swing on the porch and drink tea. So she can smoke a cigarette and watch the smoke dance away through the trees and not have to think anything except there's nothing to do or worry about any more.

I see it all and she looks at me sharp, like she's seen me see.

Somehow, she gets the person up and it's a big girl, not an old lady. Her lips are cracked up and when the blanket comes away her body's thin and bony and pointing in strange directions like it's trying to make itself into a puzzle. I remember Melody turning into a doll.

'This happens,' says the apron lady. '"Spasticity," the doctors term it.'

Celie's hand comes out again and I see it properly this time and her skin looks so ill at first I think she's wearing a wrinkly purple-black glove. The blankets are down now and Celie's got on a baby-blue nightie with frills everywhere. I can see how her body hurts her. In her big round eyes she's frightened like an animal is – not understanding anything. I feel bad, then, for thinking of her as just a lump in the bed.

Gramps opens his Bible but he puts his hand flat on the page and uses his own words: 'This is a call, a call on You, Lord, for healing this afflicted soul . . .'

He goes on and on till my ears fade him out and the insect buzzing at the window fills me up, louder than Gramps. So loud the room buzzes with it, then I am too, like me and the insect are the same thing, and I want to shake out my wings or rub the back of my neck with my legs.

Gramps is asking the spirit to enter the girl. He looks up at the ceiling at the dusty fan that's going around and around. For a second, I think it's funny, like he's talking to the fan and asking it for the spirit.

Gramps tells me to sit on the bed and it gives a creak and I can feel the buzzing going through that, too.

There's something in the room with us. It's soft and jellyish, you can't see it but it moves around us making sparkles in the air. I'm scared now, it's like ghosts are here with us. If I sit still, maybe they'll go away.

'Our hands will be the instruments . . .' Gramps is talking quietly.

He puts his hands on Celie's head, on her thick black hair, and my palms start itching.

'Do the same as I do, child.' He's giving me instructions like a teacher. 'Do exactly the same as I do.'

I kneel on the bed and do the same because I have the feeling real strong to try and help her. And it's not being a zombie this time. I really want to. I try to be gentle – it looks like her face and head get hurt easily. My hands go under his so I'm holding her ears and I can feel them curly in my hands. Everything hums and buzzes hard then, the insect shakes its wings in time. Me, the bed, Celie, the light – all hum with it. The ghosts fly through me. It feels like I'm going to get thrown off the bed so I hold on tight to her ears and close my eyes.

Then the lights. They seem to be in her body, ropes of them inside her, and as I reach toward them they jump up and get brighter. I make them flare like fireworks. The buzzing's calmed down now, not drilling in my head, but long and low, and it's making us stick like two magnets.

I don't know how long we're there.

All of a sudden I get unstuck from her. The room's gone quiet. The apple-apron lady opens up a window and I can hear birds singing from outside. My hands on Celie's head are wet. There's sweat over her face and head and her blue nightie's wet too.

I open my eyes properly and look into hers. They're clear brown marbles. She smiles at me and I don't feel afraid of her any more. She was a girl like me all along. I feel light and quick like I could fly up to the ceiling and talk to everyone from there.

'Take your hands away now, child,' says Gramps.

They've gone stiff but I move them anyway.

Celie blinks. She reaches over and lifts a glass of water from the table next to the bed and drinks it down in one go. We all watch her as she does this. She pushes the blankets off her bottom half so we can see her brown feet sticking up. She puts both hands on her head and smoothes down her hair. Then she lifts her legs up and swings them over so her feet are on the rug on the floor.

'Oh my Lord, I never see anything like it in all my born days. That child has cured her. Celie has been cured, so God is my witness,' shouts the lady in the apron. She falls down to the floor and kneels there in the middle of the room with both her hands together, holding them up. She rocks on her knees, saying, 'Praise be, praise be, praise be . . .' over and over again.

I have trouble walking back I'm so tired. Gramps stops off at a shop by the side of the road and buys Dorothy a bag of groceries and a new stove. It's got a bottle of gas that makes it work and he carries it on his shoulder like it doesn't weigh anything. His face is the most pleased I've ever seen it, he's smiling and looks super super strong and he's ignoring his limp so much he can walk almost properly.

Dorothy takes the groceries out of the orange net bag and groans with happiness. There's fruit, swollen up, green, purple, yellow. A bottle of something brown. A box of candy, double-decker, in pink cardboard. Dorothy's fingers squeeze the fruit and touch the blue shiny knobs on her new cooker with love.

Silver holds out the candy to me. Her lips are already shiny chocolate brown but I don't want any.

'You look real white, Carmel,' she says. 'You look like you're going to throw up. Are you going to throw up?'

I shake my head and then even though I'm sitting down on the steps my eyelids start to close and Mercy is behind them. Her head, stamp size, looking at me – twice over because she's behind each eyelid. Her face wants to tell me something, but she can't speak.

The next day Gramps's phone rings; he walks away from us to talk into it. After: 'The doctors have seen her and they are amazed,' he tells Dorothy.

Dorothy sits on the stripy camp chair. 'What did they say?'

'They say they can't believe it. Though men of science are generally unbelievers, that is well known. But they say the evidence is before their eyes.'

Dorothy's tapping her nose. 'So it's confirmed? There is a confirmation?'

He nods.

'Medical confirmation?'

'Yes, yes, I told you. They say they don't believe it was the child, that something else must be at play. But they can't explain what, they can't explain because they are faithless.'

Tap, tap, tap. 'This is all for the good, this confirmation. Forgive me, Dennis, but I couldn't be sure before, not truly in my heart. But we can make good now, it'll be easier now that we know for ourselves the truth of the matter. Carmel . . .' she calls out to me, 'you must be a very obedient girl for us from now on. No more waywardness. Think of our house, the one we could have, and three ponies, one for each of you.'

I don't know what she means so I keep quiet. I keep looking at my hands, though in amazement now I've felt what they can do. I sniff at them to see if they smell different and even lick my palm but there's just salt. It's the same as the time with Melody – there's still shocks in them. Before that, too, when I was little, except I didn't know what it was then.

Only it's not what Dorothy says about doctors and it's not Gramps that's shown me. It was Celie.

Some people come and throw stones at the truck.

'They think we're chancers, itinerants,' says Dorothy – same as she said before. 'You'll have to get us into a proper park.'

Then us children see a man taking photos of us. We decide not to tell, that it's our secret. We make up stories about him. I say he's a spy, Melody says he's the devil and Silver says he looks like a rat's ass. That makes us laugh so hard we roll around on the ground.

We cut ourselves with a knife sneaked from Dorothy and swear never to tell and drip our blood into each other.

'Now we're sisters,' says Melody.

I feel warm all over when she says that. 'Honest? What d'you say, Silver?'

'I guess.' She doesn't sound sure but she wipes the knife on her knickers and then holds my hand. We run back laughing and put the knife back.

But Dorothy says she knows about the man with the camera anyway – she's seen him too. Then the people with stones come again and us children are so scared we hide under the bunk beds. While I'm lying there squashed I have a daydream about Nico coming to rescue me. Later, we creep out and there's dents in the side of the truck where the stones landed. So Gramps drives us off to a park. He says it's better anyway because he's made a contact nearby.

38

ONE YEAR, 43 DAYS

ALICE HAD FADED from my life. When I saw her again I realised how long it had been. We'd often bumped into each other before; this was small-town life. Then it occurred to me she could have been avoiding me all this time – jumping up side alleys at the sight of me.

The farmers' market: the hall blowsy with sunshine, the smell of apple juice sharp in the air. And there she was, darting around, with a basket on her arm. Her busy little figure in a short purple cloak seemed to form and reform around the vast echoing room. Just the sort of silly thing she'd wear, I thought. But I didn't exactly feel the same fury on seeing her again. More an electrical memory of it, a shower of sparks as a live cable falls.

Then she was close, picking up essential oils, sniffing at the sample bottles. I went right up.

'Alice.'

She nearly dropped the blue bottle when she turned. 'Beth.' Her eyes started sliding, looking for escape.

Then it did hit me, a wave of rage. She saw it in my face and her mouth primped up like pastry and I saw a certain stubbornness there, a belief that she knew the truth, even if others wished to ignore it. 'I'm sorry, Beth, you didn't like what I said to you, I was just trying to tell you what happened. It's not only me that thought it, the people at the church did too. I have to go now . . .'

'What? What are you talking about? You'd better tell me – now.'

She sat across the table from me; an unlikely setting for this conversation: the teashop with its sprigged tablecloths, the whitewashed walls bowed with age. Careful polite chatter from other tables.

'I did try and explain to you before, Beth.' She twirled the herb teabag around her cup and plonked it on her saucer, leaving it there to leak green stuff.

'But I didn't know you'd actually taken her to church. Christ, Alice.'

We were keeping our voices down but people were starting to look.

'Yes, you did.' She sipped and made a face. 'I told you.'

She was right, I remembered now. It wasn't long after the split. I'd left the house for the weekend so Paul could return and pack the remainder of his things and spend some time with Carmel without an atmosphere. When I came back I was slightly irritated to find out that Alice had been there. It felt like she'd come as soon as she got wind that Paul was on his own. 'How are you coping?' she'd asked. 'Left all on your own, you poor thing, let me take Carmel out, give you some time.' Like he was incapable of looking after his own daughter, but he, busy and distracted, had said, 'Oh, all right.' Later Carmel told me Alice had taken her to church and I was annoyed at that too because we hadn't been asked. But Carmel smiled when she talked about going, and I thought, well, most experiences can be worthwhile, then it got forgotten in amongst everything else.

'All right, but I didn't know it wasn't a normal sort of service. Not the usual.' I was trying to even out my voice now, so as not to startle her. I needed to pick every fact clean.

'Yes, Beth, it was a healing service.'

'What happened?'

'Nothing, nothing happened. I just wanted her to be there, to witness what was going on. She went up the front to sit and I can still see her there, watching, with beautiful lilies behind her. Then afterward she said she'd felt a humming in her hands. I wanted to tell you before, you know. But you were so angry.' She shivered slightly.

How dare you, I thought, taking my daughter places without my permission, but I kept my voice soft. 'So who were you talking about earlier? You said "other people thought so too." Who did you mean, Alice?'

'Oh,' a smile broke on her face. 'He was a lovely man. He said Carmel looked full of light and we chatted about her . . .'

'Chatted?'

She was starting to relax, tell her story. 'Yes. Handsome, too, for an older man. You know, charismatic, that type. The most amazing blue eyes. I can't remember really what we talked about, Carmel, yes, and . . . I told him about the time I took my mother to Lourdes, he was really interested in that.' I realised then that she was attracted to anyone who was vaguely nice to her.

Something went off in my head. A watery light seemed to run down the walls for a moment. Then everything clear, bright like it had been painted; the flowers a box of jewels on the table.

'What else did you tell him? What did he want to know, Alice?'

She stopped, startled, and looked at me.

'Honestly, I really don't remember. It was nothing . . .' Her smile had started slipping over her face again. Her wrists arched to lift her cup in both hands and my eye caught on those bracelets. I can see them now. So unusual – leather, fastened with a popper and a saddle of plaited multicoloured silks – an identical one on each wrist, covering something up . . . My heart unexpectedly turned over for her, for us all, how could I never have fathomed it before? They'd just seemed part of the rest of her: the crystals and the dream-catchers; her talk of spirituality; conversing with the universe; kabbalah – at least my parents' religion had a heft to it, it never wavered.

Blood of Christ. I closed my eyes and a red wave of it engulfed me.

'Alice, am I a bad person?'

'Beth, I don't know . . . I don't know what you mean.'

'To have deserved this.'

I opened my eyes. She was pale and quiet now. 'You do realise,' I said, 'we're going to have to go to the police with this.'

Alice was interviewed along with the people who ran the church. Alice didn't know much beyond what he looked like; she'd done most of the talking.

They were a motley crew, Maria, the liaison officer, told me, that ran the church: old ladies with long floating scarves and bottles of holy water in their pockets. There'd been a lot of strangers there the day Carmel went, they said, but then there often were, their little church was so popular and quite well known 'on the circuit.' 'Yes, there was a man, that's right.' Oh, but they were sure he wouldn't have meant any harm, not in their church. He'd got there early. 'Mary, didn't you speak to him?' 'Yes, that's right. I think he was from away, not sure from where. He did tell me his name, but for the life of me, for the life of me . . . So long, dear. Memory not what it used to be, and after all no harm, not in our church, couldn't be. All good you see. That's what we deal in here, all good . . .'

I lay in bed pondering it all, remembering the light running like water down the walls when Alice told me. It's the movie of her life, I thought, that's the reason it knocked me sideways like that – unseen footage. Like the clown's face you imagined she might have seen that day at the circus, floating high up between the flaps of the tent. It's the film curled up in a canister that's never been played.

I saw us then, almost as in a vision, as if we'd never escaped the maze that day but were still stuck there. Me and her separated by walls of yew and only from above can it be seen how close we are.

'We'll pray,' the old ladies told Maria as she left, smiling their ingratiating false teeth smiles, willing her away so they could go back to their arranging of flowers, their moving on arthritic legs around the church to tidy the chairs back into neat rows. Back to their magic spells. 'We'll pray for the little girl, what was her name again?'

Carmel's map was yellowing now on her bedroom wall, the corners beginning to curl. There'd been no new additions for a long time. I drew a careful line from Alice's name then marked in *Church women*, the letters tall and skinny like I imagined the women to be.

Then another line which ended in a question mark.

39

GRAMPS IS EXCITED. There's a man wants to see me who he says is important.

'We'll meet the pastor in town. We'll dress up and you need to be the best behaved you've ever been,' says Gramps.

'Can we come?' asks Silver.

'No, just me and Carmel.'

'Oh, I see.' Silver's eyes go hard on me. She's still not as friendly as Melody, even if we did swear to be sisters. Today the sky is white and hot and Gramps takes me to a lovely hotel that looks like it's from Hollywood with white pillars either side of the door and trees in pots. Gramps holds my hand tight and his is shaking. Inside it's cool and the carpet looks like it's made of red velvet.

Gramps goes up to the desk. 'We're here to see Pastor Munroe.'

'Why yes, he's waiting for you.' The lady behind the desk is pretty and has tiny gold leaves hanging from her ears. 'Hello sweetie. What a little doll she is.'

She leans over the desk to smile at me and I get a whiff of her delicious perfume that smells of fruit and cakes and I stuff as much of it up my nose as possible I'm so greedy for it.

'Yes, yes. Thank you. We'll see the pastor now. Where is he?'

She points to her left. 'Through there, having coffee. Bye sweetie,' she calls after me as Gramps leads me off. I look over my shoulder and see her getting smaller and smaller as I walk away.

'Dennis.'

Gramps freezes. The voice has come from behind a plant. 'Munroe? Are you there?'

A man's head pops up above the plant.

'Dennis. Over here, come sit down and bring the child.' We go and sit with Munroe. His skin is very clean, even the pink flappy bit that goes from his chin to his white shirt collar. His teeth look too big for his head.

A lady dressed in black and white brings over a silver teapot. 'Can I get something for you, child?' she asks. She's got a lovely slow voice.

Gramps says, 'Milk, she'll have milk.'

They pour the tea, but guess what? It's not tea but coffee that comes pouring out – I can tell by the smell – and I've never seen coffee coming out of a pot before. All the time Munroe is looking at me and smiling.

'So, this is Mercy.'

I'm about to say, no, actually this is Carmel, but Gramps butts in really quickly and says, 'Yes that's right. Praise the Lord.' I press my nails into my palms until they hurt and stare at him hard, but he doesn't take any notice.

'Yes. Praise the Lord.' Munroe almost shouts it out and I find it quite embarrassing because people turn their heads to look.

They talk together, their heads close and their voices dipping down low. I sit looking at my milk and not drinking it, watching the surface turning thick and creamy. I'm remembering – there was a calendar behind the lady's head at the counter, one where the numbers fall down every day. Today, it said, was May 30. I start feeling sick.

'Gramps,' I say. I didn't even know I was going to say it, it was so sudden. 'Have I had my birthday?'

They look up and both their sets of eyes are shiny, like they've been drinking beer. 'Your birthday?' He looks confused.

'It happens in March and I can't remember it . . .' We had Christmas and went to a church. It was a horrible day missing Mum and all the Christmas things we used to do. 'My birthday always comes after Christmas.'

'Birthdays . . .' He bends his head down to Munroe again and they both chuckle old-men chuckles and shake their heads in a way that means: kids, eh? All they ever think about is presents and balloons and surprises.

A tiny fly – very black – circles around the glass and falls into the milk.

Their voices are low but once Gramps says in a louder voice, 'No, not television.' Munroe spreads out his hands to show him to calm down.

My hands and feet tingle with strangeness. Am I nine now? Have I gone and been nine and not known? Is that possible? I know the fly's struggling. It tries to swim across the glass, its legs keep poking up out of the white and look like nose hairs, but it's drowning under the milk. I think, I should rescue it, I really should, take the spoon from Gramps's coffee cup and spoon it out. But I don't. I start getting that guilty feeling but I just watch and watch and I can feel some sweat above my top lip growing. Munroe stops talking to Gramps and looks over at me. When he smiles his teeth look plastic. I wipe my top lip and water comes away on my fingers. I think of Munroe in the milk drowning with his arms and legs sticking out. I imagine they're swapped around and he's tiny and the fly is as big as him and sitting in the red velvet chair twitching its legs and sucking up coffee through its beak.

'What are you doing, child?' Gramps asks.

I've taken his silver spoon and I fish out the fly from the milk and dollop it onto the white saucer that my milk came on. It lies in a puddle twitching. It's trying to shake the milk off its body so it can be free again.

Munroe says, 'These things breed dirt and destruction.' And before I can stop him he reaches over and squishes the fly in his paper napkin and all that's left is black bits squished on the white.

Back in the truck. I'm on my bed and shoving my face hard into the crochet covers. The doors are open and Melody and Silver are playing outside even though it's starting to rain.

'Come out and play,' calls Silver.

I don't answer. I don't want to talk.

'What's the matter with her now?' I hear Dorothy's voice saying. She's farther away than the twins so her voice is thinner.

'It's 'cos she didn't get a present on her birthday.'

'It's not that. It's not, it's not.' I thought I'd never speak again but now I'm shouting.

'Oh Lord,' says Dorothy, like I've added one more thing to her problems.

But Silver won't stop. I wish she'd shut up, I really do.

'She's mad – she didn't get a cake with candles. Or people coming to a fancy big party bringing gifts tied up with pink ribbons.'

I'm guessing that's how Silver would like *her* party to be.

I hear Melody's voice. 'I'll make you a cake, Carmel. I'll get one of the patty tins and stir up some grass and we'll use twigs for candles . . .'

Melody's whispering voice is near. She's probably right by the door and staring in. But I'm lying down again and burying myself in and wishing and wishing I wasn't there. I don't care about the cake. I don't care about the presents. But how can you be nine and not know about it? How can that even be possible? Mum said nine was important because it was the last one before I went into double figures and come what may we'd do something really special.

'Leave me alone,' I shout into the bed cover. It goes hot and wet from my breath. 'I was nine and no one bothered to tell me. Leave me alone all of you. I want my mum.' The longing for her is hurting me it's so bad.

I hear Dorothy again. Her voice floating over on the wind. 'Leave her be, girls. Just leave her be and she'll get over it.'

Later, Dorothy walks us to the gas station to get an ice-cream cone. We all have green except for Dorothy who has white. We sit on benches by the gas station to eat them, Dorothy and the twins on one bench and me on the other.

She's got her arms around both of them and eats her ice cream with long slow licks. They lean against her, one either side, and sometimes she puts the underneath of her chin on top of their heads. I know when she does this she's liking the feeling of their sun-hot hair and how much she loves them. Melody twists her head and smiles up at her and Dorothy kisses her right above her eyes.

'For one, then always for the other,' she says, and makes sure she kisses Silver in the exact same spot. 'My beautiful peas,' she calls them.

Then she starts talking to them in Spanish – laughing and hugging them tight.

I suck most of my ice cream up in one go.

'Where are you going?' asks Dorothy, as I get up.

I toss the rest of the cone in the bin. 'To see if they've got a bathroom.'

The old man we bought the ice cream off watches me pass and his head looks like it's floating behind the window. The toilet's in a shed out the back with a string instead of a chain to flush. A fly's licking something off the wall. When I've flushed I close the toilet and sit on the seat and listen to the fly. Each time it moves to another bit of the wall it buzzes and it just seems real happy to be there – like it doesn't even know it's trapped in a dark cold box where people come and do their business. I feel for the pen I keep now in my pocket and spend ages scratching on the wall – *Carmel Was Here* – and I draw a little heart underneath and when I'm done the fly does a walk around the *C* and for some reason that makes me happy, like we're having a small celebration together.

Outside Melody's there and I wait while she goes.

'You been writing on the wall again, Carmel?' she says when she comes out drying her hands on a paper towel.

'Uh-huh.'

'Well, I hope Mom doesn't need to go 'cos you'll be getting it again.'

Dorothy went crazy when she found my name written in glitter glue on the truck number plate. I thought I'd done it too small for her to see but her eyes are sharp as anything. I flick a bug that's landed on my arm. 'I don't care.'

We sit on the concrete by the two old gas pumps. The blue paint of them is starting to flake away and I stick my thumbnail under a peel and scratch some more off, wondering why it always feels good to do that.

'I'm sorry Mom didn't remember your birthday.' Because it's starting to be evening she's got a jumper on over her dress that Dorothy knitted, but I don't know where Dorothy got that colour wool from. It's in between pink and orange and it's so bright it makes your teeth hurt as much as pushing them into ice cream, but Melody seems to like it; she wears it a lot.

'It doesn't matter,' I say. 'It's not your fault anyway.'

Behind the shop hut is a jungle of trees and there's monster red flowers on some of them.

'No, but it's not fair.'

'But . . .' I don't know how to say I don't mind any more. I look over to where Dorothy's still holding Silver on the bench.

'Your mom looks a bit like Jesus's mother, except she's got twin girls instead of a boy.'

I've just realised that Gramps talks about Jesus a whole lot and God of course but Jesus's mum never gets a mention.

'I guess. They've both got long hair.' She's quiet for a bit.

'Do you feel different knowing you're nine?'

'I think so.' I lift my nose up and smell the petrol hanging about: I like it – the smell is like spirit. Or like a lady's perfume, but dangerous. Here – with the blue paint, the red flowers and Melody's tooth-hurting jumper and the smell of gas and the floating head and knowing I'm nine – I've grown up, not slowly, like you usually do, but in a rush.

And I'm not even just nine; I'm nine and a bit – maybe even nearly up to a quarter. I press my hands flat on the hot blue metal of the gas pumps.

'Gramps says there's some mighty power in those hands,' says Melody, her face all serious.

My hands look bigger than I ever remember them. Nine-year-old hands. 'Yes. I can feel it now when I lay them – what they're doing.'

'What does it feel like?'

'Like shocks. I can make it happen.'

'D'you like it?' She's picking the paint off too now.

I shrug. 'It makes me dizzy.' I get a good peel of paint under my fingernail and pull off a whole strip.

I lean back and let the hot metal of the gas pump warm my back. Everywhere feels alive, even the air, and the feeling goes inside me and hurts but in a way that's nice. I know now that Dorothy loves her twins, but not me, even though I've been trying to make her, and I realise that, maybe, it's a relief because she's not my mum. And if she tried to be, and we loved each other, that would be only one life, with her – she would become my mom for ever and I'd have to be the way she wanted me to be. The way it is, I'm not her daughter – so I can have any life. It could go any way.

In the end we do have a party. Dorothy buys a cake with pink icing and puts nine pink candles on it. She gives me a present wrapped up in birthday paper; it's a white dress, with silver nylon lace around the neck, the front and the bottom, and some stickers of ladybirds and butterflies. I share those with the twins and we stick some on our faces. I put a butterfly in between my eyes.

'You can wear the dress today,' she says. 'Because being nine's so special Pastor Munroe is going to take you to his church. They're all expecting you.'

At least I got red shoes to go with it. When we went shoe buying I tucked my legs under the chair and wouldn't try anything else on. I thought, no more crappy patent leather for me because now I know I'm nine I can think like that. Dorothy just gave in. She probably remembered the coat.

Gramps says, 'It'll be a great day. Word is spreading.'

'All right,' I say. Going to Pastor Munroe's church doesn't sound like the sort of thing you do on your birthday. I like going to mazes and things. Mum said for my ninth birthday she might even take me on a ferry somewhere. *Don't think about that, Carmel.*

Dorothy says, 'Take those off your face. And look at your hair, child. We need to fix that. You look like you've got a bird's nest on your head.'

I put my hands up to feel the bird's nest. My hair's got all long again so the curls are more stretched out. She gets a brush and brushes it really hard. I still like it when she does things like this for me in spite of how mean she can be. She scrubs my face so the stickers come off.

My hair goes snap, crackle and pop from the brushing. 'Look,' I say to the twins, pointing at my head.

They both laugh a lot. 'It looks like you've had an electric shock,' says Silver, and I laugh too. She's got a ladybird on her face that looks like it's crawling up into her eye. She calls it a ladybug and I like that a lot. That's what I'm going to say from now on.

Dorothy doesn't think it's funny. She gets a spray out of the truck and sprays water over my head.

'Now stand still and get dry in the sun and don't run about. Or eat any more cake. Or put any more of those stickers on your face. I've never seen a child who can turn as messy as you in five minutes flat.'

I stand and the twins run around and around me and this makes me laugh again.

Pastor Munroe turns up in a big car with lots of silver bits on it that shine. He stands outside the truck and Dorothy gives him a slice of pink-and-white birthday cake. He stands there with the plate in his hand looking like he doesn't want it.

'And how's our miracle child today?' He's looking at me.

'I'm fine, thank you,' I say, very polite. I look down. I've got my birthday dress on and it comes nearly to my ankles. I've forgotten what it feels like to wear trousers.

Dorothy takes the plate off him – it's obvious he doesn't want it. He pats his tummy at the place where he's wearing a brown leather belt in the trousers of his white suit. 'Started the day with a big breakfast. No space left for cake.'

He's looking into our truck. 'How the heck d'you live in there, the five of you . . .' Then he stops, like he's said it without thinking.

I look at Gramps. I know he gets ashamed about things, about how we live, our clothes.

'It's fun,' I say quickly, and the three grown-ups turn around to look at me.

'Fun?' says Pastor Munroe.

'Yes. It's better than a house – you can go where you want.' I hate it when Gramps has to look ashamed. It's like when Dorothy goes on at him about the condo she wants.

That mortgages are easy now and they're giving them to anyone, even people like us.

'Well, yes.' Pastor Munroe rubs his hands together. 'Shall we get going then? Time to meet the faithful.'

Before we go we all pray there and then with our eyes closed and with people walking up and down the path next to us on the way to the toilet block. It's so hot I think we're going to melt but then we get into Pastor Munroe's car and it turns into a lovely cold fridge in about a second. I wave to Melody and Silver through the window, them and Dorothy aren't coming with us. I think, they're my very best friends now.

'Gramps,' I ask, 'what was Mum like when she was nine?'

He thinks for a while then doesn't turn around when he answers. I notice his best black suit has gone scraggy on the collar. 'She was like you, Carmel. Just like you. A little angel.'

I'm not, I think, so I bet she wasn't either. As we start driving I wonder if Nico is going to be at the church. I think that whenever we're going somewhere new, even though it was ages ago I met him.

Gramps and Pastor Munroe are talking in the front. 'I thought we could start with the blind beggar who was made to see,' says Pastor Munroe.

'Yes, and we could –'

Munroe interrupts. 'It's always good to get the feeling going. Maybe you should let me look after things this time.'

Gramps says OK and looks out of the window.

Thinking about Nico makes me go into the dream I have about him. I don't see what's outside the window because inside my head I'm arranging the house for me and Nico to live in together, just us. There's orange curtains like at home and a big comfy sofa where we can cuddle up and watch TV. I make me and Nico cook spaghetti for dinner.

I have to stop when the car pulls up outside a church. It's made of shining new stone and there's the smoothest greenest grass I've ever seen. Stuck into the grass are two bright white crosses, one on each side of the path.

'Here we are,' says Pastor Munroe. He drives around the back to where there's a car park.

'You have a truly beautiful church here, my friend.' Gramps is squeezing his neck around so he can look out the window. 'Very impressive.' Pastor Munroe makes a noise in his throat that means: 'I know.'

Even though there's a door at the back we walk around to the front. Gramps goes on one side of me and Pastor Munroe on the other.

'Ready?' Pastor Munroe asks. Gramps doesn't say anything but he must have nodded as Pastor Munroe opens up the church door. Inside, there's a red carpet up the middle. The seats are full of people and when the door gets opened they all turn around to stare at us. They stare for a moment then start shouting out. Some of them stand up.

I can tell from his voice Munroe is smiling. 'Welcome,' he says to us. This time he makes me and Gramps go first so he's last in.

40

ONE YEAR, 162 DAYS

IT WAS THE SEA that saved me.

I took to swimming – up and down the beach at Cromer, the same place I'd tried to drown. It was an act of defiance. Death, you won't have me. Not while there's a chance, not while there's hope. My body had grown weak and elastic from grief, from too many cigarettes and not eating or sleeping, or when I did in snatches. I needed to get strong again.

I ploughed up and down under the huge skies – moving, constantly changing, with big white clouds flying across them, or pinky-grey ones that burst into rain showers on my head while I was in the water.

Sometimes pure blue.

Pure blue, like the sky was on the morning I knew I had to change things; that I'd been steadily retreating into a world that I didn't recognise, and where I couldn't be reached.

My first day – the induction day for nurses' training. Too soon, everyone said. I responded by saying I was afraid I might already be too late. That maybe I'd fallen through some cellar door and I was trapped there and the only way I could think of getting out was by doing this. Actions: for other people.

All the same I nearly turned back that first day. I'd parked my car and I was walking toward the building – a one-storey sixties block. It'd been raining and the water shone on the tarmac, making doubles of the others turning up for *their* first day. They looked so – how can I say? Ordinary. Good ordinary. In the way I felt I'd never be again. They swung their bags, weighted with books, onto their shoulders and splashed across the wet ground and up the three steps to the entrance. I hung back. How could I possibly join them in all their glorious ordinariness? Suddenly this seemed a crazy enterprise.

I turned to go.

Then, as my vision was swinging away from the three steps, the people and back toward the car park, I changed my mind again. *Courage*, I told myself, *courage*. *Courage*, I made one foot go in front of the other. *Courage*, up the steps. I found the room number, *courage*, I opened the door.

Some people looked up and smiled and I smiled back.

I settled into a chair at the back and got out my notepad and pen and lined them up on the desk. This is the only way, I told myself. I have to do something. It's the only way to survive. If I can do something good then maybe it will go a tiny way to right the balance of what's happened. It was magical thinking, but it's what I figured – if I put some good into the world then that's what might bring her back, not incessant looking. It might tip some scales that exist in the natural order; it might tip them in our favour. I couldn't sit – day after day – in that big lonely house, with the floorboards sighing and asking where she was, the beech tree knocking at the wall to enquire if she was back yet. And someone like Graham, who I liked so much, being kept at arm's length.

Besides, there was something I hadn't told anyone about. The real reason I was sitting there. The reason I couldn't go back.

One day I woke up on the sofa. It was afternoon already and I was muzzy from whisky the night before. I flicked on the TV without getting up and I saw planes flying into towers. I saw it and sat up with a gasp and my only thought had been 'Thank God.' I think I even shouted it out loud, 'Thank God.' Because it seemed to me that for the first time something was happening that was equal to the rending of the universe that had happened to me.

Later, I went for a walk. I saw all that and I was pleased, I told myself. What kind of person would Carmel find if she returned now? Whisky-smelling, baying at tragedy like a half-starved dog. When I got back to the house, sloshing up the path in my muddy wellingtons, I realised something else too.

It had been the first time I'd been out of the house and not looking.

41

THE SMELL OF SICKNESS stops being like lamb's blood. I get used to it.

Carmel gets lost sometimes from being called Mercy so much in church. When that happens I get some paper and write 'My name is Carmel' a hundred times. I keep it in my pocket.

Not all the people look sick. I hear them say 'cancer' out of the sides of their mouths to Gramps. He's always next to me. I lay my hands on them and feel for the ropes of light and scrunch up my eyes tight so I can concentrate on making them flame up.

Sometimes I think about how my dad never believed in God and my mum wasn't sure. It makes me worry; everyone says you go to hell when you die if you don't.

Tonight, we're going to a hospital even though it's the middle of the night and dark. Gramps and Munroe take me to a door by the side. The light over the door isn't shining, more leaking pale green stuff onto Munroe's face as we wait. A man in a uniform that looks like blue pyjamas comes to meet us. The uniform is tight across his fat stomach.

'I'll check the coast is clear,' he says.

'Who is he?' I ask Gramps when he's gone.

Gramps smiles down. 'A nurse.'

The nurse comes back. 'OK, but we have to keep it real quiet.'

We follow the nurse down long shiny corridors. There's rooms on each side with people sleeping.

'Are we here for healing?' I whisper to Gramps. 'There's too many of them.'

'It's all right,' he says. 'Just one.'

We stop by a room and go in. Machines hum insect sounds, doing the breathing for the old man in the bed.

'Oh no. No. Not him, not this man,' I say under my breath.

The nurse stands by the door. 'We don't have long,' he says over his shoulder.

Gramps takes his Bible out from his big coat pocket and starts to read. Munroe smiles at me.

'I can't,' I say. They haven't heard me.

Then Gramps stops reading. 'OK, dear. Lay your hands.'

'I can't,' I say, louder.

'Why ever not, child? This is no time for shallying, we have to get this done quick.'

Above the bed is a dark shape, turning, flopping over – lazy but strong.

Munroe and Gramps can't see it. 'I don't like him. I think, I think . . . he did some bad things.'

'What are you saying, child?' Munroe's getting cross now. 'Mr Peters was a true believer, a good and faithful servant.'

My brain's working fast and this is what it's telling me – *they can't make you because they can't do what you do, Carmel. It's from your hands, not theirs* – and it's the very first time I've realised this. It comes to me like a big beam of light shining on something that was there all the time, I'd just never had a chance to see it before.

'I won't do it. I don't want to make him better.' They look at me in shock.

'Listen, girl.' Munroe's taking steps toward me and I look again at the black thing and my stomach turns over.

'No,' I say. 'I –' I try to think of the right word, 'I refuse.' I hold my breath; I've never refused before.

Munroe flips his jacket open and slides his hand in and it comes to me maybe there's a gun in there. I freeze solid to the spot, but all he does is say, 'Take charge of her, will you, Dennis?'

But Gramps doesn't get a chance to do anything because we hear a shout and there's a nurse with a little white hat pushing past the man at the door.

'What the hell . . . ?'

Munroe takes his hand out of his jacket and puts both hands up to calm her down. 'Now then. We just need to do what we can for our brethren. We . . .'

She doesn't give him a chance to finish. 'I've got specific instructions from the family – none of you people. Now get out. Get out and take your hocus-pocus and your hell and damnation with you. One minute more and I'm calling security.'

Her cheeks get two red spots on them and a piece of hair comes away from her hat and goes over her eye. 'And a child too. In the middle of the night. Does she even go to school? What's her name?'

'I'm Carmel,' I say, as quick as I can. 'My name's Carmel.' I always especially want ladies to know that.

'We're going,' says Gramps. 'Be it on your conscience you denied this man succour and the healing gift of the Lord.'

'I'll live with that.'

The lady nurse watches us leave from the top of the corridor, frowning and with her arms crossed. On the way out the rooms float past me, each one with its person sleeping inside, like a picture of a beehive I once saw in school. Gramps and Munroe's backs stretch up in front of me and I have the awful feeling I'm following the wrong way, that what I should really be doing is turning right around and back to the nurse. I think of how nice and calm it would be to have a hat and a white dress and be able to lay hands in a place like this with her and get to choose all the time, but Gramps turns around just at that second and says, 'Don't dawdle.'

We stop at a diner even though it's the middle of the night. I have a Coke to drink. They're both stirring their coffee and saying how terrible the lady nurse was. She reminded me of my mum – the same brown hair and getting cross if she thinks something bad is happening to someone – so I don't like them saying how the nurse is going to burn in hell.

'Goddam bitch,' says Munroe and the way he looks at me as he's saying it makes me think he's not just talking about the lady nurse.

Gramps's hot coffee spills over his fingers when Munroe uses that B word – one thing you can say about Gramps is that he never swears or curses and he doesn't like it when other people do. He climbs out from next to me to get some napkins from the counter and then it's just me and Munroe looking at each other over the sugar shaker.

'Since when did you get so uppity? You need to be kept on a tighter leash so you do as you're told. This healing's a gift that needs to be put through the proper channels, you can't just go about deciding who and what you'll see.'

'Not Mr Peters, that's for sure,' I say it under my breath but he's heard.

'The old man lets you speak to him like that?'

I just blink.

'Mercy, I said – he lets you speak to him like that?'

And the Coke I've drunk is there right in my throat and in the back of my mouth because when Pastor Munroe leaned forward his jacket puffed out and I really did see a gun inside.

Gramps is back and looking at our faces. 'What's up?'

Munroe leans back in his chair and I wonder if I imagined seeing that gun in his jacket, even though I've still got the picture of its golden teeth around the middle of it.

'Nothing, my friend.'

Gramps sits down and they start talking again but I can hardly even hear what they're saying because now the empty chair next to Munroe isn't empty any more. There's something, turning, lazy.

I suck on my straw and the Coke comes up, rolling toward me, loud as a train.

'Goddam bitch,' says Munroe again. He takes a sip of coffee

and wipes his mouth with the back of his hand and the sound of it is like his face is tearing open.

Gramps says, 'Now then, there's no need. No need . . .'

My eyes turn gummy. The shape is rising, rising above Munroe's head. It pumps out, bigger. It's in no hurry. Even though I can't see it, I know deep inside there's an eye somewhere and it's turning, looking up and down and sideways in a searchlight. It's from the hospital.

'They shouldn't let unbelievers set foot inside a hospital, Dennis. They should be cast out to work in the places where they belong – bars and casinos.'

'I have to go to the toilet.' My voice sounds as if it's in another room.

'Go ahead,' says Gramps next to me. He's leaning back on the red seats and wiping his face with a hanky.

My feet are heavy like there might be pieces of iron strapped to their underneaths. Halfway to the bathroom I get stuck. I don't know if I'm going backward or forward. It's another face – Mercy's – on the back of my head and she's walking opposite to me so we're stuck in glue.

I make my feet lift up one by one the way *I* want to go and it's so hard my face goes wet with sweat. At last: the bathroom and the door shushing behind us. The plastic behind the mirror, around the basin, is sparkling like a million diamonds are stuck inside. It's dark: except for a light above the mirror that shines on the face there. A pale small face. Eyes are round dead stones. Mouth – full of things to say but always quiet. Carmel's gone. I turn: just hair on the back of my head. Not there either. It's Mercy's face looking back at me in the mirror. In the room somewhere is the dark thing and the search eye is looking for us.

It wants me. It wants me like Gramps and Munroe do. They want the Carmel who is Mercy. They want us to be one girl.

'Sorry,' I say to the girl. 'But I need for Carmel to come *right back* this minute.'

I start talking and I say it real fierce. I have to say it before it all gets forgotten.

'This is what you must remember. *My name is Carmel Summer Wakeford. I used to live in Norfolk, England. My mum's name was Beth and my dad's name is Paul. He has a girlfriend called Lucy. I lived in a house with a tree by the side and a spider's web by the back door. My mum had a glass cat she kept by her bed. There was a picture up that said* THERE'S NO PLACE LIKE HOME. *The curtains downstairs were orange. My teacher's name was Mrs Buckfast. One time my dad took me sailing. My name is Carmel. My name is Carmel Summer Wakeford.*'

I stop and look around me.

I'm Carmel. I'm alone.

42

2 YEARS, 210 DAYS

MY NEW ANATOMY BOOKS had shiny, brightly coloured covers. I sat with Lucy on her sofa and scoured them for information about the baby swelling in her stomach. 'Look, look,' I said, 'there's the umbilical cord, see how it attaches.' She ran her fingers over the lines of the diagram in wonder.

'I don't want to know the sex,' she'd said before her scan. I didn't have to ask why. Secretly, I'd sighed with relief when their child was born a boy. Jack: a healthy squalling savage package of strong limbs and early-sprouting teeth. I searched his little face for clues; as if he might bring news from the primeval soup from which he came, that unseen land where babies spring from and little girls disappear into. But all I found was more mystery.

'She doesn't have any relatives close by,' Paul had said. 'Having you around will fill the gap.' It wasn't just kindness this time, the way they drew me in. That day, I rolled up in my clapped-out car with the emergency calendula cream in my glove box. Lucy had sounded desperate on the phone.

'Thank God,' she said, answering the door. 'He won't stop screaming.'

Jack was on the floor on a plastic changing mat and the room smelled faintly of sick.

'Take his nappy off and put some of this on,' I said. 'And let him kick with his skin exposed. That'll calm the rash down.'

She leaned over him and stripped off his babygro and plastic nappy and smeared the cream on the red angry rash.

'It's awful, isn't it?'

'Ah, just needs some fresh air.'

The room was unkempt, scattered with teething rings, a tower of clean baby clothes not yet sorted and a baby bath half full of cooling water, the surface slightly scummy from cream and talc. Lucy's hair was frayed at the ends now there wasn't time for fortnightly visits to the hairdresser and she was still in her dressing gown. It wouldn't bother Paul, this new Lucy – but I imagined it would bother *her*, who'd always been so smooth and tidy.

'Thanks for coming,' she said. 'This is so hard, he's teething badly too.'

'Any time. You know that.'

She slumped onto the sofa with a towel still tucked over her shoulder. 'Lorna was around last week. We used to be such mates but I don't seem to have much in common with them all now. Jack threw up down my back and she couldn't wait to leave. I feel much more comfortable with you.' She laughed. 'It's strange, isn't it?'

'Baby sick is nothing now compared to what I see in my job.' Jack had quietened and was kicking his legs, the rash already turning from red to pink.

'I bet.' She paused. 'Graham was asking after you again.'

'Oh yeah?' I looked out of the window. I hadn't told them of my one night with him and was sure he wouldn't either. Maybe for me, I was ashamed – I didn't want them to think I'd treated their friend badly.

Jack started to cry again. 'He needs taking out,' I said, 'a dose of air will sort him out.'

'Probably.' She was quiet for a minute. 'Would you have time to do it? I'd kill to get my head down for half an hour.' Instantly I was on my feet and the room was tipping around me, threatening to slide Jack from his mat. 'I don't think so, Lucy.'

'OK, OK. That's fine, it was just a thought – you probably have things to do.'

'No, it's not that. It's . . .' I fumbled around for words, my hands hanging uselessly by my sides. What I wanted to scream was: *I lose children, don't I?* Instead, I pressed my lips together and stood mute.

'Beth, it's fine, either way.' She'd guessed. 'If you like we could take him out together.'

'You'd trust me, you really would?' I burst out.

'Yes, of course. Gladly.' I saw the gesture she was making – *it wasn't your fault, Beth* – and I wanted more than anything not to fail.

I took a deep breath to ease the fluttering in my stomach. 'I'll do it.'

Lucy wrapped him up in a quilted jacket and hat and pulled and adjusted the knobs and levers on the impossibly expensive bucket-shaped pushchair.

'You sure you're OK?'

'Yes, yes. You get your head down. Look,' I gripped the handles of the pushchair, 'we're great. Aren't we, Jack?'

Then I found myself outside with the front door clicking shut and me and Jack contemplating each other in the cold grey light. It had been raining and the ground was still wet.

Outside, he stopped crying, like I knew he would. Once in the fresh air he forgot his niggling pains and gripes and calmly watched the world go by his pushchair, the wheels making two lines on the wet pavement. I spoke to myself in my head, saying reassuring things – 'There we go now, nice and easy. We're just out for a walk to help your mummy. She's tired.' All the time trying to drown out that other voice, the one that was saying: 'You've lost one, you could lose another. You have to blink – it could happen in that moment.'

Two, three streets away, all the newbuilds started to look the same. I thought of making my way back. 'Stop it, you've only been gone five minutes,' I scolded myself. Jack liberated a hand from his blankets and waved to me. His mitt had dropped off and was dangling from his sleeve by a thread. Up ahead I spotted the bright blue railings of the park Lucy had mentioned.

I'd never been there before – it was brand new, chunky play equipment in Lego colours. As I wheeled him in I tutted at the dog shit bagged up and hanging from the railings: 'Why do people do that, Jack? Naughty, isn't it?' I was muttering anything, to keep calm.

The playground was deserted and I wheeled him over to the slide, wiped the rain off it with my scarf, and sat on the end. Jack waved madly and grappled with his straps like a prisoner. Dare I? I stood and did a 360-degree turn. We were alone. My fingers shook slightly as I unclicked the buckles, lifted him from the pushchair and cradled him in my hands on my lap.

'Hello, Jack.' I smiled down at him and he gurgled and reached for my hair, delighted at last to be free.

I tried to discern Lucy and Paul in his blue eyes, his strong little nose but could see neither.

'You're yourself, aren't you?'

How strange, I thought. This new little boy who is almost part of me through Paul; he doesn't know Carmel. There's no mark of all this on him. As he grows up her name will be that of a girl from a fairy tale. He'll grow up and the world moves on, and on and on. I glimpsed something, the future moving in a blur ahead.

'Perhaps I should call Graham,' I said. 'What do you think?' He seemed to point at me and I laughed. 'No, I don't think so either.'

'You two look happy,' said Lucy as we returned. She'd got dressed and put her hair up in a ponytail.

'Yes, yes – we are. I'll do it again soon,' I said, 'if you like. Give you a break.'

Climbing into my car to leave I had a kind of singing energy that was almost a discomfort. The feel of Jack in my hands had unscrambled something in my heart, tugging at its dense knot, and a strand had come loose.

43

GRAMPS SAYS: 'Idaho is the last place in this land you can be free. No government interference here.'

Government interference doesn't sound a good thing when he says it. That's why we've come here. I know it's also because he wants to get away from Pastor Munroe – that he was turning into Gramps's boss too much. I know because Gramps told me, 'He'll have you for his own if we're not careful.'

I asked him, 'Why d'you say that when you're my grandad?' But Gramps just covered his eyes up with his hands like he was really worried it could happen.

We don't need him anyway now because there's plenty of money. The dollars spill out of the cut-out Bible. We can't even close the cover. Dorothy tucks away the spare ones underneath her pillow, then pats the top of the pillow, like she's putting babies to bed.

I look over the fields and all the plants there look like they're waving to me and Melody sitting on the steps. What with the sunshine and everyone being in such a good mood I realise I'm happy. At first I don't recognise the feeling, it's been so long. I feel guilty again for a moment, about being happy when Mum's dead, but I know she liked me being happy and when I think that I feel peaceful again.

Ahead I see the old farmer; we're parked in his field. He's walking over to Dorothy and there's an orange pot under his arm with a lid.

'Bite of supper for you and your family.'

He peeks over at me and I think he looks scared.

Dorothy asks, 'How is she?'

Last night I laid hands on his wife. Her skin felt as dry as an old bit of paper. Their house smelt strange but when I said this to Silver after, she giggled and said, 'Pig feed.' I didn't know what she meant till I saw the pig in the garden this morning.

'She's brighter today. Asked for breakfast. I swear, I haven't seen her eat an egg for I don't know how long.'

He looks over again and ducks his head down so he doesn't have to see me. I feel creepy all of a sudden. The feeling doesn't go until he's gone back to his farmhouse.

'Melody, if I tell you something will you swear to keep it secret?'

Her eyes have gone big but she nods.

'When I'm grown up I'm not going to do this for Munroe and Gramps any more.'

'Why?'

'I'm going to do it somewhere proper – where there's no praying and singing – somewhere like a hospital.'

'Do Pa and Pastor Munroe know?'

'No. You're the only person. Promise not to tell?'

'I won't ever. But you have to be careful, I don't think they'll like that.'

Dorothy comes over with the orange pot under her arm. 'Looks like you're getting to be the star of the show.' She says it like it's not a nice thing. Like I'm showing off on purpose. When I don't answer she heaves the pot farther up in her arms.

'Well, no time for chat. Let's see what the old man's gone and provided and whether we want to pass it through our lips.'

There are bright spots on her cheeks and she seems to be in a hurry for something, though we're not going anywhere. In the morning I find out what.

•

I know, as soon as I wake up – Dorothy's gone.

It's too quiet. I'm remembering things happening in the night too. There was creeping about and whispered voices. I sit bolt upright in bed gasping, the truck feels so weird. The bunk beds are empty. Most of their things are missing. 'Gramps?' I call out. Maybe he's gone too? Maybe I'm on my own.

I tiptoe over and stand outside his curtain, seeing if I can hear anything. I do – I can hear breathing.

'Gramps,' I call a bit louder. 'Is it you?'

There's no answer so I crawl under the curtain. Gramps is just one big lump in the bed – on his own.

'Gramps, wake up. Something's happened.'

He's got a tracksuit on in bed and he looks different when he's just waking up. His face is pinker and it's funny seeing him not wearing glasses. I realise I've never seen him in bed before even though he's so close behind the curtain.

'What is it? What is it?' He reaches up to the shelf and feels about for his specs.

'Dorothy and the twins. I think they've gone.' I feel like I'm going to cry.

He sits up and puts his glasses on. He looks more normal then.

'Perhaps they've gone for a walk, or to get something.' He gets out of bed, swinging his feet onto the floor so they're resting on the bunch of roses on the rug. His toenails look a bit old and crusty. It feels funny being so close together with him – I can even smell his sleep. He comes out of the curtain just in his sleep tracksuit and he's never done that before.

'Look, lots of their things have gone.' I'm opening their closet and there's only a couple of their really old dresses. I start sniffling. Even if she was mean sometimes and I'd decided she'd never be like my mom, I didn't want Dorothy to go – and specially not Melody. I don't want to be on my own with Gramps.

His face goes tight and I see his forehead pressing out under his white hair that's messy because he hasn't combed it yet.

'In the night like a thief . . .' he says quietly.

'Maybe she'll come back?' I say, and I wipe my nose on my nightie sleeve.

He goes behind the curtain and comes back with the money Bible. When he opens it up it's as empty as a coconut and he stands there staring at it for a while. We look around to see what else has gone and call out to each other.

'The new saucepans.'

'The good pillowcases and the backpacks.'

'My watch,' his forehead looks like it's going to explode this time, 'and my notebook.'

'Why would she take that?' I wanted to read that notebook again.

He goes behind the curtain and I hear 'evidence' – though I don't know if I heard right. He gets dressed and I do the same on my side. Then he tells me to get in next to him, in the front of the truck where Dorothy normally sits, and we drive around for a long time looking for her. We go to a coach station and walk around and there's people waiting with cases and backpacks and coaches coming in and out but no Dorothy. No girls.

'Perhaps she's gone back to Mexico, she liked it there being warm all the time,' I say. We're back in the truck now. It feels funny being in her place in the front. It feels like everything really has changed.

'They must have been carrying a lot,' I add. I can imagine them, walking down the dusty road with saucepans tied to their backpacks.

'She's probably got husbands, being fattened up in the sun, for the twins,' Gramps says. His mouth has gone into a thin line. I can't see his eyes, the white of the sky is on his glasses.

I gasp. 'They're only eleven. Eleven is too . . .'

'They marry them off early there. Goddam Mexico. They're heathens, barbarians.' I've never heard him say 'goddam' before. I think of Dorothy's skulls and wonder if that's what he means. If he knew about them all along.

Gramps is still talking: 'Heathens. Those girls will be married off by the time they're twelve. That was her plan, that was the plan right from the start. Lying thief.'

I look out of the window. Poor Melody, poor Silver. Being married to a man when you're only twelve. I think about them on their wedding day, in identical white dresses with great sticking-out skirts. They'd be marrying hairy grownups – maybe Dorothy would even find twin men for them to marry, so they'd match. They wouldn't really love them even, they wouldn't feel the way I do about Nico. They'd be shuddering inside those dresses.

And it's silly but the very worst thing that I can't stop thinking about is: Melody won't be able to have her writing lessons now. She was starting to get good at it too. She liked it more than anything.

When we get back to the campsite and Gramps has gone to get water I look around at all the gaps they've left and remember those flittering butterflies in Dorothy's eyes – the thoughts she kept from Gramps. I sit on my bed and it feels so quiet and lonely without them I don't know if I can bear it. I get my pillow so I've got something to hold on to.

That's when I see it. The book with Mercy in it that's a passport. It was hidden under my pillow and I know, I know it must have been Melody who slid it under there before she left.

She wanted to leave me with someone. For me not to be all on my own without another child. I open it up and Mercy's white little face looks back. I slip it inside my pocket and decide to keep it for ever. She can be my sister now, that's what Melody meant.

44

TWO YEARS, 301 DAYS

FIFTEEN YEARS SINCE I'D BEEN to my parents' house.

The path tiles shining black and white from the rain ten minutes before and not touched by my feet since I was a teenager. West Hampstead. A villa.

The hallway just the same. The same greenish submerged light, the small cross-legged gilt table under the mirror, the fat white lips of the silk orchid pursing down at the avocado-green telephone below. The phone I'd used to make my calls to Paul, tucking my hair behind my ear and smiling down the little black holes of the receiver and turning my back on the closed sitting-room door where I knew my mother's ear would be cocked inside. I'd met him on a backpacking trip with girlfriends – '*Oh, I knew we shouldn't have let you go, I knew.*' It was university in Edinburgh or to the east coast to him, and in a passion it was him I flew to. Somehow it seemed it had to be one or the other and secretly I worried *his* passion wouldn't survive me being in a cold Scottish town for four years.

The same smell lingering around the bottom of the stairs, never identified then, never even really registered, but now, after the years of not smelling it, so clear in its constituent parts – tinned fruit and spray polish.

In the living room I sat with my mother on the spotless grey velvet suite with the green fringing on the cushions. We both perched near the edge. Her eyes, blue, sweeping up and down on me as if she couldn't quite believe it, that I was finally back here after so many years gone. Her eye colour so similar to my father's that sometimes growing up, indecently, they'd seemed to me more like brother and sister rather than husband and wife. But the same blue colour as mine, after all. Packing cases were stacked up against the wall. They were selling up, splitting the money and buying a flat in London and a tiny cottage in Norfolk. I was so grateful for the support they'd shown me and had come to help.

'How's the packing going?' I asked.

'Oh, fine. You know how things gather over the years. So strange to get them out and look at them.'

Silence again. Being down in Norfolk was different; we'd come to be easy with each other down there. But me coming back to the family home after such an absence seemed to have ignited some half-buried spark. I sensed she felt embarrassed over what had happened; that families like ours didn't have unseemly feuds. But of course they did – and missing daughters too. It can happen to anyone.

I noticed the drinks trolley and as a diversion said, 'What about a drink? Let's toast the move.'

The drinks trolley had only ever got stirred on its castors for visitors, the shining array of bottles and glasses shivering over the olive-coloured carpet at them. She hesitated and I said, 'I'm not an alcoholic, you know, I only meant it might cheer us up.' And I closed the lid on evenings spent in a whisky haze – even days sometimes – because they were past.

'Oh, why not?'

She went to fetch ice and gave the trolley a nudge toward me, persuading its wheels out of the nests they'd made for themselves in the carpet. Behind it, pushing, she gave a little wiggle to her hips in parody of a hostess, and it was just to make me laugh. And

I did, I laughed. 'You have a great figure still,' I said, because it had struck me that minute – her neat hips in tasteful grey wool trousers.

'Thank you,' she said, flushing slightly and her hand fluttering for a moment at her collarbone.

Then there was fizzing and caps being unscrewed and glasses tinkling and it seemed funny somehow, like she was conducting a chemistry experiment, so I laughed again. We sipped and breathed in juniper fumes, then glass in hand I started wandering the living room, exclaiming over the familiar, and – when did that crack in the huge Chinese plant pot happen? And the Persian rug with golds and salmon pinks; that was new – the boring London light falling over everything.

I moved to the packing cases, not yet crated up, and ran my fingers over cookery books, slightly silty from being in the kitchen; figurines – faces pressing against bubble wrap; the brass branch of a light fitting sticking out like an antler; and the thick fabric of a photo album. Afterward, it felt as if my fingers had been searching it out all the time, feeling their way toward it. The brush of it against my skin, and flipping open the cover and the photograph of Carmel: black and white, pearlescent, close up.

I'd never seen this photograph before. Carmel's eyes, soft and luminous in some studio light. She looked about eleven, twelve – so older than . . .

My mother appeared at the doorway and I realised she'd gone to fetch more ice but one look at my stricken face and she was by my side, cubes melting in her hands.

'Beth, darling, that's my mother. Don't you remember me telling you how alike they looked?'

I shook my head.

'Darling, you've had a shock. Go and sit down.' I took the album with me.

She made another drink – without the flourishes this time – and put the wet glass in my hand.

'I always thought, I thought she looked like her dad.' The

black-and-white face looked up at me from the sofa, not smiling, not severe, not even serene. I couldn't describe what.

'Superficially, at least.' The little turn of her lip when talking about Paul had never quite gone. 'But as soon as I saw the pictures in the paper, I couldn't believe it.'

'Tell me about her, about your mother.' I wanted to know, urgently.

'Oh, I don't know what to tell.'

'Anything, you hardly ever mentioned her when I was growing up.' It had only just really occurred to me.

'No. I suppose I didn't.'

'Well, why? Come on, I'm burning to know about her now – now I can see the resemblance.'

'Oh, she was . . . she . . .' I could see the shadows on her face, from the tunnel of memory she was entering. 'She was . . . I can always remember, walking behind her, and the hairpins dropping from her hair and clattering on the ground. See,' she smiled into the ice in her glass, 'she was always different from the other mums.'

'In what way different?'

'Hectic, I don't know, in her mind. She'd put on her beautiful purple coat, but not fix the collar on properly so it dangled by a button. She'd make cakes and forget to put the eggs in. Silly things, I suppose. But I was embarrassed by her – there, that's the truth of it. I never liked talking about her because she was an embarrassment and that made me feel guilty because after all she was my mum so it was easier just to forget about it. I wanted her to be ordinary, you see.'

'And she wasn't?'

'No. It got worse, as we grew up. Dad was in the navy so she carried on as she pleased. She'd got it into her head, well, she'd fallen in with these people. Some sort of spiritualists I think. We were carted about from pillar to post. People's houses, some so poor and terrible you wouldn't believe it. The war was long over but, you must remember, people were still living in filthy conditions and disease was rife in some parts of London. She had some sort of fantasy that she could help somehow. It was all in her mind of course. She'd go into bedrooms and the door would be shut and we'd be sitting there – me and my brother – staring at some dishevelled husband and trying not to breathe in the smell. Then after a while I refused, and she made me wait outside in the car, with the doors locked.' She gulped at her drink. 'Then when I was older and your dad came along and I saw he did things the way I liked them – shipshape, you know . . . What a relief.'

'What happened to her?'

'She died, quite young. In pain – some kind of female cancer. I never quite found out what because people minced about things like that then. And her "friends,"' she snorted, 'nowhere to be seen that I knew of. Not that there was anything they could do, of course, where medical science had failed.'

We sat for a little, mulling the ice around our glasses, and I excused myself. I wanted to be with this knowledge, to put it in some kind of order, and make sense of it alone in the coolness of the bathroom. But along the corridor I got distracted, by the slightly open door, the orange flush to the light inside.

I pushed the door to my old bedroom and my heart turned over for the second time that day because not one thing had changed. The diaphanous sari I'd hung at the window still cast its tropical light, the photos of my girlfriends in a collage above the chest of drawers, all smiling, posing for the camera. The great gold canister of Elnett hairspray and my brush for backcombing. The jumble of junk-shop beads and cheap necklaces in a basket on the bedside table. I sank onto the bed, onto another sari – pink and gold, I'd been forever trying to sneak a bit of colour into that house – and tried to think. First Alice, now this. But however much I tried to stack my thoughts up they'd rattle down like pieces of a game collapsing.

I took a CD from the stack by the bed, the Pet Shop Boys, and brushed the plastic cover with my thumbs and I thought – it's clean, perfectly clean. She must come in here and dust. Do we ever give up? I looked around the room, so preserved and spotless, and had the idea –

Maybe it's not just me, perhaps many women keep shrines for their daughters.

45

WHEN I START MY FIRST PERIOD I know what it is because I remember Mum telling me about them, that it's something that happens to every girl sooner or later.

I don't know if thirteen's the right age – I can't remember that bit. For the first time in ages I miss Dorothy. She'd take charge and tell me what I had to do. All I've got is Gramps and you wouldn't even want to mention things like periods to him.

I stick a wodge of toilet paper down my panties.

'Can we stop here?'

Gramps peers through the window at the one-horse town – basically a street with stores.

'Why?'

'I need to get some stuff, OK?'

The toilet paper makes me waddle like a duck as I walk into the store. The lady behind the counter wears a check pink coat over her normal clothes.

'I'm looking for some advice,' I say. 'On how to go about things when you have your first period.'

'Oh, my dear. Don't you have a mother to help? Don't you have a lady relative?'

I grab some gum off a display stand and toss it on the counter. 'Nope. I'll have that too, thanks.'

She looks sad for me, then it's boxes and tight-packed plastic bags on the counter.

'It's best if you start off with pads,' she says. 'For comfort.'

When I get back into the truck Gramps asks, 'What have you bought?' She's put the pads in a big candy-striped paper bag so people won't see what I'm carrying.

Stuff like this is difficult to talk about with Gramps. I have to think very hard about what to say. 'Things for women,' I say finally.

He looks amazed. 'But you're not old enough.'

I don't answer and he drives off looking like he's had a shock.

I think about the lady in the shop and how nice she was. How sad she looked when she found out I didn't have a mother to help. She shouldn't have minded though.

I've gotten used to looking after myself.

We drive till we're somewhere outside a city. I try to remember which one Gramps told me it was but I don't want to ask him again. He gets lots of pain these days, in his bad leg and in his hands too. When he wakes up they're folded, like they've turned into wings in the night. It takes two hours for them to unfold properly but even then they hurt. Sometimes, we try to lay hands on him. I close my eyes and wait for the hum to go through me but it never does, not with Gramps. He doesn't get angry now though, like he did that first time at the tree. He just seems sad that I can't help him like I do with other people.

When we've gone past the city, with all its smoke rising up into the air, Gramps asks me to drive. I do this sometimes. He taught me because now and then his hands hurt too much to hold the wheel. We only do it when there's not many people around to see. I asked when I could have a driving test but the answer was never. Never: because I'd come into the country as some kind of illegal alien. And that means we have to be careful, or I'll be deported. So it'll be real hard for me to ever get a job or anything like that.

Through the window the countryside looks dirty, like it's been coated in black stuff. There's machinery in the fields that Gramps says are mine workings.

'Let's stop,' I say. 'I'm hungry, let's get something to eat.'

We stop and change places then we drive into a diner. I know it, I recognise where we are now, it's a diner we generally go to if we come this way. Me and Gramps aren't so good with the supplies and the cooking as Dorothy was, so we eat lots of pizzas and chicken wings and stuff like that. I take my wash things in with me.

'Order me a Margarita, Gramps. I'm using the bathroom.'

I fill the washbasin with lovely hot water and take off my jacket and hang it up on the towel rail. My jacket now is like a soldier's. It's got bright golden buttons and flaps on the shoulders. I found it in a thrift store. I've stuck to wearing red all through. It reminds me I'm Carmel and I like to wear red. I always make Gramps call me that when we're not working. I take off my T-shirt and soap myself standing in my jeans and vest. I dunk my whole head into the basin and scrub at my hair. Then I dry myself off under the hot blower.

Two women with thick make-up all perfect stare at me while they're washing their hands, but I can't worry about that. I have to keep clean. Now I've got my periods it's even harder to keep that way, especially as I have to hide it from Gramps. The women staring don't know anyway – they don't know what it's like to be me. They go back to proper bathrooms every day of their lives I expect. They splash about in hot water like dolphins.

I make hard eyes at them and they stop staring and look down at their hands with their coloured nails flashing under the running water.

In the diner I have to help Gramps with his sachet of ketchup because of his hands. He sits and looks out of the window. He's been real quiet lately.

'What you looking at, Gramps?' I'm oozing ketchup onto my own fries now. I like it so much I use three whole sachets just to myself.

'Only watching the comings and goings.' I look outside and there's cars and trucks pulling up or leaving as people finish eating and others arrive. There's pizza in his hand that's been there for about ten minutes.

'You better eat up, your pizza will be stone cold,' I warn. But he grunts and looks at it in his hand like he's forgotten it was even there.

'What are we going to do now?' I ask. I worry about things a lot. We make money often when I use my hands but usually Gramps gets anxious then. Whenever we settle in one place he says we're getting too well known, that someone will try and take me off him. When it starts being like that we climb back into the truck and drive and that means we have to start again from the beginning. It means we get right down to the last dollar in the Bible.

Gramps clears his throat. 'There's a gathering of the faithful I've been informed about.'

'Oh yes?'

'I got in touch with Munroe, he's organising it.'

'But I thought you didn't want anything to do with him?'

'Beggars cannot be choosers.' I think about this. I guess we are a bit like beggars. 'We should go, it would be a chance for us to shine.'

'I don't like the sound of it.'

'You should really not be so independent. You should listen to me.'

'No. I don't like big crowds, you know that. They freak me out.' We're scratchy with each other today. It's like we can't help it.

He pays and goes out to put some gas in the truck so I put our plates and stuff on a tray with the empty sachets and take it up to the counter for something to do. There's a man there coming on shift and putting his apron on.

'Hey,' he says, 'I've got something for you.' He reaches behind him, to the shelf where there's paper models of chickens and spare salt pots, and he brings down a letter. 'I knew you'd come around this way sooner or later. I remember you.'

The letter is addressed: *Carmel Mercy Patron. (The girl who wears a red coat – always with an old preacher man) Stu's Diner. Nr Pittsburgh. USA.*

I want to tear it open straight away but Gramps is outside, telling me with his hands to come on, hurry up, so I stuff it in my pocket so he won't know.

46

FIVE YEARS, 105 DAYS

AT NIGHT, ON THE WARD, people became lumps under thin hospital blankets.

Night in the hospital was another world. A netherworld: the dim lights, burning through the night; the squeak of doctors' shoes on disinfected floors; the tense crisis of health where staff and patients diced with death; the coughing heard down the corridor; the stirrings in the sleep; the sudden bursts of giggling by the nurses' station.

I preferred the nights. I felt better in an environment that said: normality is eggshell thin. Peer around the corner of it and there is this – just out of view.

All my searching had not found Carmel, instead it had brought me here; and I'd gained a reputation for being capable, calm, professional. When I thought of her now it was as a glittering needle: this great wide world and she one tiny point in it.

Twice I thought I'd seen her in the hospital out of the corner of my eye.

Once, standing by the bed of a gravely sick child. Her head was bent down and was sombrely looking into his face, her fingers in the pockets of her red coat. The other time, down the end of a corridor, holding her hand up in a kind of greeting, or farewell.

But most times she was the absent sort of ghost: a cut-out hole in the air.

At first I thought my studies could answer some question about the human puzzle and how we came to be and how we fit together . . . *living protoplasm is created from other pre-existing living protoplasm* . . . Instead what was there was another baby. Paul came to find me the night Lucy was brought in for her second labour.

'She'll be quick,' he said. 'Well, last time was.' His eyes were shiny bright.

Though, unusually, her second labour was protracted. I forced myself to focus, filling in charts, ready for the doctor's rounds in the morning. Every time the nurses' station phone rang I pounced on it.

Light was tingeing the windows by the time he came to find me again.

'She had a hard time,' he said. Black circles were daubed under each eye. 'Beth, it's a girl. A little girl.'

'A girl,' I repeated dumbly. He reached out his arms for me and over his shoulder I focused on the drugs trolley that it was my responsibility to wheel around that night – the red and blue plastic tops ranked in rows. I felt the air being sucked from the building, as if it might be a bomb wrapped in a blanket and tucked inside the see-through plastic cot upstairs in the maternity ward.

'A girl,' I said again, and we both clung to each other then, wetting each other's neck with tears, though whether it was joy or grief was hard to know, the two streamed together.

'Come and see her.'

I shook my head and grabbed on to the handle of the drugs trolley. 'Lucy will need to rest.'

'Just for a minute, please. It's better you do this right away. I want everything to be right, Beth. I can't have anything holding over her, she's just a baby.'

The wicked witch arriving at the christening, I thought, the one that leaves a curse on the girl child: that's what they're afraid of – deep down, underneath. They want to make sure it's a blessing I leave.

Lucy gave me an exhausted smile and held out the baby in her arms, pink and sleeping. 'Meet Flora,' she said, as I took the living warmth into my hands.

'Hello Flora,' I whispered to her, and of course it was not a bomb but another warm baby, tired out from being born. 'Bless you, bless you,' I said.

When they left I waved to the three of them from the front steps and turned back inside – back to all the actions, the tiny actions: the drink of water held to the lips in the middle of the night; the smoothing out of bed sheets; the whisking away of the bedpan for dignity and hygiene.

Driving home, the green dawn over the sky and the house, half expectant she could be in the back seat, coming home. *Is she back yet?* No, no, not this time. *Then when?* I chucked my keys in the copper bowl by the door and caught a glimpse of myself in the mirror. Hair: cut short and bobbed, suitable for a nurse. My face: thinner than before. With the money I now earned I'd spruced up the house, bought paint and made the walls downstairs glow warm melon yellow. *She'll love this colour.*

Up in Carmel's room I added *Flora* to her map in bright pink. Jack, Flora, Graham – all new – and I sensed how our maps were splitting, diverging, forming and reforming as people and places came crowding in.

I looked around her room, remembering my own room at my mother's. Every night, going to bed, I paused at the top of the stairs outside. Mostly the door stayed shut, but there were moments when I slipped inside to look at her folded T-shirts, her drawings, her books and her duvet, and touch them gently. I would fold the tissue paper back and look at the unworn red shoes. While I had them, she couldn't walk away from me completely.

47

ALL DAY I'VE WANTED to read my letter but I won't while
Gramps is there and now disaster's struck. The truck's died right
in the middle of nowhere.

We get out and walk and I take a blanket at the last minute in
case Gramps wants to sit down.

'Let's flag down a car,' I say, 'and ask for help.'

Gramps stops in the road. 'We wouldn't know who they were.
Whether they would be friend or foe. No, I remember there's a
town a few miles over that way.' He jerks his head toward some
hills. 'We'll find help there.'

We carry on walking and maybe he's right anyway because
when the odd car does go past, the people inside just look and I
guess they're thinking 'itinerants' like Dorothy used to say they did.

It gets so quiet it feels kind of spooky and the sky seems to be
pressing down on us hard. The hills around us start turning black.
I'm walking right behind Gramps. I think: it's just the two of us
rattling around this lonely world now. We might as well be in
our own little chain gang of two. Even if I had a sharp saw in my
hand I couldn't cut through metal like this. It puts its dead weight
around your leg and holds you there.

I decide to concentrate on Gramps's back, large and heavy in
his black coat. There's drops of cold moisture growing on the felty
fabric.

'What can you see?' I ask eventually.

He scans ahead. 'Not much, there's a light some way over there
though.'

I duck out from behind him and look. The lights are twinkling bright but they look like a long way off.

'That looks farther than a few miles. Maybe we should have gone the other way. Back toward the city.'

'Oh no, no. That was even farther and we'd be walking into the city with no vehicle or weapon. We might be set upon. We might be robbed and beaten.'

'I suppose. Well, we'll have to carry on walking then.'

So we do, we leave our footprints in the mud beside the road. I feel glad for some reason – that we're leaving some sort of trace. We stay as far off the road as we can in case a car comes past and can't see us in the twilight and runs right over us. Ahead of me Gramps starts slowing down, his limp is making his body judder and the drops on his jacket swing about as if they were hundreds of children and he's their father and they're clinging onto his back for dear life.

'Gramps, let me go ahead of you. You can't see anything with your head all bent down like that, except for your shoes.'

'I can't,' he pants. 'I'm done for. We'll have to stop.'

'We'll stop for a rest and maybe you'll get your energy back so we can carry on. Or maybe we should get back to the truck and sleep there for the night and think about what to do in the morning?'

'No, I'm done for,' he says again. 'I can't take another step – my hip feels like it's on fire. We should say some prayers. We've never needed help so much.'

I can see his face in the fading light, twisted in pain, and truly I'm worried then, we're so alone.

'Here, sit by the side of the road,' I say, and Gramps slowly lowers himself down so he's sitting on a grassy bump. He holds onto my arm as he does this so he doesn't lose his balance and fall onto the ground.

'What have things come to, Carmel? We're being sorely tested. When I think of how things could have been.'

'We could pray like you said. For help?' He's forgotten about doing that.

'Yes, yes. Only . . .'

'What?'

'I'm so weary. Do you think you could lead the prayers? This one time?'

I think about it for a minute. This will be unusual for us.

'Yes, I guess. If it would help?'

I crouch down next to him so he can hold my hands in between his. I know he likes to do this and I think it might be him trying to catch some healing from me, on the sly, but I don't mind, not really.

'Say whatever comes into your heart,' he says.

I close my eyes. 'Dear world.' I think hard about what I want to say. 'Sometimes you are a very difficult place to live. Please if you could – will you send us a new truck. And some more dollars would help us too.' I go quiet because I'm praying about seeing Nico again and I don't want Gramps to hear that bit. I open my eyes then and see Gramps looking at me and he doesn't look pleased.

'That wasn't a very pious sort of prayer.'

'But you said to say what came into my heart.'

'You can't ask for worldly goods and for them just to be delivered to you, Carmel. God is not a catalogue. He doesn't own a car lot.'

I sigh. 'OK, I'll try again.'

'No, I think that's enough from you.'

'But –' I don't want to say it but I've got the real urge to pray about Mum now. And to say I hope she can see us here, even though I know she can't.

'No more praying, I don't know if God would want to hear that sort of prayer.'

I decide to save my prayer about Mum for later. I stand up then and that's when I notice something.

'Look, Gramps, look. There's a ditch behind you.' It's just as well we stopped praying when we did as there's not much light left and if it had gone completely dark I wouldn't have seen it.

I've never been so excited to see a ditch in my whole life. I go and jump right into it and crouch down, feeling with my fingers.

'It's dry. Dry as a bone.' I jump out again. 'We can sleep here for the night.'

Gramps seems almost pleased someone is telling him what will happen.

'Well, if you say so, child.'

I help him climb into the ditch. There's even some ferny plants at the bottom so we're not sleeping on bare earth. I tuck the blanket around him and make a pillow out of a corner of it for his head. He's so tired he falls asleep almost straight away and I think about my letter and I think, dare I? Very quietly I take it out of my pocket. The sound of ripping paper makes him mutter and stir so I freeze solid. But I have to see who it's come from. So I wait till he goes back to sleep again, hoping there'll be enough light left when he does. I can only just see it by the time he's snoring.

La Casa Rosa
Durango
Chihuahua
Mexico

Dear Carmel,
I sure hope this reaches you, I sent ten letters in all to different places we used to go so with luck one of them will make it into your hands.

Oh Carmel, you see how good I write now? I made sure I went on with it and now I can write pretty good in Spanish and English. I think about you a lot Carmel.

Mom's got us a house here. It's got two stories and is dark pink and it's got the most colour in the whole village. People use it when they explain directions – turn right at the pink house, or turn left at the pink house because indeed we are on a cross-road. Mom says she's got everything she ever wanted now and

doesn't have to do nothing for nobody and never will again.
Our father tried to come back when he heard we got a house.
He sat outside for three whole days till she poured boiling water
on him from the top window and he went howling down the
street. It was sure scary and I thought we'd have to run away
like before, but we never saw him again. Mom says she is in
paradise. She grows flowers by the front door and tomatoes in
the back yard. I dream about you sometimes. Once, you were an
animal that could talk, but I don't know what kind, it wasn't
clear.

Sometimes Mom says we should have brought you with us.
I think she misses you too and she says that you could have made
a fortune here on account of the Mexican mind being so gullible
to religion. Then she says it would have only brought in trouble.
I miss you all the time Carmel and wonder if you still write
your name everywhere and if you still want to go work in a
hospital, like you told me.

Silver puts on a fancy dress most days and goes and sits on
the bench outside hoping to attract boys. But it's so quiet here,
most days there's only the old yellow dog walking by and all
that happens is that he might decide to stop and have a scratch
at his fleas. I don't care about it being quiet and all but I would
like you to be here Carmel and we could read and write stuff
together. Sometimes I wonder if we'll ever see each other again
though I guess not,

Your loving sister,
Melody.

I touch my finger to her name and think of their pink house
in the bright sunshine which must have been got with all the
dollars Dorothy stole. I'm glad for Melody but it doesn't seem
quite fair what with me and Gramps and the truck dying. I
creep under a spare corner of the blanket with Gramps and say
a prayer for Melody and then one to Mum. I tell Mum I love
her still and hope maybe she can see us here if she's made it into

heaven. But then I change my mind about that because I'm not sure I'd like her to see me sleeping in a ditch with only a blanket over me.

In the morning I wake up much sooner than Gramps. There's a strange and beautiful colour in the sky – grey and purple – and it seems to make the air around us that colour too. I slide out from underneath the blanket that's got tangled around us in the night. I'm stiff and cold from sleeping on the ground so I pull my knees up to my chin and blow on my hands to try and warm up.

Gramps is sleeping peacefully. The blanket moves up and down as he breathes. A bird jumps on top of him and it's bobbing its tiny head and pecking at the blanket, as if it's going to find food there. There's a soft lovely wind blowing around us that makes the grasses rustle. Then Gramps starts to wake, muttering and grumbling, and the bird jumps off him and flies away. Gramps sits up with the blanket half falling around him.

'Where are we?' He looks around us, then remembers. His face goes all hard and gloomy. 'What now, Carmel? What now for us?'

I don't know how to answer this so I blow on my hands some more.

He turns his eyes up toward the sky. 'Please God, look upon our time of need . . .'

I look up too and watch the purple-grey clouds shift about. He carries on, praying beside me. He runs out of prayers in the end.

'You should put your hands together when we pray,' he says.

I shrug a bit instead, hoping we can change the subject. Thinking we should be deciding what to do now, not praying. Anyway, I feel angry with God today and sometimes I remember how Dad didn't believe there was one and even Mum said she wasn't sure.

Gramps takes his glasses out of his top coat pocket to clean them. Without them, his eyes look naked and pale. 'Wilful child. God is listening to us, how can you think He's not?' Sometimes he seems to know exactly what I'm thinking. It's creepy.

I don't want to have an argument with him – even though I can see he does. I start doing star jumps to get some feeling back into my legs.

'Well. What have you got to say?' He doesn't want to leave me alone. I can feel I'm getting annoyed now.

'All this talking to the sky – the sky doesn't care about us, it just cares for itself. And pretty soon it's going to rain on us so we better make a move.'

But he buries his head in his hands. 'How can you, you of all people, say such a thing? I've taken you on, I've nurtured you and now you utter this nonsense about talking to the sky. To deny when God has chosen you to be His instrument. It's a desperate sin, child. You'll kill me with this talk. I'm half dead from it already.'

I don't like it when Gramps makes out I'm an angel or a saint. I just want to be a real person.

'It's the people, Gramps, I think it mostly comes from the people themselves.'

'And me? What does that mean? In all these years nothing could be done for me.' His shoulders are heaving and I think he's about to start sobbing.

All I can say is, 'That's the way it is; it just is, is all. I don't know why.'

We go quiet for a while, then he starts talking through his fingers because he's still got his head in his hands.

'Sometimes I think someone is after us, Carmel.'

'Whatever do you mean?'

'I see him. I catch glimpses of him. In the mirrors of the truck, or through a window . . .'

'Who, Gramps? What are you talking about?'

'He wants you. He wants what's mine. He'll go to any lengths . . .'

I shout then, because it seems that's the only way anything will get through to him. 'Gramps, who? Why would he be after us?'

'To rescue you. To take you back.'

'Rescue me from what?

'From me . . .'

'Gramps, you're not making any sense. Who is he? What does he look like?'

He opens up his fingers so I can only see one eye. 'I don't know. All I've seen is a hat. Sometimes a raincoat. He looks different every time.'

I sigh. 'Gramps, I think you're imagining things. You have to stay calm, you can't go around thinking about men in hats. Why are you always thinking that I'll be taken off you?'

'You're right. You belong to me.'

'No, I don't *belong*.' I kick at some tall grass. 'I'm not a parcel. Anyway, I've never asked why you got to keep me?' *My* forehead might look like a garlic bulb now.

'You know why, child. Your father didn't want you. I took on the burden, the responsibility, that he was too selfish to bear.'

'But,' I've been thinking about this a lot lately, 'he might have changed his mind by now?'

I stick my toe in the dirt and scrape it around because I know I shouldn't have said all this but he's silent and when I look down at him again the expression on his face makes me freeze. Without warning, the prickles are there, racing right over me.

'Maybe we should just end it here,' he says.

'What d'you mean?'

'I mean, end it. For both of us, for once and for all.'

I really shout then. 'Shut up! You stupid old man. You –' He stands up like his hip's not hurting him at all, and the blanket falls to the ground. I see a terrible flash of his old power then and his shoulders go back and his arms seem to grow bigger.

'You're not a child, you're a fiend.'

Then it flies out of my mouth. 'Who's Mercy, Gramps? Who is she?'

'She's you.'

'No, the other one. The real one in the passport. What did you do with her? Where is she?'

He goes quiet and still. 'What do you know about Mercy, snooper?'

The prickles nearly make me fall over they're so strong.

'Nothing. I want to know she's all right. Is she? You hurt her, didn't you?' I'm yelling now. 'What happened?'

He looks like if he punched something now it would fall down dead. 'Be quiet, fiend,' he roars.

But I don't stop, I can't. 'So I'm a fiend now? Suit yourself, then,' I yell, and I shove my hands in my pockets and jump out of the ditch and start marching down the road. Then I stop and look back. 'You know what? I reckon Mum was right all along not talking to you. It was your fault you fell out, wasn't it? *She* wouldn't have wanted you to keep me.' I turn and start walking off again.

'Carmel,' he calls after me. 'Carmel, come back. No one else wanted you. There – that's the truth.'

I feel my head drooping as I walk.

'Carmel, please. Please.'

I hear his pitiful cries and I walk on a few steps farther, then the energy seems to run out of me. I look back – he's standing there, bent and huge, and I can only see him from the knees up because he's standing in the ditch. But it doesn't make him look funny. It makes him look creepy and powerful, like a wizard.

'Carmel, help me. Help me to get out. You can't leave me here.'

I don't feel angry any more, just limp and useless.

'Carmel, let me phone the pastor. At least at the gathering we'll be fed and watered, they'll take care of us.'

I don't know what it is. Whether it's the years of being with him and trying to remember I'm Carmel and not Mercy. Or all the missing Mum and Dad I've done. Or being dressed up and shown about like someone from a circus. But all of a sudden I feel perhaps one night he'd done this thing to me. He'd cut me open and taken Carmel out and she'd looked like the solid doll in the middle of Russian dolls. She had my face. And he'd put in its place a doll with *his* face painted on and set it with a timer, ready to go off at this exact moment at the side of this road.

I start feeling sorry for myself. How I long to be normal. To chat with my friends and try on scarves and shoes, and have proper birthdays with presents like mobile phones. To sleep in a proper bed with coloured fairy lights around it and my school bag ready for the next day. I see these kids in every town we go. They're inside the diners and giggling about secrets, the way me and Sara used to. As they talk and laugh they stir their tall ice-cream drinks with the long spoon in their hand. Their nails are pink, the colour of sweets, and their eyelids have sparkly stuff on them.

I feel the Gramps doll inside of me and I wonder how I'm ever going to get it out. He doesn't look powerful now, he's bent over, making little cries like a kitten.

'It's OK, Gramps. I won't leave you here.'

I sigh and my energy inside seeps onto the road, ready to drip, drip into the ditch and around his feet. I close my eyes and feel the wind on my face. 'Don't worry,' I tell him. 'Everything will be all right.'

'That's my girl,' he says, and holds out his arm to be helped out of the ditch. 'Now then, we mustn't fall out like this again. Now it's only the two of us – we have to take care of each other.'

48

GRAMPS SAYS Munroe's been waiting for us all this time, waiting to welcome us back into his fold. He seems to have forgotten how we wanted to get away from him. When I think of him waiting, though, it's more like he's a spider. He's got his web in Texas and that's where we are now.

'I always knew we'd end up back with him,' I'm muttering as we walk up his drive with our few belongings in our arms.

'What was that? What was that?'

Gramps may be half deaf in his right ear but he can hear all right when he wants to.

I say, 'What a lovely house our friend Mr Munroe has. Was it bought with all the money he made from those poor folks he brought along to me to lay hands on – the babies with spina bifida and the man with the shrunken arm, the woman that couldn't stop miscarrying and the fella who thought losing his hair was worthy of a healing . . . ?'

Gramps stops in the middle of the drive and fixes his pale eyes on me.

'Mr Munroe is a man of God. He should be respected by us. He's taking us into his home at this time of need. You have to behave, Carmel. This could be the start of a new life for us. If Mr Munroe decides he wants us around, it could be the answer to our prayers. Don't go ruining it by being snippy. Honestly, I don't know what's got into you lately.'

I say I don't know either and I mean it.

'This is important for us, Carmel, real important.' He's standing right outside Mr Munroe's front door though he hasn't rung the bell yet. There's a white pillar either side of the door – like at the hotel where we first met the pastor years ago.

I look at the sticking plaster Gramps had to mend his glasses with on the coach ride here because they broke when he took them off to clean. I see the way his hands tremble as he holds his things – his spare shirt, his Bible and his socks stuffed into an old sports bag. I see the way he's putting off ringing the doorbell.

'All right, Gramps.' I need to calm him down now. 'Everything'll be A-OK.' And I press on the doorbell myself.

Munroe drives us to the gathering in his great big SUV. Me and Gramps are like the king and queen riding in the back, we've even got a cosy check blanket covering our knees. We're so high up I want to wave to the people walking on the road beside us, their faces look up at us as we pass and I smile down at them.

Munroe's driving but he keeps looking back over his shoulder because he's so excited and wants to talk.

'Hey, just ye look at them, Dennis. Just ye look. Our little Texas gathering and see them come. It's biblical. That's what it is. It's like the crowds that followed Jesus into Jerusalem.'

''Cept they didn't do it in SUVs.' Gramps gives me a look when I say this. A warning look. I wish he'd get his glasses mended. They're embarrassing.

Gramps changes the subject to get away from what I've said though I don't know what's so bad about it, it's just factually correct. Actually, that's a lie. I knew how it would annoy him.

'I heard on the radio there's weather coming. Blasting on down from the north.' He sounds worried.

'Oh that. It's 'cos of the fact they're so Godless there. It'll stop dead in its tracks before it gets to us. Its icy breath'll lick at their toes to show them how hell is and how one day it'll be fire licking there.'

Gramps chuckles. He's always been led on by Munroe, even though I think Gramps is sort of cleverer than him. Somehow all the hell talk makes Gramps feel big and safe. He thinks he's one of the chosen ones who's not going to the fiery lake. But I know there are times when he's not so certain.

'Sure. There'll be a wall of ice around us and those on the outside will see us within. They'll see our shapes moving around inside and wish they could be with us, but it will be too late. We'll be in the inner circle and they'll be on the outside . . .'

Munroe glances over his shoulder. Truth be told, Gramps often sounds a bit weird these days with the stuff he says. He can't quite hit the mark. It's like he's trying to play a part that doesn't quite suit him, even though he wants it real bad. I feel a bit sorry for him then, with Munroe looking over at him and probably thinking 'What a freak' – which is something, coming from Munroe. So I shout out, 'Amen,' and Gramps nearly jumps out of his skin I've been so quiet up till now.

Munroe's chuckling. He's forgotten about Gramps being weird. 'Amen,' he yells. 'Hallelujah.' And Gramps looks out of the window like it's hurting his ears. I can see he's going into one of his moods and he turns and looks at me.

'Are you wearing cosmetic products?' He's right, it's lipstick and some powder I found in Munroe's bathroom that belonged to his wife and I tried such a teeny bit on that I didn't think they'd be able to see or notice it had gone.

'No, Gramps. Where would I get make-up from?'

He grunts and leans closer to me. 'You look like a woman today.'

'Well, she's a growing girl.' Munroe tries to interrupt but Gramps is deep in one of his moods now. He knows his trying to impress Munroe has fallen flat again.

'The devil has a special place where he makes cosmetics for women to paint their faces. There's a workshop where demons make lipstick colours and give them names like "Flaming Heart" when the only flaming heart belongs to Jesus.'

Oh Gramps, I think, with your devils like Santa's elves making presents to tempt ladies with. Besides, that make-up belongs to

Munroe's wife and by saying it's evil you're calling her evil. So I say – and I know it's going to annoy him – 'Oh, is that right? I thought it was made by L'Oréal.'

And to my surprise Munroe gives a snort of laughter and I think – you like Gramps looking stupid because it makes you feel like you're on top. Gramps is looking out of the window again and I feel sorry for him, with Munroe in his big house and us with nothing because Gramps is short on how to be in the world. So I sneak my hand under the blanket until I find his and I let it rest there on top of his, that feels all dry and gnarly.

The crowds get thicker walking beside us. In front of us there's a bus and painted on the back doors of it is a great big cross with flames coming off it.

We park in a special VIP section that's roped off. Lots of the cars have things painted on the side, like *I've given my heart to Jesus, have you?* – and a picture of a great big heart that's like a ball of flame. When I see that I have to put my hand to my chest because there's a burning there too.

I look up to the sky.

It was blue before and now it has gone white. Today is one of those days – like the day of the ditch – where feeling hangs heavy and the air is full of all sorts of stirrings.

Gramps is getting his battered blue sports bag out of the car.

'I've got your dress in here.'

It's the one I got for my not-real ninth birthday. It was good and big then, like things always were when Dorothy bought them new, but I have to squash myself inside it now. One good thing about Dorothy going – I get to wear jeans again.

'That old thing.' I can't believe he's dragged that trash here. 'What d'you bring all that stuff for anyway?'

I've seen it, spilling out over the top of the bag, when we were staying with Munroe. My old frilly white dress that looks like an olden-day petticoat. Scarves. The hollowed-out Bible. Stuff from our Dorothy days.

'You can change before if you like.'

'We'll see about that,' I grumble to myself. Not that they'd hear anyway. They're both striding ahead pretending to themselves they're young and full of – what d'you call it? – vigour. They both have on long black coats and Munroe his hat and they take up so much room as they walk through the car park toward the tents people step out of their way. Gramps's limp is a lot better today, like it always is when he's excited.

I look to the sky again.

'What you waitin' for?' Munroe is turning back and calling out to me. His smile has gone so I can't see his big teeth any more. Without them his face is a smooth pink melon with blinking mean eyes.

But I couldn't even move if I wanted to. The sky is so strangely white and my feet are stuck to the ground. I see a curl of icy breath unfurling and it brushes my face. The white sky thickens and the shadows flicker and in a flash Gramps and Munroe are by my side. In no time. I haven't had no time for ages. I told Gramps about it in the end and he said it must be after-effects from the drugs I had when I was ill and first came here – but I thought it'd gone away.

'She does this sometimes.' Gramps is grunting and kneeling painfully on the floor trying to shift my feet by the ankles. 'S'OK. It doesn't last that long these days.'

Munroe is shoving his big hands in his pockets; the curl of cold spirals around him like it's sniffing for something. He can't see it like I can but he feels it and shivers.

'I sure hope not, Dennis. I had my doubts but I put my reputation on the line. If she's gonna flake out . . .'

'She won't. She won't. C'mon, Carmel, help me out a little.' Whoomf. I'm back inside myself and my feet get unstuck. 'Don't worry, Gramps.' I reach out and touch his white hair; it feels surprisingly silky, like he's been filching Munroe's Pantene conditioner. Maybe we're not so different. 'Look.' I lift a foot off the ground.

Gramps's bad side means Munroe has to give him an arm to help him up.

We cross the road to where the tents are. There's a dusty path between them. The icy shafts haven't been here yet; or maybe they have, high up where my head doesn't reach. In the tents I can hear singing and preaching. The sounds go mmm mmm mmm – shout. Mmm mmm mmm – shout, and I know it will be some preacher mmming about the Lord and the crowd will be shouting back Hallelujahs.

'Look, Gramps, look.' I stop and Gramps looks worried that no time is happening again but I'm pointing to the other side of the field where a huge black cross juts out of the ground and cuts into the white sky.

Munroe grins. 'Quite a feature, don't you think?' I nod, but then I see Gramps and he's standing like he's been frozen to the bone seeing that great black cross.

'It's the path to judgement.'

'What is?' Munroe's a bit annoyed by us both now, I can see. All this stopping and starting when he wants to hurry us along and get going.

'Today. I will be judged today.' Gramps is shaking all over and truth be told it makes me feel a bit frightened. I know he's old and feeble but he's the closest thing I've got to a mum or a dad. Lord knows what would happen to me without him.

'What in heaven's name for?' asks Munroe.

'For Mercy. For leaving her there like that . . .'

'But she's standing right here.'

Gramps focuses on my face. 'Oh . . . yes.'

But I know he's not talking about me and the prickles start up.

'C'mon, old boy.' Munroe sounds like he's coaxing cattle. 'Come on, old boy. There's no judgement today. It's just a feature is all.'

We're in a tent right at the corner of the field. I sit on the stage swinging my legs against the bright blue carpet tacked over it.

A noise booms out of the speakers. 'Can you hear me?'

Munroe and Gramps are out back fiddling around with the microphones. I hear them giggling then. They sound like two naughty schoolboys until Gramps's giggling turns into a cough and a wheeze.

I look at the empty chairs. Soon they will be filled. Gramps will sermonise but they will be restless, impatient. Waiting for the main attraction. Me. They'll be coming now. Dragging along their limps and tumours. Their sick babies. Their unhealed bones and the burns left unattended due to no insurance. I can feel them clamouring already, gathering up, and the weight of them all makes me want to lie down right here on the stage and fall asleep.

49

FIVE YEARS, 201 DAYS

THE HOUSE IS AGITATED TODAY. Everything stirs. I don't know why but neither I nor it can calm down. The wind makes the tree knock on the wall. Floorboards creak and groan and even the walls seem to sigh.

Into that the phone ringing down the hall. The tenor of the sound is different: sharp, insistent, and I hurry down the stairs to answer it. There must be an open window somewhere; coats hanging by the stairs stir like restless spirits wear them, the yellow leaves of the phone book that the phone sits on riffle open and closed enough to make me worry the ringing phone will be pitched to the floor.

I wonder if it's Graham because I did phone him that day, the day I first looked after Jack. We've not been lovers again but around once a month we meet and walk or eat dinner together. He reminds me how he once smoked a cigarette for me. But it won't be him: it's daytime, he'll be teaching gangling youths in a big airy classroom.

When I lift the receiver I get the feeling I'm just in time, that the caller was about to give up and the line click dead. It's a terrible line, pops and hisses sound in my ear.

'Beth?'

'Yes.'

More whooping noises.

'It's Maria. Beth, I need to come and see you, I've got –' Then the whoops chatter so much they drown her out. I shake the receiver in my hand as if I could rattle them to the floor.

'What is it?' I shout down the receiver. 'What have you got?' Then click, buzz. The line's gone dead.

'No, no.' My voice echoes up the stairs. I put the receiver down then twice it rings again. But it's worse now and the phone's been colonised by evil mocking noises – half electric, half ghostly – so they're all I can hear.

For a moment I stand frozen. A fantasy pops in my head – unwanted, unbidden – of the phone ringing and a voice asking: 'Mum? Mum, is that you? I'm coming back to you now. I'm getting closer, Mum. Mum, Mum, Mum, Mum.'

Maria calls back on my mobile and says they're reviewing the case and will be out to see me. 'Your house phone has a life of its own,' she laughs.

I pace and prowl the sitting room. There's a feeling of events gathering pace. I tell myself I've felt that before; it's my imagination. The house agrees with me, it's gone silent now. Sulking under thin cold sunshine.

'How can you bear staying in that house?' a friend had asked me once.

'But how could I ever leave? One day I might open the door and there'll she be,' I'd replied.

But the next morning there's a sour taste of whisky in my mouth when I wake up on the sofa. Something I haven't had for a long time. The armrest's bent my head back so it feels sore and stiff. I feel dull, flat. It's probably nothing, like the rest of it. See, this is how I got here. Over the years, slowly, slowly. Signs and clues emerging like seals' heads among the waves only to disappear again, leaving me scanning the horizon. The first few years: the sightings – Scotland, Belgium, South America. The police tried to weed the craziest ones out but still they came, sometimes thick and fast. Sometimes nothing for weeks on end. The red coat was what people remembered and it was seen everywhere: a special army of red-coated children popping up all over the globe. It became a distraction, one that the police tried to veer away from because who knows what happened to that coat? But long after she'd vanished she was known in the papers as the Girl in the Red Coat.

Of course, every time I reached a state of breathless anxiety. But each time the sightings faded to nothing – it was another little girl, someone else's child. Or never to be seen again: an apparition that appeared across the world from time to time, like a sighting of the Virgin Mary in the clouds. Paul started a local fund to pay for the private detective. We're onto something exciting, they'd say, a sighting on a bus in Luxembourg, in Sweden, in Brisbane. Often I'd get letters – *Sweetheart, I know where your little girl is. I've been a psychic for twenty years and I can see her clear as day. She's still wearing a red coat.*

I've had so many false alarms I'm immune to them. But who am I kidding? Coffee gets me wired and awake. Graham calls and I tell him what's happened.

'Would you like me to be there?' he asks. 'I have a free period.'

I surprise myself by saying, 'Yes.'

I'm showered and changed and waiting at the window for half an hour before they both end up arriving together. I feel a rush of affection for Maria as I see her coming up the path, the wind tugging at her raincoat. Her hair is cropped close to her head and I get the feeling she couldn't be bothered with the femininity even of a neat bob any more, and got rid of it once it became a distraction. Graham bends his head and smiles as he says something to her and an unexpected wave of tenderness for him leaves me almost gasping.

'Beth, how lovely to see you,' she says. Close up, she looks older, of course. But something else too. She's given in to her serious nature. Funny how if you don't see someone for a while you can observe how their character and their daily thoughts have seeped into their bones, sunk into their muscles.

She sits on the edge of the sofa. 'How are you, Beth? You're looking well.'

'My job keeps me going these days. I don't know what I'd do without it.'

'That's good. Listen, it's mainly a review but I won't beat about the bush because I know you'll be anxious about this. It's a slim chance and I don't want to get your hopes up.'

I smile; the platitudes haven't changed. I've grown to like them. She uses them because she's not confident about forming her own words, I can see that now.

'Of course.'

She takes a folder out of her case, the plastic kind with a zip all the way around it. There's a photo inside, blown up to A4. Graham perches on the arm of my chair and puts his hand on my shoulder.

'I want you to take a look at this and see what you think.' It's the face of a girl. Her head's half turned from the camera, revealing one eye. There's a look in it I can't quite fathom, or put my finger on. A clump of hair, curled in a loose corkscrew, blows across her face. It's shadowy, taken from a distance.

A terrible pain grips my stomach, sudden, unexpected. It makes me cry out.

Maria is by my side in a flash. 'Beth, what is it? I'm so sorry if this is upsetting you . . .'

She's crouching down on the floor, looking up, and her face is full of concern.

'It's her.'

'Now, then, we can't be so sure. We've done a computer model from a photo you gave us. It seems to match, but honestly, Beth, we can't be sure. The hair in the way, the coat collar on the other side. It stops us measuring the jaw . . .'

I'm gripping the photo so hard it's shaking and Maria gently prises it from my fingers.

'Where was this taken?' I reach up for Graham's hand and his strong slender fingers weave with mine.

Maria's back on the sofa now. She's worried, I can see, worried she's taken this too far, too soon.

'It's a group of drifters in America. The police there took photos of them, a good few years ago now, before they moved them on. They've got a database and a friend of mine's been working out there. They'd forgotten to stop her access to the database so she does a trawl now and then. Just looking, really. I guess we're a nosy bunch by trade. When she saw this she called me up.'

'Oh God, let me see again.'

She lets me have the photo but she's reluctant now. I sense it in the way she hands it over. The photo's black and white so I can't see the hair colour. But it's better like this; you can see the bare bones of a face. I put my finger onto the cheek in the photo. I'm not so sure now. Is my memory of her fading? The idea is terrible.

'She's lovely.'

'Yes, Beth. She is.'

'What else? What else can they tell you?' I'm frantic now; I need to calm down to show her she can pursue this without me falling to pieces.

'Not much. I've spoken to the policeman who took the photo. It was in the southern states and they were camping illegally. He thought they might be gypsies, or Mexicans without visas. It was a couple of years ago now so his memory's a bit hazy. He remembers the girl because she didn't seem quite the same as the rest of them. But the next day they were gone and I suppose for him it was problem solved.'

'Why did he take photos?'

'I guess it's a bit . . . well, it's a tactic I suppose.'

'What, to intimidate them?' Already I want to protect this girl.

'To persuade them to move on.'

Tonight, everything stirs. I go to the window but I can't see out. The light's on and inside the glass there's just my reflection.

'It's all right, darling,' I say fiercely. 'I know you're there.'

50

THE DRESS IS LAID OUT on the stage. Gramps must have done it when I went to the toilet. It makes me feel funny looking at the dress all empty. It's in a spotlight, blue on white. Around the neck and the bust there's the silver nylon lace and it glitters in the light. For a moment it's like it's me lying down on the stage flat and empty and the real me, the one that's looking, isn't there.

I guess I'll have to put it on. The forces saying I have to are too much again. They are Munroe and Gramps. They are the waiting chairs. They are every Bible for sale and every believer in this field. But if I do that right now I'm worried I'm going to disappear and the dress will be everything.

I go outside to get away from it all. What I'd like to do is tear the dress to shreds but I'd get into so much trouble I hardly want to think about it. I realise I'm still frightened of Munroe and re- member Mum saying if you're frightened of someone then you should think of them in a silly situation – like in their pyjamas brushing their teeth – and they stop being frightening. When I was little I'd think of people with poo on their faces, that seemed the silliest thing you could think. But the picture of Munroe with shit over his face somehow just makes him scarier so I blank the thought out and shove my hands into the pockets of my red jacket and wander down the path kicking small stones.

Then I hear this lovely voice and for a second I can't see who it is and I really think the archangel Gabriel has come down from on high and is speaking to me directly.

'Carmel.'

There's no one in front of me.

'Carmel, Carmel. Is it you?'

I look around and it's Nico. I'm sure it is. It looks like him only taller, and real handsome. He's leaning against one of the entrances to the tents, so tall and good-looking he's better than the archangel Gabriel.

My breathing goes all funny when I see him. I've waited years for this to happen.

He comes right up to me and he's so tall I have to bend my neck to look at him. 'Hey,' he says, 'haven't seen you since we were little kids.'

For some reason while I speak my hands waggle either side like I'm trying to swim because I feel I need to balance or I might fall over. 'Nico. You sound like a proper American now.'

'So do you.'

'Do I?' It's funny but you don't really know how you sound to your own ears.

I remember about his sister, I'm not sure if I should ask – in case. But I do anyway. 'Is your sister, is she . . . here?'

He smiles and it runs over me, nice prickles. 'No, but she's still surviving.' He wants to change the subject, he's thinking of something to say. 'Look at you – all your buttons are done up the wrong way.'

Then slowly, slowly he undoes the shiny brass buttons on my jacket and does them up the right way. All the time he's doing this I'm shaking and I hope he doesn't notice.

'Carmel?' Gramps's voice comes floating out of the tent toward us. I do so wish he'd go away.

'The old man and Dorothy still taking you on the road?'

'Dorothy's gone now.'

'Carmel . . .' Gramps is sounding twitchy now.

'Bye, then.' Nico reaches over and flicks one of my buttons and makes a pinging sound. 'Catch you around.'

'Carmel . . .'

I watch Nico walk away with his hands in his pockets.

I want to call him back or run after him but I stand there watching. And I feel so sad to see him walking away, so deep-down sad, like he really is an archangel and he's the only one that could ever save me.

'Carmel, we need you here . . .'

Now Nico is small in the distance and it's the sky taking my attention away from him and from Gramps. What strange light. Is it only me that can see it? There's quiet over the camp for a minute. Over the tent selling alarms that remind you to pray and T-shirts that say 'SAVED' across the chest. Crucifixes to dangle in your car. Tiny white Bibles to bury with dead babies. The big tent at the entrance to the field where a prayer service is held every hour, on the hour. Even hush from there. Then floating down on the wind. A voice. It sounds like it doesn't belong to anyone. It sounds like it's leaking from a radio.

'The doctors who took away Chandler's bandages could not believe their eyes. Where there were third-degree burns only two days before, the skin was completely clear. They were astonished . . .' It's Munroe rehearsing, I realise. The voice floats and twists down the path like a plastic bag in the wind.

There's the dress again. Waiting.

'Where have you been, girl? Folk'll be here soon.' Gramps has taken his coat off and rolled his shirt sleeves up like a workman.

'You look worried today, Gramps.'

His forehead's crinkled up into a frown and it's shining with sweat under the lights. Because of where he's standing on the stage there's a green spotlight on his face. A little explosion of a giggle escapes me.

He looks up, sharp. 'What's so funny, Carmel?'

I wish I hadn't've laughed. Now I'll have to explain. 'You remind me of something. That's all.'

'What thing?'

I don't want to say. He doesn't like me talking about *before*. 'Course he never says this, I just know, and *before* gets blurry for me now even if I did want to talk about it.

'Mum took me to a pantomime . . .'

'Pardon?'

'It's like a play. There's a princess and a prince. And two funny women that might be men . . .' I'm trying to remember now. 'But the thing I liked most was the genie. He came out of nowhere in a puff of smoke and the light on him was green and so were his clothes. But I can't remember if he was supposed to be bad or good . . .'

He cuts in. 'Sounds like a pile of Godless fakery to me.'

I knew it would make him cross.

'Time to get changed, Carmel.'

Then he's gone but his face seems to flicker still in the green light. I walk up to the dress and Gramps's face is there too in the folds – where a tummy should be. I sweep it off the stage with one hand and give it a good shake. It's only a stupid old dress, I tell myself, far too small for me now.

A waft of icy air drifts through the open flaps of the tent. I unbutton my jacket but I'm not going to take anything else off, not today. Anyway, I don't want to feel the dress against my skin – to feel all the summers, all the people that have grabbed on to my hands. I don't want to feel Dorothy right next to me. So I slip it over my jeans and my T-shirt that says 'Frank's Chicken Shed' on it that we got free one time for eating chicken wings.

'There, there she is. My girl, my girl.' Gramps's voice is almost a wail coming from the back of the tent. 'Come, child, do it up. It's half falling off you.' And he comes over and starts buttoning me up at the back and nearly choking me.

'You've got your other clothes on underneath.'

'I'm cold, Gramps. Can't you feel the cold sneaking around?'

He shakes his head and wipes the sweat away from his forehead to show he doesn't know what I'm talking about. 'She's trussed up in that dress like a killed deer. 'Bout time you took her shopping, Dennis,' Munroe grumbles and Gramps wants to answer him back, I know he does, but Munroe's turned away already and he's slotting a CD into the player and cheesy music fills the tent. We face each other in a triangle with things unsaid in each of our mouths and it's almost a relief that a family arrives, pushing a girl about my age in a wheelchair up the aisle.

Then there's fake smiles plastered over Gramps and Munroe's faces and I go sit on the steps of the stage to be quiet.

Then they come and it's like they're never going to stop – until all the seats are full and there's people standing at the back and crowding into the aisle and Munroe's rubbing his hands together. The sneaking cold is driven away and the tent feels like the roof is going to melt right off.

Finally, Munroe takes the stage and the coughing and the talking and the shuffling stops dead. He starts pacing up and down, silent – working himself up. When he goes past the microphone you can hear his breathing – heeeehaaaaw heeeeehaaaaw.

When he's worked up enough he launches himself at the microphone all spitty and excited.

'I can feel the holy spirit right here. Right now. Hey, I'm expecting the roof to blow off any second the power of it's so mighty . . .' There's lots of shouting from the crowd but then the music changes. He times it all beforehand – I've seen him do it.

'Now there was this little boy. Name of Chandler. One day when his parents were out back little Chandler decided to do a very wicked thing. He decided to play with a box of matches. Little children here – don't you be doing this. It was also a foolish act and when you hear what happened next you'll find out why. What Chandler didn't know was that his pyjamas he was wearing – 'cos it was nearly bedtime – were of the flammable variety . . .'

I stick my fingers inside my collar and give my neck a good scratch. I see the girl that came in first, the one in the wheelchair, is staring at me, she's parked up right at the front. She gives me a wispy smile. Her skinny knees in black tights are half covered with a red-and-white polka-dot dress so she looks like Minnie Mouse. She's got the most gorgeous shoes; they rest on the metal platform of her wheelchair and they're gold with red jewels on them and they even have really high heels but I don't suppose it matters, she doesn't walk on them anyway. They're just for show.

I love her. I don't know why but I love her on sight and she's looking at me and smiling and I smile back and put my hand up and give her a tiny wave and she lifts a skinny hand and waves back.

Munroe's finished his story about Chandler who went up in flames so even his fingers had a flame coming off each one so it was like his tenth birthday had come early with each finger lit like a birthday candle. He's onto something else now.

'. . . it's like we've all got personal cell phones we can keep in our pockets and in the directory under G there's a direct line to God and we can talk to Him any time, any time . . .'

Him talking about phones gets me thinking. There's a secret pocket in my coat with some money Gramps doesn't know about – an old lady gave me a couple of dollars extra for laying hands on her husband – because I've been planning one day to have my own phone. I haven't got nearly enough but I might have when I'm older and then even he won't be able to stop me. And maybe I could try and phone my dad. Can I remember his number? Only the very beginning bit but there must be a way of finding numbers out. And he might be pleased and he might not. He might have another little girl now with Lucy – but it could be just to say hello, surprise, how you doing?

But then the people facing me come back pin sharp into focus and all the steps I have to go through to phone Dad seem so big and confusing I wonder if I'll ever be able to manage it.

It's Gramps's turn. As they change over I hear Munroe saying, 'Keep it short, Dennis,' and my cheeks burn for Gramps. He doesn't say anything for a good while and the crowd gets restless. Get on with it, Gramps, I think, you're losing them, and I nearly jump up and shout Hallelujah or Amen like I did this morning in the car. But finally Gramps has started.

'Acts Eight. Twelve to sixteen – "So they carried out the sick on the streets and they laid them onto beds and pallets that, as Peter came by, at least his shadow might fall on some of them."'

His finger is pointing up to heaven and he gets carried away so he moves without thinking out of the white spotlight so he's green again. I sigh.

And then the girl and me are staring at each other. We can't stop it. It's like we've fallen in love or something. Only not like it is with Nico. Not trembly and excited. I love her like I'm a knight on a horse and I want to gather her up and make everything better for her – to look after her and keep her safe. She peeps out under her long red fringe at me with her big soft brown eyes. Now my palms are burning, itching. I concentrate on her to see what light she has burning inside her but it's hard with the spotlights being different colours. I think there might be light enough inside her, I'm not sure. Everything's wrong today. What with the green lights and Munroe and his story about little Chandler who I've never heard of.

I feel a stab in my heart as a thought pierces – what if it's all not true? What if this thing, this thing I think is a gift, is only an idea Gramps has put there? I bring the thought up to my face and look at it and it lies an ugly lump in my hands. I don't want the thought to be right and I try to rub my hands together to squish it and make it disappear, but I get covered in it and it's terrible. The one time I really want to feel the swelling warmth in my fingertips, the hum going through me – the one time when I want to reach out to this lovely girl and lay my hands on her and say, 'You can get up now. Take off those high heels because they might be hard to walk in at first, but walk, walk right out of that wheelchair' – I can't because all I can feel in my hands are cold dead stars. I have to concentrate on not moaning I feel so bad.

Gramps must have finished now without me realising, the coloured spotlights are drowned out by big white ones and I hear him saying, 'Whoa now, each will have their turn. You have to line up,' because people are pushing and pressing forward and some have dollars in their hands that they're waving about; Dorothy would've loved it.

They've let in too many people – the ones lined up at the

back are pressing forward and I feel very tiny squashed against the stage. Where's Gramps? I look around for him and catch a glimpse of his face, he's come off the stage and he's trying to fight his way through the crowd but he can't and his face is all pushed out of shape. Then there's a terrible screeching sound from the microphone and the crowd around me cover their ears and hang back and at least I can breathe a bit. I put my fingers up to my face and I must be crying, it's wet around my eyes. Because I've realised the one person I need to heal – to lay hands on and rearrange the torn and twisted insides – is Mum. And I never will, but if not her, then it has to be this girl.

The feedback screeches again and then it's Munroe's voice booming out. 'Stand back, folk. Stand back right now. Mercy will be seeing everyone today. You need to wait your turn.'

And the crowd turn from a pack of baying wolves to ones that are sniffing about and thinking what to do next. There's a smell coming off them too. A smell of warm hair. I think, it's not me that's wrong – it's this. If I could just be calm and quiet I'd be fine. I decide something: this is the last ever time I'm going to lay hands for Munroe or Gramps. I'm going to tell Gramps today and however much he wails and shouts he's not going to change my mind because if I carry on like this it'll go away.

Then Gramps is by my side and all I can say is, 'Where is she? Where is she?' Because I don't want to see any of the wolves. I only want that girl with the gold stilettos and for everyone else to go away and leave us on our own.

'Carmel, come back, come back,' I hear Gramps's cry as I fight through the crowd. But I won't. I won't do anything till I find her. It feels like my life depends on it and I catch a glimpse of her through the bodies – red hair and a gold shoe in between people's legs.

'Stand back now.' It's a roar from Gramps, so loud the crowd actually do start hanging back like cowed dogs. But the stink they've made stays, hot and heavy.

As I push past, people reach out to try and touch me but I shove them off. Some even wave paper money at me but I push that away too. For a horrible minute I think she's going to get squashed by a tall man in a frayed old suit who seems so overcome by spirit he looks like he's drowning. But he lurches off toward the door and I'm beside her clutching at one of her skinny hands that feels like a broken bird in mine. I look down and I think flowers are bursting out of her fingers and then I realise they're coloured rings and I'm nearly cutting myself on the petals of plastic roses.

'S'OK. S'OK. Sorry.' I loosen my grip and say right into her ear, 'What's your name?'

She says something back but her voice is a wisp so I have to put my ear right next to her mouth.

'Say again.'

'Maxine.'

I want to help Maxine so much but the ugly thought that got smeared all over me is there and to try and make it wash off I say, 'It's true. It really is true. I can heal you, Maxine. I can.'

And she says nothing but smiles at me and nods and her hand trembles in mine and I get really, really close to her and she smells of baby powder.

I kneel in front of her. At first the stupid dress gets caught under my knees, just about slicing my neck at the back. I grab on to the hem and yank it up without letting go of her with my other hand, scared that this horrible crowd will separate us, because they think she's not important at all – and it doesn't matter if she's forgotten as long as they get their money's worth that will go into the sack afterward at the door.

'Let me touch your stomach,' I say. She unbuckles the harness and I can feel how hollow her stomach is under the polka-dot dress. I close my eyes and I try to grope around for what I'm always looking for, the glow, the ropes of light, but I can't feel anything. When I open my eyes she's there patiently waiting. I'm crying and I press harder trying to find the glow but I don't want to hurt her so I don't press too hard.

She's saying something again so I lean in to hear. She says, 'Don't worry, it doesn't matter. It doesn't matter.'

I scrabble my tears away. 'No, no. It does, it does, it matters more than anything.' I'm shouting and crying now but I don't care. So I focus this time. I let the crowd around me melt away and instead of their dog smell I catch onto the wafts of baby powder coming off Maxine and float on them. This lovely girl, I think, with her Minnie Mouse costume and her sweet baby smell, let me help her. If I never help anyone again, let me help her. And slowly there's a glow and a humming, faint at first, and I concentrate hard, fanning away at it with my mind, trying to get it going like a bonfire on a rainy day.

Keep going, I'm thinking, keep going. And the fire jumps up, flaring beneath my hands.

And I'm falling into her. Her flesh is collapsing around mine as I fall and the liquids in her body wrap themselves around me, red and gold. I'm right in the middle of her: worming through her body, around the pipes of her veins, bumping against bones and wriggling through her guts.

Then I pop my head into her head and I'm working her body from the inside, or we're working it together. So I open her eyes and I can see – I can see *me* kneeling down in front of us.

I can feel her mouth on my face and it's smiling. But Carmel in front, she's crying again. There's tears slipping off her face and we're saying, 'It's all right, everything's gonna be all right.' And I can see Carmel – because I know her so well – feels bad. She's thinking – it should be me saying that, I'm the one that can get up and walk about on my two legs, not her.

Soon, I think, any minute I'll inflate and put my arms through hers like I'm putting on a jumper, and wriggle my legs down into hers like they're jeans. We'll kick off those high heels, and they'll fly across the tent and land – clonk, clonk – on the stage, and when I've done that I'll surge forward and stand up wearing her body like a dress. I'll walk about in it, and as I do, she'll find *she* can do it too. And somehow, I haven't figured out how yet, I'll be able to step back out and she'll be left standing and walking but strong this time, strong as a tree, and after we've separated she'll keep my energy inside her and it'll stay there forever.

But there's a ripple of disturbance through her body and I get shaken about like a bottle of milk. And I bounce around so much I end up bouncing right out of her till, whoomf, I'm back inside myself, kneeling on the floor in front of her wheelchair.

Mayhem is breaking out. I look up to find Maxine and some person I can't see is spinning her wheelchair around. The wheelchair arm whacks me in the face, whipping my head sideways on its stem.

I put my hand up to my face because I really got a thump there and the voices and tumult around is like the tower of Babel Gramps is always talking about. From the floor all I can see of Maxine – through people's legs – is her shoes bumping up and down on the footrest of her wheelchair as she's shoved out of the door and as she reaches daylight, the sun flashes on her gold shoe as it kicks into the air. Then gone. I kneel there holding my face and crying and people keep falling over me. Eventually I say to myself, 'Get up, Carmel.' And I do.

Gramps is nowhere to be seen.

I join the crowd and they're taking no notice of me now – Mercy, the miracle girl. I'm just another body getting squashed as we all fight each other to get out into the open air.

Outside, the cold stings my cheek and each gasp of fresh air is so freezing it hurts inside. At first I can't work out why everybody is leaving in great swarms like ants marching toward the gate. But then dotted around I see even bigger, blacker ants and these ants are police in uniforms. One is holding up something to his mouth and speaking through it and his words come out in a robot's voice.

'This is an illegal religious gathering with no permit. Leave immediately . . .'

There's a buzzing of angry voices because there's people who don't want to leave. They want to carry on buying Bibles and getting healed and they were probably looking forward to the worship at four o'clock around the giant cross. Munroe said he was expecting transcendence and epileptic fits and all manner of things caused by the holy spirit alighting down. People falling flat on the ground dead even. I could tell he'd been looking forward to it.

I see Nico coming toward me – I'm so glad to see his face I want to throw my arms around him and kiss him. But I've wanted to do that since I was about eight, so no change there.

Then Nico actually puts his arm around *me* and I'm nearly dizzy with the feel of it, strong, like a man's almost. It's like I've been dreaming about all these years.

'Quick. You're gonna get crushed here, Carmel. People are getting mad.'

I say, 'Yes, Nico.' Because all of a sudden it's like we could be boyfriend and girlfriend together and we're making decisions just the two of us.

People are gathering around the policeman with the voice machine and someone tries to throw a rock at him and it misses but even so he takes his gun out and waves it around in the air.

'Disperse immediately. Disperse immediately. This is a gathering with no permit.'

One of the crowd yells out, 'And Jesus Christ didn't have no permit either. You sayin' he's an illegal?'

The crowd around the cop jeer at him and some are praying with their eyes rolling back into their heads and the cop starts looking scared and I know how he's feeling because when I first witnessed the speaking in tongues I could hardly believe my eyes and I was scared too. Even though I'm over that now and sights such as those are as normal as breathing to me.

I can feel Nico's hand on the small of my back and it's setting the bones there shivering clackety clack, rippling up and down like my spine's turned into a snake. 'OK, honey. Let's get you somewhere that's safe.'

I nod at him and the crowd pushing and pulling us melt away for a minute. Even the cop with the gun melts because Nico called me 'honey.'

'Over here.' He grabs my hand and leads me to one of the corners of the tent where it's pulled tight with ropes staked into the ground. We both crouch down behind the rope and use it as a guard but people's legs knock against it, nearly falling on top of us. And quite truthfully I think I could have found a better hiding place on my own, though I don't say because I love having Nico looking after me like this, and I don't ever want him to stop being behind me with his warm chest against my back.

Because I'm thinking about hiding places the hobbit houses at the place Gramps first took me pop into my head.

'I remember hiding . . .'

Nico says, 'What?' I was talking to myself almost.

I turn my head. 'It's not important. I've just remembered hiding when I was little. There was a row of tiny houses with doors and the doors had round holes cut in them.'

'Was it a place where they put poor people?'

'I guess.'

'They had them in Romania too. I saw them – my uncle told me they used to lock people inside and they'd have to bash away at a rock and they only got something to eat when the rock was small enough to push through the holes.'

I don't know why this shocks me so much. 'So they were for locking up? Not hiding?'

'If they were the same.' Nico's breath tickles my ear as he speaks.

Then I see Gramps. 'What's he doing?' He's rushing up to one of the cops, one of the ones who's got his gun out.

'Stop it, Gramps, stop it,' I shout out, even though I know it's useless because the noise of the crowd is too much. But Gramps is pulling on the cop's sleeve now and he looks like he's trying to explain something and for the life of me I don't know what he's playing at.

'Gramps, don't,' I shout. 'Come over here.'

'Calm down, he can't hear you,' says Nico in my ear. 'He's probably explaining how this is just a gathering of the faithful so they'll leave us alone.'

'No, no. He wouldn't do that. He's mortally terrified of cops. He'll do anything to avoid them.'

Gramps's eyes are everywhere and at the same time he's pulling at the cop's sleeve and babbling at him. The policeman's big and muscled and he's jutting his chin toward Gramps with one great meaty hand fingering the butt of his gun. His fair eyebrows the colour of sand pull tighter and tighter together, but Gramps can't seem to see any of this happening and won't stop his babbling.

'I'm worried about him. What's he up to?'

Nico holds me tight in his arms. 'Nothing you can do there, Carmel. You leave them both to it, looks like trouble to me.'

Gramps's eyes don't stop scanning and searching and I wonder – is he looking for me? There's this expression on his face that's not only wild and afraid but something else – like he's drowning in some kind of relief. The cop does some talking on the radio with one hand and with the other he's reaching for his belt.

Then I see him locking a metal band around Gramps's wrist.

I want to jump up and say, 'Ta-da, surprise,' like I used to when I was a little kid, to make everything better, to calm everyone down. And I do jump up and Gramps sees me, I know he does. But all he does is lift his hand that isn't cuffed to the cop in a kind of wave that isn't really a wave. It's more he's giving me some kind of blessing from a distance, sending it winging over the field. Then the cop cuffs his other hand and tugs on the cuffs making Gramps jerk – a fish on a line. He walks away leading Gramps, who's like a bull now, not a fish, because he has no choice but to stumble after.

'Oh no. No.'

'What's happening?' Nico's standing up behind me now.

'Gramps said he was going to get judged today.' For a moment

I feel like one of the tents has fallen on top of me and I don't care even that Nico's there or not.

'What's the old fool done?' he says, and when he says that it doesn't seem to matter about his strong arms or his lovely eyes.

'Don't call him that,' I say, tears stinging my eyes.

He shrugs. Now it's not like we're boyfriend and girlfriend, but we're like Mum and Dad were in the old days, getting ourselves geared up to have a fight. I've got my nose in the air pointing up at him and his eyebrows are curling down. Then his mother's coming toward us and calling his name like he's a five-year-old. Her gypsy earrings have gone and she's wearing a jacket with fluffy white fur around the hood and stretchy pink slacks over her great big American behind and we're back being kids again.

'Bye Carmel.' He leans down and kisses me on the mouth so quick it's over before I know what's happening.

'Go find the other one you came with. Go find him – he'll look after you.' That's the last thing I want to do but he steps over the rope to join his mum and I watch until they get lost in the crowd and I can't see them any more. I realise then that Nico's probably not thought about me, like I have him, all the time, for years and years.

A freezing wind is blowing. It blows in from the direction of the cross and as it blasts it seems to peel people away, they blow on past toward the car park. Back to their cars where they can crank up the heating and take themselves back to where they belong. Back to their homes where they've got beds and microwaves where they can heat up pizza for their dinner. Back to gardens with swings, or trampolines that are tumbling across the grass in the wind.

A fat lady blows past me. 'Ice storm coming,' she calls. 'Better find your folk, child. Better find them and get safely out of here to your home, the Lord willing.'

'I have no folk,' I call back. 'There is no home.'

But she doesn't hear me and then she's gone. Ice crystals shimmer in the gap she's left. I shiver; only Nico's kiss is still there to keep me warm – my first ever kiss – burning on my mouth, melting the air around it.

I walk across the field. Everyone's nearly gone now – just a few stragglers moving toward the car park. The cold wind sounds like a song and at first I think the words are like my name. Then I realise the song isn't meant to be understood, unless you're ice or wind. Its words are creaking and humming in a different language. I'm thinking of another song though. One that my mum used to sing sometimes when the wind blew around our house and the tree tapped on the wall – 'The North Wind doth blow. And we shall have snow. And what will poor robin do then, poor thing?'

When I was little I felt sorry for the robin once I was tucked into my warm cosy bed, thinking of it shivering out there and pecking away at the cold ground. So Mum told me to put on my dressing gown and together we went out the back door and scattered some crumbs on the garden that was all black and frozen.

My jacket – my nice warm jacket. I go back through the tent flaps that are rolling in and out like a wave from the wind. Inside there's tipped-over chairs scattered across the floor. One lady's hat has been stood on so it's a flat pink cake. The lights are still on, shining on the spot where I fell inside Maxine's body, the green one on the stage where Gramps stood trying to summon up the spirit. Too cold for spirit here now, with the sides of the tent making noises like a boat in a storm.

I find my jacket folded up at the back of the stage among the coiling wires. There's a heaviness making the jacket lean to one side when I feed my arms into the sleeves. Gramps has put a drink in the pocket. It's something he does sometimes; he knows this can be thirsty work. The can of Coke is freezing in my hand but I pop the tab anyway. The icy bubbles are hard and shining, the taste of brown diamonds, bursting on my tongue.

I sit on the edge of the stage sipping Coke with the tent flapping and blowing around me. I think – I won't see Gramps again. He wanted to go with that cop. When he left there was relief on his face. The metal cuff went around his wrist and he wanted that – to feel its cold grip tightening around his skin and bone. I'd thought he was raising his hand to bless me somehow or give me luck. But now I realise he was saying goodbye and that I was never going to get to tell him how I wouldn't work for him again.

Goodbye, Carmel, and after he had gone I'd felt a certain gladness for a moment – that everything might be different now.

The wind's died down outside. The tent is still at last. When I lift the door it's stiff and hard and there's a shattering like tiny glass is breaking and I realise the canvas is iced up hard.

Outside the world is white and for a minute I don't recognise it. The tents look like a row of ships stuck in a frozen sea. I think – I've gone in one door and come out of another into this beautiful place, though of course I know that can't be true. My feet spin around in crazy circles and I have to reach out to a pole and my hand nearly sticks to it.

I shiver and pull my jacket close around me and I realise I'm still wearing the white dress over my jeans – its frilly bottom is sticking out under the red. It hardly matters – there's not a soul about to see. I'm like the queen of Iceland here alone in this strange land. I slip and slide back out onto the path. There's the cross at the end against the sky and I start to feel afraid. I walk slowly up to it huffing out smoky breath. It's turned into a cross-shaped glacier with icicles hanging from its two branches.

I wonder what I'm going to do now with Gramps gone probably for ever. I want to cry but I can feel the water freezing in my eyes before it gets out and I think soon I must leave or I'll die like the robin in winter. I wonder if I'll be found – frozen to the spot – and sometimes I feel scared and sometimes like I'm going to fly because I can't decide whether I'm alone, or free.

51

OR PERHAPS IT'S NOT like that. Perhaps, after all, you can be free and not have to be all alone. I think of Mum and Dad. Melody. Nico. Gramps. I don't want to have to die to be free – I could stay alone here and turn into an icy statue, or I could start walking. So that's what I do.

I start walking back.

On the highway the cars are driving slowly, crushing the ice and sending it up in a great spray. I walk on the grass at the edge because there's no sidewalk. The light has started to fade.

I wrap my jacket closer around me and wonder where I'm going. It's going to be dark soon – I think of the ditch I spent the night in with Gramps. But I can't see any ditches by the side of this road. And the idea of sleeping in a ditch again is bad, but not as bad as the thought that Munroe might be cruising around looking for me in his SUV to catch me. This could be my chance, I think. Take it, take it.

I turn a corner and there's a house. It's set back from the road and it looks like it was there before the highway and everything else got built around it and that's why it's on its own. There's light at a downstairs window.

I stand in the front yard. The window is open a crack and the height of it is about the same as my head. I hear dishes clattering inside and water running. I tap on the window.

'Who's that?' It's a woman's voice.

'Please. Please help me,' I call through the crack.

A figure appears at the window and looks down. It's a woman with grey hair and a large face. She looks startled, angry even.

'Can you help me?' I say again. But I'm not sure if she's hearing me, my voice is like a squeak in my mouth.

'Get away.' Her voice is fearful.

'Please,' I say it louder, 'if I could just use your phone. I need to try to call my dad. If you know how to find numbers . . .'

'Get away. Get out of my yard. Go, or I'll call the police.' The window slams shut.

I walk away and rejoin the highway. It's getting proper dark now and the traffic flows past me, chucking up melted ice.

Then, lit up like Christmas, a diner – 'Last Stop' – the name in neon pink and the words shining upside down on wet ground. I'm so weary now I have to stop.

Inside is red Formica everywhere and I'm the only customer. A man stands behind the counter looking out. There's a big clock on the wall above him. He stands there like he's been waiting for me.

I go to the counter and fumble with frozen fingers in my breast pocket for the few dollars there. 'Pie, please,' I say.

'What was that?' My voice has gone so small again he has to lean over to hear.

'Pie, please.'

'Cherry or apple?'

'Cherry.'

'Cream or ice cream?'

'Cream, please.'

He cuts me a slice of pie and spoons cream on and I take it and climb up on a high stool and start to eat, each mouthful warm and sweet. I look down and see the white lace at the bottom of my dress hanging down over my jeans black with dirt, and wet. I touch my face and feel a bruise coming where I got hit with Maxine's wheelchair. I think about writing my name on a napkin and feel about in my pocket but my pen has gone. All the times I've written it: in salt from little packets on diner tables; on the walls of restrooms; at the bottom of menus; in the dust on the sides of trucks. There must be nets of it criss-crossing this huge land by now.

I turn away to eat my pie so the man won't see my face all broken and scared and it's so quiet the clock above us fills the room with its tick.

When I finish I turn back again and the man behind the counter hasn't moved. He stands, his face yellow in the light, watching me.

52

FIVE YEARS, 209 DAYS

ARE ALL MYSTERIES finally solved or do some last forever? What happens when we die. What became of my little girl. Do they end? Or can unknowing go on for always?

The night shift has just finished; I'm at home, the winter dawn breaking outside. I'm wearing the white cotton uniform and white clogs from work.

I'm sitting on the sofa when I hear something upstairs. This is an old house, it has its own repertoire of noises but this one I haven't heard before – it sounds like someone running across bare boards. I try not to be alarmed; the house leads a life of its own.

There's a loud rap at the door.

I open it to see a man and woman on the step. They are both turned away, looking at the breaking orange on the horizon. When they face me I don't recognise either of them. But they're police, I know that.

The woman is introducing them. 'Detective Inspector Ian Carling . . . Annie Wallace . . .'

They have come unannounced: they have news. I don't know yet if it's bad or good. But unannounced, something's happened. I'm sick, suddenly, and light-headed. There's a buzzing in my ears.

'May we come in? We need to talk . . .'

They have news. They have news.

Then – I didn't know it could happen in real life – my legs turn to water beneath me and I fall forward.

The man catches me deftly, managing not to drop the file that is tucked beneath his arm. I look up at his freshly shaven jaw, and see the plugs of dark hair he can never quite get rid of. He helps me inside, back onto the sofa. He fetches me a glass of water and I drink, my teeth chattering on the glass.

'May we sit?' asks Annie. I notice she's wearing a poppy on her black coat – it must be November already.

I nod, my teeth still chattering on the glass. They sit in formal fashion. The man is broad and tall, dark with pale skin. The woman – Annie – is slim in her black coat, her blond hair in a neat ponytail.

'Are you OK?' she asks.

'Yes,' I mumble. 'I need to go to the bathroom.' I stumble upstairs. I'm delaying things. In the bathroom I jackknife over the basin and deposit a burning spurt of sick on the white porcelain. I turn on the tap to wash it away and dab cold water around my mouth. I have the sudden urge to escape out of the bathroom window, and never have to know.

Downstairs, they're waiting, in the same positions. The woman starts to speak.

'Beth, we know it would have been better for someone you're familiar with to come. But Maria is away on holiday and we can't wait with this information. I'll tell you quickly – a girl has been found and . . .'

'Is she . . . is she alive?' I burst out.

'Yes, yes.' She joins me on the sofa and puts a hand on my arm. An engagement ring glitters there. 'Yes, Beth.

She's alive and we can't be sure . . .'

'Is she alive?' I already asked that.

'Yes, alive, but . . .'

I can't think. I focus on the glowing red spot of the poppy.

Ian clears his throat, interrupts. 'A girl has been found. We have reasons to believe it may be your daughter.'

'Oh my God. Oh my God. Oh my God . . .'

'We're not sure yet. But we have to tell you. A girl has been found alive and well in the States. We have reason to believe, to be confirmed, it might be Carmel.'

'Where is she?'

'The States. A man was arrested the same day . . .'

'The States! Is she all right? Is she all right?'

'Apparently well. Though alone . . .'

'So she's well and the man . . .'

'He was arrested for another offence. He confessed to another offence . . .'

'Where is she?'

'The States, I said . . .'

'No. I mean now, right now.'

'She's being prepared to fly back . . .'

'And a man confessed to taking her . . .'

'No. He confessed to another, previous, offence. But it transpired . . .'

'She's coming home . . . ?'

Annie is nodding and smiling next to me. Her eyes are filling with tears. I focus on her poppy and try to breathe.

'But . . . how do you know? How do you know it's her?'

The policeman opens the file and begins reading from it.

'*My name is Carmel Summer Wakeford. I used to live in Norfolk, England. My mum's name was Beth and my dad's name is Paul. He has a girlfriend called Lucy. I lived in a house with a tree by the side. My mum had a glass cat she kept by her bed. There was a picture up that said* THERE'S NO PLACE LIKE HOME. *The curtains downstairs are orange . . .*'

53

FIVE YEARS, 215 DAYS

SO MY MYSTERY is to end here. 'Here' is a police facility: two hours' drive from home.

Last night I dreamed of the three of us – Paul, Carmel, me. And for the first time in years she was no longer walking backwards. Instead, she was her eight-year-old self sitting on a swing between us. There was an explosion, nuclear in ferocity. Our figures first bleached white then flashed to black outlines. The ground rocked underneath my feet. I can still feel the sway from the dream as I stand looking through the glass partition down the corridor. Graham, Lucy and the children wait for us at home. We want to keep it simple.

Behind me, Paul sits. He veers between seething with murderous intentions – wanting to get the man and 'just give us five minutes on our own' – and a sort of subsumed tearfulness. Strangely, I appear calmer than him.

I dressed this morning with care. My best gold earrings. My nice blue dress. Mary Jane shoes. I want to show her I'm all right.

But I worry that she won't recognise me. I've aged, a lot. Hair short now and grey coming through.

And closer. She must be getting closer. We toy with coffee in plastic cups and sandwiches while we wait. I go to the bathroom and look in the mirror. How can I look more myself? I fluff my hair out to look longer and put on some lipstick.

Back with the empty coffee cups and uneaten sandwiches. Closer still. I have a strange image of the two of us. That all these years we were tiny insects and the world was made of a huge beast – some kind of cattle. That we roamed and roamed across its back and even climbed up, one on the tip of each horn, and from there we tried to wave to each other. But being tiny we could not see, and the chasm was too great, and there wasn't anything that could bridge that gap. And all the time, on her map on her bedroom wall there she was – in the cradle of that single question mark.

Footsteps come down the corridor and send rumbling noises underneath the closed door at the end. I lick my dry lips and watch the door through the glass. I want to leave this glass room and walk toward the sound but find I can't move.

And the door opens and a girl – a young woman – walks through, a policewoman by her side.

The girl has short curls. She has beautiful eyes. Too thin. She wears black jeans and a red jacket with brass buttons that makes her look like a girl soldier. The eight-year-old embedded in my memory is gone. I have the sensation of looking down a time telescope and seeing into the future.

She sees me and not meaning to I lift my hand in a kind of greeting and she does the same. And I shouldn't have worried about her not recognising me, not at all, because we know each other at once.

ACKNOWLEDGEMENTS

Star billing in these acknowledgements has to go to my agent Alice Lutyens and my editor at Faber, Sarah Savitt. They have both been named as rising stars recently and frankly I'm not surprised. I feel very blessed to be supported either side by two such extraordinary women. Alice, you have a fantastic creative editorial eye and a super sharp business sense – what a combination! I feel very blessed for having landed with you. I lucked out again when it came to my editor, Sarah – I know that your incredibly wise, creative and perceptive editing has made this a far, far better book. You are both so on my wavelength and I thank you from my heart.

Sophie Portas, the brilliant publicity manager at Faber.

Anna Davis, who runs the Curtis Brown Creative course – your clearheadedness, advice and integrity have helped me enormously as did the wonderful course you devised. Chris Wakling for the wonderful teaching on the course.

To all the autumn 2011 Curtis Brown Creative group – I get the sense we are all going to be part of each other's writing journey – you all certainly have been part of mine. Thanks to James Hannah, Theresa Howes, Lisa Berry and Julie Malamute in particular for reading the novel and giving such helpful feedback.

All the staff and tutors at the creative writing MA at Aberystwyth University. I'm so glad I made the decision to go here!

To the great organisation that is Literature Wales – your support has been invaluable.

Ulrike Ostermeyer, the editor of the German edition, for your wonderful, inspiring enthusiasm.

Melissa Pimentel and Sven Van Damme at Curtis Brown for all your help. Thank you both!

Eleanor Rees for your elegant and astute copyediting. Luke Bird and Mark Swan for your stunning, hugely creative cover design – I love it!

To my parents – Christine and William – you are both an inspiration. To Lucy and Sophie, who are friends as well as sisters and such creative people. To my grandmother D.F. Southcott – I wish you were here to see this. To my two lovely children. To my husband Mark. In his book *On Writing*, Stephen King mentions how often a writer turns out to have a supportive partner and I have that in spades. You have always encouraged me and never once suggested I might be crazy for wanting to write. This book is for you.

The author wishes to acknowledge the award of a New Writer's Bursary from Literature Wales for the purpose of completing this book.

READING GROUP GUIDE

1. In the beginning of the novel, Beth briefly loses Carmel in a maze. What is the significance of this moment? How did it influence your reaction to the scenes at the festival?

2. Beth tells Carmel that, regardless of what happens, Carmel must stay uniquely 'Carmel' inside. Are names an important aspect of this story? Can you think of any examples where names play a significant role in the text?

3. Families, or, more importantly, family difficulties, are central to *The Girl in the Red Coat*. What are the various family dynamics at work? Where are there parallels and where are there inconsistencies?

4. Discuss Beth and her ex-husband's shifting relationship. Consider how it is strengthened and changed by Carmel's disappearance. As Beth says, 'We were brother and sister united in this strange bond.'

5. Early in the book, Carmel's teacher, Mrs. Buckfast, refers to Beth as 'yet another single mum.' Think about the friendships Beth has with her female friends and how they support each other. Are those relationships surprising in any way? How do they evolve?

6. Fairy tales play an important role throughout *The Girl in the Red Coat*. Discuss the fairy tale imagery (the woods, the significance of Carmel's red coat) and how it elevates the novel into the realm of the supernatural. Did this affect your reading of the story?

7. How does Beth handle the loss of her daughter over the course of the novel? Did you notice examples of 'tiny actions' that helped her cope? How do those actions compare to the more major developments in Carmel's disappearance?

8. Gramps believes Carmel possesses a divine gift. Do you see evidence of this divine gift throughout the text? Are you convinced by it? Look closely at pages 225–27.

9. Gramps and Dorothy tell Carmel a number of lies in order to keep her with them. These lies escalate as Carmel becomes more and more suspicious. What are

some of these lies and how do they affect Carmel? Is there one that feels like the breaking point, or is it more a matter of accumulation?

10. The word 'courage' is a refrain throughout the novel. Discuss the ways in which the book's protagonists – Carmel and Beth – display courage. How do those demonstrations compare to the 'courage' we see in Gramps, Dorothy, and Paul?

11. Beth says she feels 'better in an environment that said: normality is eggshell thin.' How does the world move on as Beth struggles with her grief? Did you notice historical or cultural clues that gave you a sense of when the narrative takes place? Did it matter? Look closely at page 247.

A Q&A WITH AUTHOR KATE HAMER

The Girl in the Red Coat *is partly about mothers and daughters. Beth's daughter is taken from her and this causes Beth to reconcile with her own mother, from whom she has become estranged. Is the mother-daughter relationship a subject you're particularly interested in, and if so, could you say why?*

I've always found the mother-daughter relationship to be incredibly rich territory. I wanted to write about it honestly – not some chocolate-box version. My own experience of both roles has been close, fraught, loving, disapproving, anxious and sometimes hilarious, as in my own daughter telling me – when she was about twelve – that I was 'too feminist.' Often we want our mothers to be some perfect version of saintliness and feel aggrieved when they don't comply. In the book, Carmel sometimes complains about her mother and even as a young girl has begun to feel urges to be her own person. But I think it's a sort of yo-yo relationship: despite everything, you nearly always end up coming back. I saw something on Twitter recently that really touched me – on Mother's Day someone said something like, 'When you get irritated by yet another call from your mother, remember the day will come when you just wish that Goddamn phone would ring and for it to be her.' As Beth gets older and subject to terrible trauma, her mother scoops her up and they get over their feuding. Grandmothers, mothers, daughters – I see them as a thread running down the generations, arguing, laughing, worrying and always urging the next generation to 'be careful.' Though of course we never are!

Do you have any favourite mother-daughter relationships in fiction?

It surprises me how often mothers can be quite tangential in fiction, and I wanted in *The Girl in the Red Coat* for both mother's and daughter's voices to take up as much room and be as loud as each other. Two of the books that have stuck in my mind have actually been about mothers and sons – Donna Tartt's *The Goldfinch* and Lionel Shriver's mother of a high school killer in *We Need to Talk About Kevin* (I do love an unsympathetic female character). *The Lovely Bones* is moving in its account of being a parent, and I absolutely adore the meddling Mrs. Bennett in *Pride and Prejudice*. But the one that really got me recently was Edna O'Brien's *The Light of Evening*. Her mother and their close, often scratchy, relationship came alive for me in those pages. It was tender and searing, and you could tell it totally came from the heart. I burst into tears as I closed the book.

Beth is a single parent and she worries about the impact on her daughter of the breakdown of her marriage. Was this an important topic for you to write about?

I didn't want to open on a scene of cosy, domestic paradise that the serpent enters and destroys. Beth and Carmel's closeness is already slightly at odds as Beth tries to protect and Carmel longs to be her own person. Beth is still pining for her ex-husband while at the same time trying to forge a new life for herself and her daughter – but it's a pebble in her way compared to the rock when Carmel disappears. She feels guilty then that maybe her attention wasn't where it should have been. I very much wanted to write from the reality of modern family life and not some idealised version of it.

A child being abducted is a parent's worst nightmare. How was it for you, as a writer and a parent, to imagine this situation?

When you have children, this fear is often at the back of your mind – it's pretty universal, and as a parent I guess I was working through these fears and putting them into an imaginative context. At times, I did find it difficult to write – I'd think, 'You can't do that to them!' It's not an easy subject and I worked hard to not be exploitative with it. It's a book about love as much as about loss. Having said that, the book takes you in a direction maybe the reader won't expect. I didn't want to write a misery memoir and I wanted to surprise the reader because that's what I like in a book.

In her new life, with the man who claims to be her grandfather, Carmel finds courage and solace in remembering and repeating her name. How did you come to name the characters in the novel?

The first chapter of the book was written in one go. For ages I'd had the images of a young girl in a red coat; all I knew about her was that she was lost. Then one night I sat up in bed and wrote the first chapter of the book, and that first chapter has actually changed very little. The girl was Carmel in this first writing, and although I experimented with other names I always went back to it. After I'd done some research it seemed to fit too – it's often a Catholic name (Carmel's grandparents are Catholic) and is the name of a sacred site in the Holy Lands. It's not a particularly usual name but somehow it stuck – it's got an interesting shape, and as you say, her own name becomes increasingly important to her as she tries to hang on to her identity, and it seems to me that would be easier to do if your name was a bit out of the ordinary. Plus she is quite an odd character – she couldn't have been a plain old Kate!

You used to be a TV producer. How is the process of making a TV programme different from producing a book? Do you think your TV experience has been helpful in terms of writing fiction?

For me the initial writing process was completely different. Writing a book, you delve into your imagination for the story, and in making a programme, you have to go out into the world to find it. But I found the editing remarkably similar – having to step outside of a piece of creative work and try to look at it objectively. Working with other people at this point with the narrative – in TV it might be tightening up an interview or putting certain music under something, polishing, cutting some things, emphasising others – that felt akin to the edit of a book. Although I suppose the difference is that writing is much, much more personal so you have to work a bit harder at that objectivity! Having two people like Sarah Savitt (editor) and Alice Lutyens (agent) really helped; it always felt more like having an interesting conversation than anything else.

You studied creative writing at Aberystwyth University and on the Curtis Brown creative course. What did you gain from studying creative writing? Have you been following the recent debates about whether it's worthwhile, and what would you add to the conversation?

For me it was about opening my work up to others. It can be quite a big step. I remember the first piece I read out to a group at university and my voice did that quavery thing when you're really nervous. But you get over it and that's important. I think both courses taught me to look at my work as a reader as well as a writer. The Curtis Brown course also helped immensely through its talks by agents, publishers, etc., etc. – to find out how publishing actually works. Plus the joy of mixing with people who have the same passions as you is immense. I remember thinking, 'I've found my tribe!' I would do it all again. Having said that, I'd hate to think people might believe you have to get on a course to get anywhere. It's certainly not obligatory – you could just join a writing group or do the most important thing of all and read, read, read. With our libraries (long may they continue!), it doesn't even have to cost anything.

Who are some of your favourite writers?

Maggie O'Farrell's work always blows me away, as does Hilary Mantel's. Jane Eyre and *Wuthering Heights* have stayed with me – like a lot of people – since I first encountered them as a teenager. Graham Greene, Rose Tremain and Kate Atkinson are old favourites. Lionel Shriver because she always seems to show you something new. Ian McEwan. Donna Tartt. I tore through *The Hunger Games* trilogy in about three days (so one day per book, I guess). New 'old' discoveries – I recently read John Le Carré's *The Spy Who Came in from the Cold* for the first time and loved it. Emma Donahue, Kathryn Stockett and Sue Monk Kidd for their great stories with women and children at the heart of them.

*Read on for a sneak peek of Kate Hamer's next novel,
coming from Melville House in Fall 2017*

THE DOLL FUNERAL

2 JANUARY 1970

Anna takes the turn up to the main road. It's a bright day
and the sky appears eternally high as it always does in
winter when it's clear and blue.

Fear quickens her step. There's been no period for –
how long – she counts out loud – seven, eight weeks? Is it
her imagination but does she feel a little swollen already;
her flat stomach curving out slightly, visible from the side,
like the bulbing of a convex mirror? She's convinced that
she can feel something tiny but determined clamping
onto her insides, sticking there, strong and hardy.

She shoves her hands deep in her pockets as she passes

the telegraph pole and the shed by the side of the road. The copper beech is winter threadbare now. Old Turner used to be there every day with his fold-out chair and thermos. He'd built the shed himself – back in the day, back at the dawn of time. He puttered about on the common land, growing potatoes, swedes, cabbages, half of which he gave away. Nobody cared: things were freer like that when Anna was a child. Today there'd probably be a council eviction for building without planning. Now the structure looks ready to collapse so she sidesteps it in case it happens the moment she passes.

She walks faster, making her boots ring out on the road and swinging her arms vigorously beside her. Perhaps she can break the thing loose, shake it out from its soft, pink nest. She starts trotting, purposely banging the soles of her feet onto the rough country road so the vibrations jar through her body; as the hill steepens she turns the trot into a run – a hobbled movement because of her skirt. At the top of the valley road she stops, cheeks flushed, out of breath, and looks out at the forest below. Bare branches bend and creak in the breeze. She checks her body again, exploring her stomach in its pencil skirt with her fingers. No, it's still there; she knows it'll take much more than a brisk run to break this loose. It's much stronger than she is.

23 AUGUST 1983

I felt sure, the more I thought of it (and that's about all I'd been thinking of since my birthday), that my real parents did not want to give me up. I expected that went double for my mother because mothers shouldn't want to give their children away. I refused to believe it could've been easy. There must have been a reason for it, something completely terrible. They'd chosen my name, Ruby, and – the way I saw it – why would you choose a name like that for a child you didn't want?

Three nights after my birthday the moon rose as fat as a peach. I watched it from my window turn the forest canopy into a shifting silver sea. Now I had a name for the big white emptiness burning like a desert inside. It was called 'Mum and Dad' and tonight it felt bad enough for my bones to crack.

Anything seemed possible in this light. My real parents, my flesh and blood, could be near, even living right here in the Forest of Dean. I just needed a way to find them.

I left the pillow bunched in my bed, took the pillowcase with me and crept through the moonlit spaces of the house. On the bookshelf were two books from my Gran – an aged book that used to belong to her – Pilgrim's Progress – and the Alice's Adventures in Wonderland she'd given me for my ninth birthday. I had the idea to open one on a chance page and see if somehow there might be a message from her there within the story. I hesitated, then picked Alice thinking even at that moment I'd probably chosen badly with these tales of disappearing cats and lizard gardeners. I put it in my pillowcase sack. I found the same sharp kitchen knife that had diced up my birthday cake and took it. As I left the house I used it to delicately fillet some ears of barley from the dusty flower display under the mirror in the hall and dropped them in the sack among the other things – a ball of red wool, some horse chestnuts, rags.

The flowers of the evening primroses were wide open and floated pale above the grasses. The back gate creaked on its hinges. It led directly into the trees. As I glided through the forest in my plain white nightie I thought, with my sack and this knife sticking out in front of me, if anyone sees me they'll think I'm a robber, and it made me brave, this looking-like-a-robber-girl and the belief that I could strike fear into the hearts of others.

Murderer, though. Murderer too, walking through the dark with a knife and sack. The badness in me rose up and made me think I could be a murderer. The knife began to bounce and wobble in my hand so I carefully dropped it into the pillowcase, hoping the blade wouldn't slice right through and cut my legs.

I walked deeper then stopped by a tree whose outline had something human about it – its slender trunk – and I put both hands there. I caressed the sandpapery bark; it felt like an ash – us foresters know how to tell trees so well I could do it even in this light. Despite the night the air was warm and soft. I sat cross-legged under the tree and unpacked my pillowcase among the saplings that grew haphazardly wherever seeds had landed: some forcing their way, springing up from the ground even where there was hardly any light at all. The forest was a strong body pushing out life wherever it could. I put everything out on the smooth white of the pillowcase one by one: the ears of barley; horse chestnuts from my bedside drawer; torn up grass; cloth and red thread from Barbara's workbox.

When my Gran was still alive she'd shown me things

behind the others' backs. She'd drop a leaf into the stew when Grandad wasn't looking and wink – a quick sly movement. Girls came to see her sometimes, always when Grandad was out. For girls who wanted to catch pregnant she'd make miniature babies out of string and straw for them to drop in their pockets and keep there, secretly. That's what had given me the idea. She called it 'invoking' and said it had to be kept quiet because Grandad would disapprove. Everything you'd ever need was right here in the forest, she said – she'd never been away, not even as far as Gloucester. She died outside her cottage underneath the sycamore tree. They found her like a fallen doll against the trunk and said how sad it was she died alone. I think she'd decided it that way. There were sycamore keys in her hair. She had a lapful of them as if she might have to try a hundred different doors to find where to go next.

When I was little I used to copy her. I'd bunch leaves and herbs together and mutter over them. I'd put a stone by the door for evil wishers to stumble on. Then I was only playing, but tonight I felt life tingle in my fingertips as though if I stuck a branch in the ground it might spurt green leaves.

The knife winked as I lifted it up.

ABOUT THE AUTHOR

KATE HAMER is a winner of the Rhys Davies Short Story Prize. *The Girl in the Red Coat* is her first novel. It was a Costa First Novel Award finalist, a Dagger Award finalist, and a winner of the *ELLE* Lettres Readers' Prize. Hamer lives in Cardiff, Wales, with her husband and two children.